Born and raised in Brighton, Jeff Funnell left school at sixteen and joined a London insurance company. After a series of junior positions over the next ten years, he joined a Lloyd's broking firm and worked as a broker in the non-marine market until his eventual retirement some thirty-eight years later.

This work is dedicated to my grandson Toby, whose arrival in 2011 inspired me to create something that might last a bit longer than I do.

Jeffrey Funnell

SIMON BLUNT

THE TRAINEE

AUSTIN MACAULEY
PUBLISHERS LTD.

ISBN 978 184963 492 2

www.austinmacauley.com

First Published (2014)
Austin Macauley Publishers Ltd.
25 Canada Square
Canary Wharf
London
E14 5LB

Printed and bound in Great Britain

Acknowledgments

I am indebted to my good friend and one-time wine-drinking companion Patrick M Ardis, trial lawyer based in Memphis, Tennessee, whose knowledge and work on the behaviour of suspects, and the detection of deceit, as described in *Bad Lies In Business* (Comer, Ardis and Price), McGraw-Hill, Maidenhead, 1988, I drew on for chapter 26.

Chapter 1

The London insurance firm of Nathan Henry was known in the Lloyd's market as a specialist, or niche broker. This was because of their preference for areas of business that generated the highest revenues. They were founded in the first decade of the twentieth century by a man of the same name, now long since departed. The current chairman, and major shareholder, was Brian Peterson. Already a millionaire by the age of forty, but now in his mid-sixties, Peterson was an astute boss, slightly eccentric, demanding of his senior staff, but generously supportive of everyone. His office door was always open to any staff member who needed guidance and, when increased commitment was required, he preferred the carrot rather than the stick. He drove an old London taxi around town, imagining he wouldn't get ticketed whenever he parked where he shouldn't. His deputy was minority shareholder and managing director Robert Woodhead. Peterson and Woodhead often disagreed, sometimes quite vociferously on matters of policy and direction but despite themselves, they had managed to run the company very successfully for over twenty years. Woodhead's inclination was for the stick, not the carrot. Reporting to them were the operating divisions, six in all, specialising in marine cargo, yachts, aviation, oil and gas, reinsurance and international property. Each divisional head was a main board director and minority shareholder. There were no outside shareholders. The total staff count was two hundred and forty-one, soon to be increased by one, due to the arrival of eighteen-year-old school-leaver Simon Henry John Blunt. He was to be a trainee broker.

Simon was from Brighton. He lived a couple of miles from the centre of town in an area known as Westdene with his father John, an accountant, and mother Angela, a local magistrate and charity worker. John Blunt had his own firm in

Brighton. He and his son were members of West Brighton Golf Club and ever since Simon was twelve, they had played most weekends. He was not a typical teenager. He did have a few friends, but not the sort that would hang around in the centre of town and, generally speaking, he was always well turned out and smartly dressed when he needed to be. He had dated a couple of girls from school on and off, but nothing serious. Now, though, he was quite interested in seventeen-year-old Emma from Hove, daughter of George Claremont, who was a senior civil servant in the Foreign Office. The Claremonts were also members of West Brighton Golf Club and knew the Blunts well. Daughter Emma was a beginner at the game and was taking lessons from the club professional. Golf was Simon's principal leisure activity and his passion, though he also excelled at cricket and tennis. Both father and son were single-figure handicap golfers and their respective aspirations were to become club captain and club champion. Blunt junior was still clinging to a childhood dream that one day he would become a professional, but realistically he was not quite good enough for that.

Simon did not do very well at school, a local co-educational establishment called Varndean, which at one time used to be a grammar school. He had been popular with the other pupils because of his sporting skills, but not with the staff. Those who taught him regarded him as a bit lazy, just doing enough to get by, but no more. His number one critic was long-serving deputy head Herbert Gorringe, known to the entire school as 'Jaffa'. Nobody could really remember why, except Gorringe did rhyme with orange. Other staff members used it to his face, pupils behind his back. He was a member of the same golf club as the Blunts, but not nearly as good at the game. This was the main reason for his aversion to, and constant criticism of, the younger Blunt who was considerably better. Jaffa had a reputation for fiddling his handicap higher than it should be so as to improve his net scores and achieve better results in club competitions, but he was pretty bad anyway, so no one bothered to take much notice. For the most part, he and Simon chose to ignore each other in the clubhouse, but in school it was a different story.

"Blunt you are a layabout," Jaffa had once said. "Your geography grades this year make me wonder how you ever manage to find your way to school. Just muddling through will not do."

"Really. It's worked for you all these years," thought Simon, wisely choosing to keep it to himself.

"No Sir," was what he actually said, emphasising the 'Sir'.

Simon had scraped a handful of GCSE 'O' levels and had stayed on for his 'A' levels, the results of which were not yet known. He was not expecting grades good enough for a university education, which pleased him rather, since he had no wish to prolong his academic agony any further. Maths was his worst subject, which probably excluded him from joining his father's accountancy firm, so he made the decision to look for suitable employment elsewhere. He had seen the job at Nathan Henry advertised in *The Independent* and decided to apply, hoping he could bring his school days to an end as soon as possible. After 'A' levels were finished and the results were awaited, the school timetable was abandoned and daily life was a little more haphazard. Thus it was not difficult for him to absent himself for a day to go for his interview. At the offices of Nathan Henry he had met Lynne Green, director in charge of human resources who, after a series of general questions, asked specifically about his academic achievements.

"I have just finished sitting three 'A' levels but, of course, I do not yet have the results," he explained. "I am, though, quite confident that I did the best I possibly could and that I shall not be disappointed with the grades. They will be a fair reflection of the work I put in during the past two years."

Thirty minutes later, when the interview was over, Lynne Green said, "I shall write to you in a few days, Simon, but before you go, I'd like to introduce you to the person you will be reporting to, if we decide to offer you the job."

She opened her office door and in came a middle-aged lady who was introduced as Mrs Jacqueline Whitehouse. She was chief broker in the division dealing with international property. Her proportions were ample and she was somewhat taller than Simon's five feet seven inches. She was dressed in a smart business suit and exuded an air of great authority.

"Hello," she said "I'm Jackie. Everybody calls me Mary."

Her voice was loud, deep and piercing and she had a very prominent cockney accent.

"I hear you play golf," she boomed. "Are you any good?"

"I'd like to improve a bit," he said diplomatically.

"What do you play off?"

"Actually it's three," he offered meekly.

"Now that is good," she said, smiling. "You're from Brighton I understand?"

"Yes, that's right," replied Simon.

"Tell me, how's that new football stadium that everyone's talking about?"

"Oh yes, the Amex. It's absolutely awesome. I went there for the opening game, but golf takes up my weekends most of the time."

"I'm a West Ham supporter. Go to every home game. Well it's nice to meet you," she said, and with that she left.

Interview over, he found his way back to London Bridge Station, not really able to judge the likely outcome. On the one hand, the questions seemed a bit bland but on the other, why would they bring in his potential boss if they were going to turn him down?

On the Wednesday of the following week, and six days before the official end of the school summer term, he received a letter offering him the job and asking him to start the following Monday. He sent his letter of acceptance by return and decided not to make any further appearances at school.

On the Saturday before his first full day of gainful employment, he went to the golf club. There was just one other person in the changing room. It was Jaffa.

"Blunt," he yelled, "I didn't see you in school these last two days."

"That's because I wasn't there," replied Simon confidently. "And from now on it's Mr Blunt."

"What?" screamed Jaffa. "Now listen …"

"No, you listen, Jaffa." Jaffa's face seemed to change colour in an instant. "I left school last Wednesday. I'm over eighteen, so you can now call me Mr Blunt. As of Monday I shall be a Lloyd's broker," he added, carefully omitting the word 'trainee'.

"What?" roared Jaffa. "You're joining that bunch of idle, thieving, good-for-nothing scroungers? That load of self-justifying, toffee-nosed, con-men? Well, at least you've found somewhere that perfectly suits your talents. And at least we won't have to put up with you at school any more. Leaving is your best contribution yet."

"As soon as I'm earning more than you, I'll let you know," retorted Simon. "Shouldn't be too long. And by the way, isn't it time your handicap was adjusted downwards? You won't get so many points then, will you? I must have a word with the committee."

Jaffa left the room, fuming. Simon was smiling, but quietly pondering the disparaging reference to Lloyd's. If this perception turned out to be wide-spread, it was something he would have to be aware of and careful about. Perhaps his father would know.

That evening he was able to raise the Lloyd's issue at home.

"Yes," said Simon's father, "I do remember something about this. About fifteen or so years ago, it was discovered that certain underwriters had been feathering their own nests. There were several complicated scenarios, but the gist of it was that profitable business went one way and unprofitable business another. The good business was channelled into syndicates belonging to the underwriters and their buddies, while the bad business was left to the ordinary members, or names, as they are known. There were bribes floating around, offshore facilities and all kinds of other shenanigans. When the bad catastrophe losses accumulated, as they do every four or five years, many outside investors lost vast sums of money, including their houses. It was a huge world-wide scandal."

"How did they get away with it?"

"For the most part they didn't. The wrongdoers were eventually caught and prosecuted wherever possible. Others were expelled, never to work again. The losses abated for a while and Lloyd's slowly recovered. Remember that each syndicate is a legally constituted entity in its own right and can transact whatever insurance business it likes, subject to the overall rules of governance. Lloyd's is regulated by an act of parliament, but it is merely a place in which to trade. A bit like the Stock Exchange."

"So is it ancient history now?" Simon asked.

"I suppose so. And I think the constitution of Lloyd's was restructured so as to prevent anything like that happening again. There's still a lot of cronyism, back-scratching, special favours for friends and all that stuff, but the regulatory environment is tight now and malpractice on that scale is practically impossible. The syndicate structure remains, but much of the capital is now corporate rather than individual. Why do you ask?"

"Oh, it's just something that Jaffa said when I told him. I thought I'd check it out."

"Well Jaffa's right, in a way, but out of date. It was the general view at the time but most people have forgotten about it now."

John Blunt was an early starter. Thus he was able to deliver Simon to Brighton Station in time for the 7.32a.m., which would get him to London Bridge at 8.41a.m., all being well. The evening journey home from Brighton Station would have to be by public transport, as his father's day would have long since finished, but the bus service out to Westdene was good and frequent and his mother could always pick him up if need be. So it was that Simon duly boarded the morning train on his first day. Since Brighton is at the beginning of the line, he got a seat but the train soon filled as it picked up passengers at all stations to Haywards Heath, then one more stop at East Croydon before it rattled into its final destination. From London Bridge it was a fifteen minute walk to the offices of

Nathan Henry at 30 Mark Lane, EC3, where he arrived just before 9.00 a.m. and presented himself at reception.

"I'm here for Mrs Whitehouse," Simon said to the receptionist, who without looking up, lifted the telephone receiver and punched a number.

After a few seconds she said, "Mary, your new man is here."

Turning then to Simon, she said politely, "Please take a seat and she'll come and get you."

Within a minute or two chief broker Jacqueline Whitehouse breezed in and thrust out a hand.

"Hello Simon. Welcome," she said. "Nice and early, then."

"Yes," replied Simon. "I get a lift to the station from my dad. He starts early."

"Great," she said. "Follow me."

Simon duly followed her, hardly able to keep up. They went to the nearest lift which took them to the third floor, then into an open-plan room with five desks. She looked at her watch.

"It's just on nine o'clock. Let's have a chat before the others get here. Our official start time is nine-thirty. Staff who live in town tend to drift in about that time, then stay later in the evenings. I come in from Basildon so I like to arrive early and get away on time if I can. Now I take it you're pleased to be here."

"Oh yes," said Simon enthusiastically. "But I am a little surprised I got the job."

"OK. There were others under consideration, but there were three factors that influenced us in your favour. Firstly, the answer you gave about your 'A' level results."

"I didn't have them," interjected Simon.

"Exactly. What you said was very good, yet when we analysed it afterwards, you had given us no information at all. Just spin. Sometimes that's precisely what we have to do as brokers. Secondly, you're a golfer."

"Oh, you want me to play golf?" he said, showing surprise.

"Not play, no," she explained. "But it tells us you are very familiar with etiquette and manners and all that stuff. Lloyd's is a place where that still counts for something."

"I see," he said.

"Then there's your nice cosy middle-class schooling and up-bringing. We liked that. We felt you would fit in nicely. Lloyd's is no longer a refuge for upper-class, public-school types. They're still here, of course, but there are as many of me now as there are of them. I'm an Essex girl, with virtually no academic achievements, but I'm street-wise, quick-witted and I have a big mouth. I don't like it when I'm patronised and I tend to over-react."

"How do you cope with etiquette, then?" asked Simon, trying to think of an intelligent question.

"Not very well," she replied. "But you'll need to see me in action."

They both laughed.

"Right," she said, "you can stick with me for the first week then we'll go from there. Things are typically busy. We're a bit like jugglers trying to keep ten balls in the air all at once and everything has a deadline. We are a group of five, all broking in the Room, that's the underwriting room at Lloyd's, and we are the engine room of the international property division. The grafters. Our divisional managing director, and the man I ultimately report to, is a chap called Nigel Watkins, known as Crowbar. He's opened more doors for this company than anyone who's ever worked here. He and his senior colleagues are responsible for client servicing and business production. They don't spend much time in Lloyd's but they're there if I need them, when they're not travelling. Almost all our business comes from overseas, so they're away a lot of the time. We are wholesalers, in other words we work for other insurance professionals, mostly foreign brokers, by going into the market on their behalf. We share the commission, but we deal mostly with big-ticket items, so our turnover is quite high. Back office is centralised and processes paper-work for all six operating divisions. Our claims department functions in the same way."

At that point, two smartly-dressed, fresh-faced young men burst in. It was just on 9.30 a.m.

"Morning," they said, almost in unison, as they made their way to their desks. "Are we all well?"

"Yes thanks and good morning," replied Mary. "By the way, this is Simon Blunt who starts today. I told you about him last week."

"Oh yes," one of them said. "Great. The golfer from Brighton."

Turning to Simon, she said, "These two are James Piper-Bingham and Craig Hughes."

The former was a tall, slim, hard-looking man in his early thirties, while the latter a short, plump, agreeable fellow in his late twenties. They shared a flat together in Kensington.

"John is our other broker," Mary continued, "but he's on holiday now for two weeks. He's effectively my deputy. Did you have a good weekend guys?"

"Yes, I was invited to my uncle's place in Hampshire for a shooting weekend," replied Jamie. "Couldn't get there until Sunday, though, as a crowd of us were at Goodwood on Saturday."

"I went to Goodwood with them," said Craig, timidly, "but I turned down the invitation to the shoot."

"Good for you", said Mary. "Was it Uncle Sir Andrew, the baronet, Jamie?" she added in a mocking voice. "And did you kill anything, or anyone?"

"Yes it was and no I didn't," he snapped. "It was a clay shoot. How was your weekend then?"

"Shopping, cleaning, washing and ironing. Don't forget I'm a wife and mother as well as your boss."

"How can we?" mumbled Jamie.

"OK guys, let's get the week started. You two have plenty to keep you going." Then turning back to Simon, she said "I'll take you over to Lloyd's shortly. You need to have a pass. The general public are not allowed in so the ticket, as it is called, is of paramount importance. You must have it with you at all times. I've arranged a temporary one for you which we'll collect from reception and I'll then give you the guided tour.

Underwriting hours are from eleven-thirty to one and two-thirty to four-thirty, so we'll have some time. I've one urgent item to deal with this morning so you can tag along and see how I get on. I should have done it Friday afternoon but the underwriter cleared off at lunch time. I'll explain later."

Chapter 2

Mary gathered a bundle of papers together and placed them in a thick, brown leather folder. Simon noticed that it did not zip up round its three open sides, but that it was held together by two small straps that clipped over the front and one end.

"This is a slip case," she explained. "We'll get you one in due course. Let's go."

They turned right out of the main door, up Mark Lane into Fenchurch Street, then across the road into Billiter Street, left into Fenchurch Avenue and into Lime Street, where Simon got his first glimpse of the Lloyd's building. It was a huge, odd-looking structure that seemed to be mostly opaque glass and stainless steel. The lifts were on the outside.

"When this place first opened," explained Mary, "we used to say that Lloyd's began in a coffee house and it's now in a percolator."

As they came to the main entrance, they passed a doorman in a red, full-length robe.

"It's what they used to wear in the eighteenth century," explained Mary. "These guys are called waiters. You'll also see chaps in navy-blue, tailed suits with red trimmings. They're the messengers."

The reception desk was manned by three clerks and the area immediately behind it was blocked by two more waiters – heavy-looking chaps – who were there to deny access to anyone without a ticket. Mary went straight up to one of the receptionists.

"I'm from Nathan Henry. You have a temporary pass for Mr Simon Blunt, I hope."

"Yes. Here it is," she replied.

"Thank you. This is yours, Simon. It's valid for one week until we get you a permanent one. You'll need to be photographed but we've plenty of time for that. It can all be done in twenty-four hours. Let's go through."

As they passed the two doormen, one said, "Good morning, Mary. Good morning, Sir."

It was the first time Simon had been called Sir. Once inside they made their way to the lower level underwriting floor. It was a huge area, dotted about with large heavy tables with high-backed benches either side. The space above was a vast atrium, around which were several galleries up to fifth floor level. Between the ground and upper levels was a complex series of escalators, the sides of which were made of see-through materials so that the working parts were visible. Towards one end of the ground floor was a heavy, dome-shaped wooden structure supported by four columns. A large bell was suspended from the underside of the roof under which sat a red-robed waiter. In front of him were a microphone and a computer screen.

"This is the Rostrum," Mary explained. "It houses the Lutine Bell. It used to be rung when there was a major disaster or a recovery from one, once for bad news, twice for good. It's not used much these days, really only for ceremonial reasons. The only time we hear it now is on the Friday before Remembrance Sunday when two military bandsmen come in and play *the Last Post* on their bugles. When things get going, which is about eleven-thirty, you'll hear the constant calling of names over the loudspeaker. This is to enable brokers to contact each other or for their offices to contact them. I'll show you how it works a bit later."

"Now," she continued, "let's find somewhere to sit and I'll explain what I have to do this morning. The underwriter I need won't be here until at least eleven-thirty, so we have a few minutes."

"They have a short day, then," commented Simon.

"Oh no," she explained. "They've plenty to do in their offices beforehand. While we're keeping ten balls in the air, they'll have fifty. They only spend half their time in the underwriting room."

From her slip case she took out a document, consisting of several pages of lightly-coloured card, A4 in size, held together by a ring binder. On the front was pre-printed the name Nathan Henry.

"This is a broker's slip," said Mary. "It's the whole basis of the contract. This client is a hotel chain based in Australia and you can see here that the total amount of insurance is one hundred and eleven million Australian dollars, spread across fourteen locations. It's an annual policy due to be renewed tomorrow at a premium of eight hundred and thirty-six thousand, a slight increase from last year. The client is not entirely happy and wants more time to consider. Here you can see the underwriters' stamps. When they participate, they stamp the slip and write the percentage they want. The leader typically takes the largest share, because he sets the terms, then the others follow or not as they choose. Today I have to get the leader to extend the policy by thirty days, which he won't want to do. He's called Martin Jackson, known as the Tellytubby, in view of his shape. I don't want him to know that we're looking elsewhere, so it will be a tricky conversation. I must answer his questions truthfully, otherwise I will be formally reprimanded, but he doesn't need to know everything. Only what he asks. Right, it's time to get going."

They took four escalators up to the third gallery and wended their way past several groups of people who were standing around chatting. Simon noticed an increase in the noise level as the place began to fill up.

"Tellytubby's box is over here," said Mary, shepherding Simon towards one of the large tables. "But he's not here yet."

"Box?" queried Simon.

"Yes", she replied. "That's what the tables and benches are called. Each syndicate has at least one. The underwriter and his deputies position themselves at each of the corners waiting for brokers to bring the business to them. Much of the time there is a queue to see them, so it's important to get in here early. Their support staff sit on the inside recording everything they do. They're called entry boys, except this one's a girl. She's called Jane."

"If brokers have to wait around," asked Simon, "isn't that a bit inefficient?"

"In some ways, yes," answered Mary. "But then we get to see the decision-maker face to face which makes up for it. Excuse me a minute."

Mary moved towards the girl busy entering data into a laptop.

"Is Tellytubby coming this morning?" she enquired firmly.

"If you mean Mr Jackson, he's on his way," replied Jane, without taking her eyes away from her screen.

"I know who I mean," retorted Mary, sharply.

A few other brokers were gathering round the box, identifiable to Simon by their slip cases. Within a short time a portly, round-faced, man was spotted lumbering towards them. As he neared, the assembled group began quietly humming the Tellytubby theme, reaching a crescendo as he closed in on them and provoking a scowl. He parked himself at the corner of the box nearest to the waiting brokers and the girl moved to the inside position next to him.

"Who's first then," he yelled. "Is it you, Mary?"

"Yes me," she said briskly. "Martin, this is my new trainee Simon Blunt. I'm showing him the ropes this week."

"Bad luck," he said turning to Simon. "Now what have you guys got for me today?"

"It's my Australian hotels. They want more time to consider your increased renewal premium. They have to get their management committee together to approve the order and that won't be possible for a couple of weeks due to other commitments."

"Well, Mary, it's time your client got their committee and their act together. I gave you my price weeks ago. What are they doing? This is an important issue for us all and I'm surprised they can't be bothered to deal with it. I bet they're swanning off and spending a lot of time on the beach."

"It's winter there now," said Mary, calmly. "So that's just not true, is it? And I want a thirty day extension."

"Well I'm not giving you one. They're playing for time. They're shopping around aren't they? I just hope …"

"Listen, Sir," she interrupted, emphasising the Sir. "They are a loyal client but other important issues are going on out there. Had you not increased the premium this year, renewal would have been automatic. But you did, so it isn't."

"The answer's still no," he snorted. "That's it, Mary."

"No it isn't. I'm staying here until you agree. I really do need this extension."

"Still no. Go and get me the order."

"Listen, before you make your final decision, you should know I'm under a lot of pressure here. Renewal date is tomorrow and they're already nine hours ahead so it's almost midnight out there. That means their cover expires in a couple of hours."

"Well, you should have thought of that before, Mary. You're a bit last minute, aren't you?"

"I did. I tried to see you last Friday but you were swanning off somewhere. I hope you weren't on a beach – the British public couldn't handle that."

"OK, OK," he said, laughing. Those waiting nearby in the queue were laughing too. "If you can absolutely assure me that your client is not looking around I'll agree the extra time, but there'll be a penalty charge for it if there's no renewal."

"Thank you Martin. And yes, I give you my word that my client is not looking elsewhere."

"Now clear off," said the underwriter as he initialled the short, written agreement that Mary had prepared. He then handed it to his girl who photocopied it and returned it to Mary without removing the sneer from her face. Mary and Simon made their way down from the third gallery and returned to the ground floor, where they found somewhere to sit.

"Right, Simon," said Mary. "What did you make of that?"

"Heavy stuff, I think," he ventured. "A bit touch and go?"

"Yes, I suppose so. He just wanted to give me a hard time because he enjoys it, but he couldn't really refuse in the end. He knows when I call him Sir I mean business. The relationship historically is one of master and servant, but underwriters can't function without brokers. They know that. I was relieved to get his scratch, though."

"Scratch?" asked Simon, intrigued.

"Oh, it's the act of scrawling their initials on something to signify agreement. Goes back to the days when they all used quill pens."

"And everyone around can hear what's being discussed."

"Yes. Sometimes the underwriter will agree to a private meeting if it's really confidential, but not for the kind of session we've just had."

"One thing, though," asked Simon with a serious look on his face. "He asked you to assure him that the client was not looking around and you did. You gave your word."

"And I was right," said Mary, laughing. "They're not - we are. He didn't ask me whether we were."

"Wow, I don't think I could ever do that," said Simon.

"You will one day," she commented. "But there are many different approaches a lot better than mine. You'll learn."

"What about the penalty charge?"

"Something I'll have to talk him out of later. If I do place the renewal elsewhere that conversation will be a bit tricky," she said. "Now let's go and get you photographed, Simon."

They took one of the lifts to the sixth floor and went into a small office fitted with camera and screen. Mary presented a completed form to the receptionist, explaining that her new charge was here for his first ticket. Straight away he was photographed, his form was processed and they were on their way in a matter of minutes. The ticket would be ready for collection the next day. Once back on the ground floor, Mary stopped at the Rostrum and whispered something to the waiter.

"Nathan Henry Whitehouse," was immediately announced over the loudspeakers for all to hear, all over the building.

"That's how you contact me if you ever need to," explained Mary to Simon. "Or there's a number you can phone from the office. The caller will then add the word telephone."

"OK," said Simon.

As it was approaching lunchtime, they made their way back to the office. At the corner of Fenchurch Street and Mark Lane, Mary stopped at a snack bar.

"I normally get a sandwich for lunch," she said to Simon. "Is that OK for you?"

"Oh yes, fine," he replied.

They went inside, at least as far as they could, since it was chock full of customers. It was run by Italians. Mary was immediately recognised and acknowledged by one of the counter staff.

Turning to Simon, she said "Any preference?"

"No, I'll have what you're having."

"TWO. CORNED. BROWN. YES. PLAIN. TWICE," she yelled at the top of her rasping voice, startling everyone.

Within a few minutes her order was being passed to her above the heads of the crowd in front. Mary and Simon paid at the till and hurried back to the office.

"I thought we'd be there for ever. How did you get away with that?" asked Simon.

"I've been doing it for nearly twenty years. It's a routine that most people are familiar with."

"I got everything except 'Yes'. What was that?"

"Mustard."

"What about all the big lunches we hear about?" enquired Simon confidently.

"Only when guests are involved and in our case one of our directors must to be present. We have a constant stream of overseas visitors who need to be fed and watered, so we have our own dining room. And sometimes it's necessary to entertain an underwriter when we want to discuss more general issues. I don't get invited very often, which I'm quite pleased about, but occasionally an underwriter will invite me out. Generally speaking we get on well with everybody, but we do need to look after our clients when they're in town, or someone else might. There are tens of thousands of brokers and underwriters in this market and it's very, very competitive. I love it. It's the best job."

Simon sat quietly, munching on his corned, brown, yes and wondering what he had got himself into. He couldn't imagine ever being able to handle things the way Mary just had. On the other hand, they seemed to want to train him to do that and seventeen thousand a year, minus the cost of his season ticket, was very acceptable indeed. Better make a go of it. There's no way of muddling through this time.

Chapter 3

The second week of Simon's working career began much as the first, except he now had five day's experience. He was next in after Mary, who was busy organising her desk. At precisely 9.30 a.m. in came Jamie and Craig, closely followed by divisional managing director Nigel Watkins.

"Ah, Mary," he said. "Good morning."

"Good morning Nigel," she replied. "By the way, this is our new recruit, Simon Blunt."

Simon jumped to his feet and nervously exclaimed "Good morning Sir."

"Hello Simon," said Nigel. "Welcome. And it's OK just to call me Nigel."

Turning back to Mary, he said, "We've got something on. I was contacted last week by an old school mate, Mike Edwards, who now works in Dubai for a local insurance company. He's got something important he wants me to have a look at. Apparently one of the Saudi princes is taking a wife and he's having a load of jewellery shipped in from Paris for her. It's a very valuable collection indeed. If my chap, through us, can win the account, then there's a stream of profitable business likely to follow. I'm on my way to Heathrow now, back on Wednesday. In the meantime, could you have a snoop around and see if anyone's in the market already. There's likely to be some heavy competition for this one. Problem is we don't know any names yet. It's a big secret which is why they don't want it insured locally."

"Right," said Mary, as her boss hurried away.

"OK lads, listen up. You heard all that. This is a job for you two Jamie and Craig," Mary said. "What are you working on?"

"I'm renewing the Spanish supermarkets and the South African finance company," replied Jamie, "as well as updating the Hong Kong stockbrokers' scheme with new members."

"Craig?"

"I'm getting quotes for the museum in Lisbon – it's stacked full of fine art - and I'm placing the jeweller in Monte Carlo."

"OK," said Mary. "As you go round see what you can sniff out. Cover the market, check out all the likely suspects and we'll re-convene at the end of the afternoon."

"I think this might be one for Biffo," said Craig. "I'll have a crack at him – I was at school with him."

"That'll be Charterhouse," interrupted Mary, looking at Simon.

"I may need some time with him in a wine bar, though, if I think he knows anything."

"Then do it, Craig," said Mary, "but check with as many as you can."

Simon's eyebrows were raised. "Biffo?" he enquired.

"Yes," explained Craig. "A chap called John Whitfield, an underwriter who insures a lot of jewellers, both manufacturing and retail. If there's anything big going on anywhere in the world, he'll know. He just happens to display more than a passing resemblance to the bear from the Beano comic."

Nigel Watkins went by District Line from Tower Hill to Embankment, then the Bakerloo Line to Paddington, from where he took the Heathrow Express. He then found his way by shuttle bus to Terminal Five and checked in with British Airways for the one o'clock flight to Dubai, scheduled to arrive just before 11.00 p.m. that evening local time. He was used to these trips and kept a passport in the office in case visas were needed urgently. In due course he was boarded, seated and ready for take-off. He was in an aisle seat in the third row of economy on a Boeing triple-seven. Across the aisle, and to his right, was a man in his mid-forties whom Nigel acknowledged when he arrived. He was smartly dressed in a business suit. After take-off, Nigel took out a bundle of papers, his division's management accounts reflecting the previous month's trading, and began to study them. Eventually the man to his right introduced himself.

"I'm Hari Kahn," he said. "Just Dubai is it?"

"Pleased to meet you. I'm Nigel Watkins and, yes, just Dubai," he replied. "Short trip, actually. Just one day."

"What business are you in?" enquired his fellow passenger.

"Insurance. Lloyd's broker. You?

"Oh, I have many business interests. Property development, transport, freight forwarding and a couple of hotels. If you're with Lloyd's, I'd be interested in talking with you more formally. Shall we swap business cards?"

"Sure," said Nigel. Cards were duly exchanged.

After the meal was finished and the conversation had subsided, Nigel fell asleep. The flight was uneventful and slightly ahead of time, arriving at its destination at 10.50 p.m. As they rose to disembark, Hari Kahn said "Which hotel?"

"Intercontinental," replied Nigel.

"Me too. Shall we share a taxi?"

"Sure," said Nigel having established that they both only had hand luggage.

In the taxi Hari Kahn expressed a wish to meet up again, suggesting that it might be best to arrange something in London.

"I spend a lot of time in the UK," he explained, "as well as here in Dubai. I have houses in both countries. I'll give you a call sometime."

"OK," replied Nigel.

After checking in at the hotel, Nigel went straight to his room, turned off his phone and settled down for the night. He was sure there would be news from Mary when he awoke the following morning.

Back in the London office, the international property broking team were re-convening at the end of their day.

"What news?" enquired Mary.

"I've got something," said Craig. "I saw Biffo. It's not his quote but he did see it going the rounds. The Lloyd's brokers are Baxter Taylor and Black and it came to them from an agent in Bahrain. More importantly, the rate they've got is two per cent. He thinks the schedule of jewellery was more than twenty million dollars, including some of the top pieces in the world that have staggering royal histories. That's a premium of over four hundred thousand dollars."

"Nice work," said Mary. "And what has that cost us?"

"Two bottles of Sancerre and a smoked-salmon sandwich," Craig replied, smiling. "The sandwich was for me. Biffo isn't into solids at lunchtime."

There was loud laughter from everyone in the room.

"Good stuff. I'll text Nigel. He'll be very pleased to have the information before his meeting tomorrow. Thanks guys."

Their day now ended, they all left for the evening.

At 7.30 a.m. the next morning in Dubai, Nigel came down for breakfast, armed with the news he wanted from London. He noticed Hari Kahn there with two other business people, one of whom he recognised as a Lloyd's broker. He kept away from them and found a table at the opposite end of the restaurant. After a short while, he was joined by his old friend Mike Edwards.

"How are you, Nigel," exclaimed Mike, with enthusiasm. "It's good of you to come. I would normally have sent you a package by courier, but this one's highly confidential and my Bahraini agent and his Saudi contact are joining us later."

"Thank you for inviting me," replied Nigel, "and I'm very well, thanks. I just hope we can crack this one for you."

"I have every confidence in you. Now what is your itinerary?"

"Oh I'm just here today, Mike. Taking the overnight back into Heathrow. There's no one else I need to see."

"Right. I'll show you round first, then we'll go to the office and look through all the details. We will probably learn more when the other two arrive. After we're done, we can spend the afternoon and early evening at the house, have a bite to eat, then I'll drive you to the airport. You remember Janice, my wife, don't you?"

"Yes Mike. I was at your wedding don't forget. And Louise sends her best regards to you, by the way."

"It's a great life here, by the way. You should think about it. I'm the only expat in the place and all my staff members, who are locals, are trained insurance professionals. Some of them worked in London for a while."

"Not for me, Mike," replied Nigel, solemnly.

They finished breakfast and took a drive around the city. Nigel had been there before, but not for some years, so it was interesting to see all the new developments that had sprung up. They arrived at the tall, elegant glass-fronted building of the Al Talyani Insurance Company of Dubai and Nigel was given the obligatory tour before they settled down into Mike's large and well-appointed office.

"Right, let me tell you where we're at," said Mike. "Through the people I've mentioned, we've been asked to quote for a load of jewellery being bought by a Saudi prince for his new wife. It's his first, so I guess he's one of the younger princes. It's being gathered from various parts of the world into one central point in Paris before it gets re-valued and shipped to Riyadh. Take a look at this list of items, Nigel. They're very special indeed. Some of them are hundreds of years old. There'll be a load of paperwork with them, of course, so the provenance will be unquestionable."

He handed over a single sheet of paper on which was written:-

Tiara	$1,700,000
Necklace	$3,700,000
Necklace	$1,800,000
Bracelet	$12,400,000
Gold Ring	$3,000,000
TOTAL	$22,600,000

Nigel studied the content carefully.

"Naturally, these amounts may change after valuation, but not by much I'm sure," continued Mike. "This one's too heavy for my company to take, so we want to act as agents. We've probably got about two or three weeks before all this kicks off and there are still a lot of details to clarify."

"Are there any other quotes around?" enquired Nigel, with the previous night's text from Mary very much in mind.

"Yes I think so," said Mike cautiously. "Someone in Bahrain has been to the market but the quote hasn't yet gone to Riyadh. I don't know the rate, Nigel, but there is an unacceptable condition. All these items are required to be in a bank when not being worn. The new princess is not going to be impressed with that and it's unlikely the family would be prepared to go along with the inconvenience. What do you think?"

"I agree," said Nigel. "We did find someone in the market going at two per cent – that would be slightly more than four hundred and fifty thousand dollars on these values. But I expect it will end up lower than that. Right, I think we can do something for you here."

"Good man," said Mike, happily. "Now, let's see if the others have any more details. They should be here any minute. Mahdi Al Hadda is my Bahraini agent and he's bringing his Saudi contact Saleh Said Al Othaim. Both men of high regard in the region."

After a short while the new arrivals were shown into the room. Mike made the introductions and handed over to Nigel, who began by asking for information concerning security at the palace.

"In the Kingdom of Saudi Arabia," began Saleh Said Al Othaim, "royal palaces are regarded as highly secure. They are constantly occupied, if not by the royals themselves, then by their many, many staff, not the least of which are bodyguards. We do believe there is nowhere more secure. Also, theft is not prevalent in the Kingdom in view of the penalties incurred. In summary, nowhere is as secure as a royal palace."

"I see," replied Nigel. "Thank you. What about when they travel, particularly abroad? How is this level of security maintained?"

"It is a little more difficult, of course, but they would never be alone. There would be a huge entourage, including bodyguards, who would take over the whole floor of a top hotel. No member of the hotel staff would get anywhere near to them and the public certainly wouldn't."

"Again, thank you," said Nigel. "Now the big question is the transit. How is it going to be made?"

"This has not been decided," said Mahdi. "We could use a courier service specializing in high-values, or we could employ one of our own. In either case the people involved will need to be thoroughly vetted and the final details will need the prince's approval."

After more background discussions, the meeting concluded. Nigel promised some news by the end of the week and Al Hadda and Al Othaim left. Mike then drove Nigel to the house, a mansion by western standards, where wife Janice was waiting for them. She showed Nigel round their large, single-storey, modern hi-tech dwelling complete with swimming pool and tennis court.

"This is provided for us by the company," she explained, "along with a housekeeper and gardener. They also paid for our kids to go to boarding school back in the UK and, of course, there is nothing like the pressure on Mike that there used to be at home. In short, it's the perfect life. The company's directors are mostly high-ranking locals here in the Emirates who generate pretty much all of the business. We wouldn't give this life up for the world."

"I can see why," replied Nigel. "Guildford's been pretty good for us, though. Louise has a boutique in the High Street and the boys went to the local school. They're both off at university now."

Back in the house, Mike was busy organising the food for later. As the lady of the house and their guest re-joined him, he went to the fridge, took out three bottles of beer and opened them.

"Let's just relax in the garden for a bit then I'll get the barbeque going later. OK Nigel?"

"Yes, fine with me. By the way, do you know a man called Hari Kahn," added Nigel.

"Yes I do," replied Mike. "He's originally from Pakistan, then spent some time in Lebanon, now he has interests here as well as back in the UK. Has a reputation for being a bit sharp, but he's never done anything illegal, or more likely just hasn't been caught. Why, do you know him?"

"Not really," explained Nigel. "He sat next to me on the plane. Said he wants to get together in London for a chat."

"Well it might be worth your while. Watch him, though, he can be very slippery."

"OK, Mike. Thanks."

Later that evening Mike drove Nigel to the airport in good time for his return flight, due to depart at 1.55 a.m. local time, arriving back at 6.20 a.m. Heathrow time. Nigel confirmed his commitment to the new business relationship and they said their goodbyes. The flight left on time and after declining the evening meal he settled down for a night's sleep, but something in his mind was keeping him from doing that. He was still puzzled about his exchange with Hari Kahn. Eventually he dozed, then suddenly it was 5.00 a.m. and breakfast was being served. They landed slightly later than planned, at around 7.00 a.m. and after clearing immigration, Nigel made his way straight to the office, taking the Heathrow Express and the underground. He arrived there at 8.15 a.m. He spent the first hour composing a detailed summary of his meeting in Dubai before making his way over to the office of his broking team. Mary and Simon were there as usual.

"Right, these are the details," Nigel explained, handing over his report. "You'll see that there's an issue with security as well as price. The two per cent rate you found is bound to be beaten, so if we are to stand a chance, then we'll need to be going at about one-point-five. See what you can do and give me an up-date at the end of the day. Today's Wednesday and I want to put our final quote to Mike by the end of the week."

"Right," said Mary. "We'll get on to it."

At that point, and just before 9.30 a.m. as usual, Jamie and Craig arrived. Straightaway Mary gave them, and Simon, a copy of the report and talked them through the details quickly and succinctly.

"Ok, here's what we do. I want us all to hit the market at the same time, seeing as many underwriters as we can today. Try to get the rate down as low as you can. You're likely to find other brokers working on it, so it won't be easy. We'll compare notes at lunchtime. Simon, I'd like you to have a crack at Tellytubby. He likes to banter, as you've seen, but I don't think he'll give you a rough ride first time in. Anyone else, guys?" she added.

"We'd better see Biffo the jewellery expert, just to see if he'll have a go," said Craig. "After that I'll get to as many as I can."

"OK guys, let's get up there early and remember, this is one we really do need to win."

Back in his office Nigel checked his mobile phone and saw that he had a text. It was from Hari Kahn and it read:-

'Will be back in London Wednesday evening. Could we meet on Thursday? I'll be at the Mayfair Hotel. If you're free, I could buy you lunch at, say, 12.30. I have something to talk to you about.

Hari Kahn.'

Nigel was surprised at this and more than a little wary. Very much on his mind was the chance meeting on the plane, seeing him at breakfast with a man from Lloyd's, plus the comments that his friend Mike had made. On the other hand, wouldn't it be better to know, rather than not know, what it was all about? He sent the following reply:-

'Yes. I could do lunch. See you there tomorrow.

Nigel Watkins.'

Meanwhile, Mary and her team were on their way to Lloyd's. It was just after 11.00 a.m. Simon was extremely nervous and felt quite daunted at the prospect of going it alone for the first time. One day, perhaps, he would be able to take it in his stride like the others. But not yet.

Chapter 4

Later that morning, the phone rang in Nigel's office. It was Mike Edwards calling from Dubai.

"Good morning Nigel. I trust you're well."

"Yes thank you. How are things?"

"Well, we have some more information about the transhipment. However, we're under instruction not to put it in writing in the interests of security."

"OK, Mike. I'm happy with that."

"First of all the jewellers in Paris will, when they're ready, deliver the items to the Saudi embassy. That transfer will be by armoured van and will be at their risk, not ours. We are not being told the name of the jewellers because the insurance won't be involved at that point. One of the prince's bodyguards will have flown in from Riyadh and will be waiting in the embassy. When the delivery is complete the prince will be told and the funds will then be transferred to the jeweller's bank. Once confirmation of that has been received, the items become the prince's property and the insurance kicks in."

"With you so far," said Nigel.

"The chosen method of shipment will be by private courier, though we don't know who that will be yet. He will also be at the embassy. After handover, he and the bodyguard will take a Saudia flight to Riyadh. It will be kept low key so as not to attract attention. Embassy staff will ensure that passport control and customs are made aware of these arrangements at the highest level, of course. Similar measures will be in place at Riyadh airport where two of the prince's personal aides, and possibly the prince himself, will be waiting. Most likely they'll be airside. From there it is a short drive to the palace."

"Understood, Mike, but you have no idea who the courier will be?"

"No. What I can tell you, though, is that the decision has been taken not to use a professional security company, nor to entrust the goods to the airline itself. The individual will be known to the prince and to the guys who will be waiting at Riyadh airport. We'll know who he is soon I've no doubt."

"OK. I've got all that. Our guys are in the market right now, so I'll get this information to them when they get back. By the way Mike, Hari Kahn has been in touch. We're meeting for lunch tomorrow. Says he has something to talk to me about."

"Watch him Nigel."

"Oh yes. Anyway thanks for all that. I'll be back to you on Friday, hopefully with a good price. Bye for now."

"Thanks Nigel. Cheers."

In Lloyd's, Mary's team were going their separate ways so as to see as many underwriters as they could in the shortest possible time. Simon made his way to Martin Jackson's box on the third gallery but there was no sign of him. He asked Jane whether the underwriter was on his way.

"No idea," was the terse reply. "You'll just have to wait and see."

"Thank you so much," replied Simon sarcastically, provoking yet another sneer.

Meanwhile, Craig was queuing to see his old school-friend. After a wait of about twenty minutes he was in.

"Ah, Hughes," was the opening shot. "Hope you've got something good for a change."

"Morning Biffo. It's great to see you too. Now it's the jewellery for the Saudi prince. There's about twenty-two million dollars of it."

Craig handed over the list of items together with a single piece of A4 card headed 'Quote Sheet'. On it the basic details of the proposed policy were outlined.

"I thought it might be this," said the underwriter.

"What we want is an annual policy and I need a rate a good bit under two per cent. Cover starts in Paris so we're on for the transit to Riyadh. After that the stuff will be housed in the palace for the new princess to wear when she feels like it."

"I don't like it," mumbled Biffo after studying the details carefully. "There are three reasons for that. Firstly, you can't tell me how the shipment will be carried out. Secondly, general security in Saudi Arabia seems a bit vague and, thirdly, you want world-wide cover, which indicates overseas travel. I'd like to know more about all that. You need to be a bit more precise."

"OK," said Craig. "I can deal with most of that. Just because we don't have details of the shipment yet doesn't mean poor security. I can guarantee that it will be of the highest level. What's more we will know all the details before we go on risk. Next, we're talking about the Saudi royal family here. Their palaces are highly secure and what's more, no one who values their body parts is going to steal from them."

"That's just the theft angle," interrupted Biffo. "You want comprehensive all risks cover. What if something is just lost or mislaid?"

"Right. There will be a place of safe-keeping in the princess's apartments in the palace. A vault. All items will be stored there when not being worn. It's safer than a bank vault. When they travel there would be a huge entourage that goes with them. And when they book into a hotel anywhere in the world they take a whole floor. Hotel staff are not allowed anywhere near them. Instead they take their own servants to fetch and carry. Also, Saudi embassies would be on full alert, as well as the local police. It doesn't come more secure than that, Biffo."

"Yes, I understand all that. OK, I will quote for this. I'll go at one-point-seven-five per cent but there are conditions. One, I will need to approve the details of the transhipment and if I think security is not top of the range, I will not cover it. Two, all items must be kept in the vault when not being worn and, three, not all these items are to be out of the vault at the same time. That applies particularly to overseas travel. Understood?"

"Yes I understand all right," said Craig. "I don't know how acceptable your conditions will be, though, given who the client is."

"Then you'll have to provide better information. Otherwise tough."

The underwriter scribbled his comments onto the quote sheet, initialled it and handed it back to Craig, who went on his way.

While Mary and Jamie Piper-Bingham were scurrying round the underwriting room, Simon was still waiting for the appearance of his man. The team had arranged to meet at lunch time, not back at the office but in a nearby public house called the Cheshire Cheese, situated at the corner of Crutched Friars and Lloyd's Avenue underneath Fenchurch Street Station where, by 1.15 p.m., they had all assembled. Mary had pre-ordered a platter of sandwiches and a bottle of wine, though she herself would only have a soft drink. She offered wine to the others which Simon declined in preference to orange juice.

"You don't drink then?" Jamie enquired of Simon.

"Not very much at all," he replied. "Special occasions only."

It was left to the other two to share the wine.

"Right. Where are we at?" asked Mary. "Simon?"

"No sign of Tellytubby at all this morning. I'm in the queue for this afternoon, but he has a carryover, whatever that is."

"It's people who were waiting yesterday but didn't get to see him," explained Craig. "He'll see them first this afternoon, then you afterwards."

Mary then turned to Craig, who recounted his experience with Biffo.

"I doubt that's going to be much good," she said. "Especially with the conditions he's imposing. Jamie?"

"Not much interest so far. I'm banking on Honeymonster to come up with something, though."

"Honeymonster is a chap called Richard Chandler," explained Mary to Simon. "So called because of his enormous appetite. We once took him to a carvery for lunch and he went through five full plates of food. Didn't speak at all – just ate."

Laughter from all.

"Now I'm doing OK," she continued. "Two rejections first of all, but I then got a quote of one-point-six per cent with no conditions. I still think we need to get below that though."

"It's not easy," said Craig "when we don't have enough information, especially about the shipment."

"I know," conceded Mary, "but we will have it soon, I'm sure. This is a priority case, but we mustn't let our other work fall behind. That's just as important. Have a good afternoon and we'll have another chat at the end of the day."

With that they finished their lunch and made their way back to Lloyd's.

Simon headed straight back to the Jackson box on the third gallery, where three other brokers were already waiting.

"We're the carryover," one of them said. "You follow us."

"OK," he replied, assuming he had no choice.

After an hour's wait there was still no sign of the underwriter. Then at 3.15 p.m. he appeared.

"Sorry lads," he said. "Something came up."

An hour later and Simon was still waiting. The guy in front of him was taking his time. At 4.35 p.m. he was finally in.

"Simon, isn't it?" ventured the underwriter.

"Yes Sir," he replied.

"Look, I'm afraid I haven't much time. Is it something quick?"

"Mr Jackson, Sir, we'd like you to quote for this," said Simon, handing over the list of jewellery and his copy of the quote sheet. "It's the property of a Saudi prince who's getting married and it's his wedding present to the new princess."

"Wow," commented Mr Jackson. "That's an impressive collection of sparklers. I can't deal with this now, but I will see you tomorrow morning. Say here at eleven o'clock? You can regard it as a firm appointment."

"Thank you Sir," replied Simon somewhat despondently. "I'll be here."

Back in the office he explained to his colleagues what had happened and how his day had been completely fruitless. A whole day's waiting and nothing to show for it.

"It happens," commented Jamie. "In some ways it could work well, though. Tellytubby is the sort of chap who will try to make it up to you if he feels a bit guilty. I got the rate down to one-point-five from Honeymonster, but he wants the stuff in a bank vault when not being worn. He might relent as far as the palace is concerned, but he won't budge when they're travelling overseas."

At that point Nigel entered the room.

"There's a bit more information," he announced, and then proceeded to outline the full details of the shipment.

"That's helpful," replied Mary. "I'm not satisfied with our progress so far, but we'll do better tomorrow."

"That's not all," said Nigel. "I had a second call from Dubai a few moments ago and it looks like this is all going to kick off in about seven or ten days from now. That gives us very little time. We need our best quote by close of business tomorrow and if we then get the order, the cover will have to be in place by next Tuesday latest. Can you handle that?"

"Yes, of course," replied Mary. "No problem."

"I have an appointment in the west end at lunchtime, so we'd better re-convene at the end of the afternoon tomorrow. That's it for today."

At precisely 11.00 a.m. the following morning Simon presented himself to underwriter Jackson who was already waiting for him.

"Good morning, Simon," he said. "Sorry about yesterday. Now, let's have a look at this jewellery schedule again. I thought about this overnight, but first of all will you do something for me?"

"If I can," replied Simon, sheepishly.

"I hear you're a bit of a golfer. Single figure handicap and all that. Well, every so often, a group of us from the market have a day out at the East Sussex National. One or two are quite good, the rest are not. I fall into the second category, but

I'm determined to win one day, so I wonder if you would be my partner?" It's Friday of next week. How about it?"

"I really don't know," said Simon, even more sheepishly. "I'm familiar with the course, but it's a work day. How can I do that in only my third week?"

"Tell Mary it's for me and that we raise money for charity. I'll talk to her if you need me to. I'll let you have the arrangements a couple of days beforehand. Where do you live?"

"Brighton," said Simon.

"Oh that's easy enough then. Do you have transport?"

"I can probably borrow my mother's car, or get her to drive me, I suppose."

"Good," said the underwriter. "That's settled then. I live in Forest Row, which isn't far from the club. One of our group is a member there."

"OK, I'll tell Mary when I get back and see what reaction I get."

"Thanks. Now I'll have a go at your jewellery. What rate do you need?"

"Er, not entirely …," spluttered Simon, unsure whether he should divulge someone else's quote.

"Oh come on. I'm trying to help you here," interrupted the underwriter impatiently.

"Well, our best so far is one-point-five per cent but there are conditions about where the stuff must be kept."

"Don't they understand how well it's going to be looked after? This is the Saudi royal family after all. It'll be like insuring concrete underground. I know we've got an international transhipment but I presume that'll be highly secure?"

"Certainly will," said Simon, slightly more confidently. "Private courier accompanied by a bodyguard, both known personally to the prince. Handover will be at the Saudi embassy in Paris, then by scheduled flight to Riyadh. All very low key. No flashing lights or sirens."

"Good. Right, here's the deal. Firstly, I'll go at one-point-four. Secondly, I want to see the jewellery and have the valuations and provenance verified by my own expert. In Paris if need be. What do you think?"

"The rate is good," said Simon, "but I don't know how the conditions will be received. There's been a lot of discussion about that in the office."

"Ah, but think of them not as conditions, rather as an additional service. Think how the princess would feel knowing her goodies have been properly authenticated by Lloyd's. The prince might be pleased to tell her that. For my part, I just want to be absolutely sure the items are what they're supposed to be and not being over-valued. And I think it will help you get the order."

"Oh I see," said Simon. "OK, I'll report back. Thank you very much. And I'll let you know about the golf day."

"Good man," said the underwriter, as he recorded his comments on the quote sheet. "Incidentally, do we know which prince it is?"

"No Sir. It's still a secret. I expect we will in due course."

With his new slip case tucked firmly under his arm, Simon made his way back to the office. Mary was there but the others were out.

"Well, how did it go?" she enquired.

Simon showed her the underwriter's written comments and explained in precise detail what he had been told.

"Tellytubby's excelled himself here, hasn't he," she said, smiling. "Good rate, but we'll need to think carefully about what he wants to do. Timing will be the main concern."

"He sees it as an added benefit," explained Simon. "And by the way, he wants me to play golf with him next Friday."

"Oh no. Someone's told him about you. Well I guess there's no option. You'd better go ahead, otherwise it might jeopardise the deal you've just got. You'll need cash, but I'll make sure you have some the day before. It's not a day off, incidentally – you'll still be working."

"Yes, I understand," said Simon.

"Well done, by the way. This is good stuff. We've got a few hours before the quote has to go to Nigel, so I'll put my mind to it. There is an angle here about additional security which might go down well if we put it to them the right way."

"That's precisely what Mr Jackson thinks," confirmed Simon.

"OK, now get back up to Lloyd's, find the other two and see what you can do to help them. We need to clear the decks a bit and concentrate on this one, if we get the order. I think we will, by the way, so we'll have a busy time next week."

"Even more than now?" said Simon.

"Oh yes," said Mary, smiling. "Our feet won't touch."

Chapter 5

Nigel Watkins left his office shortly before noon on his way to the Mayfair Hotel to meet Hari Kahn. He walked to Tower Hill underground station and took the District Line westbound. He changed at Westminster onto a Jubilee Line train, which took him the one stop to Green Park. From there he walked up Stratton Street and into the foyer of the Mayfair Hotel. It was coming up to 12.30 p.m. but there was no sign yet of his host. His mobile buzzed to let him know there was a text message. It was from Mary. It read:-

'Good news. We can go at 1.4%. Need to discuss though.'

He replied:-

'Great. See you this afternoon and thanks.'

A few minutes later Hari Kahn arrived. They shook hands and made their way into the restaurant. They ordered sparkling water, orange juice, the soup of the day and sea bass.

"There's something I want to run past you," said Kahn. "One of my companies is in the business of international freight forwarding. It handles all types of goods, including valuable and dangerous. Now I may be speaking out of turn, but I hear there's a big shipment of some sort bound for Riyadh soon."

"What of it?" interrupted Nigel. "Why talk to me?"

"Because I want my company to be involved. I hear Lloyd's is going to be insuring the transit and you're one of the brokers involved."

"Well, Mr Kahn, if that's true and if I were, then there is absolutely no circumstance that would permit the release of that kind of confidential information. It would be a complete breach of protocol and probably get me fired."

"I understand that, Mr Watkins and I don't want you to do that. I'm trying to get to the right people but I don't know who they are. I want to make a formal approach to them. Can you point me in the right direction?"

"No I cannot," replied Nigel firmly.

"That's a shame. I could put a lot of business your way."

"The answer's still no," said Nigel emphatically.

"In which case, I'll have to work on a few assumptions. I think the key to this is your recent visit to Dubai. I'll make a few enquiries there. Nothing underhand, I assure you, but the business community has a tendency to gossip a bit."

"That's up to you," said Nigel, "but don't involve me again or there will be repercussions. Now if you'll excuse me, I'll be on my way."

With that he left, even though the main course had not arrived, and made his way back to the office. Immediately he put a call through to Mike Edwards in Dubai and recounted in detail the substance of his conversation with Kahn.

"Doesn't surprise me," said Mike. "What I can tell you is the Lloyd's broker he was having breakfast with here in the Intercontinental on Tuesday was a chap called Darren Black from Baxter Taylor and Black. Kahn does business with them from time to time. I guess that's who told him about your involvement."

"So he probably knows exactly what's going on," said Nigel. "If so, why come to me?"

"Undoubtedly. But he probably wants to be able to say he'd discussed the matter with you. He may still do that."

"OK Mike, thanks. I'll be on my guard. In hindsight it was probably unwise to have gone. Anyway, we have the quote so I'll call you again later this afternoon."

"Thanks Nigel. At least you know what he's all about. Bye for now."

At the end of the afternoon Nigel made his way over to Mary's office, where her team had all assembled. She explained to Nigel the full extent of the terms that Simon had got, giving him full credit for the impressive result. Everyone knew, though, that she had masterminded it by sending in a trainee on his first mission.

"The rate is good," commented Nigel, "but let's talk a bit about what he wants to do. The way I see it he has to go to Paris. There's no way the stuff can be brought to him. He'll need to go soon and one of us will be obliged to go with him."

"That'll be you," interjected Mary. "We'll have enough to do when the order comes in."

"Sure," said Nigel. "But I'm still a bit concerned how this might go down with the client. I know it's supposed to be helpful, but it might be seen by others as interference, not to mention the extra people who will know about the transaction. The client is trying to keep that to a minimum."

"There's another angle here, though," said Jamie. "Once the jewellery has been authenticated on behalf of Lloyd's, there can be no dispute as to value or provenance in the event of a claim, unlikely as that may be. It's almost as though the claim amount has been pre-agreed."

"Good point," agreed Nigel. "But I'm still concerned about the timing. We can't do any of this until we get the order, which won't be until Monday at the earliest, since our weekends don't coincide."

"How about this," volunteered Craig. "You go on the day of handover. You could, say, arrive at the embassy in the morning, do the evaluation, wait there while the funds are transferred then watch the stuff while it's packed away for dispatch."

"Another good idea," said Nigel. "That might work well. I think I'm happy with it all now. I'll put the quote to them tonight. Good work everyone."

"I'll second that," said Mary. "Fine job of work all round. Let's have a couple of jars to celebrate."

They hurried out of the office to a wine bar in Great Tower Street called The Broker, where they shared a bottle of Pinot Grigio. After about an hour, Mary and Simon left for their respective stations, leaving the other two, along with a significant section of the Lloyd's community, to enjoy their evening. A short while later Biffo turned up, not unexpectedly.

"How's it going lads?" he enquired.

"Not bad at all," replied Craig. "Had quite a good day as a matter of fact. You?"

"Usual. By the way, word has it someone's got a quote of one-point-four for your jewellery. Saw it going round this afternoon."

"Yeah? Who was it?" asked Craig.

"Can't tell you that," said Biffo, laughing.

"Fair enough," said Craig. "Fancy some more wine?"

The following morning, Jamie and Craig were in the office early.

"This is a surprise," commented Mary. "Did you enjoy last evening?"

"Yes," said Craig. "But I'm afraid we have a problem. It seems that Baxter Taylor have matched our quote of one-point-four. Got it from Biffo just before seven o'clock."

"OK. Who paid the bill?"

"I did," said Jamie. "Came to just over seventy quid."

"Right, let me have the receipt and I'll bill it as a business expense. Meanwhile here's what we do. I'll tell Nigel, while Simon gets back to Tellytubby to see if he can get a rate reduction. Won't be much, but it doesn't need to be."

Simon then joined them and was briefed as to his next role in the assignment. He made his way to Lloyd's just before 11.00 a.m. and was lucky enough to find his man already in place at the box.

"Simon," said the underwriter. "How are things?"

"Good, thank you Sir," replied Simon. "The golf is fine. Mary is happy with that, but we do have a slight problem."

"What's that?"

"Someone's matched our one-point-four rate for the jewellery. We're wondering if there's any leeway at all."

"Well, if absolutely necessary I suppose I could shave a bit off. How about one-point-three-seven-five?"

"That's what we were hoping for. Thank you for that," said Simon. On his way back to the office he sent a text to Mary giving her the new rate. By the time he returned she had relayed the news to Nigel who immediately telephoned Mike in Dubai. They were just in time, as it turned out, as the quote had not at that stage been passed on, it being Friday. Now all they could do was to wait.

At home that evening, Simon was discussing the first two weeks with his father, explaining that it was quite unlike anything he had expected. They both expressed surprise that trading, or broking as it was called, was still face-to-face and not electronic, that underwriters could sometimes be more than a little pompous, that brokers were treated a bit like servants and that everyone seemed to know each other's business. Or at least they could quite easily find out if they wanted to. And yet, strangely, the system seemed to work.

"It's the same wherever you get a concentration of similar businesses in a small area," explained John. "Smithfield, Hatton Garden, even fruit and vegetable markets. People all know each other, so it ends up being very intense and extremely competitive. The thing to remember, though," he went on, "is that the client benefits from it. Take your jewellery, for example. Without that level of competition, your client would have got the higher rate rather than the lower one."

"Yes, I see," said Simon. "But I still find it very odd. Incidentally, I have to play golf next Friday at the East Sussex National. I'm partnering an underwriter in a charity match. I don't have the details yet so I don't know about the timing. My boss says I have to do it, so I'll need some transport, if that's OK?"

"Not sure what your mother's doing that day, but one of us will get you there and back for sure."

"Thanks Dad," said Simon. "I'll get a bit of practice in tomorrow, I think."

The following day Simon went to the golf club. After an hour on the driving range he joined three other members for a round of eighteen. The driving range had obviously helped, as Simon carded a very creditable two over par. He then made his way into the clubhouse where he saw Emma Claremont, on her own and sipping a glass of orange juice.

"May I join you?" asked Simon, oozing confidence.

"Yes of course," replied Emma. "How did it go?"

"Two over."

"Wow. That's impressive," she said. "I hear you're working now. How is that going?"

"So far very well," replied Simon. He then proceeded to give a detailed account of his first two weeks, the intensity of it all, the urgency with which things need to get done and the bizarre trading system that despite its cumbersome nature, seemed to work very well.

"The inner workings of markets like Lloyd's are a mystery to most people," explained Simon. "Of course, it's the client that benefits," he added, borrowing the line from his father's summing up the evening before.

"Yes, I see," she replied, already mystified.

"I wonder Emma," he ventured, "whether you'd like to come out one evening soon? Perhaps next Saturday we could go to a film or a show, then have a bite to eat?"

"That's very kind, Simon," she replied. "I'd like to do that."

"Excellent. I'll see what's on and let you know. Are you having a sandwich here."

"No, Simon. I'm just waiting for my dad to pick me up. He'll be here soon."

"OK."

Mr Claremont duly arrived to collect his daughter.

"Hello Simon," he said. "How are you?"

"Fine thank you Mr Claremont. I hope you don't mind but I've just invited Emma out next Saturday. A show and a bite to eat."

"Did she accept?"

"Yes, she did."

"Good. That's a very good idea. Right Emma, if you're ready we'll get on our way. It's nice to see you Simon."

"You too, Sir," said Simon.

The following morning, a working day in Dubai, Mike Edwards was preparing the details of the quote ready for transmission to his agent in Bahrain. He was a little unsure how the verification procedure would be received, but seemed a good idea when he talked it through with Nigel and it was going to be by Lloyd's in any event. Eventually he decided to go ahead with it. He telephoned Mahdi Al Hadda and relayed the information to him. There was a very positive response.

"I like it," said Mahdi. "Very much indeed. I'll get hold of the Saudis and get back to you as soon as I can. Are you sending me the written quote?"

"Yes," replied Mike. "There'll be a package coming by air courier on the next flight. Should be with you by this afternoon."

"OK thanks. Talk to you soon."

Later that day Mike got a return call from Mahdi Al Hadda in Bahrain.

"Mike, they like it," he announced enthusiastically. "We've got the go-ahead. Handover day will be next Thursday and the courier will be none other than Saleh Said Al Othaim, the guy you met, who is one of the prince's closest aides. He will be accompanied by a bodyguard called Yacoub, also on the prince's pay-roll. Yacoub has considerable experience at this kind of work, apparently.

They're going to be driven to the airport in an embassy limo and one of the officials will be going with them. At check-in they will be met by the airport's services manager who will shepherd them through security and passport control. Once airside, they will be met by an official from Saudia, who will accompany them as far as the departure lounge. I've asked that the Saudi embassy in Paris be alerted to the underwriter's visit, that it should coincide with the pick-up and that there will be three people in the group. We will need to provide names in advance of their arrival. One slight problem, though, the Saudia flight leaves at 11.20 a.m., which means being out of the embassy and on the road by about 8.00 a.m. You might like to get your guys to think that through again."

"I will," said Mike. "And well done. This is good news. I'll tell London as soon as I can. Did the package arrive yet?"

"Yes Mike. I have it."

"Great. Let me have confirmation in writing in due course but I'll get on with this in the meantime. And thanks. Are we being told the name of the prince yet?"

"No Mike. They want to keep it a secret for as long as possible, at least until the goods have arrived."

"OK. Understood. Bye for now."

It being the end of his day, Mike made his way home.

"Janice, do we have Nigel's home number?" he asked. "I need to contact him."

"Yes. I'll get it for you."

He made the call.

"Nigel it's Mike. Good news, mate, we have the order."

He then proceeded to outline the details, emphasising again the need for as much secrecy as possible, despite the number of people now involved and confirming the Saudi embassy in Paris would be made aware in advance of the impending visit.

"We need names as soon as possible," he reiterated, "along with confirmation of exactly when you plan to arrive. Also the couriers will have to leave the embassy by eight in the morning."

"Understood Mike. And thanks. The underwriter is a chap called Martin Jackson. I will be going with him but I don't know who the other one will be yet. Should know tomorrow."

"OK Nigel. Our company have been asked to keep our name out of this transaction, so it will be a direct placement into Lloyd's. We'll take our commission into one of our sub-agencies but the paperwork will bear the Lloyd's name. What is the commission, while I think of it?"

"We'll get twenty-two and a half per cent from Lloyd's," confirmed Nigel. "We'll keep seven and a half per cent ourselves, leaving you fifteen per cent to share with Mahdi."

"Fine," said Mike. "One small snag, though. They don't want to tell us the name of the prince. I don't know how to get around that."

"We'll think of something, I'm sure. I'll be onto it first thing. Is there any more news of Hari Kahn, by the way?"

"Not here, but he has been sniffing around in Bahrain."

"Mike, I'm a bit surprised he hasn't been to see you."

"So am I, Nigel. He may have sounded out one or more of our directors, though, but they wouldn't necessarily tell me."

"OK Mike. Thanks for that. We'll talk again tomorrow. Bye."

"Bye Nigel."

Chapter 6

On Monday morning the team assembled as usual and were soon joined by Nigel Watkins.

"Good news," he proclaimed. "We have the go-ahead."

He then proceeded to outline the order, emphasising the urgency, explaining the need to identify the group that would be going to Paris on Thursday, plus the fact that the prince's name was still a secret.

"I'll leave you guys to work out how that can be done," he said. "Let me know how it's going, won't you."

"Of course," replied Mary. "You can leave it to us."

At that point John Marshall, the final member of the team arrived, having just returned from holiday. He was a man in his mid-fifties, tall and well-groomed, who came from Borehamwood in Hertfordshire. Mary introduced him to Simon and gave him a quick up-date as to the matter in hand.

"I'll prepare the slip for the jewellery," she said. "Any ideas how to get around the identity issue?"

"We could use a code," suggested John. "Then at some suitable time in the future the real name can be substituted. Or it could just be left as it is, if the prince prefers to remain anonymous. That way no location will be shown on the documents."

"What, something like 'NHSP01'?" said Mary. "In other words, 'Nathan Henry Saudi Prince 01'."

"Yes. That'll do."

"Lovely," replied Mary. "Right, here's the plan. Simon, you need to see Tellytubby first thing. You need to get his line down on the slip. Hopefully his share will be in the region of fifteen per cent, otherwise we might struggle a bit. He also needs to tell us who he's taking to Paris so the visit can be organised. Once you've done that get a message to me in Lloyd's. Craig, you and I will have photo-copies of the slip so we can scoot round and cover the following market. We'll get their lines down in pencil to start with, then the original slip can be formally stamped by the entry boys later. It'll save time. I want this finished by the end of tomorrow if we can. John, you and Jamie can carry on with our other stuff. Everyone happy?"

"I'm a bit lost with these percentages," said Simon. "Where does the fifteen per cent come in?"

"Right, remember the slip I showed you on your first day," explained Mary. "No underwriter ever takes the whole of the risk. Each one takes a share. The more the leader takes, the easier it is for us to get to one hundred per cent. Fifteen per cent would be a good start."

"OK," replied Simon. "What's the one-point-three-seven-five per cent then?"

"Multiply that by the amount insured and you get the premium. That's for a twelve month policy."

"Right," said Simon, still puzzled.

"OK. Meet back here at the end of the afternoon," said Mary. "Good luck everyone."

The Al Talyani Insurance Company of Dubai was known for its support of local enterprise. Its directors were prominent members of the community who took a keen interest in all business affairs within the Emirates. They had a reputation for integrity and were well-known in the London insurance market. The company served Muslim and non-Muslim businesses alike and welcomed enquiries from the expat community. The chairman, Sheikh Abdul Rahman bin Aziz Al Talyani, was a keen follower of sport and from time to time, his company would sponsor professional golf tournaments and international cricket. He was related to the ruling family of Dubai and, as a result, was very well connected in the region.

The day after receiving the order on the jewellery, Mike Edwards paid a visit to the chairman at his office in the Dubai Financial Centre. He gave him a full account of the deal he had just negotiated with Lloyd's, explaining what was and who were involved and the need for secrecy.

"This is good news," commented the sheikh. "Why did the Bahraini agent come to us?"

"He has no intro into the Lloyd's market, but he knows we do and we're better placed to get decent quotes."

"OK. Actually I think I know who the prince is, but I suppose I'd better keep it to myself."

"I guess so," replied Mike.

"While you're here," continued Al Talyani, "have you ever met a man called Hari Kahn?"

"No I haven't," replied Mike. "I've heard of him, though. Why do you ask?"

"He's a man I don't want our company to do business with. Anyway, Mike, thanks for keeping me informed."

"Pleasure. See you soon."

At 11.30 a.m. back in London, Simon was waiting for Martin Jackson to arrive at the box. Within a few minutes he appeared.

"Morning Simon," he exclaimed. "All well?"

"Yes thank you Sir. We have the order on the jewellery."

"Excellent. Now about the golf. We're meeting at around nine o'clock for coffee. We'll play nine in the morning, break for lunch, then do the other nine afterwards. There'll be eight four-balls. The cost is eighty quid, of which fifty will go into the kitty for the charity. The winners get to choose which charity the money goes to. Happy with that?"

"Yes," replied Simon. "No worries."

"Good. Right let's see the slip. I'll lead you off with ten per cent I think."

"Actually Sir, we were hoping for fifteen. Otherwise we think we might struggle to finish. Several underwriters have already declined to participate."

"OK well I could go to twelve and a half, but no more. This is a lot of jewellery. Fifteen per cent would give my syndicate too much exposure."

With that he stamped the slip, wrote his share alongside and handed it to Jane, who referenced and photocopied it then handed it back to Simon. At no time did she either speak or smile.

"Thank you Sir," said Simon. "Now we need to know about the Paris trip as soon as possible. The Saudi embassy wants names in advance."

"Understood," said the underwriter. "Who's going from your place?"

"Nigel Watkins," replied Simon.

"Ah Crowbar. I thought this might be one of his. I'm probably going to use Sotheby's jewellery expert in Paris. I don't want a valuation. That would cost me two arms and two legs. He'll just tell me that the items are what they're supposed to be and that they aren't being overvalued. He'll photograph them as well. My sister-in-law works at Sotheby's in London so she will be able to set it up for me. I'll confirm it all later today. Pop by at about four-thirty, would you?"

"Yes Sir," said Simon. "Thank you."

With that he headed back to the ground floor, made his way to the Rostrum and asked the waiter to call Nathan Henry Whitehouse. Within a few seconds Mary was leaning over the railing of the second gallery waving frantically. She motioned Simon to come to her.

"I'm in a queue," she explained when he got there. "How did you get on?"

"Twelve and a half per cent," he replied.

"OK. Not too bad. Now see what support you can get. What about the trip?"

"He's working on it. He's asked me to stop by at half past four," explained Simon.

"OK. See you later."

On his way back to the office at the end of the afternoon, Simon stopped at the Jackson box as agreed. The underwriter stood away from the box, interrupting the broker who was there and came over.

"Right, it's all agreed. The local expert is Marcel Dubois. He's well known in the jewellery trade. Someone will need to let me know what the arrangements are."

"Yes of course Sir. And thanks again."

Back in the office they were summarising their day. In addition to the twelve and a half per cent from the leader, Simon had collected a further fifteen per cent, in two lines of seven and a half each.

"How about you, Craig?" asked Mary.

"Ten per cent each from Biffo and Honeymonster plus a couple more fives."

"OK. I've got two more tens and a three. Let's see, that gives us a grand total of eighty and a half per cent. We should easily knock that off tomorrow. What about the trip, Simon?"

"Yes I have the details. Someone needs to call Tellytubby with the arrangements."

"Perfect. I'll go and see Nigel now. Good-night guys. Bright and early in the morning."

At 4.45 p.m. on Wednesday, Nigel Watkins met Martin Jackson at his offices in Gracechurch Street and from there they took a taxi to St Pancras. They were booked on the 18.01 departure to Paris. On arrival at Gare du Nord, some two hours and sixteen minutes later, they took a taxi to the Holiday Inn, close to the Champs Elysees, checked in and went for dinner. Having agreed to meet the following morning at 5.30 a.m., they turned in for the night. They had not wanted to disrupt the consignment's departure for the airport at 8.00 a.m., so had arranged to be at the embassy by 6.00 a.m. This they duly were. Shortly afterwards Marcel Dubois arrived and a little while after that the armoured van arrived. The assembled group now consisted of Jackson, Watkins, Dubois, Al Othaim, Yacoub, two Parisian jewellers and three officials from the embassy. Witnessed by all, Marcel Dubois commenced his assessment. He examined each of the five pieces in detail, taking his time. He then repeated the process. Then he photographed each piece several times from different angles. His attention then turned to the accompanying paperwork which he again examined meticulously. He then photographed each document. One hour and fifteen minutes later and the job was done.

"Thank you very much gentlemen," he said. "I need nothing further."

He turned and nodded in the direction of the men from Lloyd's, indicating to them that all was in order. Meanwhile one of the jewellers was on his mobile checking on the funds transfer. He, too, nodded. The embassy officials then re-packaged each item, placing them one by one into a security box which was then locked and placed into a travel bag, small enough to be taken on board as hand luggage. At 7.50 a.m. the embassy limo arrived at the back of the building, into which were escorted Al Othaim with precious luggage, Yacoub with hand luggage and one embassy official. Underwriter Jackson and broker Watkins both thanked their hosts for accommodating them in such a pleasant and efficient manner and left, along with Marcel Dubois. They decided to go for coffee.

"So it's all OK?" they enquired of the expert, almost in unison.

"Oh yes," replied Dubois. "These are well known items that have been around for a long time. They were once the property of the Romanovs but they date back beyond them to the middle of the seventeenth century. They've been in several royal collections over the years. I'll send you a written report in a few days."

"Many thanks indeed," said the underwriter. "Send me your bill at the same time, won't you."

With that they left. They took a taxi to Gare du Nord, boarded the Eurostar to London and made their way to the city, arriving at their respective offices just after noon. At 1.00 p m. Nigel headed over to Mary's room to check on progress of things.

"All done and dusted," she confirmed. "Everything in place. How was Paris?"

"Fine," replied Nigel. "They're the real thing. Tellytubby was very happy. Excellent work all round, guys, so thank you."

The following morning, armed with golf clubs, peripheral accessories and two hundred pounds of his company's petty cash, Simon was on his way to the East Sussex National Golf Club, courtesy of his mother.

"It's on the A22 isn't it?" she asked.

"Yes mother. Just south of Uckfield. Our best way is the A27 eastwards, turning left at Polegate. I've been there before, so we'll have no trouble finding it."

They didn't, and they arrived there at 8.45 a.m.

"Now give me a call about an hour before you're ready to leave and I'll come and get you. Have a nice time, dear."

Simon did not like being referred to as 'dear'. Inside the club house he saw his host Martin Jackson in an area of the bar sectioned off for coffee and buns.

"Hello Simon," he said.

"Good morning Sir," Simon replied.

"I think you'd better call me Martin from now on. Now that we're golf partners."

"OK."

The group gradually assembled, Simon recognising only a few of them. They were given details of the groupings and handed their cards. Scoring was to be by the Stableford system, each pair adding their points together to determine the winners. Simon noticed there were two other underwriters making up his four, Cyril Jones and Brian Fielding, but he did not know either of them. They made their introductions and at the appointed time headed for the first tee. Their group was second off. They wished each other good luck and shook hands. Cyril drove off first, slicing the ball into the bushes a short way down the course. Martin then hit a presentable drive down the middle, but not very far, while Brian shanked his ball left of the fairway and out of bounds. Simon hit his drive very straight and an extremely long way towards the green, almost reaching it. The others looked on in amazement.

"I've heard about you," said Brian. "You've recently joined Nathan Henry, haven't you?"

"Yes, that's right."

"In that case, welcome to Lloyd's."

"Thank you," said Simon.

The rest of the morning round continued in more or less the same fashion and by lunch time Martin and Simon were way ahead of the rest. Simon had most of the points, but Martin had managed to raise his game a bit, no doubt due to the illustrious golfing company he was in. Back in the club house they supped a well-earned beer, while waiting for the stragglers to finish. Then it was time for lunch.

"You've joined a good team, Simon," said Martin as they were eating. "High level of integrity. How are you, Darren?" he added, looking at the chap opposite.

"Fair, I suppose," he replied. "We just lost out on a big one to Nathan Henry though. Don't know how they did that."

"I do," replied Martin, grinning. "Darren Black, meet Simon Blunt. He's from Nathan Henry."

There was loud laughter from all those within earshot. The afternoon continued much as the morning, with Martin and Simon running out clear winners by fifteen points. They were duly presented with their trophy, a small gold-coloured plastic golfer, fixed on a wooden base and engraved *Bunker Hunt Winners 2012*. They were then invited to name the charity they wanted to benefit from the day, which they had pre-agreed should be the Chestnut Tree House, a children's hospice based in West Sussex. It being 4.30 p.m. by now, Simon phoned his mother to tell her that he could be collected. His mobile had been off all day, but now he left it on. After a while it rang. It was Mary.

"Simon, is Martin still with you?" she asked.

"Yes. Why?"

"I need to speak to him. Would you put him on, please?"

"It's Mary for you," said Simon, handing his phone to Martin.

"Martin, the jewellery's gone."

"I know, Mary. I was there, remember?"

"No. Gone as in disappeared. It did not arrive in Riyadh nor did the couriers. The Saudis haven't a clue what happened and the prince is going crazy. Thought you'd better know about it straight away. Obviously they'll keep us posted and as soon as any more information comes to light, we'll let you know."

"Nice try Mary. You can't catch me like that. You and your merry little pranks," he said, laughing loudly.

"No Martin. This is not a prank. It's for real."

"Very funny. Here am I on a golf course and you phone to tell me I'm looking at a total loss on only the second day of the policy. I don't think so. Your colleagues put you up to this. I know what you lot are like."

"No, really Martin. I assure you this is no joke."

"Yeah, and I'm the Count of Monte Cristo," he roared, handing the phone back to Simon.

"Everything all right, Mary?" enquired Simon.

"No, it most certainly is not. The jewellery has disappeared but the idiot won't believe me. Has he been drinking?"

"Yes," replied Simon. "He's celebrating his victory. He's got someone driving him home later."

"Best leave him to it, then."

"OK."

Simon was stunned for a second, not knowing quite what to do next. At that point he saw his mother pulling into the car park. He said his goodbyes, gathered his things and made a swift exit.

"Thanks for today, by the way," Martin yelled after him.

"No problem." replied Simon. "Have a good weekend."

"You too."

Chapter 7

Late on Friday afternoon in Bahrain, Mahdi Al Hadda was on his way to meet two of the prince's men, Almahdi and Fawzi, originally from Qatar and Abu Dhabi respectively. In the interests of expediency, they had agreed to meet at Al-Khobar, enabling Mahdi to drive from Bahrain across the causeway.

"We were there," they began. "The prince had arranged for us to be airside waiting at the top of the ramp as the passengers came off. Al Othaim and Yacoub were in first class, or rather they were supposed to be, and they are both well-known to us. They just didn't get off."

"Was there any other way off?" asked Mahdi.

"No," was the reply. "We checked."

"And are you absolutely sure everyone got off?"

"Yes. We alerted the captain straight away. He was the only one of the crew that knew about the precious cargo. He invited us on board and a thorough search was carried out, but no one had hidden themselves, or been hidden, on the plane. The captain then instructed his flight attendants to look for any hand luggage that had been left behind, but there was none. At that point we told the prince, who asked us to tell you."

"It was a direct flight, wasn't it?" enquired Mahdi.

"Yes it was."

"So whatever happened, it must have happened in Paris."

"Yes, we think so. The prince, of course, is outraged. At the moment he thinks Al Othaim and Yacoub, two of his most trusted aides, have simply absconded taking the jewellery with them. If they have, and when they are caught, the punishment will be very severe, as is our tradition."

"But the flight would not take off on time if it were two passengers short," said Mahdi. "It's one of the fundamental rules of airline security. There would have been extra checks causing considerable disruption and delay. Was the flight on time?"

"Yes it was," they confirmed.

"So what are you planning to do next?"

"There's not much we can do here. We have, though, told the embassy in Paris to notify the French police and no doubt their enquiries will get underway with some urgency. The prince wants it kept out of the public domain, as far as is possible, in the interests of preserving his dignity, but certain people must be told, particularly Lloyd's."

"That's been done through our contact in Dubai," confirmed Mahdi. "Naturally, they will want full details if a claim is to be made. We've placed comprehensive cover, so there's no doubt the policy will respond, it's just that a full explanation of the loss will be required, whenever that can be done."

"Understood," they confirmed.

"What about the local police?" asked Mahdi. "Have they been told?"

"Not yet. The prince is holding off for the time being until there's more information."

With that the meeting concluded. Mahdi drove back to Bahrain and put a call through to Mike Edwards in Dubai. He gave a full account of the conversation that had just taken place in Al-Khobar.

"Are you sure they're telling the truth?" asked Mike. "It all sounds a bit far-fetched to me. How can we be certain this story is right? What if the couriers did get off the plane and the reception committee just let them pass? And how do we know the prince isn't in on it?"

"Would you like to ask him, Mike?"

"Not me. He's your client," replied Mike sharply. "You do it."

"I'll think about that. OK that's it for now. Be in touch."

Mike then telephoned Nigel at home in Guildford and gave him a full account of the conversation that had just taken place with Mahdi, adding his own suspicions about what he had heard.

"It doesn't make sense to me," he told Nigel. "They insure the stuff on day one and on day two they lose it all. Not for me.

I bet those guys got off that flight and they're now holed up somewhere in Saudi Arabia with the jewels. That's the only way it could have happened. You'll see."

"OK Mike," said Nigel. "We're going to need a statement from the prince for the purpose of registering a formal claim, if he decides to do that."

"I'm not sure that's wise. I think he might have been in on it. Why, for instance, hasn't it been reported to the police in Riyadh?"

"To avoid the publicity. I doubt he's involved, Mike. We are talking about a Saudi royal here. Anyway, let me have every scrap of information as and when you get it. Bye for now."

"OK. Bye."

That evening, back in Brighton, Simon was at home organising his Saturday evening out with Emma Claremont. His mind, though, was still on the events of the afternoon.

"You're quiet, dear," ventured his mother. "Is everything all right?"

"I don't know," he replied. "Something happened at the office today which I'm not too sure about."

"Oh, never mind. It's just work," she commented. "It'll be fine. Best talk to your father if it's worrying you. By the way, the Claremonts are coming here for dinner tomorrow, so they'll be bringing Emma and taking her home afterwards. If you need transport into Brighton, I'll drive you and pick you up."

"No thanks," he replied, somewhat irritated by his mother's habit of treating him like a small boy. "We'll go by bus and come back by taxi."

An internet search had revealed there was a film on he wanted to see, so he sent a text to Emma, which read:-

'WYL 2 C Spiderman 2morrow? B4N'

To which Emma replied:-

'GR8 WFM CYT'

At that point his father came into the room.

"How was today?" he asked his son.

"Well the golf was fine, but something else happened at the end of the afternoon."

He then proceeded to describe the telephone call from his boss and the precise details of what had transpired, limited as they were.

"It's not really your fault, is it?" said his father. "You've only been there three weeks and you're a trainee. Just go along with it and learn from what they do. And remember, twenty-odd million dollars is not a large amount for these Lloyd's guys. It's not up there with hurricanes, tsunamis, earthquakes, oil pollution, airline or shipping disasters. That's the business they're in. It's the billions they get concerned about."

"Yes I know, Dad, but I still feel kind of responsible. It was because of me that we got the quote that won us the order, all because I agreed to play golf with the underwriter. It was my first ever visit to Lloyd's on my own and it's probably going to stay in people's minds for the rest of my career. I'm a bit nervous about ever going in there again."

"Don't be. It's what insurance is all about. It's exactly what your company do day in day out. There can be no criticism of your part in this affair. Lloyd's pays out over seventy-five million pounds of claims every working day on average. This will hardly be noticed."

"Yes," said Simon, "but there's only a small group of underwriters on this one. Fourteen out of the couple of hundred or more that make up the whole market. It's going to hurt them disproportionately."

"Oh, so each syndicate is on for just their own share, then?" queried his father. "I somehow thought that once an underwriter had subscribed to a slip, the whole of Lloyd's was committed to it. That's the impression we get when they boast about the absolute security of the Lloyd's policy."

"Oh, that bit's true," explained Simon. "All the premiums are gathered into a huge central trust fund which is where all claims are paid from. Each syndicate is then accountable for the premiums and losses it generates and if there's a shortfall of serious proportions, Lloyd's comes after the assets of each member of that syndicate. And members' liabilities are unlimited, of course. After that there's a further guarantee fund which runs into hundreds of millions, but by then the claims have already been paid, so it's all very secure."

"You've picked up quite a bit in three weeks," commented his father.

"Yes," confirmed Simon. "They give me loads of stuff to read in the office."

"Well it's still not your fault," said his father. "You were acting reasonably and fairly for your company in their client's interests. Don't let anyone suggest otherwise."

"I won't," replied Simon, feeling slightly better about it, but not much.

The following afternoon the Claremont family – George, wife Joanne and daughter Emma – duly arrived at the home of the Blunts in Valley Drive. It was a fine, sunny afternoon so they relaxed in the garden. Simon had decided to catch the early evening showing of *The Amazing Spiderman* and then go for an Italian meal at a restaurant nearby. He would have suggested going to one of the glitzy, seafront clubs after that, but not while the Claremonts were waiting for the safe return of their daughter back at his house. Maybe next time. At 5.00.p.m. he and Emma set off on foot, past the Withdean Sports Stadium, down Tongdean Lane to London Road, where they caught the next bus into town. They got off at the Clock Tower and made their way down West Street towards the cinema. They were in good time for the film, so walked over to the seafront and found a couple of empty deckchairs on the beach.

"So are you enjoying work?" asked Emma.

"Yes, on the whole. I'm involved in some heavy stuff at the moment," replied Simon, giving a brief summary of the events of his week, exaggerating somewhat the part he played in the jewellery matter. Emma seemed duly impressed.

"I don't think I'd want do anything like that," she said. "It sounds very intense. I'm aiming to go to university myself," she added, "with a view to becoming a teacher."

To Simon, right then, it sounded like a very good idea, not that he had the academic skills for that line of work. He was still struggling to come to terms with what had happened and was more than a little concerned at what he might have to face on Monday morning. It wasn't something he was prepared to reveal to Emma, though. His parents had sensed his anxiety and were doing their best to be supportive, without really understanding how one-to-one relationships worked in the Lloyd's market and how important they were. After spending ten or so minutes on the beach, they then made their way from the esplanade back to the cinema in time for the film.

Back at the house, Simon's new job and his transition from schoolboy to broker was the principle subject of discussion over dinner. The Claremonts knew very little of Lloyd's and its trading practices, so it took a while for John to explain, as best he could, how it all worked. In so doing, he touched on the matter of the jewellery.

"I know a lot about that region," said George. "For a while I was posted to our embassy in Kuwait, then to Bahrain and there was a lot of interaction with the Saudis. I still have a lot of dealings with those countries."

"So you'll be familiar with business people as well," asked John.

"Yes, some of them," replied George. "It's been a while now, though. These days I'm more in touch with diplomats."

"So Simon is getting involved in some really heavy matters," commented Joanne Claremont. "And it's only his third week?"

Yes," said Angela Blunt. "He's right in at the deep end."

"He's the junior member of a team of five, though," explained John. "He only follows instructions. I know he's a bit concerned, but he really doesn't need to be. It'll be run-of-the-mill stuff for his company."

At that point, just on 10.30 p.m., Simon and Emma returned.

"Nice evening?" enquired Angela.

"Yes thank you," said Emma. "Very nice indeed. The film was spectacular. Afterwards we went for an Italian meal which was first class."

"Where did you go?" asked her father.

"Donatello's," said Simon, "in The Lanes."

"Oh, very nice," commented Joanne. "Well, I think we'd better be on our way now. Thank you so much for dinner, Angela. It was delightful. You must all come to us next time. And thank you Simon for taking Emma out and for looking after her so well."

"Pleasure," he replied.

They said their goodbyes and the Claremonts headed back to their home in Woodland Drive with Joanne at the wheel. They could have walked it in about twenty minutes, but the driver was teetotal, so there were no concerns about her driving.

"They are a nice family," said Joanne.

"Yes," said George, "they are."

"And Simon's a nice lad. Do you like him, Emma?"

"Yes, I do mother," she replied. "Very much. He's very polite, well-mannered and interesting, particular now he's working. He's good to be with."

"That's nice," said her mother.

"It's the golf club that does that for him," suggested George. "Plus, of course, his background. Funny he didn't join his father's accountancy firm, though," he added.

"He can't stand maths," explained Emma. "It's a subject he didn't get on with it at school."

"And yet he's gone into Lloyd's," said Joanne, "with all their complicated calculations."

"Yes, but he's only a glorified messenger," commented George. "At least for the moment."

"That's not fair, George," said Joanne. "It's only been three weeks."

"I know," replied George. "But it'll be a while before he gets any real responsibility. It's a good start, of course, and something he can be proud of but there'll be a protocol in his company that suggests someone higher will be responsible for whatever he does, all the while he's a trainee."

"You're right, George," sighed Joanne. "As usual."

Chapter 8

At precisely 9.00 a.m. on Monday morning Simon arrived at the office. Mary was the only one there, as usual.

"So you had a good day, then," she asked.

"Yes we did, thank you," replied Simon. "We won the trophy, so the sixteen hundred quid went to the charity of our choice, a local children's hospice. Here's the money I didn't spend, by the way," he added, handing back one hundred and twenty pounds. "It was eighty pounds for the day, plus incidental refreshments, but Mr Jackson funded those."

"Not all he'll be funding, by the look of things," she said, wryly.

"Any more news?" asked Simon, cautiously.

"We're due to meet with Nigel in about half an hour. He'll give us the latest. You, I and Craig will handle that, since we were the placing brokers."

Craig duly arrived just before 9.30 a.m. and the three of them made their way to Nigel's office.

"I've asked David Locke, our claims director to join us," he told the group and at that point a young man of slick appearance with over-gelled jet-black hair entered the room. He was from Gravesend and was known for being forthright, occasionally bordering on the offensive. His tact and diplomacy, it was often said, if measured by the centigrade scale, would be below freezing. He was a leather-clad biker, the proud owner of a Kawasaki 1000, which he rode to and from the office every day. He was an extremely dedicated employee who was at his desk every morning by 7.30 a.m. and interested only in getting the job done according to the correct protocol. Because of this he had the respect of those he worked with.

"David," said Mary. "This is Simon Blunt."

"Ah yes," replied David. "You're the chap who got the quote. They won't forget you in a hurry," he added, sneeringly.

"Shut it, David," retorted Mary, leaping to Simon's defence. "He did the right thing for this company in the right circumstances, so let's have none of that."

"OK guys," said Nigel, interrupting. "Here's where we're at. I had a long conversation with Mike Edwards on Friday evening. His Bahraini agent has seen the two who were waiting at the airport and it's pretty clear to them that the couriers did not get off the plane in Riyadh. Thorough checks were made on the spot to see if there was any other way off. There wasn't. Further checks were made to see if anyone was still on board. There wasn't. Flight crew also checked for baggage left on board. There wasn't any. The Saudi embassy in Paris has been asked to notify the French police and enquiries are underway there. The police in Riyadh have not yet been notified, so as to avoid adverse publicity for the prince, but they will be told when there is more information. Mike Edwards thinks it possible that the stuff did arrive and the two chaps who were waiting for it are lying. He thinks the prince himself might be involved in the deception. I doubt that myself, but I suppose we can't rule it out. Mary, did you get the message through to the underwriter on Friday afternoon?"

"I did, yes," she replied. "But he chose not to believe me. He thought I was blagging him."

"That's up to him," said Nigel. "But at least you told him. Now, I want us to make good progress before this breaks in the press. What do you think should happen next, David?"

"I don't think," he replied. "I follow procedure. And as we don't have a claim from the client yet, that procedure can't begin. Until then I'm not able to do anything, but you lot can do whatever you like. Who is the client, by the way?"

"We don't have a name," explained Nigel. "It's all to do with secrecy."

"Oh great," he smirked. "We're flying by the seat of our boxers again."

"No, that's not how it is," snapped Nigel. "We had clear, firm instructions about secrecy and underwriters went along with it."

"Well, there's not enough here for a claim to be presented," said David. "Let me know when you have something I can work with. Now if you don't mind, I have work to do," he added, leaving the room somewhat abruptly.

During this slightly acrimonious exchange, Simon had been completely silent and somewhat embarrassed. He had not yet come to terms with his involvement in such a high-profile matter.

"That wasn't too helpful," commented Mary.

"I know," said Nigel. "The problem is he's right, a formal claim can only come from the client. We can't do it on his behalf. We'd better get a meeting going with Jackson. Can you set that up, please Mary?"

"Yes, will do," was the reply, as she, Craig and Simon made their way back to their own office.

"Who do you think's been on the phone?" asked John, when they got back.

"Himself, I suppose," said Mary, wearily.

"Spot on. He wants you in his office at 10.15 a.m. this morning."

"OK, we'll be there."

Mary put a call through to her boss and a few minutes later the four of them – she, Nigel, Craig and Simon - walked over to the Jackson office in Gracechurch Street and waited in reception for the 10.15 a.m. summons. They were not kept waiting long. After a few minutes, the underwriter burst in and with a brisk and cheery 'good morning', ushered them into the nearest meeting room.

"How are we all today, then," he began.

"Fine, thanks," was the unenthusiastic reply, almost in unison.

"We had a good day Friday, didn't we Simon?"

"Yes Sir," came the reply, rather meekly.

"So, the goodies went missing, did they?" he continued. "Tell me more."

Nigel proceeded to give a complete run-down of the situation to date, the non-appearance of the couriers in Riyadh, the enquiries currently underway in Paris and the preference for complete confidentiality. He chose, however, not to mention the suspicions held by Mike Edwards concerning the prince.

"So we don't have a claim yet?"

"No, Martin," replied Mary.

"Right. Here's what we're going to do. Firstly I want a written statement from the prince. If he prefers to go through lawyers, rather than you guys, then that's fine with me. I just want his perspective on the situation. Secondly, I want one of my men looking at all aspects of this. It's going to be Oliver Bentham, an ex-military chap based in Hereford and now a private security consultant. I'm not going to tell you the regiment he was in, but his location is a bit of a giveaway. Thirdly, I want to post a reward. It'll be a quarter of a million dollars. I know that means publicity, otherwise it won't work, but I'll get Oliver to take charge of that. He can filter it out whenever and wherever he thinks it appropriate. He'll probably want to talk to you guys, as well as the embassy staff in Paris, plus everyone else involved including, I suppose, the prince. Meanwhile, keep this well away from Lloyd's Claims Office until we get formal notification of the loss from the client. It's still possible the stuff will turn up and we don't want any more egg on our faces. There's enough there already. Everyone happy?"

"Yes thanks," replied Nigel. "I'm going to pass this information down the line, so it doesn't come as a surprise to the people involved, if that's OK."

"No, Nigel. I'd rather you didn't do that. By all means organise the prince's statement, but keep the rest quiet for now. Right, that's it. Have a good week everyone. And Simon, if there's any more golf, can I count on you?"

"Yes, Sir," he replied sheepishly. "Of course." Now he was feeling a lot better. There seemed to be no animosity at all from the underwriter and, furthermore, things appeared to be unfolding just as his father had predicted.

"Martin," ventured Mary, as they were leaving. "You didn't believe me on Friday afternoon. Why was that?"

"Yes I know. I needed to keep my weekend free from work, so I chose to ignore you. Sorry."

Back in their own office, the conversation turned to the man from the military.

"I know a bit about him," said Jamie. "He was a major in the SAS, one of their finest operatives, apparently. Carried out a lot of single-handed missions in countries where subversives were active including, I'm told, night-time halo jumps, in other words, high altitude, low opening parachute descents. I also believe he was part of the team that stormed the Iranian embassy in London back in the eighties. He's in his sixties now and he advises businesses, including Lloyd's, on matters of international security. He's an experienced kidnap negotiator as well. A few of his ex-military colleagues work with him in the company, which is said to be the leader in its field."

Simon could not believe what he was hearing. He was noticeably dazed and way out of his comfort zone. This was a world he imagined only ever existed in films or TV dramas, not in the insurance industry. And it was only the beginning of his fourth week.

"How do you know all that, Jamie?" asked Mary.

"My dad knew him from his own army days. They still see each other from time to time, mainly at reunions."

"And weren't you in the army as well for a while?" asked Craig, already knowing the answer.

"Yes, after Eton it was Sandhurst, followed by a short-service commission in the Grenadier Guards, including two tours of duty in Iraq."

"Impressive," said Mary. "You have been some use to your country, then. It might be an idea if you were around when the major comes to see us, as he surely will."

"Yes," said Jamie. "Happy to do that."

Back in his office, Nigel was quickly on the phone to Mike in Dubai.

"The underwriter is making his own enquiries," he advised, "without us being involved. We must, though, get a statement from the prince."

"I'm not sure that's a good idea," reiterated Mike. "You know my feelings on it."

"Yes I do, but we have no choice," replied Nigel, not willing to give in. "It can be done through lawyers, if preferred. Presumably the prince has a London lawyer. They could hold it in their offices for the underwriter to inspect. That way it won't get released to anyone else. We also need a formal claim to be made, which can be done in the same way, if necessary, so we can start the process officially. The sooner that's done the better. It won't be long before this all hits the press and that might hamper investigations. Will you organise it please Mike?"

"I guess so," was the reluctant reply.

Later that day, Nigel's telephone rang.

"Nigel Watkins?" enquired the caller.

"Yes. Who's speaking?"

"It's Oliver Bentham from Hereford. I gather Martin Jackson has mentioned me."

"Yes, he has."

"I'd like to set up a meeting as soon as possible. Are you free tomorrow morning at, say, 9.30 a.m.? I'll come to your office, if that's OK."

"Yes, no problem."

"I'd like to meet the rest of your team as well, if I can. Would that be possible?"

"Yes, I don't see why not. I'll organise it."

"Many thanks. See you tomorrow."

Nigel immediately passed the message to Mary and the morning meeting was confirmed.

Back in Dubai, Mike Edwards took a call from his chairman asking for a meeting, so he hurried across to the Dubai Financial Centre and presented himself at reception. The sheikh was running late. Eventually Mike was shown into his office.

"I hear we have a problem," said Al Talyani. "Tell me about it."

Mike relayed the story, including the request from London for a statement from the prince.

"I'm reluctant to ask Mahdi Al Hadda to do that," he said.

"Leave the prince to me," said the sheikh. "I'll have a quiet word with him. It's a perfectly reasonable request and I know he will want to cooperate fully with Lloyd's. I don't understand your concerns, though Mike."

"It's just a feeling," he explained. "I think there's a lot more to this than we know at this stage."

"OK. I'll deal with it from now on. I'm one of his guests at the wedding, which is in a week's time. That's how I know all about this. I'll be in Riyadh for about two weeks, so I'm in a much better position than you to handle things. I want to know everything that happens from now on. Keep me up-dated, please."

"Yes, of course."

The following morning in the offices of Nathan Henry, the group assembled in the boardroom, pending the arrival of Oliver Bentham. At precisely 9.30 a.m. he was shown into the room and formal introductions were made.

"Mr Bentham, Sir," ventured Jamie Piper-Bingham. "I believe you know my father."

"Yes I do," he replied. "A brigadier, as I recall."

"Yes, that's him. Pleased to meet you."

"You too. Now, let me explain my role here. Martin Jackson has called me in, as you know, to see if I can make some sense of these events and, more importantly, to see if there's any possibility of the jewellery being recovered. It's an information-gathering exercise to start with and I'd like to know exactly what you know. After that I plan to go to Paris and make enquiries there. Hopefully the French police will have made some progress with their preliminary investigations, but they are notoriously thorough in these matters, so it may be a bit early. I do have a contact over there who will probably be able to help. I will also visit the Saudi embassy and interview the officials that were involved in the handover. I'll then contact airport and airline staff and see, amongst other things, whether any CCTV footage might help. Depending on the results I may or may not go to Riyadh. Now would you, Mr Watkins, please run through everything that happened right from the beginning and if anyone has anything to add, please feel free to do so."

Nigel had spent the evening before preparing a written summary which he handed over, at the same time passing copies to his colleagues. They took a few minutes to read it. It included a full report of the trip to Dubai and the visit he and the underwriter had made to Paris. Mary then described her team's role in securing the quote which led to the firm order and what they had to do in order to complete the placement in the time available. In her summary, she made reference to those underwriters who were seen but had declined to participate.

"Were there any other brokers in the market?" asked Bentham.

"Yes," she replied, "a man called Darren Black from Baxter, Taylor and Black."

"He was in Dubai while I was there," interrupted Nigel. "He was with a chap called Hari Kahn."

"Oh no," said Oliver. "Not him."

"You know him?"

"Not personally, no. Let's just say he's known to the security services. Is he involved in this case?"

"Not with us," said Nigel. "Maybe with others at one time. I just have no idea."

"OK, thanks," said Bentham. "That's all very helpful. I'm on my way to Paris now so I'll leave you to get on. We may need to talk again, in which case I'll call you, Mr Watkins. By the way, you've met Al Othaim and Yacoub haven't you?"

"Yes," replied Nigel. "Al Othaim twice and Yacoub once."

"So you'd recognise them if you saw them on CCTV?"

"Yes I would," said Nigel.

"OK, that's great. Bye for now."

Chapter 9

The following day, Sheikh Abdul Rahman bin Aziz Al Talyani took a flight from Dubai to King Khaled airport in Riyadh. He had no family in the Emirates so he was travelling alone. His wife had died a few years earlier and both his sons were pursuing their careers elsewhere, one in the United States and the other in the United Kingdom. Upon arrival, and in view of his status, he was met by a royal limousine and driven straight to the King Saud Palace, which would be his home for the next two weeks. It was here that the wedding would take place and where the guests would be assembling ready for the festivities. Two palace officials greeted him and ushered him into his suite of rooms, where he relaxed and freshened up before a formal meeting with his host, Prince Fahd bin Waleed bin Mohammed al-Saud, later that afternoon. He was one of the many Saudi princes who were great-grandsons of King Abdulaziz bin Abdul Rahman al-Saud, founder of the present-day Kingdom of Saudi Arabia. At the appointed hour the sheikh was collected by an aide and taken to the prince's private apartments, where he waited in an ante-room for the summons. After a short while he was shown in.

"Sheikh Abdul Rahman," said the prince warmly. "It is a very great pleasure to see you. I am so pleased that you are here and I hope your stay is both enjoyable and comfortable."

"Your Royal Highness, it is indeed a pleasure to be here," responded the sheikh, with due deference. "I do wish you well in the forthcoming celebrations of your marriage."

Pleasantries continued for a further thirty minutes before the subject of the missing jewellery came to the fore.

"I was so sorry to hear what had happened," said Abdul Rahman. "I know how disappointing it must be for you. On behalf of my company I am happy to confirm that the insurance we placed at Lloyd's will stand firmly behind you and, indeed, according to my CEO Michael Edwards, they are already instigating their own enquiries into the recovery of the lost items. There are one or two things we should deal with now, though, and if you will permit me, I have some suggestions to make."

"Yes, of course," replied the prince. "I think, though, I'd like my business secretary to join us, if you don't mind."

"Not at all, Sir,"

They were then joined by an elderly, grey-haired Englishman, whom the prince introduced as Mr Alan Carmichael.

"Mr Carmichael deals with my international business affairs. He is extremely experienced in such matters, having for many years been the British Government's commercial attaché at the embassy here in Riyadh. When he retired, I asked him to stay on and join my staff. Please now proceed, Sheikh Abdul Rahman."

"Underwriters at Lloyd's have been made aware of the disappearance of the jewellery but there is little we can tell them at this moment about what precisely happened. The underwriter concerned, a Mr Martin Jackson, has asked that you provide a written statement of events as you see them. He is happy for this to be done through lawyers, rather than us, and has agreed to keep it confidential. Photographs of the courier and the guard would be helpful as well. At the moment your identity has not been revealed in London. At the same time, I think you should give written notice that you intend to make a claim, something that is required by the policy conditions. Are you happy to do this?"

"Yes, perfectly," replied the prince. "I think it important that we follow the correct procedures here."

"Will Lloyd's post a reward, do you think?" asked secretary Carmichael.

"Yes they will," replied Abdul Rachman. "It will, of course, need to be publicised, so secrecy will be at an end, I'm afraid. Lloyd's are familiar with these issues, though, and they will want to avoid the danger of false demands from people who actually know nothing, so circulation of any reward will be very carefully done."

"Thank you," said the secretary.

"I will prepare the papers you ask for," confirmed the prince. "I think I would like Mr Carmichael to deliver them personally to our lawyers in London. He will give you their contact details and the underwriter can view them in their offices. Aren't you going on leave soon, Alan?" he said, turning to the secretary.

"Yes, in three days' time Sir," he replied. "I'll be away for four weeks."

"I'd like you to go tomorrow instead. Go straight to our lawyers' offices and deal with this matter with them. After that is done you can enjoy your break, but I'd like our lawyers to have your UK contact details in case they need something more."

"Yes Sir," he said, "of course. I shall get onto it straight away."

"There is one further development, Abdul Rahman," continued the prince. "The two who were waiting at the airport are now missing. Attempts have been made to locate them but without success and we have no idea what has happened to them. In view of this we have alerted the police commissioner of Riyadh Province so, to a certain extent, confidentiality is now less important."

"I see," said the sheikh. "I will pass this on straightaway."

Back in his quarters, Abdul Rahman put a call through to Mike Edwards, still in his office in Dubai. He described the meeting he had just had with the prince, confirming that a statement was being prepared for Lloyd's and that it would be delivered personally by the prince's secretary, who would arrive in London the following day. He also mentioned the sudden disappearance of Almahdi and Fawzi and the fact that the police in Riyadh had now been officially informed.

"I thought something like this would emerge," said Mike. "It looks very suspicious to me."

"Well we can't jump to any conclusions here. It's quite possible they chose to vanish out of shame, fearing what might happen to them and knowing how the prince would likely react. Anyway, pass this on to London would you."

"Yes, of course. I'll do it straight away."

At home that evening, by then the third Tuesday in August, Simon was again discussing progress at work with his father John. Eventually the matter of the jewellery came up.

"There's a lot of people involved, now," explained Simon. "There's one guy, an ex-military security expert in Paris at the moment, seeing if there's any way to track down the stuff. Lloyd's may be posting a reward and the prince will be making an official statement to them about the claim."

"Amazing. I bet you never thought you'd be into something like this. But Lloyd's will pay up if it comes to it, won't they?"

"Oh yes," said Simon. "They're fully behind the prince here."

"Now, I had a call from George Claremont earlier on today. He's got some tickets for the Brighton game on Saturday. It's the bank holiday weekend, by the way. He's managed to get six seats all together and he's offering us three of them. Mrs Claremont said she'll come, but Emma wants to know if you're going before she says yes."

"Really," said Simon, enthusiastically. "That sounds promising."

"Don't get too carried away," said his father. "She may not want to be the only teenager in the company of adults. So will you come? George is organising a mini-bus there and back and he'll book us in to the restaurant for a snack. Then back to their place afterwards."

"Yes, I'd love to. Who are they playing?"

"Barnsley. Should be a good game, but if not, still a good day out."

"Great," said Simon. "I shall look forward to it."

The offices of corporate lawyers Bromley, Lockett and Jones were located not far from the Lloyd's building in Leadenhall Street. They specialised in matters involving insurance and acted principally for Lloyd's including, *inter alia*, the syndicate run by Martin Jackson and his colleagues. Bromley Lockett had been alerted by their underwriter client to the arrival of Alan Carmichael from Riyadh and they were to be contacted by the prince's lawyers, Beauchamp & Co., located in Grosvenor Square, W1. Early on Thursday morning they received the call to advise them that senior partner Ralph Beauchamp was on his way to Leadenhall Street, along with Mr Carmichael, to deliver some important documents, which were then to be held for inspection by Martin Jackson later that day. Peter Bromley was the partner arranging matters for the underwriter and after the documents were handed over, and pleasantries and business cards exchanged, he called his client to let him know they had arrived. Martin promised to call in shortly after 2.00 p.m.

There were two letters and two photographs in the package. The first letter was addressed to him personally and gave a full explanation of events that had occurred, including how the items were chosen in the first place, how they were gathered in Paris, how much he had paid for them and how he remained in considerable disbelief at their disappearance. It also described his own involvement in the arrangements and the part played by secretary Carmichael in carrying out his wishes, in other words a full and frank disclosure of everything relevant. It was signed 'HRH Prince Fahd bin Waleed bin Mohammed al-Saud'.

The second was addressed 'To Whom It May Concern at Lloyd's of London'. It gave formal notice to underwriters that their policyholder intended to make a claim for the full amount and that further information concerning the circumstances of the loss would be forthcoming in due course. The second letter was signed 'Alan Carmichael, secretary to His Royal Highness'. Martin gave instructions for the second letter to be passed to brokers Nathan Henry for the claim to be properly activated, the first he left in the lawyers' office and the photographs he took with him. Later that day he took a call from Oliver Bentham.

"I'm back from Paris, Martin," said Oliver. "Can we meet tomorrow morning? I need to run through with you what I have discovered. Then you can decide what to do next."

"Yes, certainly," replied Martin. "9.00 a.m. OK?"

"Yes, fine. See you in your office."

By the end of the day, Nathan Henry's claims director had seen to it that the claim was formally lodged with Lloyd's, prompting the appointment of chartered loss adjusters Woods & Moore. David Moore, so chosen because of his experience in the region having previously been posted to Kuwait, would now take charge. He immediately made contact with David Locke, requesting a copy of the file and any other supporting information available to date. Woods & Moore were located in an office block overlooking St Katharine's Dock, close to the Tower of London, so it was a simple matter for the papers to be hand-delivered. David Moore was a master of detail, sometimes to the point of boredom. He had a habit of using ten words where two would suffice and it had once been said of him that he called a spade a non-mechanical soil displacement facilitator. Nevertheless he had a fine reputation as a qualified loss adjuster and, over the years, had served the Lloyd's market well. He did not take sides, but aspired to fairness whatever the outcome.

"I'll review everything tomorrow," he said on the telephone to David, "then perhaps we can get together. Monday is a bank holiday, so it will mean Tuesday morning."

Meanwhile in Riyadh, police officers acting on specific orders from the commissioner, Kasim Mansur, were finding progress difficult. They were in the process of interviewing immigration officers and customs officials with photographs of the courier and the guard, but Ramadan had only just ended a few days earlier with the festival of Eid al-Fitr on the Sunday, so it was still a little difficult to locate people. They had examined all available CCTV footage along with immigration records, but to no avail. They were able to confirm, though, that the story put forward by Almahdi and Fawzi, waiting airside and who had now vanished, seemed to be true, borne out by the camera footage. The flight crew had not yet been interviewed, but Saudia Airlines officials had been visited and they had confirmed nothing untoward about the plane's arrival in Riyadh, which had been on time and without incident. In short, there was nothing at that stage to report.

The following morning at precisely 9.00 a.m. Oliver Bentham arrived at Martin Jackson's office ready for their scheduled meeting and was immediately shown in.

"I had a little help from someone I know in the French security services," began Oliver, "so I had access to places regular investigators would not have. I have been able to interview Saudi embassy personnel, the police, airport staff and Saudia Airlines officials. I have been shown CCTV footage where available, much of which is now on my laptop. I also saw your evaluator, Marcel Dubois, who confirmed he had sent you photographs of the jewellery, as well as the supporting documentation."

"Yes," said Martin. "I have them here in the office."

"Good. They will be useful. The drive from the embassy to Charles de Gaulle was pretty straightforward. The couriers were received by the airport's services manager, Jean Noël Leblanc, who accompanied them to check-in, then went with them through security and passport control, where he handed them over to a locally-based Saudia Airline official, Patrice Ducharme. She stayed with them in the lounge until the flight was called, then accompanied them to the departure gate."

"You interviewed the two airport people did you?" asked Martin.

"Oh yes," confirmed Oliver. "Now it gets interesting, though. Ten minutes before passengers were due to board, the fire alarm was activated, affecting not only that gate, but those adjacent to it as well. Passengers were herded out through an emergency exit onto the tarmac where they waited for several minutes before boarding the plane from there. There was a lot of hustle and bustle, so ground staff and airline officials were in a state of some confusion. I have some footage of this incident, Martin. Here, let me show you."

The laptop was set up and the evidence displayed, albeit not entirely clearly. What was clear, though, was that the whole situation was extremely haphazard. Boarding passes and passports were being checked as best they could be, while passengers were hurriedly shown up a flight of emergency steps onto the ramp, then directly onto the aircraft.

"Now look at this," urged Oliver. "In the distance there's an ambulance with lights flashing leaving the area. It's just possible to make out the registration plate. When I checked it with the police, it was found to be false and they did have a report of one being stolen a few days' earlier. Now, if you look at what happened in the departure lounge, you'll see the alarm being activated. The person who does it appears to be a cleaner, or is certainly dressed like one, and he smashes the glass with his mop handle. It looks to have been deliberate, because immediately afterwards he is nowhere to be seen."

"Well," commented Martin, "that's very good work, Oliver. It looks like this was a professionally organised crime, then. Is that your opinion as well?"

"Yes it is. My guess is that the courier and the guard ended up in the ambulance then, out of sight of everyone, they were substituted by two others. That's why the flight had its full complement of passengers."

"But what about the checks immediately before boarding?" asked Martin.

"The imposters could have taken both boarding passes and passports which would have got them on the plane, particularly with all that was going on."

"What about their arrival at immigration?"

"They would need to have had their own passports with them for that to be possible. If they were Saudi nationals they wouldn't need visas or anything, nor would they if they were from Kuwait, Bahrain or anywhere in the Emirates."

"So, Al Othaim and Yacoub didn't get off in Riyadh because they never got on in Paris. How do you think the switch took place, Oliver?"

"Well," replied Oliver. "I think the ambulance would have come in through the cargo area, with lights flashing, and it then drove to somewhere near the departure gate. After that there is no footage of it until it eventually drives away, presumably by the same route. So there are two possible scenarios. Either they were forcibly bundled into the back, perhaps being rendered unconscious, or they were part of the plot and simply replaced the original driver and his mate, who then replaced them in turn. It's impossible to know which, but in either case the valuable cargo goes with them. The two imposters have their own hand luggage and, of course, they arouse no suspicion when they disembark at their destination."

"So I can't at this stage tell whether it's a genuine heist, as it were, or if all this happened at the prince's behest. In other words, an insurance fraud?"

"No you can't be sure yet, Martin," replied Oliver. "But it's unlikely to involve the prince, in my opinion. Not with it being a wedding present."

"Fair point. OK, I think I'll post a reward, say a quarter of a million dollars," said Martin. "Now, though, we've got loss adjusters in charge of everything, so they'll need to know what I'm planning. I'd like you to be available to help, if you would."

"Yes, I will of course. Rewards are tricky things, Martin. All kinds of nutcases try to claim they know something when they don't, but there are ways of filtering them out. If you give me a minute I'll draft something for you now."

Oliver tapped away at his laptop for a minute or two, then showed Martin the following:-

'Substantial reward offered for information leading to the recovery of the missing jewellery. +447535534099'

"This is how I think it should read. Any callers would need to give identifying information about the crime then be given a code for future contact. That's one of my mobile numbers, by the way, the one I use for kidnap negotiation. There's more of that work around than hits the press, you know. I'm very happy to take charge of this reward situation for you, if you would like."

"Yes I would, please. I'll speak to the loss adjusters later today and also tell the brokers. Let me know when the reward notices have been posted won't you. Anyway, many thanks for what you've done so far. It's an excellent job, as usual."

"Thanks, Martin. I will keep you up to date. Have a good weekend."

"You too."

Chapter 10

At 12.30 p.m. on Saturday, a minibus arrived to pick up the Blunts from their home in Valley Drive. The Claremont family were already on board. From there they drove west into Dyke Road, then onto the eastbound carriageway of the A27 towards Falmer, the location of Brighton's new football stadium known as the Amex, short for the American Express Community Stadium. It was an award-winning structure completed only a year earlier, providing a huge economic boost to the town and generating a lot of local pride, not just from football fans, but also townspeople generally. No one who went there could fail to be impressed. It served not only as a stadium for sport, but major pop concerts, trade fairs and conferences and it was also a licensed wedding venue. As well as the main restaurant, it had fifteen other bars and refreshment outlets, each with its own cook, ensuring that the food on offer was of the highest quality and freshly prepared. It had the capacity for a twenty-eight thousand crowd, so not vast by other clubs' standards, but Brighton and Hove Albion, known in football circles as the Seagulls', had not been in the top flight of English soccer for almost thirty years. They did have planning permission for additional seating, though, should promotion ever come their way. The minibus pulled into the coach park some twenty minutes later, its driver confirming he would return to collect them at 5.00 p.m.

They made their way towards the east stand and took one of the lifts to the main restaurant, the East Central Brasserie on the first floor, where they had a reservation for 1.00 p.m. They were greeted by a smart-suited receptionist who led them straight to their table. It was a large restaurant, some two or three hundred feet in length and slightly curved, in line with the contours of the building, so it was impossible to see from one end to the other. Much of it was festooned with club memorabilia and most of its occupants were in blue and white, the colours of the home team. The group was very soon visited by their waiter and a drinks waiter, who between them took their orders. Shortly afterwards, one of the maître d's, of which there seemed to be several, came to make sure the table was to their liking and that they were comfortable.

"I didn't expect this level of service at a football match," commented Joanne Claremont. "Last time I went I had to queue for ages to get a pie and a plastic cup of Bovril."

"Yes dear," replied George wearily. "It was forty years ago, though."

"This is something special," said John Blunt. "The club has deliberately set out to provide high standards of service, as well as comfort and safety. That's why there are so many staff around the ground. And not just on match days either. This restaurant, for example, is open every day, as is the main bar, the shop, and the ticket office. So a lot of the jobs here are full time. They even bring a hawk in to keep other birds away and to ensure the seating doesn't get covered in droppings."

Their drinks arrived quickly and the food soon followed. The maître d' joined them again to check everything was fine and to assure them there was no hurry so they could relax at their table for as long as they wished. At 2.30 p.m., the bill having been paid by John Blunt, they found their way to their seats, paid for by George Claremont, in the fourth row of the east stand close to the halfway line. The seats were of blue padded leather. There were two large screens at each end of the ground showing highlights from previous games, details of forthcoming events and adverts for local businesses. The club mascot – a seven-foot seagull dressed in blue and white stripes and blue shorts – was prancing round the perimeter of the pitch chatting to, and having its photograph taken with younger members of the crowd. Both teams were on the pitch warming up. At 2.40 p.m. the voice on the loudspeaker announced the appearance of the home team's cheerleaders Gully's Girls, who performed a part dance, part gymnastic routine in the centre circle accompanied by loud music. As they began, the teams left the pitch having completed their warm-up. The atmosphere was building up, as was the crowd and its level of excitement. At 2.55 p.m. the teams emerged from the tunnel, led by the home side, to the stirring sound of the military march Sussex By The Sea, a recording by the band of the Grenadier Guards chosen specifically for use at the Amex. The applause was rapturous and the noise level deafening.

And it was set to continue. After four minutes the home side were a goal up, then two up after fourteen, ending 3-1 at half time. The ground was almost full to capacity, apart from several empty blocks at the away supporters' end, so the gate would be just under twenty-five thousand, it was suggested by John Blunt. After the fifteen minute respite, for players and fans alike, the game continued with a further two goals from Brighton, thus ending 5-1, their biggest victory ever at the Amex. John Blunt's estimate of the gate turned out to be fairly accurate, when an announcement towards the end confirmed the attendance to be twenty-four thousand five hundred and ninety-four.

"That was a good guess, John," commented George.

"He's an accountant. He probably counted them all," said Simon, prompting laughter from all within earshot.

Finally, they made their way back to the coach park and found the minibus which, after manoeuvring its way through the traffic congestion, returned them to the Claremonts' home in Woodland Drive at around 6.00 p.m. It being a fine August evening, they sat outside while George served champagne to those that wanted it, beer, wine or soft drinks to those that didn't. They talked about the team's success but, more importantly, the quality and comfort of the stadium facilities and the enjoyment of the day as a whole.

After a while the conversation turned to Simon and his work and, since he was feeling a lot more confident about things, he gave a good insight into some of the characters he had come across in the market, how nonchalant they and his colleagues seemed to be about serious business and yet how instinctively resourceful they could be when the occasion demanded. It wasn't long before he brought up the matter of the jewellery.

"For example," he explained, "we insured over twenty million dollars of stuff one day and it went missing the next, yet no one seems to get excited about it. It's all very matter-of-fact."

By now he knew better than to give specific details, but the example was a good one for illustrative purposes.

"And this is all to do with a Saudi prince, is it?" asked George.

"Yes," replied Simon. "His private secretary is over here at the moment."

"What's his name?" asked George.

"Carmichael, I think," said Simon, hesitantly. He regretted it as soon as he had said it.

"And how's the train journey?" asked Joanne, sensing Simon's discomfort.

"Oh that's fine. Expensive though," he answered. "Having a train to catch in the evenings helps me get away promptly and it's good not having work colleagues anywhere near my home life. I can keep the two worlds separate."

Finally dinner was ready to be served so they made their way indoors. They enjoyed salad niçoise for the starter, a coq au vin which had been bubbling away all day in a slow cooker and tarte tatin, all prepared by the lady of the house earlier.

When their evening was over the Blunts decided to walk home, having thanked their hosts profusely for a wonderful day and an enjoyable dinner. On the way, Simon admitted his concern at having given away confidential information to Mr Claremont.

"I really shouldn't have done that," he said. "The question took me a bit by surprise, but I hope it was just general interest. Anything more than that and I could be in trouble."

"Well, he knows the area and some of the people," said his father. "But don't worry, George is a decent chap. They're used to keeping secrets in the diplomatic service. It won't get out."

Meanwhile in Riyadh, preparations were well underway for the up-coming marriage of Prince Fahd to his bride

Princess Laila bint Faisal bin Mohammed al-Saud. They were cousins, in fact, since they shared the same grandparents, but that was not unusual amongst Saudi royals. This was a marriage of choice, though, rather than arrangement. They had met occasionally as children, but more recently they had been students together at King's College, Cambridge. As a result, they were both quite modern in outlook, but a wedding such as theirs could only take place according to long-established Saudi traditions, which they were duty bound to observe to the full. Not so, though, their future life together. The princess had no plans to accept any more wives into the household. No Sir. He could forget that tradition straight away.

It was unusual for weddings of such importance to take place during August, the hottest month in the Kingdom, but the prince had business interests that took him to Europe and America and his next trip was planned for mid-September. The princess was to accompany him, so the first few weeks would serve as their honeymoon. Her future role was to look after his charitable foundations, of which there were several, but one of them she was especially keen on, concerning itself with the advancement of professional women in Saudi society.

It was also unusual for the ceremony to take place without the dowry, in other words the jewellery, but Prince Fahd had explained the predicament to his father-in-law to be, Prince Faisal, who accepted the position straight away. In fact, postponement of the event would have been unthinkable, since there were to be five hundred guests for the celebrations, many of whom were already in Riyadh. As a senior Saudi with wealth to match, Saleh Said Al Othaim would have been there, but for his untimely disappearance, but neither Yacoub the henchman, nor Alan Carmichael the secretary, were important enough to have been invited. In any event, they were both now out of the country.

Thus the wedding went ahead as planned on Monday. The ceremony was a small affair, presided over by an Islamic judicial officer in the presence of three witnesses. Rings were exchanged, the dowry promised later and the marriage contract signed. The evening celebrations, with men and women segregated into different parts of the palace complex, began at 10.00 p.m. that evening and continued through the night. The women's party was a lively affair with music and dancing, some of which was quite informal and energetic, while the men's was more sedate, with entertainment in the form of sword-dancers dressed in traditional tribal costumes. The feasting was sumptuous in both groups. At some point during the proceedings, Sheikh Abdul Rahman Al Talyani found himself in conversation with the governor of Riyadh Province, Sheikh Mohammed bin Youseff al Thaneyan, an officer of the Ministry of the Interior and the man to whom the police commissioner reported. Though they had never met before, they soon found an area of common interest, the matter of the prince's loss.

"I'm told there is a development," said the governor, "but now is not the time to raise it with the prince. Perhaps you would be able to come to my office tomorrow and I will tell you about it."

"Yes I will," replied Abdul Rahman. "That would be very helpful."

Late the following day, Al talyani arrived at the governor's office in the centre of Riyadh and was greeted warmly.

"The police have found Almahdi and Fawzi," said the governor, "the two who went missing after the airport misfortune. They are being held in custody, but as yet they have not been interrogated. The commissioner will wait for the prince's instructions before taking any action, so they will remain in jail for a little while."

"Is there any indication of why they disappeared?" asked Abdul Rahman.

"None whatsoever. They have said nothing."

"So it is still feasible that they were just so ashamed that they did not want to face the prince?"

"Yes, Abdul Rahman. They were picked up at Al-Khobar on their way to the causeway, probably bound for Bahrain. Neither is a Saudi national and they probably thought it was good for their welfare to get out of the country, perhaps never to return."

"Right, thank you Sheikh Mohammed," said Abdul Rahman. "I will pass this information to those that need to have it. We should keep in touch I think."

"Yes," replied the governor. "That would be useful."

Back at King Saud Palace, the sheikh put another call through to Mike Edwards to up-date him with what he had just learned.

"It seems to me," he told Mike, "that these two were not part of the plot. As I suspected earlier, they appear to have been too overcome with shame to face the prince and decided to leave the country. I am pretty certain they can be discounted but, again, we must keep open minds."

"Certainly we must," said Mike. "But I will pass this on. When are you returning?"

"In about a week's time, I think," said the sheikh. "There's another party next Monday then it's all over."

"OK. See you then."

In France the search was still on for Al Othaim and Yacoub. Paris police had circulated photographs of them to all regional forces who were now on the lookout. The stolen ambulance had been located and was now undergoing forensic examination. CCTV footage had been re-examined but no further evidence about the switch had come to light. Airport staff and embassy officials had been re-interviewed, but there was no additional information that could help.

Early on Tuesday morning, the detective in charge of the case, Lieutenant Pierre Le Bret, took a call from the police in St Quentin, a few miles south of Lille.

"I think we've found one of your men," said the officer. "A short while ago a body was discovered hidden in woods near the village of Péronne. A dog-walker found it. It looks like the victim had been shot twice through the head. When the body was found, it was bound and gagged, so it looks like some sort of assassination. We think it had been there for about a week. You'd better come and see it."

"I'm on my way," replied Pierre. "And thanks for letting me know."

Two hours later he arrived in St Quentin and, with the local sergeant, drove to the spot where the body was found.

"You're right," said Pierre. "It is one of them. It's a man called Saleh Said Al Othaim. He and a colleague went missing from Charles de Gaulle eleven days ago. They were either abducted, which now looks to be the case, or they absconded, which now looks unlikely. Are you searching the area?"

"Yes Sir," replied the sergeant, "and of course scene of crime officers are all over the site, as you can see. Are we looking for anything in particular?"

"Perhaps another body," suggested Pierre, "and maybe some luggage, but I doubt it very much."

They then drove back to the police station at St Quentin.

"When the formalities are complete," said Pierre, "let me know. I want to see a copy of the pathologist's report, though it's pretty clear to me what happened. I'm curious about a lot of things here, but for the moment the most important objective is find out what happened to Yacoub. He needs to be tracked down soon. Also, they had valuable items of jewellery with them, which also need to be found quickly, since they belong to a foreign royal."

He left a photograph of Yacoub with the sergeant, who promised to keep him advised of every development, then drove back to Paris. Back in his office he set in motion a series of checks at ferry ports, airports, stations, Eurostar and Eurotunnel terminals and border crossings, hoping that Yacoub might show up on some CCTV footage somewhere. He was not too confident, though, since it was now over a week since the heist, plus the whole thing had the sniff of well-organised professional criminals about it. He sent a request through to Interpol in Lyon, with photograph, asking them for their help in the search for Yacoub, just in case he had sneaked, or had been taken, across a border somewhere. He did, after all, have a Saudi passport assuming he still had it, which might have registered with someone if he had left by a more traditional route. Le Bret sent a written interim report to the officer in charge, the Prefect of Police, who gave instructions for the Saudi embassy to be informed, since it was they who had contacted the police in the first place.

The embassy passed the news back to the Saudi Ministry of the Interior, since the prince was still in the middle of his nuptials, and they in turn informed the governor of Riyadh Province. Sheikh Mohammed planned to tell the Prince Fahd in due course, but he told Al Talyani straight away and the news was quickly passed on through his own office to London. Al Talyani also instructed Mike to let Mahdi Al Hadda know in Bahrain.

Chapter 11

On the Tuesday after bank holiday, in the offices of Nathan Henry, divisional managing director Watkins and claims director Locke were hearing from loss adjuster Moore about his proposed strategy going forward. All three were fully aware of the latest developments. Mary and her team, including Simon, had moved on to other matters and were going about their day-to-day business in the normal way, their involvement in the jewellery affair now being general interest, rather than participation.

"A reward is being posted this week, as I understand it," said David Moore. "It's being activated by Oliver Bentham, who will handle any calls that ensue as a result. He and his colleagues have some very sophisticated technology that isn't generally available to the public, so let's hope this will bring about a result. Now, what I have to do, as I'm sure you already understand, is to fit the circumstances of the loss to the policy conditions."

"Yes David," said David Locke. "We know."

"Now I understand the policy document had not been issued at the time of the loss?" said the adjuster.

"That's right," confirmed Nigel. "It happened on day two."

"So all I have to work with is the broker's slip. Is that right, Nigel?"

"Yes it is, David. The one you have a copy of."

"And the premium has not yet been paid?"

"That's right, David. It would be due in sixty days, according to the terms of trade agreement we have with our agents."

"OK. Now I see the basis of the cover is as follows, and I quote, 'All risks of physical loss or damage howsoever and by whomsoever caused', but there are as yet no qualifying conditions."

"True," said David Locke, "but they would be pretty standard. General conditions aren't something to get excited about. No need to spend any time on them."

"Maybe, but I have to be sure they've not been breached. The main issue here is whether or not we have a real claim or a fraudulent one. I have to satisfy myself, and therefore everyone else, that this was not a put-up job. If the prince has the jewellery, or knows where it is because he was part of the plot, then we have a case of fraud. And since he has now registered a formal claim, he would be liable to prosecution."

"We know all that," said the claims director, angrily.

"And do you really think," asked Nigel, "that the prince would embark on such subterfuge when his new bride was the intended recipient of the jewellery? How do you think that would go down with the House of Saud? And don't you think it unlikely to have been a plot now that a body has turned up?"

"It's not my job to guess," replied David Moore. "It's my job to find out."

"OK. What are you planning to do next?" asked David Locke.

"Firstly I'll go to Paris, spend a couple of days with the police and the embassy staff. Then I will certainly go to Riyadh to see the police and the prince. After that, and depending on what information is forthcoming, I may go to see the agents in Bahrain and Dubai. I'll need to contact the prince's secretary first, though. What's his name?"

"Alan Carmichael," said Nigel. "Here are his contact details."

"Oh yes. Right, thanks. I'll be on my way now. Let me know if you hear anything about the reward."

In his office in Hereford, Oliver Bentham was busy organising the reward. He had decided to put notices in the personal columns of *The Times* and *Le Figaro*, including their on-line versions, using the format he had already discussed with the underwriter. He might, in due course, widen the scope to include publications in other countries, but for the time being he would await developments. His mobile would operate in conjunction with his laptop using the latest hybrid positioning technology in order to trace the location of any caller. Two of his ex-military intelligence colleagues, Captain Andrew Weaver and Major Kevin Chamberlain, both of whom had a serious level of security knowledge, would work on this project with him.

He posted the notices by e-mail and paid by credit card. They would run for the next five days, with options to renew for further periods if required. Oliver and his colleagues agreed that the response to any caller would follow a specific format. They would ask a series of questions involving what, where and when in order to establish credibility then, if satisfactory answers were forthcoming, they would give out a code which the caller would use to identify him or herself on subsequent occasions. Realistically this was a procedure whereby Oliver would establish control over the conversation, getting the caller used to the idea of following instructions. They would not, at any stage during the first conversation, reveal the amount of the reward. That would come later and would be assessed according to the significance of the information given. Calls would be recorded, later to be subjected to voice analysis, and their origin traced. This was how they handled ransom demands in cases of kidnap. Oliver then put a call through to the underwriter to tell him it was done.

The following day, Sheikh Mohammed, governor of Riyadh Province, visited King Saud Palace for an audience with Prince Fahd. There were important matters he wanted to discuss, the discovery of the body, the disappearance of the guard and the apprehension of the two from the airport, Almahdi and Fawzi. He particularly wanted to know what instructions he should give to Commissioner Mansur about their interrogation.

"Your Royal Highness," he began. "It was a very great pleasure to have been a guest at your wedding yesterday and I thank you most warmly for the invitation."

"Not at all, Sheikh Mohammed," replied Prince Fahd. "I was very pleased that you could be there. What can I do for you today?"

"I have some grave news," said the governor. "A body has been found in northern France and it has been identified as that of your friend Saleh Said Al Othaim. I offer my sincerest condolences. At least we now know he did not abscond with the jewellery."

"Thank you," said the prince. "This is indeed sad news. He was a good man and I did not really believe he was the guilty party here. I know the family well. Have they been told?"

"Yes Sir. I did that myself earlier."

"I must visit them as soon as I can. He was, after all, carrying out an important mission for me. Where is the body now?"

"It's in a mortuary in St Quentin. It will undergo a post-mortem in the next few days. I believe he was shot twice through the head in what looks like to have been an execution. There is no sign of the guard, Yacoub though. The police in France are trying to find him, but so far they have not been successful."

"What do they think might have happened to him?"

"He, too, might have been killed, but there has been no discovery of a second body. He is possibly on the run, but whether he has escaped from his captors, or whether he is still being held hostage by them is impossible to say at this stage. The police in Paris will keep our embassy notified."

"I do not know Yacoub particularly well," said Prince Fahd, "but he was one of my loyal employees and people regarded him as trustworthy. What do we know so far about the disappearance of the jewellery?"

"Well Sir," explained the governor. "It seems to have happened at the airport in Paris. Just prior to boarding Al Othaim and Yacoub were abducted from the tarmac, shortly after a fire alarm was set off in the departure lounge and they appear to have been driven away in a stolen ambulance. The police in Paris are continuing to investigate, and Lloyd's are putting up a reward. Meanwhile Almahdi and Fawzi have been found and they are in police custody here in the town. They were on their way out of the country. Commissioner Mansur would like to know what he should do with them, in other words whether to interrogate them or let them go. They do not appear to have had anything to do with things, since it all happened in Paris, but we cannot be sure. My recommendation is that they be interrogated."

"I do not know them. Are they Saudi nationals?" asked the prince.

"No Sir. One is from Abu Dhabi and the other Qatar."

"OK. Interrogate them. We might find they can tell us something useful, even though they might not be involved."

"Very well, Sir."

Back in his office, Governor Mohammed passed the prince's instructions to Commissioner Mansur, who promised that the process would begin forthwith. Two officers were assigned to the task, one for each suspect, who would be interviewed simultaneously, but separately. The questioning would be along the same lines, following exactly the same format and the answers then compared for any discrepancies. Then, the next day, the whole procedure would be repeated, with different interrogators asking exactly the same questions and the answers compared a second time.

At the end of the first day, only basic information had been revealed. They were both drivers, who owned and ran a limousine service in Riyadh. They worked for the prince on a casual basis, usually being engaged by one of the staff when the permanent drivers were otherwise occupied. Though not on the permanent payroll, they did do a lot of work for the palace and knew many of the personnel there. They had been in the Kingdom for seven years and lived in apartments in the centre of town. This particular job was a little unusual, they had both said. Together, but in one car, they were to collect Al Othaim and Yacoub from the airport and drive them straight to the palace. But there was slightly more to it. They would need to be airside, so a special pass would be waiting for them at airport customer services. They were to report there and then be taken through to the gate to await the arrival of the flight. Neither could remember the name of the person from the palace who had given them their instructions.

The two stories proved to be identical when interrogators compared notes afterwards. Police had already seen the CCTV footage of the disembarkation and, together with this additional information, they were sure there was no reason to suspect Almahdi and Fawzi of wrongdoing. They would, though, be repeating the process again the next day.

In Oliver Bentham's office in Hereford, no meaningful contact had been made by the end of Thursday in response to the reward notices. Three calls had been received. One from someone who said he had information but could not give any details, another from a chap who wanted to know what the jewellery consisted of and the third from a lady who said she had found an emerald ring in Bishop Stortford High Street and handed it in to the police. Was there a reward, she wanted to know. All three numbers were traced while the callers were still on the line and their locations pinpointed, so confirming that the technology was in proper working order.

Everything changed quickly the following morning, though. At precisely 10.00 a.m. the mobile rang and Oliver answered.

"Good morning," said the caller. "You want the jewellery back?"

"Who are you please," said Oliver calmly, beckoning his colleagues to listen in.

"Not saying," said the caller. "So do you want the jewellery back?"

"OK," replied Oliver. "You need to give me something to indicate you know what you're talking about, or I hang up. What can you tell me?"

"Paris. Sixteenth August. Will that do?"

"And you have the items in question?"

"Oh yes. And it will cost you five million dollars to get them back."

"How many pieces," asked Oliver.

"Five."

"What about the others?"

"Nice try. There's only five. You know that."

"OK. Here's what we're going to do. Firstly there's a code that you will need to have for future contact. It's R7938PF. Repeat that back to me."

"What?"

"Repeat it, or this conversation ends here."

"OK. R7938PF."

"Secondly, I need you to prove you have the jewellery. Take a picture of one of the items on your mobile now and send it to this number."

"Not now. Maybe later," said the caller, who then ended the call.

"What did you get from that, Kevin?" asked Oliver.

"The call came from just outside Lille at a place called Pont-à-Marcq," said Kevin. "It's close to Lille Airport and, of course, there's a Eurostar terminal in the town. I wasn't able to trace the number, though."

"I'm not surprised. I expect he'll call again," said Oliver. "What he has said so far sounds promising. Any idea on the voice?"

"It's English, by the sound of it, but not very posh. East London, or Essex, possibly. We have it recorded, so I'll get someone on to it right away."

At that point Oliver put a call through to Martin Jackson in London and advised him of this new development. There was nothing they could do for the time being, other than wait for the next call, but between them they agreed that five million was out of the question and, provided things turned out to be authentic and it was certain that the jewellery would be returned, then somewhere between one and two million might be more appropriate.

"I will tell David Moore, the loss adjuster," said the underwriter. "He'll need to know this. Are you in touch with the police in Paris?"

"Yes. Shall I let them know?"

"Yes please, Oliver. If there's another call from the same area they might be in time to apprehend whoever it is."

"OK, I will."

In Riyadh the interrogation of Almahdi and Fawzi was continuing for a second day. The same questions were asked and the same answers given, thus it was beginning to look as though there was nothing more they could add and that they were telling the truth. Commissioner Mansur was given a full transcript of the interviews and a report from the interrogating officers. Almahdi and Fawzi would remain under lock and key.

After reviewing the information, the commissioner called in the two officers to discuss what they might do next.

"I am not entirely happy with this," said Kasim Mansur. "There is something here that does not quite make sense. Why, for example, was such an important task assigned to two such unimportant people, in other words, two drivers that are not even on the permanent payroll? I would like to know who engaged them. I will speak with the governor and see if we can find out, meanwhile keep the two of them in custody."

Commissioner Mansur went directly to the office of the governor, conveniently located in the same building and was shown in straight away.

"I need some information, Sheikh Mohammed," said the commissioner. "The two we have in custody look as though they are clear of any involvement, but what I am concerned about is why they were selected to carry out such an important task, since they themselves cannot be regarded as senior employees of Prince Fahd, quite the reverse, in fact. Can we find out who chose them and why?"

"I will try, Kasim," said the governor. "But the secretary, Alan Carmichael, is on leave at the moment and it would have been one of his staff who made the arrangements, I am sure. I will ask the prince, though."

"Thank you, Sheikh Mohammed. It would be very helpful."

In Paris, loss adjuster Moore was reviewing the progress of the police investigations with Lieutenant Le Bret, having already interviewed the embassy staff and reviewed their CCTV footage the previous day. He was covering a lot of ground in his usual meticulous fashion, but the one piece of evidence vital to the mystery still eluded him – the switch itself and whether it was abduction or misappropriation. There was no CCTV coverage of the incident, nor were there any witnesses, as yet. In either case Lloyd's would have to pay the claim, unless the prince was somehow part of the scam but, nevertheless, it was Moore's job to deliver the fullest account of the circumstances as he possibly could. If all else failed, though, his opinion would count for a lot, but he would not suggest policyholder complicity as a means to repudiate the claim unless there was clear and overwhelming evidence to support it. Such a course of action would be quite wrong, against his guiding principles and contrary to the way that Lloyd's underwriters sought to fulfil their obligations.

Lieutenant Le Bret confirmed that he would continue with some urgency the search for witnesses and for Yacoub. David Moore then left. Back in his hotel room he put a call through to Alan Carmichael's mobile and when it was answered promptly, he introduced himself and described the role he was playing on behalf of his principals, Lloyd's of London.

"I shall be going to Riyadh next," he advised Carmichael. "I would like you to let Prince Fahd know that I will be coming and that I would like a meeting with him. I shall also be seeing the commissioner of police and, at the suggestion of embassy staff here in Paris, the governor of Riyadh Province. Can you let me know when that has been done please."

"Yes, of course," confirmed secretary Carmichael. "I will deal with it straight away."

Immediately he called the King Saud Palace and was put through to the prince. He passed on the news about the loss adjuster's visit, that he was acting on behalf of Lloyd's and that afterwards he would be filing a report recommending, or otherwise, payment of the claim.

"This is normal procedure," said the secretary, which Prince Fahd duly noted.

"While you are on," said the prince, "the police here are interested to know who it was that engaged the two drivers to pick up Saleh and Yacoub at the airport. Who would that have been, Alan?"

"I think it was Yacoub himself, Sir," replied Alan. "I certainly gave the original instructions to Yacoub, but I left it to him to make the arrangements with whoever was available at the time. He may have delegated it himself."

"Thank you Alan," said the prince. "You know what has happened do you?"

"No Sir."

"Saleh's body was discovered in a field in northern France and Yacoub cannot be found. The police are looking for either him or another body."

"I am sorry to hear that, Sir," said Carmichael. "That is bad news. This is turning out to be a matter of some gravity, I think."

"Yes Alan. How is your leave?"

"Very restful, thank you. How was the wedding?"

"Just outstanding. Minus the dowry, I am afraid, but nevertheless spectacular."

"I'm very pleased, Sir."

"Thank you. We are meeting in London, are we not, in early October?"

"Yes Sir."

"Very well. Goodbye until then Alan. And thank you."

On Saturday, Oliver Bentham and his colleagues Andrew Weaver and Kevin Chamberlain were in the office, in anticipation of another call. Lieutenant Le Bret was also on alert in his office in Paris and he had a team of officers in the Lille area standing by with their own localization equipment. Kevin Chamberlain had the detective's mobile number punched into his own handset ready to make contact quickly. They did not have to wait long before the mobile buzzed to indicate there was a message. It was a photograph of the tiara. The covering text quoted the code R7938PF. Twenty minutes later the mobile rang.

"Got it, have you?" said the caller.

"What is the code," asked Oliver.

"R7938PF."

"Yes, I've got it."

"Right, you pay five million dollars in cash and the stuff is returned."

At the same time, Andrew Weaver raised his hand to indicate he had a fix on the location. He wrote on a pad 'Not same place. La Louvière near Mons. Same voice.' Kevin Chamberlain quickly activated Le Bret's mobile number and passed the information on. He in turn told his men in Lille to stand down.

"No. Here's what will happen," continued Oliver. "We'll pay one million, not five, when and only when our expert has inspected the goods."

"Think again," said the caller, who then rang off.

Chapter 12

The weekend was a busy one for the men of the Blunt household. Sunday was the day of West Brighton Golf Club's championship competition and both Simon and his father had entered. They would practice on the Saturday in readiness for the big day, which would be thirty-six holes of scratch stroke-play without handicaps being taken into account. The player with the lowest aggregate score would win the trophy and be declared club champion for the next twelve months. Only the top fifty players, those with the lowest handicaps, were eligible to enter. Simon had a better chance than his father and this was his first real opportunity, now he was a senior club member, to make a golfing name for himself. He would do well, he thought, if he could put other things out of his mind. This was not a weekend to be thinking about work, nor indeed about Emma, even though he would relish the idea of showing her his name on the honours board.

They drove to the club early and spent the first hour on the driving range. They played eighteen holes before adjourning to the clubhouse for a lunchtime sandwich. Jaffa was in the bar remonstrating with others about the closure of the course to non-participants while the tournament was being staged.

"Good morning, John," he said politely. "And good morning to you, Simon. I think I will call you Simon from now on since you're a working man, if that's all right," he added slightly sarcastically."

"Good morning," replied John Blunt.

"Good morning," said Simon. "I'll call you Jaffa, since you're still a teacher, whether that's all right or not," added Simon equally sarcastically.

There was a good deal of humour behind the exchange and the three seemed perfectly relaxed about it.

"Good luck tomorrow, by the way," said Jaffa. "I'm not playing. Not good enough, you know."

"Yes, we know," said Simon. More laughter.

"How's work, then?" Jaffa asked.

"Oh, very interesting, we get involved in some very big things that go on around the world. Quite exciting, actually."

"Good. I'm pleased you're enjoying it," he commented, before moving away to join his pals at the bar.

After lunch the Blunts played another nine holes before calling it a day and returning home to relax for the evening. Too much practice might be counter-productive, they thought. They retired to bed early ready for the following morning.

They breakfasted early on Sunday morning and made their way to the club. They were not paired together. John was in the second group to tee off and Simon somewhere halfway down the field. He would start at the tenth. The morning round went fairly well for both of them, John carding seven over par at seventy-nine and Simon, who seemed to be in sparkling form, one under at seventy-one, putting him in third place. Not a bad start, he thought.

The afternoon saw John fall away a bit with a round of eighty-three, an aggregate score of one hundred and sixty two. Simon continued his blistering performance and managed a round of seventy, making his aggregate score one hundred and forty-one. He would have to wait for the others to finish, though, before his position on the leader board would be known. Just before 6.00 p.m. the final scores were in. There was a tie for first place with aggregate scores of one hundred and forty-one and Simon was one of them. There would be a play-off of two holes, the thirteenth and fourteenth and if the scores were still tied, they would go again. Simon went one up with a birdie, his opponent only making par. They both made par on the fourteenth, leaving Simon the clear winner. There was a large crowd watching and they applauded enthusiastically as the two players made their way into the clubhouse. It was full to capacity and the reception Simon received was stupendous. What he hadn't realised at that point, but other people had, was that he was the youngest ever club champion. He saw George Claremont there, together with

Emma, who was clapping and jumping up and down excitedly. After a short interlude to allow players and onlookers alike to settle down, the presentation ceremony began. Simon was called to the front and after a speech of congratulations from the club captain, he was handed the trophy. The press were there, representatives of Brighton's local daily, *The Argus*, who photographed and interviewed him, confirming his victory would be featured in the following day's edition. Eventually he managed to break away from press and onlookers alike and meet up with Emma, who congratulated him with an affectionate hug. Her father shook him warmly by the hand and offered his own personal congratulations.

"How did it go?" asked Angela Blunt, when they finally got home.

"He won," said John, heartily. "He is the new club champion."

"Wow," said Angela. "Well done. How do you feel?"

"Quite elated," said Simon. "I never thought I would do it. I was a bit fortunate to be on good form when it really mattered."

As they relaxed during the evening, Simon began to wonder whether he could actually make it as a professional golfer after all. If all else failed, he could perhaps give it a try, but life in Lloyd's seemed to be working out quite well for him, at least for the time being.

While Simon was winning his trophy, Oliver Bentham and his colleagues were in their office monitoring the mobile and awaiting the next call. They were sure there would be one. They had not alerted Lieutenant Le Bret this time, since they were convinced the caller was moving around. Just before 4.30.p.m. the mobile rang and the technology sprang into action.

"Ready?" said the voice.

"Code," said Oliver.

"R7938PF."

"How's the five million coming along?"

Andrew Weaver indicated he had a fix, writing on his pad 'Châtelet, between Charleroi and Namur. Same voice'.

"I repeat," said Oliver firmly. "It's one million or nothing. Take it or leave it."

"Make it two and we have a deal."

"No. One million or nothing."

"Two million. We have a hostage."

"Who is it?" asked Oliver.

"Not saying. Two million."

"No, and for the final time it's one million. Accept it now or this negotiation ends here."

"No police," said the caller.

"I don't have any plans to involve the police. You bring the jewellery to be evaluated by an expert then we hand over one million dollars in cash. We keep the jewellery. That's how it will work. There is no other deal on offer."

"Where?"

"You call me Tuesday and I will tell you precisely where and when."

"And if I don't like it?"

"The deal's off."

The call then ended.

"I'll go to London tomorrow," said Oliver, "speak to the underwriter and get this organised. I'll be back ready for Tuesday."

The following morning at the offices of Nathan Henry, Nigel Watkins took a call from Mike Edwards in Dubai.

"I'm coming over to London later this week," said Mike. "I'd like to meet with you to talk about other business we might work on together. Are you free on Thursday, say?"

"Yes Mike. All day."

"Great. I'd like to meet other members of your team, so I can report back to my chairman. We're thinking of consolidating all our London business through one broker and we'd like to explore that prospect with you."

"Excellent, Mike," replied Nigel. "I'm sure we can deliver. See you Thursday, then."

"Yes, Nigel. About 10.00 a.m."

In his office in Gracechurch Street, Martin Jackson took his first call of the day from David Moore the loss adjuster.

"I'm back from Riyadh, Martin," he said. "I think it's important that we meet, sooner rather than later."

"OK David. Come here at 11.00 a.m. I'll see you then."

"Right, Martin. Thanks."

His second call was from Oliver Bentham.

"Can we meet this morning, Martin," asked Oliver. "It's important and urgent."

"Yes, of course," replied the underwriter. "The loss adjuster is here at 11.00 a.m., so why don't you join us?"

"Good idea. See you at 11.00 a.m."

In Riyadh the police were re-interviewing Almahdi and Fawzi at the suggestion of Commissioner Mansur. They were anxious to find out more about who booked them for the airport job, now that Carmichael had confirmed, more or less, that he had asked Yacoub to organise it. The two had now been in custody for over a week, but there was no limit on the amount of time they could be held, so they were not hopeful of release any moment soon. Again they were interrogated separately by the same officers as before. It was Fawzi who had taken the call and, yes, the conversation was conducted in Arabic. It was a local voice and, on reflection, he thought the caller gave his name as Yacoub. The two were admonished for wasting time by not having revealed the information earlier and, as a result, they were thrown back into their cells. The officers passed this new information to the commissioner who in turn conveyed it to the governor.

Meanwhile in Paris, Lieutenant Le Bret had received the results of the post mortem. Al Othaim had, indeed, been shot twice through the head but also his blood contained a large quantity of methadone, not enough to have killed him but certainly enough to cause extreme drowsiness, even unconsciousness. There had also been a sighting of the stolen ambulance in St Quentin on the night of Thursday, 16 August. It had been captured on CCTV in the centre of town, but forensics had not found anything useful from their examination of it. There were no fingerprints or any other clues as to any of its occupants. However, a witness had come forward, a baggage-handler at the airport who had just finished his shift and was in the corridor overlooking the departure gate. He had been on holiday for the past week and only when he returned and caught up with the news did he realise he had information that might be important. He told Detective Le Bret that he saw what looked like an emergency medical situation airside, minutes before the Saudia flight took off for Riyadh. A casualty, apparently unconscious, was being stretchered into an ambulance by two paramedics who then drove away, with lights flashing, towards the cargo area of the airport. He could not give any descriptions.

Thus it was now appropriate to conclude it was abduction. It now seemed likely that the couriers were jabbed unconscious at some point before being put into the ambulance but how they were separated from the other passengers was not at all clear. Le Bret passed the news to his superior officer, as well as the Saudi embassy before telephoning adjuster Moore in London.

At 11.00 a.m. David Moore and Oliver Bentham were shown into Martin Jackson's office.

"Gentlemen," he began. "I hope we can make good progress this morning. Who would like to go first?"

"I will," said the loss adjuster. "These are my preliminary findings. I went to Paris, where I interviewed the Saudi embassy staff and the police, then on to Riyadh. I was able to see Prince Fahd, Governor Mohammed of Riyadh Province and Commissioner Mansur of the police department. This morning I received a call from Lieutenant Le Bret of the Paris police with news about what now appears to have been abduction. His enquiries have revealed that the most likely explanation is the couriers were injected with methadone at some point, rendering them completely unconscious. They were bundled into the ambulance out of sight of the other passengers by two paramedics, and driven away in the ambulance that we now know to have been stolen. I have no evidence at all that they themselves were involved in the plot, particularly as one of them ended up dead."

"How did they get separated from the other passengers?" asked Martin.

"Le Bret has no idea. Whatever happened would have been over in seconds. There wasn't much time between the fire alarm being activated and the ambulance driving away."

"OK David," said Martin. "Carry on."

"In Riyadh I had a long meeting with Prince Fahd. There was little he could tell me, since he was miles away at the time, not only geographically, but emotionally as well due to his up-coming marriage. I also saw the governor and the police commissioner, who both confirmed no involvement from the two waiting at the airport, but they were being held in custody for the time being."

"So where does that take us, David?" asked Martin.

"It is my conclusion that we are looking at a well-planned and well-executed heist. I can find no evidence at all that Prince Fahd is in anyway involved. Far from it. There are two important factors here, his wedding, plus the fact that the theft took place during Ramadan. Imagine the shame on the family of Saud if he had been exposed as a fraudster. He would at the very least be expelled from the House of Saud and probably from the Kingdom as well, plus he would have missed out on marrying Princess Laila, his chosen bride. Also he is a very well-respected, up-standing royal, with several charitable foundations, none of which he would put at risk. I would, therefore, be recommending immediate payment of the claim, but I believe there are other developments."

"Yes, David," said Martin. "We'll hear from Oliver in a second. Is there anything else?"

"Yes, Martin. The police, both in Paris as well as Riyadh, and I believe that someone is responsible for divulging inside information to the perpetrators, either by choice or by threat. It doesn't invalidate the claim, of course, but it would be a sensible lead to follow if we are to get to the bottom of things. I recommended that enquiries should be pursued with that in mind. We can immediately eliminate the policyholder, I think, and also the underwriters. Both sides have too much at stake."

"Thank goodness for that," said the underwriter.

"Others, though, will be contacted and interviewed in due course, but I don't think it should hold up anything we want to do in the meantime. I will put all this in my report, which will be available later this week."

"Right, thank you David. Now Oliver, what can you tell us?"

"We have," began Oliver, "received an approach from someone who says he has the jewellery and will return it on payment of five million dollars. The caller has also let slip that he has a hostage, which I think we can assume is Yacoub. I have had three conversations now, each from a different location in north-eastern France. I believe he does have the goods and that there is a real chance of getting them back. I have offered one million and I'm pretty sure I've convinced him it's the only offer on the table. We have to move quickly and, if he does what I ask, he will call again tomorrow so I can set up the exchange. I do not want the police involved, despite what everyone might prefer. They have different objectives. Theirs is to catch the criminals come what may, mine is to recover the jewellery, come what may. The two are not necessarily compatible. There will be three of us – my two colleagues and I – and I'd like your expert to be there as well. We'll guarantee his safety and all that, so he's no need to worry on that score. Probably best that you don't know how we'll do that. I also need one million dollars to be made available in cash straight away. How can we do that?"

"It's too difficult for Lloyd's," said Martin straight away. "The brokers would have to get the agreement of all fourteen underwriters on the slip, plus permission of Lloyd's Claims Office, who would no doubt have serious concerns about payment of ransom demands."

"It's more like a reward, though, isn't it?" enquired Oliver.

"I suppose we could call it that," said Martin. "The policy will pay the one million, there's no doubt about that, but I don't think it can be mustered in the time available. I wonder if the Saudi embassy could organise it."

"I'm sure they would," said David. "As long as we confirm it's covered by the policy."

"Good," said the underwriter. "Can you arrange it, please?"

"Certainly. I'll contact them straight away."

"Also," added Martin, "I will tell the brokers, so as to keep them up to speed, but I'd like you guys to report direct to me from now on. OK?"

"Of course," they both confirmed.

Nigel Watkins, meanwhile, decided to let his chairman know that Mike Edwards was coming later that week with a view to channelling all the Al Talyani business through Nathan Henry. The chairman promised he would be sure to meet him and asked how everything else was going.

"Very well," said Nigel. "There's one issue we're wrestling with at the moment to do with a claim for lost jewellery that happened on day two of the policy, over twenty-two million dollars' worth."

He went on to describe the circumstances in some detail, including how they won the business in the first place, how well Mary's team had performed in completing the placement in the time they had and how he and the underwriter had been to Paris to verify and witness the items being packaged and dispatched. He also mentioned the possible leak of inside information, something the police would be investigating and that he and his team might find themselves being interviewed.

"They'll only be routine enquiries, I'm sure," said Brian, "but if you need me to help in any capacity at all, I will. In fact, I'll speak to your people at some stage soon. And if the police do come here, let me know."

"I will," confirmed Nigel, "and thanks."

Chapter 13

At the end of Monday, as Mary was leaving the building on her way to the station, she was confronted by group managing director Robert Woodhead, a man not known for politeness and good manners.

"I've just heard," he said. "What sort of mess have you got us into now?"

"What do you mean?" asked Mary.

"You know exactly. You send a trainee into the market on his own to get a quote in only his third week. Not very bright, is it?"

"May I take it this is not a formal conversation?" she asked sarcastically.

"You can take it how you like."

"Then I'll take it as an off-site ambush. And be careful, I was born and brought up in Bethnal Green."

"So what do you have to say, then, about the ridiculous stunt you pulled? Do you think that's how you should be running your team, or have you lost control?"

"I run my team as I see fit," she retorted. "They do nothing without my approval and nothing happens without my knowledge. Unlike you, I live and breathe this market. I know what the underwriters think, sometimes before they do. I know what they have for breakfast, what wine they prefer and how often they change their socks. I used the trainee for that job because I believed the underwriter would be soft on him and it would get the right result. It did. We won the business. It's worth over twenty-three thousand dollars annually in commission to us. I think that's worthy of praise, not criticism, don't you?"

"It's still not how this company should be operating," argued Robert. "What if it had gone wrong?"

"It didn't."

"It has now, hasn't it?"

"What do you mean?" asked Mary.

"The stuff got nicked on day two," he bellowed. "Word is that the police are about to investigate the leakage of confidential information and it includes us. That's what I mean."

"Well, the heist was not our fault, was it?" Mary bellowed back. "It was a good thing it was insured, wasn't it? And as for us having leaked information, there is no chance my staff had anything to do with that. I find your suggestion offensive."

"Well, the whole market is talking about us now" yelled Robert. "What do you think that will do for our reputation? And I tell you this," he added, waving his finger, "if you do anything like that again, and I find out, there will be repercussions. Got it?"

"If I do, it will be because it's the right thing, as it was last time. And if there are any repercussions, I will raise them formally with human resources. Now, out of my way please, I have a train to catch."

Simon, meanwhile, was on his way home. He bought *The Argus* at London Bridge Station and, sure enough, there was a big spread about him on the inside back page. There was a photograph of him with the trophy and a description of his performance in detail. It made reference to his desire to become a professional golfer but, for the time being, he was enjoying life in Lloyd's. Halfway into his train journey home, he took a call from Emma.

"Have you seen it?" she asked.

"Yes, I've got it," he replied.

"Cool, eh. Perhaps we should celebrate."

"Yes. Good idea. Isn't it your birthday soon?"

"Yes it is," she confirmed. "Well remembered. It's on Friday. I'll be eighteen and about to start my final year at sixth form college."

"Double celebration then. Perhaps we could do something on the Saturday? Maybe we could have an evening out somewhere. Would you like that?"

"Yes I would. Thank you."

"OK. I'll be in touch later in the week."

"Great."

At home there were several copies of the local newspaper dotted around the house. His parents were not going to miss an opportunity like this to broadcast their son's achievement to members of the family, some of whom were far flung. He mentioned to his mother that he had plans to take Emma out on Saturday, which she thought was a good idea, indicating her approval of the Claremonts who were, she said, a fine, up-standing family. Simon told her it was Emma's eighteenth on the Friday so their evening out would need to be something a bit special.

"Would you be able to have a quiet word," he asked "to see if anything else is planned. Also, I want to get Emma a present so I'd also like some idea of what she's getting from the family."

"Yes," said Angela. "I'll speak to Joanne."

"Thanks. That will be helpful. I don't want to tread on anyone's toes here."

"Very considerate, Simon," said his mother.

In Riyadh, Commissioner Mansur was considering what should be done about Almahdi and Fawzi, still being held in custody. There was nothing more they could tell him, he thought, and it was probably time for their release. He called in the two officers involved and asked for their opinions.

"We agree there is no point in questioning them further," they said. "We cannot imagine what else they will tell us. It seems certain that Yacoub was the man who booked them for the job and until he is found, we will probably not make any more progress."

"Yes," said the commissioner. "I agree with that. Shall I release them, then?"

"We think so, but it might be worth following them. Just in case."

"Yes," said Commissioner Mansur. "Do you think they might leave the country? They have a business here, do they not?"

"Yes. They run a chauffeur service. They have two cars, a small rented office and they live in rented apartments. They could easily go somewhere else and start up again."

"I think it would not concern us if they did. Release them and follow them, then. See to it, would you."

"Yes we will. Right away."

"Meanwhile, I had a call from Paris. The police there want to explore the possibility of an inside job, someone who knew all the details and passed them on. How else could such a precise and well-executed robbery have taken place? We therefore need to interview the palace staff but it is going to be difficult with Prince Fahd's secretary being on leave in the United Kingdom at present. I think, perhaps, he could be interviewed by the British police. I will suggest that, meanwhile would you see to it that the palace interviews get underway. Not many people knew about the jewellery, as it was being kept secret so as to be a surprise for the princess, but go ahead anyway. I will have Governor Mohammed alert the prince that it is happening."

"Yes Sir," they said. "We will."

On Tuesday in Hereford, Oliver Bentham was waiting for the expected call. Martin Jackson had, through his sister-in-law, arranged for Sotheby's Paris-based jewellery expert, Marcel Dubois, to be on standby ready for the exchange. He would be there to verify they were the same items, that one or more of them had not been substituted and that they had not been damaged in any way. The police were not going to be involved, Oliver had already decided, but Andrew Weaver and Kevin Chamberlain would be, their previous military experiences standing them in good stead for such a mission. He would choose a remote spot in the south of England, not letting on he knew they would have to come from France. He would insist on the handover taking place the following day, Wednesday, and he would decide what to do about the hostage at the time. His main priority was to recover the jewellery along with the paperwork and he did not want to complicate that with other matters. The police might, if they were there.

How much of it would go his way was a matter of some speculation, but he did have considerable experience in such things and was thus hopeful of complete success. His track record was second to none. But by the end of the day, no call had been received.

"What do you make of that," asked Andrew.

"Nothing much," replied Oliver. "He's probably trying to regain the initiative. He will call."

At Nathan Henry, chairman Brain Peterson asked Nigel Watkins, plus Mary and her entire team, to join him in his office. It was a large room with an antique desk, two sofas, a table and chairs enough for twelve people and a television in one corner, permanently tuned to stock exchange prices. Robert Woodhead was also there. Mary introduced Simon, her latest recruit and, at the chairman's bidding, they took their places on the sofas.

"I just want to assure you all," said Brian, "that you have this company's full support over the matter of the jewellery. Some of you may not yet know, but the police are looking for an insider, someone who had knowledge of the transhipment and who gave that information away. Everyone involved is being included in their enquiries and I am certain that you will all be contacted in due course. It is purely a matter of routine. There is nothing for you to worry about. If at any time you feel threatened by the questioning, refer to me. If necessary I can arrange for our solicitors to be present, but I doubt very much whether it will be necessary. I'm not imagining the police will find anything untoward in these offices. Lloyd's brokers do not engage in that kind of thing. They earn too much."

The assembled company laughed politely at their chairman's humour.

"Any questions?" he asked.

They shook their heads.

"Anything to add, Robert," he enquired.

"No. Nothing. Mary already knows my view."

"And are you going to share it with us?" asked Brian, trying to put his deputy on the spot.

"No. It's between the two of us. I'll keep it to myself from now on."

"Good. That makes a pleasant change," said the chairman, and with that the meeting concluded. Apart from Nigel and Mary, the rest of the team had not been aware of the latest police enquiries, but they now felt reassured nevertheless.

"What did Woodhead say to you?" asked John Marshall, as they made their way back to their room.

"Oh, he wasn't very complimentary," said Mary. "He just had a bit of a pop about sending a trainee, i.e. Simon, in to get the quote. He thinks it's damaged the company's reputation, forgetting that it got the job done."

"Ignore him," said John.

"I usually do."

At police headquarters in Paris, Lieutenant Le Bret was studying the reports he had received from his counterparts in Saudi Arabia, Bahrain and Dubai. There appeared to be nothing helpful in any of them. Commissioner Mansur in Riyadh advised that only three people in the prince's household knew anything at all about the jewellery, Al Othaim, Yacoub and Alan Carmichael. One was dead, another missing and the third was on leave somewhere in the United Kingdom. They could not, therefore, help him any further. Bahrain police had spoken with Mahdi Al Hadda, the only person in his company who knew anything, with similar results – all was well and there was nothing suspicious to report. Police in Dubai had spoken with Sheikh Al Talyani, who advised that his chief executive, Mike Edwards, was the person to contact and he was on his way to London. As far as was known, he was the only person in the company who knew anything about the jewellery. Le Bret then contacted the City of London police and gave them a full appraisal of the matter to date. He asked for their assistance, receiving a positive response from the officer in charge, who promised to commence enquiries in the Lloyd's community as soon as possible.

At 9.30 a.m. the following morning Nigel Watkins was at his desk when the receptionist rang through to say there were two gentlemen to see him, a Mr Partridge and a Mr Bennett. He asked that they be shown up and that he would meet them at the lift on the third floor.

"Good morning," one of them said. "I'm Detective Chief Superintendent Roy Partridge and this is my assistant Detective Sergeant Eric Bennett. We're from the City of London police based at the station in Bishopsgate. I didn't say so at reception, in case it caused unnecessary alarm."

"Yes, come in gentlemen," said Nigel. "I have been expecting you. How can I help?"

"Let me explain our role here first," said Detective Partridge. "We're acting on behalf of the police in Paris. As I'm sure you appreciate it's their case, since the crime in question appears to have been committed within their jurisdiction, but we have been asked to assist by interviewing London-based people in the hope they might be able to help. This is not a City of London police matter in the normal sense and no one here is under any suspicion. No one is going to be arrested or taken in for questioning unless the Paris police so instruct. We are to report back to them when our enquiries are complete."

"I understand," said Nigel. "I have no problem with that."

"Good. I'd like you to tell us from the beginning about your own involvement in this matter."

Nigel did just that. He began with the first telephone call from Mike Edwards, his trip to Dubai and the meeting with Al Othaim and Al Hadda. He handed over a copy of his trip report, explained how he had instructed Mary to organise quotations from Lloyd's and how they had won the order. He described his visit to Paris with the underwriter and how they had witnessed the verification and dispatch of the items. He was full and exact in every detail. The sergeant took notes.

"Thank you," said Chief Superintendent Partridge. "That's very helpful. To your knowledge was anyone else involved?"

"Yes," confirmed Nigel. "Another broker was looking for terms just prior to our involvement. It was a company called

Baxter Taylor and Black. I think the person involved was Darren Black, but my team can give you more information about them if you need it. He was in Dubai at the same time as I was. I recognised him as someone from Lloyd's, but I didn't meet him there, nor have I met him before or since."

"At any time, Mr Watkins, did you consider any of these arrangements unusual?"

"Yes I did, as a matter of fact," said Nigel. "I'm not normally invited to visit the agent, in this case in Dubai, just to collect information for quotation purposes. I would usually expect a courier package to be sent, but I now understand why they didn't want to put anything in writing, in the interests of secrecy. It was also helpful to have met Al Othaim and Al Hadda"

"I see. Anything else?"

"Yes. The Paris trip was unusual. I wouldn't expect to have to do that, but it was the underwriter's request."

"Why not just let him go on his own?"

"That would be a breach of protocol. If an underwriter wants to go anywhere near a broker's client, the broker goes too."

"Thank you Mr Watkins," said Detective Partridge. "That's been very helpful. I understand Mr Edwards is in London. Do you know how I can contact him?"

"Yes I do," said Nigel. "He'll be here tomorrow. I'll ask him to call you, shall I?"

"Yes please. He might like to pop in to see us at the station in Bishopsgate. Also, do you know a man called Carmichael and perhaps where he is?"

"I know of him," said Nigel. "He's the prince's secretary. He's here in the UK at present on leave. I have his contact details somewhere. Yes, here they are."

"Thank you. Here's my card. You can call me when Mr Edwards gets here. Now we would like to meet your staff. It will be the same procedure as we've just been through, but I think we can see them all together. It might help them jog each other's memory, though I doubt there's much they can add."

"Yes, Chief Superintendent, said Nigel. "If you wait here for a moment I'll find a meeting room and we can then adjourn. I'd like to sit in, if I may?"

"Yes of course," said Partridge. "I've no problem with that."

There was, as the chief superintendent had thought, nothing much the team could add. Mary described how she had organised the quotation, asking Simon to see underwriter Jackson, how other underwriters had been approached by Jamie and Craig and how, when the order was received, they went about completing the placement. Her version of events was identical to Nigel's.

"Did anything here strike you as unusual," asked Roy Partridge.

"No, nothing," confirmed Mary.

"And did any of you talk about this out of the office or the market?" he asked.

"Probably at home, but not in any detail," said Mary.

"I told my father," said Simon, "but it was in the course of normal conversation and I don't think I mentioned names or places."

"There was a bit of banter about it in a wine bar one evening," added Jamie, "but only amongst Lloyd's people."

"How about you?" said Roy, looking at John Marshall.

"I was on holiday until the day we got the order," replied John.

"OK. Thank you very much," said Partridge. "I don't think there's anything here to concern us, it all seems quite straightforward. Tell me, how do I get hold of the man Darren Black?"

"Baxter Taylor and Black is a small, ten-man firm with offices in Pepys Street, just off Seething Lane," said Mary.

"Right that's all. Thank you very much everyone. If I need anything more, Mr Watkins, I will call you. Meanwhile, I'll wait to hear from you as to the arrival of Mr Edwards. I probably won't need him for very long, but if he could just call in to the station, it would be helpful."

"I will call you," said Nigel.

Chapter 14

In Hereford, Oliver had decided to spend the night in the office, bedding down on the sofa, in case there was a late call. There wasn't. But it did come at 7.30 a.m. on Wednesday morning.

"Code?" he asked.

"R7938PF," responded the caller. "Have you thought again?"

"Here's the plan," said Oliver. "The exchange will take place tomorrow at noon. You will make your way to Cheeseman's Green in Kent, just south of Ashford and when you're there you will call me."

"I don't think so," said the caller.

"There will be two of us plus a jewellery expert," continued Oliver, regardless. "There will be no police and no trickery."

"What about the two million?"

"You will leave the jewellery at a spot where it can be inspected, within range and vision of us both, and when we are satisfied that everything is in order and the paperwork is there with it, we shall deposit a brief case containing one million dollars at the same spot and then retreat. When you have inspected the cash, which will be genuine and in used notes, you will withdraw and we shall retrieve the bag containing the jewellery. When the exchange is complete you will leave. You and I will be in constant communication using these mobiles enabling me to give you specific instructions on the day."

"Two million is the price," said the caller. "There is no other deal on the table."

"There will be one million dollars. That is it."

"And if I don't agree?"

"Negotiations end here and I shall walk away."

"Then Lloyd's will have to pay the full amount of the claim," said the caller.

"Which they will do," said Oliver. "And you will be left with items so well-known and valuable that you will be able to do nothing with them."

The call ended. Interesting, thought Oliver. They know about the Lloyd's policy. An hour later, the mobile rang again.

"Code," said Oliver.

"R7938PF."

"And?" he asked.

"Tomorrow morning," said the caller, who then rang off.

Andrew Weaver and Kevin Chamberlain arrived at that point and Oliver brought them up to date.

"Looks like we're on for tomorrow," he told them. "I'll let people know and we'll get down to Kent later. If we can, we'll pick up the jeweller from Ashford Eurostar terminal this evening and pitch up at a local hotel. Someone will have to get the cash to us somehow."

He then called Martin Jackson to advise him of the arrangements that were in place. He asked him to have Marcel Dubois take a train from Paris to Ashford and asked about the cash. An hour later he received a return call from the underwriter confirming that Marcel Dubois would be on the evening train scheduled to arrive at Ashford at 8.09 p.m.

"The loss adjuster has organised the cash," said Martin. "Through his contacts at the embassy in Paris, arrangements are in place for him to collect it from their counterparts in London and drive it down to you tonight. He'll meet you at whatever hotel you're at, stay the night and formally take charge of the jewellery on behalf of Lloyd's when you have it. I presume you will have it?"

"Almost certainly," confirmed Oliver.

"I've given him your mobile number," said the underwriter. "Good luck."

"Right," said Oliver to his colleagues. "We'll leave after lunch, drive down, find a hotel then pick the expert up. I've met him before so I will recognise him. I think we should take two cars."

At around 1.00 p.m. they set off, Oliver and Andrew in one car, Kevin in another. They headed south to Ross-On-Wye, then east to Gloucester, before picking up the A417 to Cirencester and the A419 to Swindon. From Swindon they took the M4 eastbound and joined the anti-clockwise carriageway of the M25, finding their way onto the M20 just outside Maidstone. After an uneventful journey, they arrived in Ashford more or less together just after 5.00 p.m. and booked into the Holiday Inn. After refreshments, they had an early dinner before Oliver drove to the station in time for the arrival of Marcel Dubois, whom they assumed would have eaten on the train. He had, as he confirmed when he met up with Oliver, who then drove back to the hotel. Straightaway, they convened in Oliver's room to discuss the plan for the next day. Shortly afterwards, David Moore rang to say he was in Ashford, enquired which hotel they were at and confirmed he would join then. Fifteen minutes later he checked in.

"I've been studying a local map," began Oliver. "On the edge of Cheeseman's Green there's an area known as Captain's Wood. From the main road there's a single-carriageway track that borders the wood on its eastern and northern sides. It's a dead end at its most northern point, so there's only one way in and out. It's that spot we will aim for and I want us to be in situ by 11.30 a.m. They think there's only two of us, plus you, Marcel. I want you, Kevin, to take one of the cars, park it out of sight, then watch and see what you can pick up. You'll have my laptop and all your other gismos. We'll take the other car up the track, park it where they will see it and wait. When they arrive we'll meet them in the woods. I will do all the talking. I will have two mobiles, one in my top pocket linked to yours, Kevin, so you can hear everything that goes on and the other I will use to communicate with them."

"How long will I have for the verification?" asked Marcel.

"I'd like you to be as quick as possible," replied Oliver. "I don't want them to think we're playing for time. I've said no trickery, so we need to be as slick as possible. However, if the stuff is right, then you'll be able to tell quickly, won't you?"

"Yes," said Marcel. "I'm sure I will. But where will the items be placed?"

"I'll get them to a point halfway between us, in a sort of no-mans-land. They can then withdraw a short distance, as will I, leaving you to do what you need to. You will be in view of both sides at all times. They may be armed, of course, and they will be thinking we are as well."

"You mean you're not?" asked Marcel, worriedly.

"It's best you don't know," replied Oliver. "We are very experienced in these matters."

"Well, let's hope nothing goes wrong," said Andrew, "and that it's not prime dog-walking territory."

At that point they retired to their respective rooms ready for the events of the following day.

The following morning they breakfasted together at 8.30.a.m. At 11.00.a.m. they checked out and, without David Moore, drove south from Ashford towards Kingsnorth, before heading eastwards across country towards Cheeseman's Green, where they arrived at 11.25 a.m. As instructed, Kevin parked his car some distance away, connected his own mobile to Oliver's spare, and waited. Oliver, Andrew and Marcel drove halfway up the lane, leaving their car visible and waited. At noon precisely Oliver's main mobile rang.

"Code?" he said.

"R7938PF," said the caller. "Where do we go?"

"At Cheeseman's Green there is an owl sanctuary. Almost opposite there is a turning, a small track. Take it. You will see a dark red Mercedes. Park a hundred yards behind it and walk into the woods. Then call again."

After a short while a pale blue left-hand drive Citroën pulled slowly in and parked as instructed. Its registration number was obliterated on both plates by mud. Its occupants, three in total, walked into the woods. Two of them appeared to be wearing masks and the third was bound and gagged. The mobile rang again.

"What now?" said the caller.

"Stay on the line. We're coming into the woods."

They met in a small clearing and stood some thirty or so yards apart. One of them had a bag, which Marcel was able to confirm was similar to the one the jewellery was originally dispatched in. He was also sure that the man bound and gagged was the guard he had seen at the embassy. One of the masked men drew a gun and held it to their captive's head. Kevin was at least four-hundred yards away and hidden from view.

"Walk forward with the bag and put it down halfway between us," instructed Oliver. "Now open it. Now withdraw."

When this was done, Oliver beckoned Marcel to move forward and approached the open bag. He examined each item in turn and compared them with the paperwork. He then turned to Oliver, nodded, replaced the items in the bag and withdrew.

"We have verified the jewellery," said Oliver. "We are now satisfied they are the items stolen from the airport. Stay where you are while I walk forward with the brief case. I will then withdraw. When I have done that, you will move forward and inspect the cash. We will keep our distance while you do that."

Oliver's instructions were followed to the letter. The gun was still pointed at Yacoub's head.

"Now do exactly as I say," said Oliver. "Take the brief case, leave the jewellery, return to your car and drive away. There are no tricks. You will not be followed. You are free to go."

They did so. They withdrew quickly and sped away. Oliver, Andrew and Marcel stayed where they were for five minutes, then stepped forward and recovered the bag. Kevin suddenly appeared from the undergrowth.

"What did you get?" asked Oliver.

"Quite a bit, actually," replied Kevin. "I got several pictures of their Citroën and a couple of long shots of them as they left. They were kind enough to have removed their masks by then. It looks like we are dealing with two youngish IC4 males. And by the way, their car now has a tracking device."

"Good," said Oliver. "We'll have some useful stuff we can pass to the police in Paris. We are more or less certain the hostage was Yacoub. They still have him, but our priority here was to recover the jewellery, which we did. Kevin, you stick around and track where they go. You and I, Andrew, will get back to David at the hotel."

On their way back Oliver called underwriter Jackson.

"We have the stuff back," he exclaimed enthusiastically.

"Well done," said Martin. "Good work as usual. Is everyone safe and well?"

"Yes, no problem," said Oliver. "We're pretty certain their hostage is Yacoub and they still have him, but that's for someone else to sort out. Our job is done now."

"Brilliant. Many thanks. What are you going to do now?"

"We're on our way back to meet up with David Moore and hand the jewellery over to him. We'll then drop Marcel back at the station, drive straight to London and come to your office. David will take the same route and we will be right behind him all the way. By the time we get to you, perhaps you'll have decided what you want to do with the goodies."

"Yes I will. I'd like them out of my custody as soon as possible. I think it's something the lawyers can wrestle with. I'll get them organised. See you later in the office."

Earlier that morning, Mike Edwards arrived at the offices of Nathan Henry to keep his appointment with Nigel. After coffee and preliminary discussions, Mike began to explain the reason for his visit.

"As I mentioned on the telephone, we have been considering channelling all our London business through one Lloyd's broker. My chairman, Sheikh Al Talyani, and I both feel our best interests have not been served by having several routes to the market and we think the time has come to nominate just one. We have been impressed with the way you handled the jewellery, so we would like it to be Nathan Henry. It will also help us expand our capacity for new business."

"That's gratifying to know, Mike," said Nigel. "Thank you for that."

"There are two ways in which we'd like you to help," continued Mike. "Firstly, there's our various reinsurance programmes. We think if we can expand them a bit, we'd be able to take on more business. You have a specialist reinsurance division, don't you?"

"Yes we do," confirmed Nigel. "I'll arrange for you to meet them."

"Thanks. Then there's a series of what I'd call unusual risks, ones too large for us, or too odd to fit into our own portfolio, even with the backing of reinsurance. We would prefer to run this stuff through our agency, rather than insuring it ourselves. The jewellery fell into this latter category, for example."

"Right," said Nigel. "That's me then. What sort of cases might they be, do you think?"

"Generally speaking, they could be anything, but it's the amount of insurance that would be the criterion. Any risk where we would be exposed to more than ten million dollars in one hit we would want to avoid. They could be high-value yachts and private aircraft, construction projects, high-rise hotels and office blocks, those kind of things."

"What have you been doing with them until now?" asked Nigel.

"Turning them away, mostly," said Mike. "But it's the jewellery and its royal connection that's making us think again."

"OK," said Nigel. "Other divisions deal with yachts and aircraft and you can meet them tomorrow. I'll handle the rest. How would you like to proceed?"

"We think it might be good to have one of your chaps spend a couple of weeks with us in order to assess the potential. We'll provide temporary accommodation for him. Is that something you would consider?"

"Yes it is," confirmed Nigel. "And immediately I have someone in mind. You can meet him later."

"Good. Thanks"

"Now before I forget," said Nigel, "we are all being interviewed by the police over the matter of the jewellery. The loss adjuster has suggested that inside information was leaked to the miscreants and we're all being asked about it. We're not under any suspicion here, you understand, just helping.

Detective Chief Superintendent Partridge was here talking to us and the Dubai police have been trying to contact you for the same reason. When they found out you would be here, they asked Roy Partridge to carry out the interview. Are you happy to do that?"

"Yes, of course, Nigel. When?"

"We could get it done now, if that's all right. I'll phone him and, if he's free, you can see him straight away. I'll walk over with you and wait. It should only take thirty minutes. We'll be back in time for lunch."

"OK," said Mike.

In response to Nigel's call, Partridge confirmed he was free, so they walked over to Bishopsgate. Nigel waited outside until, as anticipated, Mike re-emerged some twenty-five minutes later. The questioning, as he described it, was much in line with Nigel's own.

"Any matters of concern?" asked Nigel.

"Not really," replied Mike. "Nothing I couldn't handle. He asked me about a man called Carmichael," said Mike. "I think he's the prince's commercial secretary."

"Yes, that's right", confirmed Nigel. "He's in the UK on leave at the moment and the police here have been asked to interview him as well."

"He also asked me if I knew Hari Kahn. I found that strange."

"Now that is strange," said Nigel. "What did you tell him?"

"That I knew of him and had some idea of his commercial interests. That I'd seen him a few times but never met him. I also said that our chairman refused to do business with him. The rest of it was pretty mundane, to be honest."

"I wonder what brought his name to Partridge's attention. Did he say it was in connection with the robbery?"

"No, he didn't actually," said Mike. "It was more of an aside just as I was leaving."

"Still strange, though. Right, it's time for lunch. I've booked a dining room back at the office and my broking team are joining us. It'll give you a chance to get more familiar with how we work."

They made their way back to Mark Lane and went straight to the top floor where the dining room was located. They were the first there.

"We don't serve alcohol at lunch times, I'm afraid," explained Nigel. "It's fruit juice or fizzy water."

"Orange is fine for me," said Mike.

A few minutes later they were joined by Mary and her team, Messrs Marshall, Piper-Bingham, Hughes and Blunt. Introductions were made and after pleasantries were exchanged, Nigel explained the purpose of Mike's visit, stressing it was a good opportunity for both companies to expand their business in the region. Mike thanked them for the excellent job they did with the prince's jewellery, adding that it was the main reason why Nathan Henry was their broker of choice going forward. Lunch, all home-made on site by the in-house cook, consisted of Italian tomato and basil soup, chicken supreme with duchesse potatoes and vegetables, followed by cheese and biscuits and fruit. As the coffee arrived, there was a knock on the dining room door and a receptionist came in.

"Sorry to bother you, Mr Watkins," she said, handing over a piece of paper, "but there's an urgent telephone message."

"I think we should all hear this," announced Nigel. "The jewellery was recovered this morning and is now on its way to London. A decision will be made later today about where it goes from here. It's a good result all round. Please call me later this afternoon. Martin Jackson."

"Wonderful," said Mike. "This is excellent news. I will call my chairman and let him know. He can make sure the prince is told as soon as possible."

Simon was so out of his depth now, he was struggling to keep up with all that was going on. All the lunchtime talk, particularly with regard to reinsurance, was going well over his head. And now this. The sheer ingenuity of the people of Lloyd's had him mesmerised.

"OK, thank you everybody," said Nigel, bringing the lunch to an end. "Back to work chaps. Mary, would you and John give us five minutes, Mike has an idea he'd like to run past you."

"We think it would help get things moving," said Mike, "if someone from here were to spend two weeks in our office in Dubai getting to know how we operate, which would generate a greater understanding of our needs. We would provide suitable accommodation and subsistence."

"Mary," said Nigel. "Can you spare John for this?"

"Yes I can I'm sure," she replied.

"I would have suggested you, but …"

"But I'm a woman," she interrupted.

"I wasn't being discriminatory," he replied, slightly taken aback. "It's just that I know about your domestic commitments."

"Don't worry," said Mary. "It wasn't that. I just don't think women in the workplace are top of the agenda in the Emirates. I wouldn't feel comfortable there."

"Yes, of course," said Nigel.

"I'm happy to go," said John. "When would you like me to start?"

"I'm planning to leave Monday," said Mike. "You can come back with me."

"That's fine," said John.

"OK," said Nigel. "Thanks again."

Oliver Bentham, Andrew Weaver and David Moore duly arrived at Martin Jackson's Gracechurch Street office and the goods were handed over to him. He asked David to let Lieutenant Le Bret know, which he did immediately. Martin had already made contact with Prince Fahd's lawyers, Beauchamp & Co. in Mayfair, and arrangements were in hand for the items to be held at the Saudi embassy in London awaiting further instructions. They were being collected during the afternoon. At that point Oliver took a call from Kevin, who was still in Kent.

"Oliver," he said. "They drove to a car park on the outskirts of Hythe, left the Citroën there and transferred into a black BMW, in which they sped away in the direction of the

M2. I chose not to follow it, but I have the registration numbers of both cars. They're probably false, but I have them anyway and I got a shot of the BMW."

"OK," said Oliver. "Give me the numbers and I'll pass them onto the police."

Registration details of the two vehicles, one French and one English, were duly passed to Lieutenant Le Bret.

"This is a really good result," said Martin. "Everyone involved is going to be extremely pleased with what you've done here, Oliver. Now I'd like to get a meeting going, probably on Monday morning, so that everything you learned from the recovery can be passed on to those that need to know. The Paris police do have a murder on their hands arising from these events, so their enquiries will be continuing. We should do everything we can to help, but I also have in mind getting the reward money back. It's not right that people should profit from their crimes and Lloyd's likes to adhere to that principle. I'd like us to explore ways in which we can go about that. I know it's not going to be easy, but I would like to have a go nevertheless."

"Well I can be here for that," said Oliver. "Who else do you suggest?"

"Certainly you, David," said Martin, "and perhaps you could see if Lieutenant Le Bret would like to come. I'll tell Watkins and Locke from the brokers. They should be here as well. That should do it."

"Right," confirmed Oliver. "See you Monday morning, then."

"Yes," said Martin. "And once again thank you for what you guys have done here. It's an outstanding piece of work."

Chapter 15

When the news broke in Riyadh the following day, the general feeling was one of relief. Sheikh Al Talyani had told Governor Mohammed, who had informed Prince Fahd. The governor also told Commissioner Mansur and, between them, they decided there was no point in following Almahdi and Fawzi any longer. The two were still in Riyadh going about their business and nothing unusual had occurred since their release from prison. Within the hour the prince was on the telephone to Sheikh Al Talyani in Dubai.

"This is wonderful news, Sheikh Abdul Rahman," said the prince. "I thought the princess would never see her dowry. Tell me, how was it done?"

"Your Royal Highness," began the sheikh. "It was the work of Lloyd's. Not only did they put up a reward, as is customary, but the underwriter concerned organised an experienced negotiating team to set up and carry out the exchange. It all went exactly to plan. There is some useful information to hand over to the police in Paris, who will be continuing their enquiries into the death of Saleh Al Othaim."

"Yes, I see," said the prince, "and who is the underwriter concerned?"

"A man called Martin Jackson, Sir."

"Well, would you see to it that my compliments and warmest thanks are passed to him. Also tell him, if you would, that I am planning to be in London in October and that I would like to meet him. He sounds a very capable man."

"I will, Sir."

"Where is the jewellery now?" asked Prince Fahd.

"Currently at the embassy in London," replied the sheikh. "What would you like to happen to it?"

"I'd like it here, please, so the princess can have it as soon as possible. It is the one formal part of the wedding ceremony still outstanding."

"Very well, Sir," said Sheik Abdul Rahman. "I'll see it gets to you."

"Thank you," said the prince. "And, once again, this is an exceptional result."

Al Talyani immediately put a call through to his CEO Mike Edwards, who was with Nigel Watkins in his office.

"Mike," said the sheikh, "the prince wants the jewellery shipped out to him as quickly as possible. Can you arrange it please?"

"I'll do my best," said Mike. "It's going to be tricky, though. Technically Lloyd's are the current custodians, albeit the embassy is actually where the items are and I suspect the Paris police see it as evidence and want it kept to hand. Plus I wouldn't want to use a regular courier service and end up in the same position as we've just got out of."

"When are you returning," asked Sheikh Al Talyani.

"Monday," said Mike. "Why?"

"And is anyone coming with you?"

"Yes, as a matter of fact," said Mike. "One of the brokers here, John Marshall, will be with me. He's the chap that will be with us for two weeks looking at our current book of business."

"Right. You and he can act as couriers. I am sure Lloyd's would not object and, if you need to, assure the police all items can be returned to them whenever they need it. This is important, Mike. The prince's marriage contract is incomplete without the dowry."

"I understand," said Mike. "Leave it to me."

Mike immediately raised the point with Nigel.

"Our client's interests come first, I think, but it's an unusual step to take, with you guys acting as couriers. I'm sure your part of it will be fine, but there's one thing that worries me, the Lloyd's policy. It has remained fully in force all this time, of course, and its geographical scope is worldwide, so technically the trip is covered. I would feel happier, though, if we had underwriter approval to what you're proposing. It's a change of material information, Mike, so I think it needs to be disclosed to all fourteen participants. We'll speak to the team."

"Good idea," said Mike.

Meanwhile Mary and her team were in deep conversation, largely instigated by Simon who, still overwhelmed by the events of the previous day, had asked what reinsurance was all about.

"I don't understand it," he had said. "If something's insured, why does it need to be insured again? Is it like a bookmaker who lays off bets?"

"Oh dear," said Mary. "Who'd like to go first?"

"I'll have a go," said Jamie. "A reinsurance contract is set up to protect an insurer from unusually high claims, either by accumulation or by single hit. They can take many different forms but, essentially, they are pre-arranged finite agreements, in other words they run for twelve, twenty-four, or perhaps thirty-six months, with real premiums being paid up front and real policies being issued."

"Not bad so far," said Mary. "Now give an example."

"Right, here goes. ABC Company is an insurer of buildings, both residential and small commercial. Individually, those policies don't pose a great threat and the company would be able to cope with any claims from their own resources. But they would have a problem when faced with an accumulation of claims from, say, a flood or an earthquake. So ABC Company buys a reinsurance policy to cover them in these exceptional circumstances, one that would kick in at a certain level, above fifty million dollars, for example. Below that amount ABC pays the claims, above it the reinsurers pay. It would cost ABC a small percentage of their premium revenue, but it's worth it because it limits their exposure."

"Well done," said Mary. "That's called a treaty. There's another type, though. Anyone like to try that?"

"I will," said Craig. "It's where a single risk is too large for ABC Company, say fifty million dollars. Assume they need to limit their involvement to only five million, they have two choices. They could either share ninety per cent of the fifty million with a reinsurer, or keep the bottom five million and reinsure the top forty-five. The first costs them a straight ninety per cent of the original premium, less a commission, while the second would cost them a lot less. How did I do?"

"Pretty good," said Mary. "Did you get all that, Simon?"

"I think so," replied Simon. "I'll need to do some more work on it, though."

"Yes," added Mary. "And there are a lot more options than the ones we've just described, so you can see why we have specialist reinsurance brokers. It's an area we don't know much about, but I can tell you the main markets are here in London, in Germany and in Switzerland."

At that point Nigel and Mike came into the room.

"We have an urgent request," said Nigel. "Where's John, by the way?"

"Oh, he's gone to sort out his visa for Monday," said Mary. "He'll be back after lunch."

"Right," continued Nigel. "The suggestion is that Mike and John act as couriers and take the jewellery back with them on Monday. The prince is anxious for this to happen because his marriage contract is incomplete without the dowry. Mike and John are going to Dubai, of course, not Riyadh, so there will need to be an onward journey from there. Who do think could do that, Mike?"

"My chairman, most likely," said Mike. "I think he should be the one."

"OK. Now here's the issue," continued Nigel. "I think we need Lloyd's approval for this to happen on the grounds that it's not what was originally planned. I'd like this done today please, Mary. What else have you got on?"

"Just the usual fifteen or twenty cases we normally have each day," she replied with a smile. "But this will be done. You can be sure of it."

"Good. Thanks. Leave you to it then."

"What we do now then," said Mary after Nigel and Mike had left, "is prepare an endorsement notifying the market of the second transhipment. All fourteen underwriters need to be seen, so the leader first, then the rest, but I think I'll telephone Jackson now to let him know what's happening. With any luck he'll let the girl scratch the endorsement, which will save a lot of time. We can all work on this and perhaps have it wrapped up by lunch. That's all folks, let's get to it and good luck."

Back in Nigel's office, he and Mike were summarising the events of the week. They both agreed it had been successful all round.

"What time is your flight on Monday, Mike?" asked Nigel.

"Oh, it's the red-eye," he replied, "leaving at 8.35 p.m."

"That's good. There's a meeting with Martin Jackson taking place in the morning and I think you should be there. It's a round-up of the jewellery affair with the loss adjuster, the police, the negotiator and us. The objective is to pool all that's been learned so that the detective from Paris, Lieutenant le Bret, will be in a position to pursue his enquiries further. The underwriter also wants to explore ways of getting his million dollars back. Personally I don't think he has much chance, but it will be an interesting conversation. Do you have any other plans?"

"I did, actually," said Mike, "but now they're cancelled. I really would like to be at that meeting."

"Excellent. Now why don't you check out of your hotel this afternoon and spend the weekend with us in Guildford. Before then, though, I'll introduce you to our chairman."

At Bishopsgate Police Station, Detective Chief Superintendent Partridge and Sergeant Bennett, known throughout the force as Gordon, were wondering what they could do to make contact with the prince's secretary Alan Carmichael. They had telephoned his mobile twice so far, leaving a message each time, but as yet there was no response. He did, though, get a call from Lieutenant Le Bret, advising that he would be in London on Monday to meet with the underwriter and others and would like to call in to the station first. Detective Partridge, it was suggested, might like to be at the meeting as well.

Later that morning there was a return call from Alan Carmichael.

"I've only just got your messages," he explained. "I'm on a cruise and there's not much of a signal in the Mediterranean. We've just arrived in Naples, which is why I'm able to make contact now. What can I do for you?"

"I've been asked to interview you about the arrangements you put in place for the prince regarding his jewellery. That was because everyone thought you were here in the UK."

"I was until earlier this week," he replied. "What do you need to know?"

"Well, I'd rather not do this over the telephone. When are you back?"

"Thursday this week. From then on I'll be staying with my sister and her family just outside Godalming."

"Would it be possible," asked the detective, "for you to come and see me here in Bishopsgate?"

"Yes of course," confirmed Carmichael. "Say Friday morning?"

"Perfect. See you then."

"Right," he said to the sergeant. "He's the last one but probably the most important, being the only one that seems to know anything about all this. Let's hope he can throw some light on things. By the way, Gordon, did you see how Edwards reacted when I mentioned Hari Kahn? That took him off guard, didn't it?"

"Yes, Sir," he replied, "but what's the connection?"

"No idea," said Partridge. "Our colleagues in West End Central have had their eye on him for a while. Nothing concrete, but as he's based in Dubai and so is Edwards, I thought I'd just throw it out. When I interviewed the man Black at that company in Pepys Street, I asked him as well. He said Kahn wasn't his agent for the jewellery, that was someone else in Bahrain, but he was Kahn's preferred London broker and he knew him pretty well."

By 1.15 p.m., Mary's team were back in their office as arranged.

"All done?" she asked.

"All but one," said Craig. "One of the tail-enders wants an additional premium of twenty-five thousand dollars and won't be talked out of it."

"Why?" asked Mary. "The policy scope is already worldwide."

"I told him that," replied Craig. "He's saying it's a change of material information that increases the risk."

"Who is it?" asked Mary.

"Cyril Jones," said Craig. "He's got three per cent."

"Oh, nice one Cyril," said Mary. "Tail wagging the dog again."

"If he's only got three per cent," asked Simon, "why can't we just pay him his share of the extra premium?"

"That's completely against the rules," said Craig. "We've got to treat every participating underwriter the same."

"Would you like me to see him?" suggested Simon. "He was in the group I played golf with."

"There's no harm in trying," said Mary. "See what you can do this afternoon."

After lunch, Simon made his way back to Lloyd's and to the box of underwriter Jones.

"Hello Simon," said Cyril. "How are you? Didn't I read about you in the paper earlier this week? You won a golf tournament, didn't you?"

"If you take *The Argus*, yes you did, Sir. I became club champion last weekend."

"I do take it, as a matter of fact," said Cyril. "I live in Haywards Heath. And well done, by the way. Right, what can I help you with?"

"I'm afraid it's the jewellery Sir," said Simon. "We've got everyone's agreement but yours to the second shipment and it's causing concern, after all it's not the client's fault this is happening. I was wondering if there's any leeway here."

"I think the leader was wrong not to charge extra for this. It seems to me he's too involved with the case to focus objectively on the increased risk here. The fact that I'm the only guy who picked up on it doesn't make me wrong."

"No Sir," said Simon. "We're not saying you're wrong. It's just that it's going to be awkward to handle in the time we have available. We can't go ahead without the policyholder's agreement to the increased price and the shipment is scheduled for Monday."

"OK. Here's what I'll do. I'll suspend the additional charge until next week. If the stuff gets there safely I'll waive it, if not I'll proceed with it. How's that?"

"I think that will be fine, Sir. Thank you."

The news was well-received back in the office, not a completely successful result but for the time being it would do. Mary was thus able to confirm to Nigel that Monday's trip now had the approval of Lloyd's and it could go ahead fully insured.

"Nice work everyone," said Mary. "And have a good weekend."

Simon headed for the station, his brain buzzing yet again from the events of the week, but now with a minor triumph under his belt. Once on the train, he began to turn his attention to the weekend and Emma's birthday.

At home that evening Simon was able to catch up with his mother, whose week had been rather overburdened with charity meetings and other local matters. She had, though, managed to speak with Emma's mother and knew what was planned for the weekend.

"They have a family dinner tonight," she told Simon. "Emma, her parents, grandparents, one uncle and two aunts are all off to the Grand Hotel. Then tomorrow there's a party for her friends, and those of her family that are still around, at the house. Emma doesn't know about it yet and she still thinks you're taking her out. You're not. You are invited to the party instead and your father and I are going to keep the Claremonts company while they stay out of the way, and to help organise the food and drink. The weather looks to be good, so the frolics will be in the garden for most of the time. We'll be there in the morning, but 4.00 p.m. is the start time."

"Right," said Simon. "It all sounds good to me. I got her this, by the way."

"That's nice dear," said his mother, looking at a rather smart gold bracelet in a presentation box. "She's getting an iPad from her parents, but I don't know what else."

The following morning, Simon went to the golf club, mainly to see if his name had made it to the honours board. It had. He played eighteen holes with three other members, all of whom were delighted that he was with them, before adjourning to the clubhouse for a sandwich. He was home in time to smarten himself up for the party and when he was ready he walked over to Woodland Drive, arriving there just after 4.00.p.m. Emma greeted him warmly and he handed her the present.

"This is lovely," she said with excitement. "Thank you so much."

"It's a friendship bracelet, "said Simon. "I think we can call ourselves friends by now, don't you?"

"Oh yes," said Emma, laughing. "Let's keep it going, shall we?"

"Certainly," said Simon. "For as long as we can."

The party got underway as more guests arrived. They were mainly Emma's friends from school, plus a few younger members of her wider family, most of whom Simon had not met before.

"This is my boyfriend," she said to a group of them, pointing to Simon, who found himself pleasantly lost for words.

"I hope you didn't mind me calling you that," she explained later. "One or two of the lads get funny ideas about me sometimes and I thought it might ward them off."

"I don't mind at all," said Simon. "In fact, let's go on record with it shall we?"

"Yes," replied Emma. "I was hoping you might see it that way."

Chapter 16

For Monday morning, Martin Jackson had taken the precaution of booking a meeting room in the Lloyd's building, in view of the number of people likely to be there. Those not familiar with Lloyd's would be given the grand tour by those that were, he had decided, followed by lunch in the Captain's Room. His syndicate would foot the bill, since they were there largely to further the interests of the Lloyd's market. The meeting was scheduled to begin at 10.00 a.m., with coffee and biscuits laid on by the catering staff. For Martin, his underwriting duties at the box would have to wait until the afternoon. By 10.00 a.m. they had all assembled. At the table were underwriter Jackson and his claims man Derek Pike, Nigel Watkins and his claims director David Locke, Mike Edwards, loss adjuster David Moore, negotiators Oliver Bentham and Kevin Chamberlain, Lieutenant Le Bret, plus Chief Superintendent Partridge and Sergeant Bennett, who were there at the Lieutenant's request. Business cards were exchanged where necessary and the underwriter took the chair.

"Gentlemen," began Martin. "Thank you all for coming this morning. The purpose of the meeting is twofold. Firstly, it is to exchange information and to ensure that the police are completely up to date with everything that we know and, secondly, to see what we can do about recovering the reward money. Our priority at the time was to get the jewellery back, but we cannot let criminals profit from their crimes if we can help it. It is an informal meeting, so minutes will not be taken, but you are welcome to make notes should you wish to do so. Now Oliver, could you tell us about the exchange and, more importantly, what we can learn from it?"

"Right. In response to our advert offering a reward, we began to receive calls from someone who was able to identify the date and place of the heist and who eventually sent a photograph of the tiara. His initial demand was for five million dollars in cash which we resisted, holding out for one million. During these calls we were able to do two things, pinpoint the locations they were coming from and record the voice. The calls came from north-eastern France, from slightly different areas within the same general region between Lille and Namur. We've had the voice analysed by experts, who have concluded that it is heavily east London, with a hint of the sub-continent coming out in some of the vowel sounds. I'll come back to this point later. Generally speaking, it didn't seem too difficult to take control of these conversations, so I took a firm line with regard to the one million from which I didn't budge. By the day of the exchange, the caller was following my instructions to the letter. It also became clear they knew about the Lloyd's policy, since the caller mentioned it.

On the day itself, Andrew, Marcel Dubois and I met them at a lonely, wooded spot near Romney Marsh, while Kevin here hid himself in the undergrowth some distance away, complete with tracking equipment and other stuff you don't need to know about. When they arrived they had Yacoub with them, holding a gun to his head. The other two were wearing masks. I communicated with one of them by mobile, even though we were only thirty or so yards apart. When the exchange was done, they left but, fortunately for us, they had removed their masks by the time they reached their car, thinking they were out of our range. Kevin was able to follow them to Hythe, where they appear to have ditched the Citroën in favour of a BMW. The vehicle registration numbers were passed to Lieutenant Le Bret. We have photographs of the two of them with Yacoub and both of the cars."

At that point Kevin passed round copies of all the photographs he had taken. Oliver had deliberately avoided mentioning they had bugged the Citroën, in view of the police presence.

"Why Romney Marsh?" asked Martin. "Wasn't it risky getting them to come here from France?"

"Yes, Martin," said Oliver. "But it was a risk we chose to take, since they were following our instructions quite readily by then. I wanted them in territory they weren't familiar with and I also wanted them on a ferry or through the tunnel, where they would have to use their passports and might be caught on CCTV. It was more a risk for them, rather than us and the fact that they went along with it indicates inexperience."

"What about the stuff they had with them?" asked Lieutenant Le Bret. "High value jewellery and a gun aren't everyday travel items."

"Yes I know," said Oliver. "This leads me to think they came through the tunnel. Security checks are different from those for the ferry. The emphasis isn't quite the same. For the shuttle, it's the car that gets scanned in the search for stowaways, rather than anything else. The jewellery would probably be indistinguishable, as would the gun if it were hidden in, say, a tool box. And in any event, if they were caught then our job would have been done and the handover of cash would have been rendered unnecessary. It would have been slightly inconvenient, of course, as customs authorities would have had control of the jewellery, not Lloyd's, so it would take considerably longer for it to be released to the owner. It also tells us that Yacoub was not concealed in the boot of their car, but came through as a normal passenger, in which case he would have needed to show some sort of passport. "

"So with your experience in these matters," asked Martin, "what do you think we're dealing with here?"

"OK," replied Oliver. "In my view, we're dealing with two IC4 males, in other words men of Asian origin, who were brought up in east London or Essex, who are aged between twenty-five and thirty-five and who aren't particularly experienced. They seem familiar with north-eastern France, so may have spent time there. They have access to firearms, or maybe just imitation ones, and may have a history of petty crime. They probably crossed the channel on the morning of the exchange, since they wouldn't want an overnight stop in the UK while they had a hostage with them, if indeed he was a hostage."

"Can you explain that, please?" asked Lieutenant Le Bret.

"Yes," said Oliver. "There is something that bothers us about Yacoub's part in all this. Our experience leaves us a little puzzled as to why his captors bothered to bring him along. After all, it was the jewellery we wanted back, not him. And if they killed Al Othaim, why keep Yacoub alive? Secondly, during the exchange he didn't seem frightened about anything, even though there was a gun at his head. He stayed remarkably calm throughout. He didn't seem threatened nor was he manhandled in any way. Thirdly, only one person was seen being put into the ambulance, so where was the other one? It is still an open question, therefore, as to whether Yacoub was abducted or whether he was one of the abductors. Fourthly, it is still a puzzle how he and Al Othaim were separated from the other passengers on the tarmac. What if Yacoub was the one who got Al Othaim away from that area?"

"I see," said Le Bret. "It's an interesting theory and one which I shall bear in mind, but it can only be that until firm evidence comes to light."

"Yes," said Martin. "But we should acknowledge that Oliver and his people are very experienced in these matters. How many kidnap negotiations have you conducted now, Oliver?"

"Fifty-seven," he replied.

"And what is your success rate?" he asked, for other people's benefit.

"All but one resulted in the release of the hostage unharmed. The one failure, where the victim was killed, was an operation we went into jointly with local police. Not in Europe, I hasten to add, but in South America."

"Thanks, Oliver," said Martin. "It was an outstanding job, I think we all agree. Perhaps, Lieutenant Le Bret, you have some points you'd like to raise?"

"Yes of course," said the Lieutenant, "I am happy to bring you up to date with our findings so far, but I'm afraid I cannot discuss any new lines of enquiry at this stage."

"Of course not," said Martin, "but please tell us what you feel you can."

"Ours is a murder enquiry. Everything is relevant, of course, but it is the death of Al Othaim that is our priority here. Since we last spoke, forensics found fibres which did not come from the clothing on the body and there was also a spot of blood on one of the shoes that did not match the victim's. At the moment we have nothing to compare them with, nor are there any positive results from our DNA database. His personal belongings, including his mobile, were missing. We have CCTV of the ambulance in St Quentin, as you already know, but the images of the two occupants are extremely blurred. Nevertheless we shall compare them with the photographs we now have to determine if they are the same people. I will also interview our witness at the airport again to see if he recognises anyone. However, our priority now is to find Yacoub. He is the person we would most like to interview at this point, as we feel he has the answer to all this. For the moment, though, we are treating it as abduction, although I will take into account what you said earlier, Mr Bentham. It is still possible, though, that Yacoub's life is in danger, so the sooner we find him the better. The new information I now have may help speed up that process. Meanwhile we recovered the Citroën and its plates turned out to be false, as we suspected. Forensics are checking it over and we're looking for reports of recently stolen vehicles of that description. I've asked Chief Superintendent Partridge to run a check on the BMW and we are currently awaiting the results."

"Has anyone phoned Yacoub's mobile?" asked David Locke. "Seems like a simple thing to do."

"I have, several times," replied the lieutenant. "It appears to be permanently switched off. I've left messages but there's been no return call. It's probably been dumped."

"Thank you, Lieutenant," said Martin. "David?" he said, turning to the loss adjuster.

"My own position concurs entirely with that of Lieutenant Le Bret," began David Moore. "In addition I went to Riyadh and spoke to the prince. Nothing he said to me gave any indication that he was in any way responsible for the release of detailed information, either deliberately or mistakenly. He was very certain about that. However, as we have the jewellery back, we do not have to address that issue but I am, though, recommending to underwriters that the reward money ..."

"Ransom money," interrupted David Locke.

"… the reward money," continued the loss adjuster, regardless, "be collected from the syndicates and returned to the Saudi embassy in Paris as quickly as possible. I told them I would see to it in a timely manner."

"Yes," said Martin. "Our two claims men can get that going straight away. Derek, you need to organise the agreement for the brokers to take round the market and you, Mr Locke … I'd prefer you to be a little more diplomatic and use the term reward if you would."

"He doesn't do diplomatic," said Nigel, "but he will get it done."

"Now," continued Oliver, "I have something else to add, pure supposition again, I'm afraid. Our belief is that the inside man is someone more senior, someone who pulled all the strings and who either knew, or was able to obtain, inside information about the transhipment. He is a person of international experience, domiciled in an area where dollars are commonplace, if not the home currency. It most likely rules out Europe and points us towards the Middle East. Our caller gradually went along with all our demands and it's usually a lot tougher than that, so we think he was an inexperienced amateur, rather than a seasoned professional. And if so, then someone cleverer than him was running things."

"If that is so," said Lieutenant Le Bret, "then how was it they settled so readily for an amount one fifth of their original demand?"

"Good point," said Oliver. "We don't know whether five million was the original demand. In other words, the caller may have been under instructions to go for, say, two million but decided himself to try for five, hoping to hang onto the difference. I'll come back to this point later, if I may, it's something we might make use of."

"Any other questions?" asked Martin.

"Yes," said Le Bret. "If Yacoub was part of the plot, why would the others bother to treat him as a hostage and bring him along at the handover?"

"Probably to raise the stakes or to throw us off the scent, perhaps. I really believe this is what they were trying to do. Yacoub's involvement has all the trademarks of a put-up job and I'm beginning to wonder whether the gun at his head was loaded or not."

"Thank you Oliver," said Martin. "Is there anything you want to raise, Chief Superintendent Partridge?"

"Not really," said Roy Partridge. "I'm waiting for the results of the vehicle check on the BMW plates and there's one more person to interview, but until then I rather think I'm up the proverbial gum tree."

"Or the proverbial pear tree," said David Locke, an aside which passed everyone by except for the chief superintendent who cast him an ugly glance.

"Now Mike," said the underwriter. "I understand you're acting as courier later today. Tell us what arrangements are in place."

"Yes Mr Jackson," replied Mike. "John Marshall will be coming with me. We report to the Saudi embassy in London this afternoon and with the package they drive us to Heathrow. Airport officials have already been alerted, so there should be no problem getting through security. Ours is a British Airways flight leaving at 8.35 p.m. for Dubai, where we will be met by my chairman, Sheikh Al Talyani, who by then will have made suitable arrangements with customs and immigration. He will then board a flight to Riyadh where, upon arrival, he will be driven by the prince's personal chauffeur directly to the King Saud Palace to hand the jewellery over."

"And are you happy doing this," asked Martin, "and with these arrangements?"

"Yes," said Mike. "We know we are not couriers, but we are both experienced businessmen and seasoned travellers."

"Very well," said Martin. "Thank you. Now, can we turn our attentions to the tricky matter of the reward and how we might get our money back?"

"Yes," said Lieutenant Le Bret. "Though the handover wasn't carried out within my jurisdiction, I think it will very much be tied up with my murder investigation which is and, though I cannot be of any immediate help, I will be sure to bring it up when we locate any of the suspects."

"I think we can do better than that," said Oliver. "You remember earlier when I talked about the amount of the demand? Well, it occurs to me that a little inaccurate publicity, aimed at causing a rift between gang members, might flush something out here. We have used this technique successfully before, so let me explain how it works. Assume we are right and there is a Mr Big, to use a worn-out expression. Let's also assume that because he controlled everything, the telephone caller reported back to him between each call and took new instructions. We know they were aware of the Lloyd's policy so if he were up to speed on such things, he would expect a reward of around ten per cent. Thus he might have set the demand at two million."

"We're with you so far," said Martin. "Keep going."

"He would be disappointed to learn from his henchmen that they had settled for the lower figure of one million."

"This is all speculation," said Lieutenant Le Bret. "Where is it going to lead us?"

"Now," continued Oliver. "Imagine how he would feel if he heard they had actually been handed two million. How do you think that would make him react?"

"He'd be pretty rattled, don't you think?" said Martin. "So what do we do?"

"We put out a statement," said Oliver, "saying that a two million dollar reward was paid by Lloyd's for the return of a substantial consignment of jewellery, giving a few basic details to identify the exchange. Add to that the notion that police in France and the UK have been making extensive enquiries and are close to making an arrest."

"Just one problem," said Martin. "Lloyd's would never agree to that. They just don't put out statements of that nature."

"I thought you would say that," said Oliver. "But I can. I can have certain papers print a couple of unattributed paragraphs. I've done it before, actually."

"What I don't understand," said Le Bret, "is why the top man, if there is one, didn't do the negotiating himself."

"Ah, now here's another clue," said Oliver. "He would naturally assume we had a recorder on the go, so what if he was someone whose voice might be recognised?"

"And what do you expect to happen following this announcement?" asked Le Bret, exuding scepticism about the idea.

"My guess is there would be a lot of movement. The top man would want to catch up with his hired hands and confront them. Who knows what might happen if he finds them? So the important thing is to alert immigration officers and border control agents to be on the lookout. Now that we have photographs and a description of their car, if indeed the BMW turns out to be theirs, it just might bring about a result. And don't forget we have one guy with a non-EU passport. We have tried this kind of manoeuvre before and it does sometimes work. Not always, of course, but I do recommend that we try it."

"Sounds like a good idea to me," said Martin. "Any other views?"

"It might be an idea," said Chief Superintendent Partridge, "to wait until we have the results of our check on the BMW. If we know where it is we can put a watch on it and follow it to see where it goes."

"Excellent," said Martin. "I think that's it then. Those that would like a tour of Lloyd's followed by lunch are welcome. What are your plans, Lieutenant Le Bret?"

"I have to get back this evening so, yes, I can stay for a little while. It's my wife's birthday tomorrow."

"Ah, the French lieutenant's woman," said David Locke.

"Shut it David," said Nigel, hiding a smile.

The chief superintendent and his sergeant declined the invitation, as did Derek Pike and David Locke, preferring to get on with their work. Nigel said he and Mike would stay, but they would need to be away by 2.30 p.m. for Mike to link up with John and head off to the Saudi embassy. The meeting then adjourned.

Chapter 17

By 8.15 p.m. that evening, Mike and John were comfortably seated in business class on a British Airways triple seven on their way to Dubai. The journey from the embassy to Heathrow had passed without a hitch, as did their progression through security to the departure lounge, courtesy of an airport services manager. The boarding procedure was uninterrupted by any extraneous event and the flight departed on schedule, due to arrive at its destination the following morning at 7.45 a.m. local time. Sheikh Al Talyani would be there to meet them with all the necessary arrangements in place. They were considerably more relaxed than they had been earlier in the day, now that their valuable cargo was safely tucked under one of the seats in front of them.

Disembarkation at Dubai was as smooth as had been the boarding at Heathrow. Al Talyani was waiting for them airside and immediately took custody of the valuables. Introductions were made and the sheikh then headed off for his flight to Riyadh. The company driver was waiting for Mike and John when they emerged from the terminal and the limo took them straight to the office. Mike called Nigel in London and reported safe arrival in Dubai, promising to call again when he got news that the jewellery had finally reached the prince.

"I'll just check my desk," said Mike, "to see if there's anything here that's urgent, then I'll show you where the apartment is. Once I hear from the boss that he's handed over the prince's belongings, I'll call it a day. I suggest you do the same."

"Yes, I think I will," said John.

In Riyadh, Sheikh Al Talyani was met from his flight by the prince's personal chauffeur, who had also been given permission to wait airside. After clearing immigration, he was driven straight to the King Saud Palace and shown into the private apartments of Prince Fahd. Both were dressed formally in their finest robes.

"Sheikh Abdul Rahman," said the prince. "How nice it is to see you again."

"The pleasure is mine, Your Royal Highness," replied the sheikh. "Your property, I believe," he added, handing over the security box and key. "The honour of opening it is yours, Sir."

"Thank you," said Prince Fahd. "This will be the first time I have set eyes on the real thing, you know. I have only ever seen photographs before. The princess will be overjoyed and I thank you and your colleagues for the part you have all played in this. Will you stay a few days?"

"Thank you, Sir," said Al Talyani. "I have to be in the office tomorrow, but I will stay here tonight."

Back in his quarters in the palace, where he had stayed during the prince's wedding, he called Mike.

"All done," he confirmed. "The goods are finally in the prince's possession."

"Thank you," said Mike. "I'll pass the news on."

Mike managed to catch Nigel just as he was leaving the office at the end of his day, but he promised he would spread the word quickly to all those who needed to know.

At Bishopsgate Police Station, Roy Partridge had received news of the BMW. They were not false plates, as it turned out, and the vehicle was registered to a Mushtaq Hussain at an address in Elm Park in the London Borough of Havering. Further enquiries by the Metropolitan Police had revealed that Mr Hussain was a restaurant owner and had no police record. Living at the same address, according to the electoral roll, was Meera Hussain, wife and two sons Ali, aged twenty-nine and Kareem, aged twenty-six. Both sons were known to the police as having a history of petty crime. The local force had driven by the house several times in two days, but there was no sign of the BMW or the two sons. Chief Superintendent Partridge asked for a continuous watch to be kept on the property and any sightings to be reported. He then relayed the information to Lieutenant Le Bret in Paris and the two detectives set up nationwide alerts in their respective countries, with instructions to report whereabouts but not to approach. Within hours there was a response. The BMW had been located in a long stay car park in Barking and twenty-four hour surveillance was now in place courtesy of the local force. With that information, Partridge telephoned Oliver Bentham and suggested that now might be the time to put out his statement to the press.

In Hereford, Oliver Bentham had been putting together a short piece which he planned to release to the national press on Thursday. The text of it read:-

Massive Jewellery Collection Recovered

A large quantity of valuable and historically important jewellery, thought to be worth in excess of twenty million dollars, has been returned to its rightful owner. A source close to Lloyd's of London says that the five pieces, originally stolen from Charles de Gaulle airport in August, were recovered by a specialist team of negotiators in an exchange which took place near Romney Marsh last Thursday, in which the sum of $2,000,000 in cash was handed over. Lloyd's declined to make a statement about the specific case, but said it was not unusual for rewards of up to ten per cent to be paid by the insurance industry for the return of stolen goods. Police in France and the United Kingdom are continuing their enquiries and are confident that arrests will be made shortly.

Oliver was extremely familiar with how to get the British press onside, having done so several times previously, so it wasn't long before arrangements were in place. His piece was to be featured in all the papers that mattered starting Thursday. The French press was more of a challenge for him, so he decided to wait for a reaction from home first and, in any event, the BMW was still in the UK. The objective of this manoeuvre, though, was to flush out the mastermind and since he had no idea who that might be or where that person was, he was not entirely confident of success. He reminded himself again that it had worked a few times before.

At 10.00 a.m. on Friday morning, Alan Carmichael arrived at the police station in Bishopsgate to keep his appointment with Roy Partridge. He was shown into the chief superintendent's office where coffee and biscuits were served and they were joined by Sergeant Bennett. Partridge explained to Carmichael that the purpose of the interview was to assist the Paris police with their enquiries into a possible leak of information, that he was not under caution, but was attending voluntarily as a potential witness.

"So how was your cruise?" said Roy. "My wife and I keep thinking about doing one, but she can't quite make up her mind."

"I enjoyed it very much," replied Carmichael. "I was with friends, as I don't have a wife any more, but I wouldn't want to do it on my own. I'd be left out of things, I think."

"Where did you go?" said the detective, seemingly wanting to talk more about it.

"Western Mediterranean. Picked the boat up in Barcelona."

"Which boat?"

"*Liberty of the Seas*, one of Royal Caribbean's fleet."

"Sounds good," said Partridge. "I'll take a look at it."

"Now, I'd like you to talk me through your role in setting up the purchase of the jewellery and all the arrangements leading up to its transhipment to Riyadh. You know the latest position do you?"

"No I don't, I'm afraid."

"Well," explained Partridge. "The jewellery was recovered last week and has now been handed over to the prince. Lloyd's masterminded the exchange in return for payment of a reward."

"That is good news," said Carmichael. "Do you know how much the reward was?"

"Two million dollars I think," replied Roy, bearing in mind the press article. Only those present at Monday's meeting were to know it was half that amount and they had been asked to keep it secret.

"Wow," said Carmichael. "Well, the prince had more or less chosen the items himself after a lot of research and, with the help of a Paris jeweller, they were tracked down. He then passed the information to me to make all the arrangements. I decided to assemble the collection in Paris and, when complete, have it delivered to the Saudi embassy prior to purchase. Hearing that Lloyd's wanted to be there to verify the provenance and witness the handover was for me very helpful. It gave the whole transaction an added level of security."

"Whose job was it to transfer the funds?" asked the sergeant.

"Mine," said Carmichael. "The moment I got the call I gave instructions to the bank who wired the money straight away."

"And who else knew about these arrangements?" asked Partridge.

"Al Othaim from the very beginning," said Carmichael. "He was the chosen courier right from the start, but we didn't disclose that until the last minute. Yacoub knew later on, after the date had been set and it was then we told him he would be going as well."

"Tell me about Al Othaim," said the chief superintendent.

"He was an old friend of the prince and a long-serving staff member. He was very highly thought of and was from a well-respected family, though not titled. He was regarded as the number one aide and handled all the non-commercial aspects of the prince's life."

"And Yacoub?" enquired the sergeant.

"He's the man who fixes things for us unofficially, if you know what I mean. He's Riyadh born and bred and knows everyone in public positions below the top level, which quite often is very useful. He's been with us for about seven years and has a reputation for getting things sorted quickly and without fuss. Sometimes, though, he breaks the rules of Saudi culture, which on occasions has landed him in jail. Nothing really criminal, but he should know better."

"Give me an example," said Roy.

"Right," said Carmichael. "Every police officer would recognise him and his car, a rather old and rusty Chevrolet, which they are always on the lookout for. He was caught once driving a female passenger, a cleaner I think, from the palace to the supermarket and because she wasn't his wife, he was taken to jail. It was an infringement of the rules at the time. On another occasion he was found with a vodka bottle on the back seat and, again, taken to jail, even though the bottle contained tap water. When he's been missing from the palace for a day or two, the prince telephones the governor and asks if he can have the boy back. It works every time."

"OK, thanks," said Roy. "Now, can you tell us a bit about the reception committee that was waiting at the airport in Riyadh. How were they chosen?"

"That's something I asked Yacoub to arrange," said Carmichael. "He told me it was done, but I don't know much more, I'm afraid."

"Well," said the chief superintendent, "it came as a bit of a surprise to learn they were a couple of local taxi drivers who weren't even on the palace payroll, in view of the importance of the task. The original idea was to have personal aides do the job, guys on the permanent staff, wasn't it?"

"Yes," replied Carmichael. "I didn't know he'd done that. Those two are known to us, though, but you're right, palace staff would have been more appropriate."

"Why do you think he did that?"

"Not sure. I think they're mates and he might have owed them a favour."

"OK," said Partridge. "Now can you tell me please, who was it that arranged for the Lloyd's quote?"

"That was me initially," replied Carmichael. "First of all I asked an agent in Bahrain to come up with terms, but the result wasn't very encouraging."

"Who was the agent?" asked the sergeant.

"A man called Richard Greer. He's an expat working for a Bahraini organisation called Manama General Enterprises. They went to a Lloyd's broker called Baxter Taylor and Black, I think, but the conditions were unacceptable. Then Saleh Al Othaim said he knew someone, so I left it to him to organise. He went to another Bahraini agent called Mahdi Al Hadda and we got what we wanted."

"Who gave the order to proceed?" asked Roy.

"That was me," confirmed Carmichael. "Once the date was fixed, the prince and I approved the quotation and I asked Saleh to give the agent the go-ahead. It was then we released the identity of the courier, i.e. Saleh himself, and it was then we assigned Yacoub to accompany him."

"Did anyone else at the palace know about the insurance?"

"I think not, just the prince, Saleh and I."

"OK, Mr Carmichael," said Chief Superintendent Partridge. "That's very helpful, so thank you for that. If I need to talk to you further, might I have a contact address please and some idea of your whereabouts for the next few weeks?"

"Yes of course," replied Carmichael, handing over a card on which he wrote an address and telephone number. "This is my sister's address in Godalming. I'm staying there while waiting for the prince to arrive in London. He's due here sometime in October and I'm sure he'll be in touch soon to tell me when. After London I travel with him to New York, then back to Riyadh."

"Thank you very much," said the chief superintendent. "And thank you for coming in. By the way, do you know a man called Hari Kahn?"

"I don't think so," said Carmichael. "I've met hundreds of business people during my time as commercial attaché in Riyadh, so I could have run across him."

"OK. Thanks anyway."

Sergeant Bennett showed him out and returned to his boss's office.

"What did you make of that?" asked Partridge.

"He seemed genuine enough to me. He's clearly a very competent business operative and I found nothing untoward in anything he said. And why were you going on about cruising? You hate the sea."

"Oh dear," sighed Roy. "You've a lot to learn, Gordon. I thought I might check his story about where he had been and now we have the name of his cruise company and the ship he says he was on."

"Did you suspect anything?" asked Sergeant Bennett.

"No, not at the beginning. It's been in my mind that someone we already know has been up to no good here and it's time to start prying a bit more. I know we're only supposed to be carrying out enquiries on behalf of the Paris police, but the exchange did take place on our soil, so I think I'm within my rights to set up my own enquiry now. Anyway, as it turned out, there was something that struck me as odd. Why, do you think, did he ask me about the amount of the reward?"

"To tell the prince?" suggested Sergeant Bennett.

"I don't think so," said Partridge. "I'm just wondering whether he was checking out yesterday's press release. And another thing, did I say anything about Hari Kahn being a business man in the Middle East? No. That's something he came up with himself. Plus I wouldn't have delegated the job of arranging the guys to meet the couriers at the airport, I'd have done that myself, unless I knew they weren't going to arrive. I want you to check with the cruise company and have the local force keep a watch on his sister's house. See what car he's using, get some idea of his movements and all the usual stuff."

"Yes boss," said the sergeant. "I'll get on to it straight away."

"By the way," said Roy. "Do you recognise anyone in this photograph?"

"I think I do, boss," replied the sergeant. "Isn't it the bloke from the brokers, Nigel Watkins?"

"Yes it is. The guy he's with is Hari Kahn and they're having lunch at the Mayfair Hotel. Our friends from West End Central were tailing Kahn at the time and circulated this picture to see if the other guy could be identified. I think I'd like to question him again, but first we'll see who does what following the press announcement. With any luck, that might reveal something interesting."

"It might just," agreed the Sergeant. "So do you think that Kahn is involved in the jewellery case?"

"I've no idea, but I'd like to know what he was doing lunching with Watkins. Could be nothing in it, but I'd like to be sure. And in any event our colleagues up west would be interested. We'll come back to Watkins again on Monday morning. In the meantime I will report all this to Le Bret in Paris."

Chapter 18

In Paris Lieutenant Le Bret was making very little progress. His witness from the airport was not able to match the two in the photograph with those he had seen on the tarmac, nor was there any police record in France of the Hussain brothers, nor anyone matching their description closely enough for a positive identification. He was fairly certain, though, that they were the same two as had been caught on CCTV driving the ambulance in St Quentin, but the blood and fibre samples from the body of Al Othaim were of no use until arrests were made. Le Bret had, though, alerted all agencies to be on the lookout for any sightings of the BMW and its occupants, one of whom would probably have a Saudi passport. He would have preferred it if the British police were to arrest Ali and Kareem Hussain instead of carrying out surveillance, but he understood the desire to flush out the mastermind and was prepared to go along with the plan for a little while. All he could do for the time being, though, was to wait, hoping that the press announcement might generate some action.

There was negative news from the police in Riyadh that, despite extensive enquiries, it had not been possible to identify the two imposters who arrived at King Khaled Airport in place of the couriers. Apparently it was a busy weekend in the Kingdom and several flights had arrived within minutes of each other, thus there was no way of knowing who had disembarked from which. And despite conversations with several airport staff on duty at Charles de Gaulle, there was no information whatsoever concerning the individual who had set off the fire alarm.

All in all, he was looking at a criminal gang of at least six, maybe seven if Yacoub were included, some of whom would need to have enough passable French to get them in and out of the secure area with the ambulance.

Later on Friday afternoon, Chief Superintendent Partridge received a call from a colleague in the Metropolitan Police advising him that at approximately 3.00 p.m. an IC4 male, thought to be in his mid-fifties, had visited the Hussain house in Elm Park and, in the absence of a reply, driven to an Indian restaurant in Hornchurch. The vehicle he was driving was a Bentley, the registration number of which was in the process of being checked. The driver had spoken briefly to Mushtaq Hussain, the restaurateur, before driving to a bed and breakfast establishment in Barking, arriving there at 3.30 p.m. Shortly before his arrival, at approximately 3.20 p.m., three men were seen running from the house to a nearby long-stay car park and driving away in a black BMW, in full view of the police surveillance team. At approximately 3.35 p.m. the Bentley sped away in the same direction, eastwards along the A13. No attempt was made to follow either vehicle, since the instructions were to watch and report. Partridge thanked the officer for the report and asked to be kept informed of all developments. A short while later he received a further call telling him that the Bentley was registered to a Mr Hari Kahn at an address in Chigwell.

The chief superintendent called his sergeant into his office.

"We have some action, Gordon, and it looks like the plan is working," said Roy. "Hari Kahn has been trying to catch up with the Hussain brothers. I wonder why."

"So are you saying that Kahn is the mastermind?" asked Sergeant Bennett.

"Can't be certain yet," replied Roy, "but it is beginning to look as though he's involved in some way. Anyway, it's enough for us to pull him in. I think we'd better come in tomorrow first thing. I know it's Saturday, but things are going to get a bit lively from now on."

"OK," said the sergeant.

Partridge then called West End Central who put out an alert to all forces for Kahn's immediate apprehension, being wanted for questioning in connection with conspiracy to rob and to commit murder. He did the same with Ali and Kareem Hussain, plus or minus Yacoub, warning that they might be armed, but this time suggesting that sightings be reported to him before any arrests were made. Roy then called Le Bret in Paris and told him of the latest developments. He also telephoned Oliver Bentham and let him know that things were kicking off, all three agreeing they would be at their desks for the weekend.

"Any news yet about Carmichael?" asked the chief superintendent.

"Yes," replied the sergeant. "We've checked his phone records and there is nothing there to help us. He's hardly used his mobile since arriving in the UK and then only to the lawyer's office in Mayfair, his sister in Godalming a couple of times, the prince in Riyadh and to us here, a call which came from outside the UK. When he left us this morning he went straight back to his sister's house and is still there. He's using a red Peugeot 308 Estate registered to a Mrs Barbara Goddard at the address he gave us, so I presume she's his sister. The car was parked at Godalming station until just after lunch. Meanwhile, I'm waiting to hear back from the cruise company. They do have a record of a Mr Carmichael being a customer of theirs, but their computer went down at that point and it will be a little while before they can tell us anything."

"OK, thanks," said Roy. "Now, just so you know what's in my mind, I want Kahn in custody here as soon as possible, rather than skipping back to Dubai, or wherever he might decide to go. I want him in West End Central where our enquiries can be coordinated with our colleagues there. You and I will interview him regarding the jewellery matter, though, and if necessary I'll get Le Bret over here as well."

"OK boss," said the sergeant.

"However, with regard to the others," continued Roy. "I'd prefer it if they were arrested in France, that is to say within the jurisdiction where the crimes were committed. I don't know if it will work out like that, but I'd rather not go through the hassle of a European Arrest Warrant or extradition procedures. It would be better if Le Bret had them from day one."

"Got it."

"Right, until tomorrow then," said Roy, who then left for the evening.

In Dubai, John Marshall was beginning to familiarise himself with the working practices of the Al Talyani Insurance Company. They were open for business from Sundays through to Thursdays, their weekend being Fridays and Saturdays. The typical working day was from 8.00 a.m. until 2.00pm, then from 5.00 p.m. until 7.00 p.m. The apartment John had been allocated was a short walk from the office and came with a cook/housekeeper. He had not at that point met the chairman, but was due to do so the following week. He had spent his first Friday at the home of Mike Edwards, just relaxing and getting to know more about each other's business objectives.

"I often wonder how I would have got on," said Mike, "if I had been a Lloyd's broker. I know it can be quite intense most of the time, but I think I would have enjoyed it."

"I'm sure," said John. "Most people do, despite having to work at full speed. Where did you start out, Mike?"

"I joined the Sun Alliance in Horsham about thirty years ago and for a short while, once I'd learned the business, I was posted to their branch office in Jeddah. That's what gave me the taste for an expat life. It's very easy going here compared with what you guys have to do. I'm ten minutes from the office, I don't have the worry of train travel and most of what I need is provided by the company. I sometimes feel, though, that I just sit at my desk shuffling paper, whereas you guys are out and about all the time. The face to face style of broking definitely has its advantages, because you get the right result more often than not. What's your background, John?"

"Oh, I left school at sixteen with a handful of 'O' levels and joined a Lloyd's syndicate as an entry boy. I found it a bit boring, though, and something of a dead end job. The only way upwards was if someone above you left or died. So after a couple of years I went into broking and I've been doing that ever since."

"And the outside services that Lloyd's underwriters have at their disposal are just staggering," commented Mike. "Take the jewellery episode, for example. Who'd have thought they would get the stuff back with such ease. And now they're trying to get the reward money back as well with every chance of success it seems. It's just so impressive."

"There's talk of an inside man," said John. "We've all been questioned by the police."

"Me too," replied Mike. "Any thoughts as to who it might be?"

"Not really," said John. "I can't imagine it being anyone in the insurance business. It just wouldn't enter their minds to do anything like that. There's too much to lose. Too many opportunities for career advancement would simply be thrown away, certainly in Lloyd's. The top people in our market take home hundreds of thousands of pounds a year and that's what we all aspire to."

"Yes, you're right," said Mike. "Trouble is, it doesn't leave very many others."

"That's right," said John. "I think we're looking at someone whose life isn't quite as rosy as they would like. It's someone who wants to change things significantly for themselves, who probably hasn't done anything like this before and isn't planning on doing it again. Someone who's prepared to disappear, leaving the past behind and who doesn't have much of a family life to care about."

"Interesting," said Mike. "But there's more than one person involved, don't you think?"

"Oh yes," said John. "I was just talking about the top man. I'm sure he would be someone of substance who wouldn't be averse to getting a bit of muscle to help him along the way and, of course, having the contacts to do so. This was, by all accounts, a very amateurish job."

"Have you shared these thoughts with the police?" asked Mike.

"Oh no," said John. "This is just my own speculation, just wild thinking."

"It sounds pretty plausible to me," said Mike. "But I'm sure we won't have to wait long before we know."

Simon's weekend was following what had become the customary format, with golf on the Saturday and a day out with Emma on the Sunday. Brighton's home game against Sheffield Wednesday was played on the Friday evening, but his train home from London would not deliver him there with enough time to spare, so he chose not to go, even though his father had tickets. His mother went in his stead. Simon played his usual eighteen holes on Saturday morning, something he regarded as obligatory since he was club champion, much to the delight of fellow members. Even Jaffa, who acknowledged him enthusiastically, seemed pleased to see him.

"How are things," he said to Simon.

"Absolutely first rate, thanks. You?"

"Oh, much the same," said Jaffa. "Still jogging along. Tell me, what is the view in Lloyd's these days about the troubles of the past?"

"It's all behind us," said Simon, carefully including himself in the response. "There's no mention of it at all now. Nobody there seems to have had any part in the bad stuff and it's all gone away. It's onwards and upwards for everyone now."

"Interesting," said Jaffa. "I thought that might be the case."

"It's not what you said last time," said Simon. "You were pretty scathing about the whole thing."

"I know," said Jaffa. "I'm sorry about that. That was then and this is now."

The following day at around 10.30 a.m. Simon walked over to Woodland Drive to collect Emma, who was waiting for him. Her father was there as well.

"Tell me Simon," said George Claremont. "That piece I read in the papers on Thursday, was that to do with you?"

"If you mean the recovery of the jewellery, then yes it was," replied Simon. "It was me that got the quote that won the account. Then the stuff got nicked and now we've got it back."

"It was a hell of a price to pay, though, wasn't it?"

"Oh, the reward," said Simon. "Yes, I suppose so. As far as I can tell, though, it's quite normal."

"What happens now?" asked George.

"I'm not sure," replied Simon. "It's not something we talk about much in the office these days. We've moved on to other things, but I suppose the police will continue to investigate as there's a murder involved."

Emma was by now looking wide-eyed.

"A murder?" she exclaimed.

"Yes," said Simon. "One of the couriers was killed and the other one has disappeared. But I'm not in the loop any longer, so I don't really know the latest position."

"That fellow you told me about," asked George. "What was his name again?"

"Oh, you mean the chap who's the prince's secretary. Carmichael?"

"Yes, that's him. I think I remember him from my time in Kuwait and Bahrain. If his name's Alan, then it's the same bloke. He was our commercial attaché in Riyadh. Before that he was in Jeddah for a while."

"I don't know for sure, I'm afraid," said Simon. "I'm not a party to these conversations now."

"OK, have a good time," said George. "See you later."

They walked up the hill towards Dyke Road and took a bus into Churchill Square, in order to have a look round the shopping centre. After that they walked down West Street and made their way to the pier, where they spent a couple of hours.

"You didn't tell me about a murder," said Emma. "And there's me thinking that insurance was all a bit boring."

"It is," said Simon, "if you're in the local office of a provincial company. Not in Lloyd's though. Pretty lively stuff all round. Our boss, a chap called Nigel Watkins, actually met the chap in Dubai before we knew he was going to be the courier and again at the handover in Paris. The next thing we hear about him is he's been shot twice in the head and dumped in a field."

"You seem a bit serious today," ventured Emma. "Is something bothering you?"

"A little bit," replied Simon. "I'm a bit concerned that your father keeps raising the subject of the bloke Carmichael. I shouldn't really have divulged that name as it's a breach of my company's protocol. If anyone found out, I think I'd be in trouble and I'm wondering why he raises it."

"He's a diplomat," said Emma, "so I don't think there's any way he would breach your confidence."

"Yes, that's what my dad said."

"If you like I'll have a quiet word and see what's on his mind. He's probably just trying to reconnect with old colleagues, but he'll tell me whatever it is."

"Yes, thank you," said Simon. "It would just put my mind at rest."

They left the pier and took Volks Railway out to Black Rock, then made their way to the marina complex, where they enjoyed a late lunch. The subject of Simon's work was not raised again.

On Sunday afternoon, Chief Superintendent Partridge and Sergeant Bennett were at their desks in Bishopsgate Police Station. Nothing had happened the previous day and they were beginning to think about getting home in time for their evening meals. At around 4.00 p.m. the telephone rang. The call was from West End Central, telling Roy Partridge that Hari Kahn had been arrested at Heathrow Airport and was now being held in custody. He had been read his rights and his personal effects confiscated by the custody sergeant, including his mobile phone, his passport, one air ticket to Paris plus hand luggage. Partridge and Bennett decided to carry out a preliminary interview that evening and called Lieutenant Le Bret in Paris to let him know. Before they left for the west end, there was a second call, this time from the police in Kent, letting them know that the BMW, with its three passengers, was in line waiting to take the shuttle through the tunnel to Calais. Roy Partridge gave instructions for them not to be apprehended, but they were to be allowed to travel. That way they could be arrested within French jurisdiction in line with his plan. He immediately telephoned Lieutenant Le Bret again to let him know and he in turn alerted the police in Calais. Later that evening confirmation was received from Le Bret that they had the Hussain brothers and Yacoub in custody and they were on their way in separate police vans to Paris. They had initially been processed at a police station in Calais and their belongings confiscated, but there was no sign of either the gun or the money.

Hari Kahn was escorted into an interview room at West End Central where detectives Partridge and Bennett were waiting. They had agreed that the sergeant would lead the questioning with the chief superintendent taking notes. The conversation was to be recorded.

"You understand Mr Kahn," began the sergeant, "that you are under arrest for conspiracy to rob and murder, that you have already been cautioned, and that you are entitled to be represented by a solicitor?"

"Yes," replied Kahn. "However I have no need of a solicitor at this stage as I have done nothing."

"On Friday afternoon you were seen visiting the home and place of work of a Mr Mushtaq Hussain, then later driving to an address in Barking. What can you tell me about that?"

"I have a business proposition for his sons, Ali and Kareem, but I missed them."

"What sort of business proposition?"

"No comment."

"How do you know the Hussain family?"

"Mushtaq is my brother-in-law. His wife Meera is my sister and his sons are therefore my nephews."

"How was it that you missed them?" asked the sergeant.

"I do not know. They just weren't there when I arrived."

"What can you tell us, Mr Kahn, about the jewellery that went missing from Charles de Gaulle airport?"

"Nothing. I have no knowledge of it."

"What can you tell us, Mr Kahn, about the arrangements in place for the transhipment to Riyadh?"

"Nothing specific. I was at one stage trying to get the assignment for my freight forwarding company, but it didn't work out."

"Do you know a man called Darren Black?"

"Yes I do. He's the Lloyd's broker I use for some of my business activities. He works for a company called Baxter Taylor and Black. He's the Black."

"And do you know a man called Nigel Watkins?"

"Yes. He's also a Lloyd's broker, with a company called Nathan Henry."

"How many times have you met him?"

"Twice," confirmed Hari Kahn. "I first ran across him on a flight to Dubai, then later we had a meeting at the Mayfair Hotel."

"What was the meeting about?"

"The jewellery shipment. I was trying to put my company forward to take care of the transit and I thought he was closer to the account than the other brokers."

"And what was the outcome?"

"I didn't get the job."

"So you were a little put out by that, perhaps?"

"I suppose. Some you win, others you don't."

"OK Mr Kahn," said the chief superintendent. "We'll leave it there for now. You will be held in custody overnight pending further enquiries, meanwhile we will be getting a warrant to search your premises in Chigwell and we will also be checking your telephone records. I take it you have no objection to that?"

"I do, as a matter of fact, though you will find nothing. But I guess I have no choice?"

"Correct."

Chapter 19

The following day, Prince Fahd and Princess Laila arrived at Charles de Gaulle airport and were driven by embassy staff to their hotel, Le Meurice in rue de Rivoli, where they had reserved the royal suite. They were travelling with seven members of their household staff – two maids, three general aides and two bodyguards. Between them they occupied all the rooms on the top floor of the hotel, some of which had been reorganised by hotel staff and were available to be used as offices. Princess Laila had with her the gold ring, which she wore permanently as her wedding ring, and one of the necklaces, the total value of the two items being just under four million dollars. The remaining items from her dowry she had left at home, safely stored away in her private apartments at the King Saud Palace.

Apart from several business matters that needed attention, Prince Fahd wanted to meet the people involved with the jewellery and the investigation of its theft, but there was one important duty he was particularly hoping to fulfil. When, before he left for Paris, he met the family of Saleh Said Al Othaim, he promised he would see to it that the body would be safely returned home, as and when it would be appropriate to do so. He was very anxious that this should be done as soon as possible but, of course, that depended on the authorities in Paris.

Two of the prince's evenings would be taken up with formal dinners at the embassy involving local dignitaries, one of whom would be the French foreign minister. Though Prince Fahd was not himself a government minister, there was no doubt that the time would come when the king would appoint him to high office. For now, though, he was free from those obligations and able to further his own business interests, thus there were several dinners he would be hosting at the hotel. The princess would spend much of her time shopping, accompanied by her maids and one bodyguard, but she would join her husband on the less formal occasions in view of her involvement in the charitable foundations. And from time to time they hoped they might slip away on their own, dressed down in jeans and t-shirts, and do a bit of sightseeing, something that would remind them of their student days.

In London, Roy Partridge and his sergeant were reviewing the results of the search of Hari Kahn's house in Chigwell. They also had a list of his telephone calls and were waiting for news from his bank about recent withdrawals and deposits, but it was unlikely to be his only bank account, since his business interests were international and he was domiciled in two countries. They had still not heard from the cruise company concerning Alan Carmichael's trip around the western Mediterranean.

"The only thing we have," said Roy, "is that the local force found a quantity of US dollars in a hidden compartment of his desk, totalling eighty-three thousand. Nothing else incriminating was found that would link him to these crimes."

"What of his phone records?" asked Sergeant Bennett.

"Nothing unusual," replied Roy. "No calls made to either of his nephews, nor Yacoub. In fact, everything looks quite straightforward."

"Yes, but it wouldn't be unusual for these guys to have more than one mobile. A second pay-as-you-go would be untraceable."

"Yes, of course," agreed Roy. "We'll keep an open mind then. I wonder if we can attribute any of his dollars to the reward money. Have a word with the negotiator, Oliver Bentham and see what he comes up with. Meanwhile check out the entries in his passport and see what his movements have been in the past six weeks or so."

"OK boss," said the sergeant. "Will do."

The chief superintendent then called Lieutenant Le Bret in Paris so as to coordinate their enquiries. Le Bret confirmed that questioning of the three suspects was now underway, but as yet there was no news to report. He had already passed news of the arrests to loss adjuster Moore in London and promised to keep him posted as and when there was any positive news.

Sergeant Bennett put a call through to Oliver Bentham.

"Mr Bentham," he said. "I wonder, can you tell me what denomination of notes comprised the reward money, please? It's just that we have someone in custody, a man called Hari Kahn, who may or may not be involved and we found a quantity of dollars at his house."

"Not him again," said Oliver. "I wondered if he might be involved. Yes, they were all one hundred dollar bills in used notes."

"And does anyone have a record of any of the numbers?"

"No, I'm afraid not," said Oliver. "We were very anxious not to play any tricks on them. Our job was to get the jewellery back and nothing more."

"And do you know where they came from?"

"Yes, the Saudi embassy in London. I don't know where they got them from, though."

"OK thanks."

The sergeant then turned his attention to the passport which showed Hari Kahn's status as a citizen of the United Kingdom, surprisingly. As such there were no records of his movements within the European Union, though there had been two trips to Dubai, one on 6 August for two days, the other from 18 to 21 August. Sergeant Bennett therefore concluded that Kahn was not in Dubai at the time of the robbery, nor at the time of the handover. He could, therefore, have been anywhere in Europe but, like mobiles, it was not impossible for someone to have two passports, especially if they had dual nationality.

Meanwhile the cruise company had called to say that Alan Carmichael did have a booking aboard *Liberty of the Seas* and that he had joined the ship in Barcelona on Friday 7 September. There was, however, something strange, they had added. He had no bar bill to pay on the final day, nor had he used any of the on-board credit that he had paid for in advance. And, of course, there was no facility for him to have paid cash, as was customary on such cruises to prevent staff pilfering. The sergeant then reported these findings to Roy Partridge.

"Right," said Roy. "Let's have him back again. And let's get Watkins in as well, but before that I think we need another word with Kahn. We'll see what he says when we suggest his dollars were part of the reward."

They returned to West End Central and Hari Kahn was again brought into the interview room. They resumed the previous format with the sergeant asking the questions and his boss taking notes.

"Mr Kahn," began Sergeant Bennett. "Your premises have been searched and some US dollars were found in your desk. Can you explain where they came from, please?"

"Yes. I run international businesses and I often trade in dollars. I keep a quantity of them in cash in case I need them."

"I repeat, where did they come from?"

"I really cannot tell you that. Some of them would have been paid to me by customers and some I may have withdrawn myself from my bank in Dubai. I really cannot remember."

"And how long might you have had them?"

"It could be several months for some of them."

"Well, Mr Kahn," continued Sergeant Bennett. "What if I were to tell you that some of them came from the reward money? What would you say to that?"

"I would say you were making it up. It is simply not the case. I am willing to have a sensible conversation with you, but when you make ridiculous assertions like this, all conversation stops. I will say nothing more until my solicitor is here."

"Very well, Mr Kahn," said the sergeant. "Your responses have been noted and this interview is now suspended. We shall continue when your solicitor is here."

Sergeant Bennett and the chief superintendent then withdrew and Hari Kahn was returned to his cell, after making his telephone call.

"We don't really have anything," commented the sergeant.

"No we don't," replied Roy. "But I do think he's hiding something. What he didn't say was 'what reward?' when you mentioned it, which indicates he knew about it. Nor did he seem surprised by the question."

"Yes, but he could have got that information from anywhere. It was even in the papers, remember?"

"I know, Gordon," said Roy. "I still have serious doubts about his story, but I guess we've got to be prepared to release him. I will want a watch kept on him, though."

An hour later Mr Ahmed Zaheer, solicitor from Romford, arrived and asked to see his client, Mr Hari Kahn. Fifteen minutes later he asked to see the two officers that were carrying out enquiries into the jewellery matter.

"Chief Superintendent Partridge," he began. "My client has now been in custody for almost twenty hours and yet you have presented no evidence against him whatsoever. He has cooperated with you fully and given perfectly satisfactory answers to all your questions."

"We'll be the judge of that," said Roy.

"No, I will. There is nothing at all that links my client to these crimes and your suggestion that the cash he holds resulted from some kind of unlawful activity is totally without foundation. I insist you release him immediately."

"Very well, Mr Zaheer," said Roy. "He will be released on police bail pending further enquiries. Bail will be conditional and he will surrender his passport. He will be free to go about his business within the UK, but must notify the local police of any plans he may have to be away from his Chigwell address for more than two nights."

"Not good enough," said Zaheer. "I require my client to be released unconditionally."

"No," said Roy firmly. "I've told you what's going to happen and it will now be explained fully to your client by the custody sergeant. That's all, Mr Zaheer."

The following morning in Paris, Lieutenant Le Bret called at Hôtel Le Meurice to meet formally with Prince Fahd. He was received at reception by an aide and taken directly to the top floor, where the prince was waiting.

"Your Royal Highness, we have three men in custody," explained Le Bret. "One of them is Yacoub, but we are unsure at this moment whether he is a victim or a wrongdoer. We are continuing to question them all and I will keep the embassy fully informed as to our progress."

"There is another option," said the prince. "Yacoub might well have been a victim to start with, but then joined in with them, either by choice or under duress. There are a few skeletons in his cupboard, you know. Would it help if I were to talk to him?"

"I'm sure it would, Sir," replied Le Bret, "but our procedures would not allow that to happen at this stage. Maybe later."

"I understand," said the prince.

"In addition," continued the lieutenant, "my colleagues in London have been questioning a man called Hari Kahn, though I believe he has now been released. Have you heard of him, Sir?"

"No," replied Prince Fahd. "I don't think I have."

"He is a possible suspect, according to Chief Superintendent Partridge, so they have him under surveillance. Lloyd's underwriters are trying to get the reward monies back, so I am required to update the loss adjuster from time to time as to how things are going."

"I see. Now, Lieutenant, there is one important matter I would like to raise with you. It has to do with the family of Saleh Said Al Othaim, whom I have known and respected for some time. I have promised them I would do everything I could to have the body released and returned to Riyadh at the earliest possible moment, so he can be properly laid to rest. Are you in a position to allow me to arrange that?"

"It is probably a little early, Sir," said Le Bret. "Certainly the forensic team has finished with the body, but I would need permission from a presiding judge however, since our enquiries are at a preliminary stage, we don't have one yet."

"Is there anything you can do to help?"

"I think so," said Le Bret. "What I can do is organise an application to the court for the release, but it may take a few days and, of course, it may not be successful. I think it would be better if it was a formal request from the embassy, but I will give it my backing and I will take a close interest in its progress. I know how sensitive these matters can be. "

"Thank you, Lieutenant. That would be very helpful."

In London, Martin Jackson had called a meeting with loss adjuster David Moore. He was anxious to know how things were progressing with regard to recovery of the reward.

"So where's the money then?" he enquired of David, somewhat impatiently. "It's about time I had it back."

"That's easier said than done," replied the loss adjuster. "There are police investigations going on that I'm not a party to and never will be. I have to wait until there's a result."

"Have they found the money yet?"

"As far as I am aware they have not. But a lot of progress has been made. Bentham's little ruse does seem to have worked in that four arrests have been made and suspects are being, or have been, questioned, but there is as yet no sign of the cash. There's a murder involved here as well, you know."

"Yes, I'm well aware of that," said the underwriter. "I met the bloke, remember? My interests are those of this market, of all underwriters who participated on the slip and I don't want this matter dragging on much longer. I need you to introduce some urgency here. You'll expect your fee to be paid on time, won't you?"

"I'll do what I can, Martin, but much of this is out of my hands. And, by the way, you've always kept me waiting for my fee and I don't imagine that will change in a hurry."

"Well, get Oliver and his guys on to it. They have ways of working behind the scenes that nobody else has. If anyone can hurry this up, they can."

"I did think of that, Martin, but they are expensive, you know."

"Yes I know. I pay everyone's bills here, don't I? Let me know when there's some news."

David went back to his office at St Katharine's Dock and passed the instructions on to Oliver Bentham in Hereford.

Alan Carmichael arrived at Bishopsgate Police Station for the second time, having been summoned by the chief superintendent. As instructed, he had with him his mobile and his laptop.

"There's one thing I want to clear up," said Roy Partridge. "It has to do with your cruise. Tell me, what happened to you after you boarded the ship in Barcelona?"

"I went on a cruise. What else do you imagine I did?"

"And how was the cruise?"

"Very nice thank you," said Carmichael. "Why do you ask?"

"According to our information, Mr Carmichael, there is no evidence to support the fact you actually took the cruise. You certainly checked in, but you incurred no on-board charges, nor did you make use of the credit you had pre-purchased. Why is that?"

"Oh, I see. Well, that's because I was feeling a bit fragile, I'm afraid. I think it was a touch of seasickness, or maybe a stomach bug, but I did not feel right the whole time I was on board."

"And did you see any of the medical staff about this?"

"No, I didn't."

"Why was that?"

"Embarrassment, I'm afraid."

"And the friends you were with, they will confirm this will they?"

"I'm sure they will."

"Right, leave their names and contact details with Sergeant Bennett before you go, meanwhile we'd like you to leave your laptop here for a day or two, if that's all right?"

"Well, it's a bit inconvenient, but I suppose it'll be OK. I am expecting contact from Prince Fahd soon about his London visit, but I don't know whether he will telephone or e-mail. Can I pick it up in two days' time?"

"Yes, I'm sure that will be fine," said the chief superintendent. "That's all for now and thank you for coming in again."

"What did you make of that, Gordon?" asked Roy after Carmichael had left.

"Not sure yet," said the sergeant. "What's in your mind, boss?"

"Also not sure. Check with the names he gave us and see if his story stacks up. I don't quite know where this is leading us, but we'll pursue it nevertheless. I always like to know who's telling the truth and who isn't.

"Right, boss. I'll get on to it."

"OK, now we'll get the man Watkins back in. I want to grill him about Kahn, so it'll be the same procedure with mobile and laptop."

They walked over to Mark Lane, to the offices of Nathan Henry and asked at reception to see Nigel Watkins.

"He's in a board meeting, I'm afraid," said the receptionist. "Can you come back later?"

"No we can't," said the sergeant. "We are the police," he added, brandishing his warrant card. "We'd like you to call him out of the meeting if you would."

"I'll try," she said.

A few minutes later Nigel Watkins came into reception.

"What's this about?" he asked, angrily. "I'm in the middle of a board meeting."

"Yes, we know," said Roy Partridge. "There are some further questions we'd like to ask you and we would like to examine your mobile and laptop."

"Well, it's not convenient at the moment," said Nigel, even more angrily. "There are important issues going on today and I simply cannot spare the time. Maybe later in the week."

"I don't think you quite understand," said Roy. "We need to talk to you now and we can do this at the station under caution, if you would prefer."

"No I would not prefer", shouted Nigel. "I'm busy. I said later in the week."

"Then you are under arrest. Read him his rights, Sergeant. Have his laptop and mobile confiscated and brought to the station, while I arrange for a squad car to pick us up."

Within minutes a police car arrived and Nigel was ushered into the back seat. The receptionist who had witnessed this was considerably shaken and taken aback, but nevertheless had the common sense to interrupt the board meeting again, telling the chairman what had just transpired. The chairman then suspended the meeting and returned to his office. He immediately called the company's solicitors, Cameron, Gilbert and Leighton in St Botolph Street and told them what had happened. Senior partner Michael Leighton dropped everything he was doing and immediately went to Bishopsgate. As a corporate lawyer, criminal law was not his strong point, but if it came to it, there were other firms whom he could call on to assist. For the time being, though, he would do his best to ensure Nigel's release from custody at the soonest opportunity.

Meanwhile in Lloyd's, Simon was going about the normal business of the day. He was in a queue to see underwriter Brian Fielding, who was the leader of the Hong Kong stockbrokers' scheme that Nathan Henry ran. There were some updates to notify him of, two new members and a merger. After a few minutes, another broker joined the queue, Darren Black of Baxter, Taylor and Black.

"You lot are in trouble, I hear," he said to Simon, laughing.

"How so?" asked Simon.

"One of your directors has been arrested," he said laughing even louder. "That's not something that happens every day, is it? I wonder what he's been up to."

"How do you know that?" asked Simon.

"It's all over the market. Everyone's talking about it. It won't do much for your fine reputation, will it?"

At that point the underwriter arrived and Simon was in. He explained the changes that were required and the endorsement was scratched. He quickly made his way back to the office and told Mary what he had just heard. She immediately called the chairman to tell him what Simon had picked up in Lloyd's.

"It's true," she said to Simon. "It's Nigel. It only happened this morning and we're surprised how it's all over Lloyd's so quickly. Our chairman is on his way right now to tell the chairman of Lloyd's, meanwhile we need to carry on as normal, as if there's nothing at all to worry about. I'm sure there isn't, by the way. Anything we hear from now on we must keep a note of and we must not respond to any of the jibes that will undoubtedly come our way, both from underwriters and brokers. Any trouble, report it to me."

"Yes Mary," said Simon. "What do you think it's all about?"

"The jewellery, I imagine. Nigel's as straight as they come. He won't have been up to anything."

Chapter 20

In Paris, questioning of the Hussain brothers and Yacoub was well underway. Le Bret had secured an extension of time from the court, ensuring they were in his custody for a total of ninety-six hours. Forensics had identified the samples taken from Al Othaim's body, the fibres being from clothes worn by Ali Hussain, while the blood was Yacoub's. There was no sign of the money or the gun and the BMW was free of any other incriminating evidence. The Hussains were refusing to answer any questions put to them regarding the jewellery heist and the murder, denying all knowledge and suggesting the photographs taken of them were inconclusive due to the blurred nature of them. They were being questioned through interpreters, on the basis that neither of them could speak French, though there was doubt in Le Bret's mind whether this was actually true. When asked about their relationship with Hari Kahn, they did confirm he was their uncle and, from time to time, they did do casual work for his freight forwarding company at the depot in Tilbury. An identity parade had been organised, in case the witness from the airport could confirm they were the people he had seen on the tarmac, but he could not. They were shown CCTV evidence of the ambulance being driven in the area of St Quentin, but again denied it was them, despite certain similarities in their appearance.

Yacoub, though, was telling a different story. He was, he said, an innocent victim, having been abducted into the ambulance along with Al Othaim. He had been drugged and blindfolded, he claimed, so was unable to confirm what happened after they had driven out of the secure area at Charles de Gaulle airport. He had tried to prevent the killing of Al Othaim, but was hit in the face by one of them, which accounted for his blood being on the victim's body. After that he was held for several days in the cellar of a farmhouse which, again, he could not identify, until eventually they made their way through the tunnel to the spot where the handover would take place. He had witnessed the exchange, his blindfold having been removed in order to reveal his identity and he was then driven to an address somewhere in Essex where, again, he was held captive by the brothers. He did not know why they had made a run for it from the B & B in Barking, but that was not where he had been taken initially. On one occasion, a man in a Bentley called at the house and was given a package. Yacoub was, he confirmed, willing to testify in court to these events on the basis that he was entirely innocent and had played no part whatsoever in any unlawful activity. He made a formal statement to that effect. When asked about Hari Kahn, he said he had no knowledge of him, but had heard the name mentioned a few times by the brothers. He thought they were his nephews.

Day three of questioning began with Le Bret's team confronting each of the Hussain brothers separately with the testimony they had taken from Yacoub. Both of them, through interpreters and with lawyers present, refuted everything he had said. He was, they argued, the man in charge. It was Yacoub who had controlled the heist at the airport and it was he who had murdered Al Othaim. They were prepared to admit to theft, but certainly not murder and they, too, gave a statement to that effect. When asked about the telephone calls demanding the ransom, Ali Hussain confirmed he was responsible for that, but had done so at gunpoint, in fear of his life. And when they made the exchange, Yacoub set it up to look as though he was a hostage, whereas he was, in fact, not.

Returning to the robbery itself, Ali and Kareem were asked to describe how they were able to make it into the secure area of the airport. They confirmed they stole the ambulance and with the two substitute travellers on board, neither of whom they had met before, blue-lighted their way into the cargo area and driven at speed across the tarmac to the departure gate. Yacoub had administered an injection to Al Othaim, who was then dragged into the back of the ambulance while the two imposters took passports and boarding cards and quickly joined the waiting group. They were banking on the fact that in the chaos, their identities would not be examined too closely, which is how it turned out. There were, though, similarities in appearance, since they were of the same ethnic origin as Al Othaim and Yacoub. The ambulance was then driven at speed, with blue lights flashing and sirens wailing, back the way they had come and were waved through without any security checks, all under the close control of Yacoub, who gave instructions every step of the way. They were then ordered to drive north towards St Quentin and it was at a lonely spot on the outskirts of a village called Péronne that Yacoub took Al Othaim, who was coming round by then, out of the ambulance and shot him twice in the head. They then drove to a deserted farmhouse not far from St Quentin and, dumping the ambulance *en route,* hid for a few days with the jewellery, though they could not be sure why, they said.

After several days, Ali was given a number to call and told what he had to say by Yacoub. He was to make demands for the return of the jewellery starting with five million dollars, then fall back to two million if that didn't work, and to take instructions regarding handover procedures. When the time came, Yacoub stole the Citroën and they drove through the tunnel to the spot in Kent they were instructed to and the exchange was completed. At all times, they said, Yacoub was in total control of their movements. He had allowed them to point the gun at his head during the handover, but had removed the bullets beforehand.

Enquiries then turned to the identity of the top man, on the basis there had to have been one. Yacoub said he knew nothing of that, since he was not involved, while the Hussains said they were contacted by someone who chose to remain anonymous, but identified himself to them simply as the captain. They took instructions from him over the telephone, so never met him. When asked if they knew how and why he had chosen them, they said it was through someone that knew them, but the name of that person had never been disclosed. They had each been offered one hundred thousand dollars in cash for their part in things, but it had never been paid to them.

The lieutenant and his team then took a break to compare notes. Le Bret was due to make a report to the investigating magistrate, under whose direction the enquiries were being undertaken, but it was still unclear as to who was telling the truth. Certainly the brothers were involved and there was sufficient evidence now to charge them with both the robbery and the murder, but Yacoub's part in this was still a mystery. He was definitely there, since it was his blood on the victim, but the nature of his involvement had yet to be discovered. He was bound to say what he had, as were the Hussains, but Ali's story about the telephone calls having been made under duress did not make sense. The conversations were far too impromptu for that to have happened. And how was it that Yacoub was able to run things, when he had come directly from Riyadh with Al Othaim and had been in his company ever since? His mobile had revealed no unusual calls, certainly none to the Hussains, or any other names in the frame. Neither of their statements could be relied upon, though, until corroborated by further evidence, since they were self-serving.

Le Bret made his way to the courthouse and waited outside the office of Michel Blanc, the investigating magistrate. Once in, he gave a summary of his enquiries to date and showed Monsieur Blanc the written statements.

"What is clear," said the lieutenant, "is that they were all there. However, the Hussains say it was Yacoub who ran things and he, of course, denies any involvement other than that of hostage. Someone was pulling the strings here, but I doubt it was Yacoub. He would have known about the Lloyd's policy, though, something which came out in one of the telephone calls."

"Yes, I see," said the magistrate. "There is more to this than we know at present, however the Hussains have admitted taking part in a robbery which led to a murder and on that basis they should be charged with both crimes. The issue of joint criminal enterprise comes into play here, so it's irrelevant which one of them killed Al Othaim. Yacoub's part in this remains unclear at this stage, so I think further enquiries are necessary. How much longer can we hold him?"

"Twenty-four hours, give or take."

"Right, charge the two but keep them all in custody for the time being. We'll review the position again this time tomorrow."

"Yes, Sir," confirmed Le Bret. "I will see to it immediately."

Later that day Oliver Bentham arrived at the office of loss adjuster Moore in order to set about locating and returning the reward monies. David Moore had, in the meantime, received an update from Lieutenant Le Bret as to the progress of the investigations in Paris. He was particularly interested to note that a man in a Bentley had visited the Hussain brothers at an address in Essex and taken a package away. He immediately passed the information to Roy Partridge, who decided that Kahn should be questioned on the matter, so gave instructions for him to be re-arrested.

"Let's think about the cash for a second," began Oliver. "We know that the serial numbers of the notes were not recorded, but the Hussains would not know that, nor would the mastermind whoever it is. In those circumstances they would think they had limited choices. Either stash it away for a while, or launder it. They certainly wouldn't want to be splashing it around."

"Agreed," said David. "So what would you do with it?"

"Well, I think my first priority would be to get it out of the country. That would reduce the chances of it being identified, especially if it were in one of those banking secrecy jurisdictions."

"Yes," said David, "but they wouldn't just wander across borders or through security checks with a bag full of dollars. There's a real risk of detection there."

"True," said Oliver. "But what if they used some form of professional courier?"

"There are still disclosure procedures to overcome. The contents of packages like that have to be declared."

"Except if the courier company is in on it," said Oliver. "Then they could easily falsify the documentation. Who do we know who runs such an organisation?"

"Hari Kahn," they both said in unison.

"Right," said Oliver. "Let's start with him. We need to get the police to carry out a raid of his premises in Tilbury and see what they can dig up. I'd like to see a list of all destinations where packages were shipped shortly after the day we made the exchange. Then we can take it from there."

"OK," said David. "I'll talk to Partridge and see if he'll agree to it. By the way, what do you make of the Hussain's reference to a mastermind they knew only as the captain and that he only ever dealt with them by telephone?"

"It sounds to me as though it's true," said Oliver. "Don't forget they were in custody at the time facing charges of robbery and murder and in those circumstances I'd be very quick to incriminate anyone else involved, especially if I hadn't been paid my share. I wouldn't want to go down for these crimes on my own."

"Yes," said David. "Unless he was a family member, then I might protect him."

"True, I suppose," said Oliver. "Anyway, my guess is that Kahn is involved in this somehow, but there is still someone out there that set it all up and it's probably not Yacoub."

"You may think that," commented David. "I'm afraid I can only deal in fact. I'll get on to Partridge immediately and we'll reconvene."

"OK," said Oliver.

At Bishopsgate Police Station, Chief Superintendent Partridge and Sergeant Bennett were waiting news that Hari Kahn had been located and arrested. They had also set in motion a search of Kahn's depot in Tilbury, having received the request from loss adjuster David Moore. Meanwhile there were one or two questions still to be put to Nigel Watkins who was waiting in the interview room with his solicitor Michael Leighton.

"Mr Watkins," began the sergeant. "Do you understand why you have been brought here?"

"No, my client does not," interrupted Leighton. "This is a complete outrage and I insist that you release him forthwith. There is no indication whatsoever of his involvement in the crimes that you are investigating and if he is held for much longer there will be serious repercussions."

"Your client," replied Bennett, "has been brought in for questioning because he refused to cooperate when asked to do so and is therefore under caution for obstructing the police in the course of their enquiries."

"My client is a busy man, Sergeant," said Leighton. "You cannot wander into an office and expect an innocent man to drop everything just to answer your questions."

"Yes we can, actually," said the chief superintendent. "This is a murder enquiry, don't forget, but if your client cooperates now, there will be no need to hold him."

"Very well," said Leighton. "Carry on."

"Mr Watkins," continued the sergeant. "How well do you know a man called Hari Kahn?"

"Not very well at all," said Nigel.

"How many times have you met him?"

"Twice."

"And can you describe those meetings, please"

"The first was on a flight to Dubai. I was on my way to see Mike Edwards about the jewellery matter and he was sitting across the aisle from me. He introduced himself."

"What happened?"

"We shared a taxi to the Intercontinental Hotel and exchanged business cards. He said he would like to have a meeting in London some time."

"Anything else?"

"I saw him the next morning at breakfast with another group, one of whom was a Lloyd's broker, a man I now know to be Darren Black."

"Did you check Kahn out at all? We know you brokers like to do that."

"I asked Mike Edwards about him. He said he knew of him and that I was to watch him because he had a reputation for being a bit slippery."

"And the second meeting?"

"He invited me to lunch at the Mayfair Hotel."

"Again, what happened?"

"He only wanted to talk about the jewellery. He said he was keen to get the shipment order for his freight forwarding company and wanted me to tell him what I knew."

"And?"

"I refused on the grounds of client confidentiality and left immediately, before the main course was served, in fact."

"And have you had any contact with him since?"

"No none."

"Well thank you, Mr Watkins," said the chief superintendent. "I think that's all. I'd like you to leave your laptop with me overnight, if you don't mind and I will be checking your mobile phone records."

"No, Chief Superintendent," said Michael Leighton. "My client will not leave his laptop with you. It is needed in the course of his work."

"In which case, Mr Leighton, I will keep Mr Watkins here while we examine the laptop. It could take several hours. Which would you prefer?"

"I'd like to confer with my client," said Leighton. "Very well," he added a few minutes later. "My client has nothing to hide and is willing to leave his laptop. Are we now free to go?"

"Yes," said Roy. "You are released under police bail, requiring you to make yourself available for further questioning should it be necessary. Bail is otherwise unconditional."

Nigel and his solicitor were then shown out by the sergeant who returned to his boss's office.

"Nothing untoward I think," said Bennett.

"As I expected," said Partridge. "I just will not be pushed around by these guys who think their work is more important than ours. I never had any intention of keeping him. Is there any more word on the Carmichael matter?"

"Yes, his travelling companions have been contacted. They saw him on day one, but they also confirmed he was a bit under the weather so they saw very little of him. They're a bit hazy as to how often, but he definitely disembarked with them because they all flew back together from Barcelona."

"OK," said Roy.

The following morning Mary was in her office feeling slightly the worse for wear because of a girls' night out the previous evening. During the course of it she had picked up a piece of office gossip that was disturbing her slightly. Nathan Henry's receptionist, a lady called Claire, had been seen on more than one occasion in the company of someone she shouldn't have been with. Such matters would normally fall below the radar in most companies, but this was different. The man in question was none other than rival broker Darren Black. Was it possible, therefore, that this was how the news of Nigel's arrest had found its way to Lloyd's so quickly? And if so, what other vital information was being handed over and for how long had it been going on? After several minutes of deliberation, Mary decided this was something the chairman needed to know about. She went straight to his office.

"Morning Brian," she said.

"Mary, hello," he replied. "What can I do for you?"

"It's a matter of some delicacy, I'm afraid," she said. "One of our number has been seen in circumstances that might have compromised this company's position in the market."

"OK, tell me all, but I think I'd like Robert in on this."

"Must we?" said Mary.

"I know what you mean," said Brian, "but I think we should nevertheless."

Robert was summoned and he joined them straightaway. Mary then proceeded to outline everything she had learned from the night before. The chairman was astonished to think that one of his long-serving employees might have been responsible for the leak of such harmful information and vowed to find out how she had got herself into that situation. His deputy was more forthright, suggesting she be confronted, asked to explain herself and if the information was correct, be relieved of her duties forthwith without compensation in lieu of notice. The chairman disagreed.

"If it were a senior staff member, then I agree," he said. "Summary dismissal would be entirely appropriate. But she wasn't. It was probably a silly mistake rather than a deliberate act of sabotage."

"Too soft as usual," retorted Robert.

With Mary out of the room, Claire was summoned. She confirmed that she had telephoned her friend Darren and passed on the news of Nigel's arrest, that she was very sorry, but for some time he had been pursuing her in an inappropriate manner. Now she realised he had only been after confidential information about the company and, somewhat tearfully, promised to have nothing to do with him ever again. As expected, the chairman sympathised with her, overruled Robert's call for her dismissal and she was allowed to continue with her duties, albeit with a verbal warning about future conduct. They called Mary back in and told her the outcome.

"Thank you," she said. "Sorry to have got you involved in this but I thought it was important."

"It was," said the chairman. "Thank you for raising it. What about this chap Black?"

"You can leave him to me, Brian"

Mary then left and made her way to Lloyd's. She made a circuit of the ground floor, before taking the escalators to each of the galleries, in the search of the one person uppermost in her mind at that point. Eventually she found him waiting in a queue.

"Mr Black," she said in a quiet voice. "A quick word."

"What is it?" he enquired, moving away from the crowd.

"We know what you've been up to with Claire, our receptionist, and we also know it's you that has been maligning our company. If you continue to do that, my chairman will take formal proceedings against you and your company."

"I don't know what you mean," he protested.

"Yes you do," she continued. "Claire nearly lost her job because of you. She now knows you only really wanted information from her and that your advances were nothing more than deceitful. True, she was flattered for a while but she is a married woman and her husband, whom I know, is not a man to be trifled with. If you ever pull any stunts with her like that again, he and I will take less formal proceedings. We shall see to it that several of your bits are spread across Hackney Marshes before you have a chance to draw your next breath."

"Are you threatening me?" he said, somewhat shocked.

"Yes. Well spotted. And don't think I'm joking. I know people who will do a fine job in that regard. That's all."

Back in the office at lunch time, Mary told her team of the conversation she had just had.

"Here's how we play this," she instructed them. "If any broker raises the matter of Nigel's arrest with you, say you have no more information than they do. If any underwriter raises it, tell them the truth and make sure they know that the matter is now closed without any adverse developments."

Chapter 21

News of Nigel's arrest had found its way to Dubai, much to the surprise of John Marshall, who heard about it from Mike Edwards. John put a call through to Mary in her office.

"It's nothing to worry about," she said. "The police called at the office to ask him about Hari Kahn in connection with the jewellery matter, but he was in the middle of a board meeting and, unfortunately, refused to go with them. They took him to the nick and questioned him under caution, then released him. His so-called arrest was just a technicality, you might say, and that appears to be the end of the matter."

"OK, thanks," said John. "Sadly that's not the story that's going round in the Emirates. It's more sinister than that."

"Yes, I can imagine. It's the same here in Lloyd's. We'll just have to get through it, but I think I've sorted the man who was responsible for hyping up the situation."

"OK," said John. "I'd better go and tell Al Talyani before he finds out from someone else."

"Good idea," she replied.

John and Mike then made their way to the Dubai Financial Centre and waited for the sheikh. Eventually they were shown into his office. John passed on the information he had just received from Mary and promised to keep him fully informed if there were any further developments, though he was expecting the matter to disappear off the agenda before very much longer.

"Thank you for telling me," said Al Talyani. "I had heard a whisper about this, nothing like the truth obviously, but you know how these stories get mangled in the telling."

"Yes, I do," said John. "That's why I came to tell you personally."

"There is one thing that I must raise, though," said the sheikh. "This company will not do business with Hari Kahn. He's on our banned list. If we are to do business with you exclusively, I would like to think that your company takes the same line. Will you be able to confirm that to me?"

"We probably will in due course," said John cautiously, not knowing whether any other part of Nathan Henry was doing business with Kahn. "I will be back in the office on Monday, so I will raise it then, but I imagine it will need the approval of the board. Someone will report back to you after that."

"That's fine," said Al Talyani. "It is important, though."

"I understand," said John. "I will see to it."

Meanwhile in Paris, the questioning of Yacoub was continuing, the two Hussain brothers having been charged with robbery and murder. Yacoub's position remained unchanged and he continued to protest his innocence, standing by the written statement he had made earlier.

"There are one or two things I don't quite understand," said Le Bret. "Firstly, how was it that when you were ushered onto the tarmac following the fire alarm, you were at the back of the crowd?"

"We didn't want to merge with the other passengers in view of our valuable cargo."

"And how was it that when you and Al Othaim were bundled into the ambulance, no one noticed?"

"I don't know, I was drugged, remember?"

"So you say. And why was it that on the day of the handover in Kent, when you abandoned the Citroën for the BMW, you appeared to do so of your own free will?"

"I was under threat all the time. They were armed, remember?"

"And when you hurried away from the address in Barking, you also appeared to do so of your own free will."

"Same again. I was under constant threat."

"And the same is true when you were a passenger in the BMW waiting for the channel tunnel crossing. You didn't appear to be under any threat then, did you?"

"As I have already said, the threat was always there."

"And how was it, do you suppose, that no gun was found in the BMW when you were apprehended?"

"I have no idea. I presume they must have dumped it somewhere on the way."

"I am afraid I do not believe you," said the lieutenant. "I put it to you that you were part of this all along, that you conspired from the outset along with others to rob and then murder and that you have been lying about your involvement ever since. Rather than being a hostage under threat, you were a willing participant pulling the strings."

"Lieutenant Le Bret," interrupted Yacoub's solicitor. "Your assertions are entirely without foundation. My client has made a full written statement as to his part in this affair, that of hostage. He has now been in your custody for over ninety hours and I therefore require that he be either charged or released."

"Very well," said Le Bret. "This interview is at an end."

Yacoub was returned to his cell, the solicitor waited in reception and Le Bret made his way to the magistrate's office for the second time.

"The time has come," he told Monsieur Blanc, "for a decision to be made regarding Yacoub. I don't believe his story at all. I think his written statement is a complete fabrication of events. It just doesn't make sense that he was a hostage throughout. The only way he and Al Othaim could have been separated from the crowd on the tarmac would have been with his connivance and I find it extremely odd that Al Othaim is murdered but Yacoub isn't. I just don't think he can be released."

"Very well, Lieutenant," said the magistrate. "We'll charge him as well. If his lawyers are able to mount a successful defence then so be it but I agree, in view of the Hussain brothers' statements, we have no choice but to treat Yacoub as complicit. What's his family name, by the way?"

"Iqbal."

"Right, see to it would you."

"Yes Sir," replied Le Bret. "I will, if you agree, let the Saudi embassy know so they can pass the news to the prince.

And I will also need to inform the loss adjuster acting for Lloyd's."

"Of course," said the magistrate. "I have no problem with that."

By noon the following day, there was still no news concerning the arrest of Hari Kahn and Roy Partridge was beginning to get a little anxious. He called his colleague in Chigwell.

"I'm afraid there's no sign of him yet," said the officer. "His Bentley is still on the drive, having been there now for several days. The housekeeper comes and goes, but he is not there."

"Then he's in breach of his bail conditions," said Roy.

"Yes, absolutely."

"OK," said Roy. "I'll alert all forces nationwide that he's a wanted man, meanwhile keep me posted."

"I will," said the officer.

Later that day the police at Tilbury descended on Hari Kahn's freight forwarding depot with a warrant to search the premises. They removed order books, copy invoices, computer terminals, logged all packages ready for dispatch and checked employees' identities. There was no sign of Hari Kahn, nor did anyone know of his whereabouts. He had not been seen for several days but, said the foreman, it was not particularly unusual. The premises were secured for the night and the employees sent home. The officer in charge then called Roy Partridge to let him know they had completed their task. They were asked to hold all items that had been confiscated ready for inspection by security experts. Oliver Bentham and two colleagues, he advised, would be with them the very next day.

And so they were. They had driven down from Hereford and arrived in Tilbury just before 8.30 a.m., immediately setting about their task. They had been assigned a secure room in the basement where all Kahn's items were being held. Meticulously they listed every shipment record, both incoming and outgoing since mid-August, including destinations, addresses, customer names, weight, size, description and value. They noted that many shipments were repeat orders for regular customers and in such circumstances the destinations did not vary that much. The nature of the business was truly international, including a considerable amount of traffic into Northern and Eastern Europe, as well as the Middle and Far East, but there were no shipments at all to North and South America or Canada. There were significant numbers of incoming shipments, with deliveries made to customers all over the UK, including Northern Ireland. Oliver and his team chose not to break for lunch but carried on relentlessly throughout the afternoon. Eventually their efforts seemed to have been rewarded.

"Here's something," said Kevin Chamberlain. "On Tuesday, 4 September, four items were dispatched from the Tilbury depot, each about the size of a five hundred sheet packet of copy paper, to an address in Monte Carlo. They are listed as being documents, but no customer has been allocated to the transaction nor has any invoice been raised. Computer instructions state that the packages were to be held for collection, but it doesn't say by whom. I imagine the address is that of a courier company or a post office, but we need to check it out."

"OK Kevin," said Oliver. "It looks like we have a lead. I think we'd better carry on, though, just in case there's something else."

They continued until early evening before taking a break for dinner at a nearby hotel where they had booked in for an overnight stay. The following morning they returned to the station and finished the job, no other items of interest coming to the fore. They confirmed to the station sergeant that their task was done and that they would be reporting directly to Roy Partridge at Bishopsgate. On their way back to Hereford they were trying to make sense of what they had discovered the previous afternoon.

"So Kevin," said Oliver. "It looks as though it might have been the reward money, doesn't it?"

"Yes, it certainly does. The size and weight would be about right, the date fits, the destination is not a regular one and the fact that there's no customer involved is a really serious clue."

"Why Monte Carlo?" said Oliver, "and why bother to log it into the computer?"

"Casinos," said Andrew Weaver. "They were laundering. Whoever picked up the cash went into a casino, bought chips, played a bit then cashed the chips back into euros. Probably he, or she, or both went several times on different days to different casinos and repeated the process. The dollars have gone and now we're looking for euros. And it was logged into their computer for tracking purposes, I would guess."

"That's good thinking, Andrew," said Oliver, "if it proves to be true. What do you make of it, Kevin?"

"It sounds pretty feasible to me. It's a good way of getting rid of the dollars quickly. We appear to have identified the man with a courier company who got the dollars out of the country easily, now all we need is the chap at the other end who picked them up."

"Easy then," said Oliver, laughing.

"Oh yes," said Andrew. "Piece of cake."

"Right," said Kevin. "Where do we go from here?"

"First we report to David Moore," said Oliver, "so he can tell the underwriter and the police. All casinos have CCTV these days as well as identity checks, so one of us needs to get to Monte Carlo quickly and see if we can get access to that information. Do we know anyone in Monaco?"

"No," said Kevin, "but I do have an old contact in Nice."

"OK," said Oliver. "You'd better get out there soonest. I'll get Moore to tell Le Bret as well, in case he can help."

"Right," said Kevin. "I'll be in touch when I have some news."

At midday the following Monday, Prince Fahd and Princess Laila, along with their entourage, checked into the Ritz Hotel in London, having arrived from Paris earlier that morning. Once again they had the royal suite, together with all the rooms on the top floor. They were due to be joined later that day by secretary Alan Carmichael, whose summer vacation was over and whose attentions would now be focused on his employer's business interests. He arrived at 4.00 p.m., checked into one of the pre-booked rooms and, with his laptop now retrieved from the police in Bishopsgate, made his way to the prince's suite.

"Alan," said the prince warmly. "How are you?"

"I'm very well, Sir, thank you," said Carmichael. "And you?"

"Fine, thank you. How was your holiday?"

"It was very restful, thank you, though I wasn't too well during the cruise."

"Oh, I am sorry to hear that. We had a successful time in Paris, for the most part. Unfortunately I wasn't able to secure the release of Al Othaim's body for repatriation yet, as it is still in police custody at one of the mortuaries. I've left the matter in the hands of the ambassador, though. Nor was I able to see Yacoub, due to police restrictions, but I'll let that pass, since he's now been charged. Otherwise all went well."

"Very good, Sir," said the secretary. "How is your schedule looking?"

"I have the usual rounds of meetings and dinners at the embassy, then I want to see my lawyers and the banks that are involved in my charitable foundations. In particular, though, I want to see the Lloyd's underwriter who was responsible for the recovery of the jewellery. It's a man called Martin Jackson, isn't it?"

"Yes it is, Sir. I've made some progress in that regard. I spoke with the loss adjuster who put me in touch with Nathan Henry, the brokers who placed the business originally. We're obliged to go through them. I then spoke to Nigel Watkins, the director in charge of our case, who has arranged for us to meet at Lloyd's tomorrow morning, if that's convenient."

"Yes it is, Alan," confirmed the prince. "What is the plan?"

"An embassy car will collect us and take us directly to Lloyd's, where we will be met by underwriter Jackson and the broker Watkins and given the grand tour, followed by lunch in the Captains' Room. The catering personnel have been made aware of your dietary requirements. We shall be joined by the loss adjuster David Moore, whom you've met, as well as Oliver Bentham, who was the man who organised and carried out the recovery of the jewellery. He is an ex-military security expert who specialises a lot in kidnap negotiation."

"Will the princess be joining us?" asked Prince Fahd.

"Oh yes, Sir," confirmed Carmichael. "I think they would like it if she were with you. After all, it's her jewellery that this is all about."

"Good. And will you be with us, Alan?"

"Yes I will, Sir, but I think the bodyguards had better stay in the car."

"Yes, I agree. What form of dress might be appropriate, do you think?"

Well, Sir, it's deliberately being kept low key. It's not an official visit as such, so my suggestion would be for western dress. There won't be any formalities, just the tour and the lunch. We should be away by 2.15 p.m."

"Excellent," said the prince. "I shall look forward to it."

Meanwhile, in the offices of Nathan Henry, Mary and her team were planning their schedules for the day. John Marshall was back from Dubai and was in the process of compiling his report for Nigel and the board.

"Now, I know it's only October," Mary announced, "but I have a memo here about the office Christmas party."

"Oh no," groaned Craig.

"It will be on the second Friday in December at the Café Royale. Wives, girlfriends, boyfriends are invited, but only one per employee and this year tickets are a fiver each."

"Why is that?" asked Jamie. "It was free last year."

"Well, as you know, the chairman pays for this bash himself out of his own personal funds. It's his way of saying thank you. What used to happen when it was free is that some people would put their names down but not turn up. So the idea is that if you buy a ticket, albeit at only a token cost, that won't happen. Simon, do you have a partner?"

"Yes I do," he said. "I've a girlfriend called Emma and I'm sure she'd love to come with me."

"That's the spirit," roared Mary. "Right everyone, names down and fivers in then."

"Yes, OK," they said in unison.

"And don't forget, the Employee of the Year award. It's a week's family holiday somewhere exotic. Main board directors are not included, you'll be pleased to know."

"Whoopee," said Jamie, sarcastically. "Will your better half be coming, Mary?"

"I am the better half."

"Yes of course. Silly me."

"Now, there's something else," continued Mary. "The prince and his lady are in town this week and they're paying a visit to Lloyd's tomorrow. I don't suppose they'll come here, but you never know, so best behaviour and all that stuff. And if you happen to see them wandering around the market, ignore them, even though Nigel and Martin Jackson will be with them."

"Is that wise?" asked Jamie.

"What do you mean?" said Mary, sharply.

"Well, in view of recent events I would have thought he was the last person to be showing guests round Lloyd's."

"Ah, I see," said Mary. "Yes, we did think about that and the chairman did ask me for my opinion. I thought it was absolutely the right thing to do because it demonstrates there is nothing for us to worry about and that it's business as usual. It's a good time for Nigel to show his face round the market. The chairman agreed with me and that's why it's happening."

"Fair enough," said Jamie.

That evening at home, Simon called Emma and told her about the Christmas party. She did not hesitate and accepted the invitation straightaway.

"I don't quite know what the format is, but I expect it will be a late finish," said Simon. "I'll make sure we have suitable transport home, so we're not rushing for the last train."

They agreed they would spend some time together at the weekend, probably at the golf club, then perhaps dinner in their favourite Italian restaurant in The Lanes. Then Emma said something that intrigued him.

"My dad says he has something he'd like to talk to you about. Some information you might find useful in connection with your work."

"Any idea what?" he enquired.

"No, he hasn't told me, but perhaps we could plan to be here sometime during Sunday?"

"Yes, of course. I'd be happy to come."

Chapter 22

The following morning, Kevin Chamberlain took a flight from Birmingham to Nice, where he checked into the Dante Hotel, a two-star establishment about a mile from the centre of town. He put a call through to his old colleague from the military, Archie Prendergast, whom he had known for many years. They agreed to meet for lunch. Kevin outlined in detail the purpose of his visit and hoped that Archie would be able to lend a hand, in return for a fee, of course. Their principal objective was, he explained, to uncover evidence that might lead to the recovery of the reward monies and the eventual apprehension of the guilty party. The first port of call would be the address in Monte Carlo where the four packages had been sent. Archie advised that they make themselves known to the local police, letting them know they were pursuing enquiries on behalf of Lloyd's underwriters who were following up on a theft of property. With Kevin in full agreement, they then drove across the border into Monaco.

They went straight to the address they had and discovered it was the parcels office of the local post office, where they asked to see the person in charge. They announced themselves as investigators acting for Lloyd's of London who were seeking information concerning certain packages that had arrived from Tilbury for collection. The manager was at first rather reluctant to reveal anything at all on the grounds of confidentiality, but when it was explained to him that criminal indictments were likely to be involved, including one for murder, he quickly acquiesced. Yes, he confirmed, four packages that were all part of the same shipment were collected on Monday, 10 September by a person unknown, but who was able to produce the proper written authorisation in the form of a copy of the original consignment docket with the correct code numbers. He asked them to wait for a few moments while he found the clerk who had overseen the transaction. Shortly afterwards they were joined by a middle-aged lady who was able to confirm that a well-dressed Englishman in his late fifties had collected the parcels and taken them away by taxi. When asked to describe him, she remembered him as being tall, grey-haired and well-spoken, perhaps with a military air about him. He wore a dark grey business suit, with blue shirt, striped tie and black shoes and took the packages away in a large hold-all. The taxi was from a local cab company, she also remembered.

The manager confirmed it was slightly unusual for packages to arrive for anonymous collection, but it did sometimes happen and that it was not in their remit in such circumstances to ask any questions. Kevin and Archie thanked them both for their assistance and drove straight to the police station, where they asked to see one of the senior officers. After a wait of some twenty minutes or so, they were shown into the office of Capitaine Pierrefonds, to whom they explained the exact reason for their presence in the Principality.

"Thank you for letting me know," said the capitaine. "I am grateful that you have come to see me. I'm not sure what I can do to help you at this stage, since I have no evidence that a crime has been committed within my jurisdiction. Lloyd's of London, you say?"

"Yes, Capitaine," said Kevin. "There are serious crimes involved here, theft and murder, that are under investigation by Lieutenant Le Bret of the Paris police. Lloyd's assigned us the job of recovering the jewellery, which we did, and now we are being asked to track down the reward monies, or ransom if you prefer. We believe the sum of one million dollars arrived here and was laundered through one or more of the casinos. Please feel free to call Lieutenant Le Bret, if it will help."

"Yes, gentlemen, I think I will do that. Why don't you wait in an interview room and I'll have some coffee sent in to you."

After another wait of some twenty minutes or so, they were summoned back into the office of Capitaine Pierrefonds.

"I had a long conversation with Lieutenant Le Bret," confirmed the capitaine, "and he has given me a lot of detail as to his progress in this matter. He also vouched for you, Mr Chamberlain, and spoke highly of your professional expertise in matters of security. I think after all there might be something I can do to help."

"Thank you," said Kevin. "That would be extremely useful."

"As you may know," continued the capitaine, "Monaco is one of the most secure territories of all. We have one police officer per hundred population, the whole of the Principality is monitored by twenty-four hour video CCTV and we take all crime very seriously. Like you we have a royal family to protect. All major buildings are under constant surveillance, including hotels and gambling establishments. We have no homeless, no underclass and we have the ability to secure our borders within minutes. Where this is leading me, gentlemen, is to money laundering. Again, it is something we take very seriously in view of the number of casinos we have, so security in that regard is extremely tight. Players are required to produce identity cards and records are kept of everyone who comes in."

"Capitaine," asked Archie. "British people don't carry identity cards as such, so how would that work?"

"They would need two forms of identity, typically passport and driving licence."

"I see," said Archie. "Thank you. Now with all that in mind, how do you suggest we go about tracking down our miscreant?"

"Well now," said the capitaine. "That's the tricky part. If, of course, we knew what he looked like, or what his name was, then we could examine all the CCTV, even though there's a lot of it. But we don't. What I can do, though, is ask the officers who were on casino duty at the time. So we're looking for a tall, well-dressed Englishman who, during the week of the 10 September, frequented a number of casinos, who bought chips with US dollars, played a bit but not much, then cashed his chips back into euros. Is that it?"

"Yes Capitaine," said Kevin. "That's certainly where we'd like to start."

"Right," said the capitaine. "Give me twenty-four hours and come and see me this time tomorrow. Where are you staying?"

"Oh, we're driving back to Nice," said Archie. "But we'll be back tomorrow."

On the way back they decided to call at a couple of the casinos, just out of interest to check out the level of security for themselves, though they imagined it would be just as Pierrefonds had described it. At the first they were confronted by two doormen who immediately asked for their identity documents, which they obligingly produced.

"We wonder if it would be possible to see the manager," asked Archie in fluent French.

"What about?" enquired one of the doormen.

"It's a private matter."

"Wait here."

Several minutes later the doorman returned and showed them into the manager's office. Having decided to conduct the conversation in French, Archie explained why they were there and who they were working for, taking care to stress the serious nature of the crimes involved and the importance of what they were doing for Lloyd's.

"I'm afraid I'll have to stop you there," said the manager. "I am not willing to divulge any information to you whatsoever. These matters are governed by our rules of confidentiality. I would be prepared to talk to the police but not you, so I think it best that you leave now."

They fared little better at the second establishment, the confidentiality issues seeming to be universal. They tried a third. This time the doorman introduced them to the head croupier, in the temporary unavailability of the manager.

"I do remember someone like that," he said, "but I'm afraid I cannot let you have any specific information. These matters are subject to the rules of confidentiality, you know."

"Yes, we know," said Archie. "However, our enquiries are of a formal nature on behalf of Lloyd's of London and as such there could be a reward involved. Perhaps when you've had a chance to review things you might give us a call?"

"Yes, perhaps I will call you later. Where will you be?"

"We're staying in Nice," said Archie, "but we will be back here tomorrow. Here are our mobile numbers. What's your name, by the way?"

"It's Massimo, and I will try to call you tomorrow afternoon. I'm working the late shift tonight, so I don't finish until 4.00 a.m."

Meanwhile the royal visit to Lloyd's had gone well. The prince, princess and secretary had arrived by embassy limo at the main entrance of Lloyd's in Lime Street just before noon and were met, as planned, by the underwriter and the broker. They were ushered past the red-robed waiters, who had been pre-warned of their arrival and shown around all floors of the underwriting room before making their way towards what was known as the Nelson Room, a series of large display cabinets containing priceless works of gold and silver.

"What we have here," explained underwriter Jackson, "are trophies presented by Lloyd's to sea captains over the centuries for successfully defending British shipping against foreign attack. Many of them are engraved with the captain's name and the action in which his ship fought. Nelson himself did much of that on our behalf and over the years these items have found their way back to us."

"What's this?" asked the prince, pointing to a strange-looking fork, nestling amidst an array of cups, bowls, decanters and tureens.

"That's a piece of Nelson's own cutlery," explained Martin. "It's a knork."

"A knork?

"Yes," said Martin. "If you remember, Nelson could only use one hand, so he commissioned a solid gold fork with a sharp edge to double up as a knife, which he would use to cut first then stab, much like the Americans do today."

"Wonderful," said the princess.

"And here's the original log from Nelson's flagship with the famous England expects message sent just prior to the Battle of Trafalgar."

"Fascinating," said the prince. "There's so much history here."

Yes," said Martin. "Right, time for lunch I think."

They moved into the Captains' Room and were greeted by the maître d', who showed them immediately to their table. David Moore and Oliver Bentham were already there and introductions were made. The royals declined the wine, as was their custom, but had no concerns if others in the group wished to partake. They had, after all, been students here, they said.

"Now, Mr Jackson," said the prince. "On behalf of Princess Laila and myself, I would like to thank you and your colleagues for all that you have done here. You see that some of the jewellery is here today, items which I never imagined we would ever see again. We really do commend you for your ingenuity and resourcefulness. I didn't know that Lloyd's had so many support services at its disposal."

"Yes," said Martin. "As underwriters we share in the fortunes of the syndicate we underwrite for. It's a bit like owning shares in the company you work for, so we are inclined to take it a bit personally. When there's a loss, we see if it can be put right, rather than just pay the claim and, yes, we are well-placed enough to have access to many unusual services. Oliver is one of them."

"Yes," said the prince. "I understand you are a specialist kidnap negotiator."

"That's right, Sir," confirmed Oliver. "I did a lot of covert stuff in the military when I was younger, so when my commission came to an end, I offered my services to the private sector. Lloyd's was the obvious choice."

"Well your skills are exceptional," said the prince, "so thank you too for what you did. But we mustn't forget, though, that a life was lost here. I wonder how the police are progressing with their enquiries on that front."

"As I understand it," said David Moore, "three people have been charged in Paris while enquiries continue, but there is still the feeling that someone else, as yet unknown, is behind all this."

"So I understand," said the prince. "What do you think, Alan?"

"It seems likely," said secretary Carmichael, "that there is, but I'm struggling to think who it could be. I was shocked, though, to learn that Yacoub was somehow involved, as I always found him to be completely trustworthy. Perhaps he will be exonerated in the fullness of time."

"Perhaps he will," said the prince.

"It seems to me," said Oliver, "that Lloyd's was targeted here, that the thieves never had any intention of keeping the goods, but what they were after was an opportunity to demand a ransom, or reward as we prefer to call it. So whoever it was, knew about the insurance. They could never have shifted the items without them being recognised, in view of their historical importance."

"Good point," said Martin.

"And I understand you're trying to get the reward money back," said the prince.

"Yes," said Oliver.

"How is that going?" asked the secretary.

"Slowly," replied Oliver, not letting on about his colleague's activities in Monaco. "But we do have one or two leads we are following. It won't be easy, but we have done this kind of work before."

"Well," said the prince. "I make this promise to you, Mr Jackson. If you are unsuccessful in your efforts to recover the reward, I will return the dollars to you myself, since you did that just as much for our benefit as your own. It's the least I can do. Your work here has been outstanding and the princess and I are so grateful. We are forever in your debt."

"Your Royal Highness," said Martin, formally. "Thank you for your very kind offer, which I will keep in mind. I'm hoping it will not be necessary and we shall, of course, not let up on our efforts. Let's hope it all ends up with a satisfactory conclusion. Thank you very much for coming here today and we wish you well for the future. If there's ever anything we can ever help you with again, be sure to let the brokers know."

"I will," replied the prince. "We thank you most warmly for your hospitality today and again for your fine work. And if you're ever planning to be in Riyadh, be sure to let me know."

With the meeting over, they made their way out of the building into Lime Street and the limo took them back to the embassy.

That evening during dinner at the Dante Hotel in Nice, Archie took a call on his mobile from Massimo.

"I believe I can help you here," he said. "I think I have discovered information that might help you in your enquiries. But first of all, I'd like to know more about the reward. How much is on offer, do you think?"

"That depends on the information," said Archie, cagily. "What is it you can tell us, Massimo?"

"I'd prefer to talk to you face to face, if you don't mind. I'm on a coffee break at the moment, so I don't have much time. Can we meet up tomorrow?"

"Yes, where?"

"There's a café in rue Compte-Félix-Gastaldi called the Crêperie du Rocher. Meet me there at 11.30 a.m."

"OK, we will be there," confirmed Archie.

The following morning Kevin and Archie drove back to Monte Carlo from Nice and made their way directly to the café. Massimo was already there.

"Let me explain," he said. "I think I can help you, but I want your assurances that my identity will be kept entirely secret. There are very strict rules in the casinos about customer confidentiality which I will be in breach of, however you should know that this is my last week here, before I start a new job on a cruise ship. My employers have given me a good reference and I do not want to jeopardise that."

"Then why do it?" asked Archie.

"I'm broke. I need cash, so the reward money you are offering will help me. This is why I want to know how much it is."

"As we have said, it will depend on the information you give us."

"Give me a rough idea."

"It could perhaps be in the region of five hundred euros."

"Oh, that's not going to be enough. Not for what I can give you."

"Tell us, then," said Archie.

"Before I do that," said Massimo, "let me say that I have spoken to several croupiers I know in other casinos and I believe I have built up a very comprehensive picture of the guy I think you are looking for, including his description and, more importantly, his name. He made several visits on his own to all the casinos here, each time bringing a bundle of dollars and exchanging them for chips. He would then play for a while, sometimes winning sometimes losing, before changing the chips back into euros."

"Didn't anyone find that a bit suspicious?" asked Archie.

"Well yes," said Massimo, "but as long as he provided satisfactory proof of identity, which he appears to have done, then we don't mind what form his money takes."

"And his name?"

"Ah, for that I will need more than five hundred. A lot more."

"How much do you have in mind?"

"Ten times that amount. Five thousand."

"No way. We might go to a thousand, but five is far too much. We can always find someone else, you know, just like we found you."

"Two thousand or I walk now."

"OK, we'll make it fifteen hundred," said Archie, "provided we like what you tell us."

"Right," said Massimo. "He was English, probably in his mid-to-late fifties, tall, grey-haired with moustache and glasses and he was always well-dressed, typically in a grey business suit. He produced a British passport and driving licence for identification purposes."

"His name," said Archie, impatiently.

"Fifteen hundred, wasn't it?" said Massimo.

"Yes, yes."

"John Goddard. Now what about my money?"

"You'll get it," said Archie, "but I'm afraid this is not a name we know. We need time to check it out. Is there any chance of getting a copy or at least a sight of the CCTV? If there were, we might add another thousand."

"None whatsoever," said Massimo. "We're under more surveillance than the clients. We're frisked on the way in and on the way out and our uniforms have no pockets at all. They're worried about chips being pilfered."

"OK," said Archie. "Meet us back here in a couple of hours."

Massimo reluctantly agreed, hoping he would have enough time during one of his breaks. After he had left, Kevin put a call through to Oliver in Hereford.

"We have a name," he said, "but it's not one we've come across before. It's John Goddard."

"Leave it with me," said Oliver. "I'll make a few calls and let you know."

Oliver then telephoned Martin Jackson and David Moore, neither of whom had heard the name mentioned. He then contacted Roy Partridge who, after checking with the sergeant, confirmed that a Mrs Barbara Goddard of Godalming, Surrey, did come up in their enquiries as being the owner of the car driven by Alan Carmichael, her brother. It was a long shot, indicated the chief superintendent, but it could be that John Goddard was Barbara's husband and was, therefore, Alan Carmichael's brother-in-law. The question was, though, did he fit the description.

Roy Partridge decided it should be checked out, so arranged for the local police to visit the house and ask about his whereabouts during the week in question, beginning 10 September. Two hours later he received news that John Goddard was indeed Barbara's husband, that he was a tall, grey-haired man with moustache and glasses but, more importantly, he had been in hospital for seven days from Wednesday, 5 September having a minor heart irregularity checked out. It wasn't him then, thought the chief superintendent, who immediately called Oliver Bentham and relayed the news. Oliver then called Kevin in Monte Carlo and passed on the result of the police enquiries. He and Archie went back to the café and waited for Massimo, who eventually arrived but was in a hurry.

"Are you completely sure about the name?" asked Archie.

"Yes absolutely sure," confirmed Massimo. "All my friends confirmed it. Now I do need the money today, as I'm leaving on Friday and you won't be able to contact me after that."

"OK," said Archie, handing over an envelope. "We'll leave it there."

He and Kevin then drove to the police station for their meeting with the Capitaine Pierrefonds. Again they were kept waiting for twenty or so minutes before being shown into his office.

"Gentlemen," he said. "I have made a few enquiries, but I'm afraid there is nothing I can do that will help you. It has come to my attention that you have been going it alone, behind my back in other words and I do not think that was at all appropriate. What do you have to say about that?"

"Yes we did do that," responded Archie. "We are experienced investigators and we are acting in an official capacity for one of the world's most prestigious insurers, Lloyd's of London, to whom we are obliged to report our findings in the fullest possible detail. We are sorry if that has interfered with your own investigations, but it is our job to explore all avenues, official or otherwise."

"Well, I would have preferred it if you had waited until after I had made my own enquiries, when I might have been more help to you. As it is I cannot be. Any further requests will have to come from the Paris police, when I shall give the matter my due consideration. I now bid you good day."

"It's a pity about the CCTV," said Kevin during the drive back to Nice. "That would probably have clinched it for us."

"Yes, I agree," said Archie. "But the police would have access to it, I'm sure. Not if the request were to come from us, though."

"No," said Kevin, "but they would do it for their Paris colleagues. That's what I'll recommend when I get back. Meanwhile, I wonder if you could do a bit more snooping and see if the name John Goddard has been recorded anywhere else in the vicinity, hotels, car hire companies and the like. Meanwhile, we'll suggest to Le Bret that he looks at the CCTV of the casinos. The sooner we get a fix on this chap, the more likely we are to get the reward money back, or at least some of it."

"OK," said Archie, as he dropped Kevin off at the airport. "I will be in touch."

Chapter 23

By the first Saturday in October, Brighton was relatively calm compared with the height of summer. Holidaymakers and day-trippers were no longer piling onto the seafront and The Seagulls were away at Derby County, so things were quiet. Simon and Emma were thus able to enjoy a leisurely afternoon on the pier before finding their way to Donatello's in The Lanes for their now customary Italian meal. Afterwards they took a stroll along the promenade before taking a bus back to Woodland Drive. Emma's parents were at home and they were both pleased to see Simon.

"How are things going?" enquired George Claremont.

"Oh rather well, thank you," said Simon. "Things are quite hectic at times, but I'm beginning to get the hang of how to cope with it all."

"And how's that business with the jewellery? Any more news?"

"I think there are three guys under arrest in Paris and the prince and princess are in London at present, along with several of their staff. They made a visit to Lloyd's earlier in the week."

"That's what I want to talk to you about," said George. "You will remember that I had an interest in that chap by the name of Carmichael?"

"Yes, I do."

"Well, he is someone I've heard of. He's the Alan Carmichael that was in Jeddah for a while, before moving to Riyadh as commercial attaché. And he has a bit of a history. He did not retire from diplomatic service, as he likes to tell everyone, but he was asked to resign. That's the equivalent in our circles of getting fired. I did a bit of discreet checking and it seems there was a bit of a scandal. He had been in financial trouble for some time following a messy divorce and used to spend most of his free time living the high life in Bahrain. He

221

would drive across the causeway at weekends and get up to all the things that were not available to him in Riyadh."

"I see," said Simon, wondering where this was going.

"Now here's the interesting part," continued George. "He was found to have been taking bribes from businessmen who were looking for trading partners in the Kingdom. It had been going on for a while and it's very much against all diplomatic protocol."

"Isn't that how business is done there?" said Simon, recalling some of the news items he had seen in recent years.

"In a way, yes," said George. "But it's slightly more formal than that. For businesses to trade there, they must have a local sponsor, who takes a share of the income. It's a sort of licensing procedure, but the money goes to the individual rather than the authorities. The sponsor is usually a well-connected Saudi national, often a sheikh or a prince, whose role it is to promote that business, to ensure that local customs and practices are adhered to at all times and to see that there is no profiteering."

"So what was Carmichael up to then?"

"It appears that from time to time he was receiving brown envelopes for the advice and help he was giving to businesses, entirely against our rules of conduct, of course, but he was in cahoots with some pretty slimy characters who were determined to get a foothold in the Kingdom. He got caught when, having taken a bribe to put a foreign business in touch with a potential sponsor, the deal went sour, but he refused to hand the cash back. The businessman tipped off the embassy and he was quietly dispensed with."

"I see," said Simon. "That's pretty damaging stuff then. Do we know who the businessman was?"

"Yes, we do," said George. "It was a Pakistani by the name of Hari Kahn."

Back in Hereford, Kevin was giving Oliver and Andrew full details of his findings in Monaco, adding that Archie was continuing to look for further evidence left behind by the man they knew as John Goddard. It was a mystery, they all agreed, as to how he could have been in two places at once, if indeed it was the same person.

"We need to get hold of the CCTV footage from Monte Carlo," said Kevin. "I'm afraid we blew it with the local police, but perhaps Le Bret can ask them to make an official request."

"Couldn't you have hacked into their computer?" asked Andrew.

"Yes, but I would have been spotted. The whole area is under video camera surveillance at all times, so I didn't want to risk it."

At that point Kevin's mobile rang. It was Archie from Nice.

"I think I have something," he said. "The local Hertz here in Nice rented a Peugeot 208 to a John Goddard on Sunday, 9 September and it was returned the following Wednesday late in the afternoon. It took a while, but I managed to persuade the girl to give me a copy of the driving licence that was produced. It's a bit blurred, I'm afraid, but I'm e-mailing it over to you now."

"Good man," said Kevin. "What address does it show?"

"Portsmouth Road, Godalming."

"That'll do. Thanks Archie."

Within a few minutes the e-mail arrived. Kevin was able to enlarge the copy of the driving licence which displayed an image similar to the descriptions he had been given in Monaco.

"I think we'd better tell Partridge," said Oliver. "Then we'll talk to Le Bret."

The chief superintendent was able to confirm that the address was that of John Goddard, brother-in-law of Alan Carmichael. He was somewhat surprised to learn that his driving licence had been used in Nice, since Goddard was in hospital at the time and his whereabouts had, in fact, been checked out by the local constabulary. He was admitted to The Royal Surrey County Hospital in Guildford on Wednesday, 5 September, before being released the following Wednesday, the 12th. It was also confirmed that when the police called and he was asked to check, Goddard confirmed his passport and driving licence were in their usual place in his writing desk. And Carmichael was on a cruise ship in the Mediterranean, Partridge reminded them.

"So if it wasn't Goddard," said Kevin, "who was it that borrowed his driving licence and passport without him knowing, that looked vaguely like him, hired a car in Nice, played the tables in Monte Carlo, then returned and put the documents back where they came from?"

"I think we should take a close look at the man Carmichael," said Oliver. "He was there in the house, after all. Let's see if what he told Partridge really checks out, meanwhile I'll get Le Bret onto the matter of the CCTV."

Andrew Weaver went on-line and looked at the itinerary for the Royal Caribbean Mediterranean cruise that Carmichael said he joined on Friday, 7 September. It left from Barcelona that same day, before arriving at Nice two days later early on Sunday morning. It then left for Italy, before returning to Nice on the Wednesday the 12th on its way back to Barcelona.

"Oliver," said Andrew. "I think I have something. The itinerary of the cruise seems to tie in very neatly with the hiring of the Peugeot and its return three days later. It looks to me as though Carmichael could have boarded the cruise, got off at Nice, made his way to Monte Carlo and back to Nice in time to pick the ship up again. It would also explain why he wasn't seen much and suggest his story about being unwell is a bit of a cover up."

"It certainly does," said Oliver. "But why him? He has the perfect life, a tax-free income, accommodation and transport that comes with the job and very little stress as a result. And the penalties for committing such a crime out there are pretty severe, aren't they?"

"Yes," said Kevin, "except he wouldn't have committed the crime in that jurisdiction, would he?"

"Fair point," said Oliver. "The prince would be pretty miffed with him, though and that would mean the end for him."

"Yes. And how does Hari Kahn fit into all this?" asked Andrew. "Do you think they might have been working together?"

"All possible," said Oliver. "We'll just have to find out."

Lieutenant Le Bret was on his way from Paris to see Capitaine Pierrefonds in Monaco, having called ahead to indicate an interest in seeing the CCTV from the casinos. With any luck he would be able to come back with some of the footage transferred to his laptop, or at least one or two stills. Rather than drive the thousand or so miles, he was on a TGV from Gare de Lyon that would deliver him directly to his destination in just over six hours. He would rest up overnight so as to be ready for his meeting the following morning.

"My officers have completed their enquiries," said the capitaine, as they sipped their morning coffee, "and we have several stills taken from the CCTV footage of the person I think you are looking for. I take it you will be able to recognise him, Lieutenant?"

"I'm afraid I won't," said Le Bret. "I've never seen him, however my colleagues in the UK have and with your permission I'd like to e-mail these photos to them straight away."

"Yes," said the capitaine. "I have no problem with that."

The lieutenant was then shown into a small office which he was at liberty to use for as long as he needed, confirmed Pierrefonds. Straight away he called Oliver Bentham.

"I have some stills taken from the CCTV footage," he said to Oliver. "I'm going to e-mail them to you now and perhaps you would call me back when you have a chance to study them. I will stay here as long as I need to, until that is we're satisfied we have a positive identification."

The e-mail arrived in Hereford within minutes and, again, Kevin was able to enlarge the images using a very advanced photo-enhancement programme, before sending copies through to Roy Partridge in Bishopsgate. They were looking at a man who fitted the description of the one described to them by Massimo but, on detailed examination, it did not appear to be a close likeness to the image on the driving licence. True they were both grey-haired and in their fifties, with moustache and glasses, and to the naked eye, could just have passed as the same person, but clearly they were not.

"Let's see what happens if I remove the moustache and glasses," said Kevin, who then proceeded to do so. "Does that help?"

"It certainly does," said Oliver. "It looks very much like Carmichael now and it seems as though our latest theory might prove to be correct - that Carmichael is our man and he will lead us to the reward monies. OK, send a copy of the latest image to Partridge and I'll talk to Le Bret. And well done, guys, we're making real progress now."

With everyone up-dated as to the current position, Roy Partridge set in motion the apprehension of Alan Carmichael, who was still at the Ritz in London. Once again the chief superintendent's colleagues from West End Central would formally carry out the arrest on suspicion of conspiracy to rob, murder and pervert the course of justice. Within the hour Roy received confirmation that he was in custody. There was, though, no encouraging such news relating to the arrest of Hari Kahn, who now seemed to have gone to ground. He had not been to his house in Chigwell, nor the depot in Tilbury, nor had he been seen anywhere in the region of his sister's house or brother-in-law's restaurant in the Hornchurch area. His Bentley remained in the drive, where it had been for several days.

Carmichael had been read his rights, his personal property handed over to the custody sergeant and was now being held in an interview room. The one telephone call he was allowed he made to the prince who, after recovering from the surprise, promised legal representation within the hour. He was sure, commented the secretary, that these were just routine enquiries. Later that afternoon he was joined by Peter Butler, a solicitor from the firm of James, Butler and Foley of Brook Street, W1, his attendance having been requested by the prince's solicitors Beauchamp & Co, who themselves had no experience in the field of criminal law. Within minutes Roy Partridge and Eric Bennett themselves arrived and the interrogation of secretary Carmichael began, with Sergeant Bennett asking the questions and Chief Superintendent Partridge listening, watching and taking notes.

"Do you understand that you are under arrest, Mr Carmichael, that this interview is being carried out under caution and is being recorded?" asked the sergeant.

"Yes," replied Carmichael.

"We do not, however, accept the position," interrupted solicitor Butler. "As I understand things, in the short time you gave me with my client, he is here on suspicion of crimes that were not committed within your jurisdiction. That is so, isn't it?"

"Explain further, if you would," said the sergeant.

"The robbery and the murder, neither of which my client was involved with, both took place in France. At the time these events occurred, and for a considerable time leading up to them, my client was out of the country, in Saudi Arabia in fact, so I fail to see how you have any right to hold him in custody in the UK. Any alleged conspiracy would have been way outside your jurisdiction, so I demand that this interview be terminated forthwith and that my client be immediately released."

"Your position is noted," said Roy Partridge, "however your client has lied to us during a previous interview thus perverting the course of justice and that was here in the UK. So no, he will not be released. He will be questioned here on behalf of the police in Paris and if and when appropriate, he will become the subject of a European Arrest Warrant in order that he may stand trial in France. Is that clear, Mr Butler?"

"My position stands," said the solicitor, "and I will be making formal representations on the basis of jurisdiction."

"Noted," said Roy. "Carry on, sergeant."

"Now, Mr Carmichael, tell us again where you were between Friday 7th and Thursday, 13 September."

"On the cruise ship *Liberty of the Seas* in the western Mediterranean."

"And did you get off the ship at any time?"

"Twice, as I remember. Once when we docked at Nice and again at Naples."

"And why was there no bill for you to pay at the end of the trip?"

"As I have said before, I was taken ill. I ate very little and drank nothing."

"How is it, then," continued the sergeant, "that you visited several casinos in Monte Carlo between 10 and 12 September?"

"I did not."

"For the record," said the sergeant turning towards the microphone, "I am showing the suspect several photographs of himself taken in Monte Carlo between the dates mentioned. What do you say to these, Mr Carmichael?"

"I object to this line of questioning," said the solicitor. "Again you are asking questions way beyond your remit concerning matters well outside your jurisdiction. I advise you not to answer, Mr Carmichael."

"Well it isn't me in any event. I do not wear glasses and I do not have a moustache."

"Both of which could be used as a basic disguise," said the sergeant. "Try this one, with those items removed. It's you, isn't it?"

"No it isn't."

"Very well, do you know a man called John Goddard?"

"I have a brother-in-law by that name."

"And you have been staying at his house while here in the UK?"

"Yes, that's right."

"So how was it that his passport and driving licence were used to hire a car in Nice and the same documents then used to gain access to casinos in Monte Carlo?"

"I've no idea."

"Now, Mr Carmichael," said the sergeant. "I think it's time for you to tell the truth. I put it to you that though you checked in for your cruise, you left the ship in Nice, hired a car using your brother-in-law's identity, drove to Monte Carlo where you collected four packages from the local parcels office containing cash amounting to about a million dollars, laundered it through several casinos, before returning the car, re-joining the ship at Nice, disembarking with your friends at Barcelona and flying back to the UK."

"A nice story," said the solicitor. "I would like a moment with my client in private."

The sergeant suspended the interview and he and his boss left the room, taking the opportunity to top up their coffee intake.

"What do you make of it, Gordon?" asked Roy.

"I think we have him. I reckon he's going to make a full statement, but what that will include remains to be seen. Of course, we don't know what he did with the euros, but perhaps he will tell us that as well."

Thirty minutes later they were ready to resume.

"My client has decided to make a full statement," announced solicitor Butler, "which he is prepared to do voluntarily. We would prefer it if you were to leave any other questions to the end."

"Very well," said the sergeant.

"A little while ago," began Carmichael, "I was contacted by a man called Hari Kahn who said a friend had given him my name and asked if it would be possible to meet me in Bahrain. This would have been some time during the week of 6 August. On the Thursday afternoon, when my duties for the day were finished, I drove across the causeway and checked into the Hilton Hotel. He told me he knew about the jewellery and wanted an opportunity to bid for the transportation of it from Paris to Riyadh. I told him the couriers had already been chosen. He persisted with his interest and, during the evening, I believe I let it slip that the job was being carried out by two of the prince's own staff, Al Othaim and Yacoub, something which I now regret."

"Would you like some water, Mr Carmichael?" asked the sergeant.

"Yes please. After that we talked about anything and everything, including my forthcoming Mediterranean cruise and he said there was something I could possibly help him with at a later date which he would contact me about when he had more information. We exchanged business cards, but I thought nothing more of it."

"So that meeting was in Bahrain on Thursday, 9 August, was it?"

"Yes. Then while I was here in the UK he called me. He asked if I would help with a business transaction involving foreign exchange. There was some cash he was trying to hide from the authorities which he wanted converted from dollars to euros. He would pay me one hundred thousand for my assistance. I was attracted by the prospect of such a handsome sum that I agreed to help him. I wish now that I hadn't."

"I bet you do," said Sergeant Bennett, provoking a scowl form the solicitor. "What happened next?"

"We met in Croydon shortly before I flew to Barcelona. He told me where to collect the packages and gave me the authorisation documents. I decided to try to conceal my identity, so I took my brother-in-law's passport and driving licence – I had my own as well, you understand – and for the purpose of the exercise, changed my appearance slightly so as to look a bit like him. Both his photos are a bit out of date so it wasn't difficult. I left the ship in Nice, hired the car, went to Monte Carlo, dealt with the cash, returned to Nice and re-boarded the ship, exactly as you suggested earlier."

"Very interesting," said Roy. "Now, what has happened to the euros?"

"Ah, yes. I took my share and couriered the rest back to him in Tilbury."

"And did you ever wonder what the transaction was all about, that it might have been the reward money following the recovery of the jewellery?"

"Not at first, but I did think that later."

"And what do you know of the robbery itself?" asked the sergeant.

"I know nothing at all. I had no idea that it was going to happen. It seems clear to me now that the man behind it all was Hari Kahn. He had his two nephews do the murky stuff and it was one of them that killed Al Othaim. Yacoub is the innocent victim here. He, like I, knew nothing of their plans."

"Right, Mr Carmichael. Is there anything else you would like to add?"

"I don't think so, thank you."

"And are you willing to sign a statement confirming everything you have just told us?"

"Yes I am."

"Right, Chief Superintendent," said Butler. "If we're done here, I'd now like my client released."

"Not possible," replied Roy. "We are going to check everything that has been said and we may have further questions. Your client will be detained here until that process is complete. He has just confessed to money laundering, after all."

"Yes, but again not within your jurisdiction."

"Not relevant," said Roy firmly. "That's all."

Chapter 24

At home Simon was mulling over the information he had been given by Emma's father. He was rather concerned as to what he should do next. Should he tell someone and, if so, who should that person be? Should he go directly to the police or should he share it with someone at the office? In the end he decided to speak to his father about it.

"First of all," said John Blunt, "I think you can trust that Mr Claremont has given you accurate information. Secondly, I can't think for one minute that his motives are anything other than straightforward and that he is trying to help you somehow. Thirdly, it seems to me that he believes the information is going to be important to someone, though he doesn't know quite to whom."

"Yes, I see all that," said Simon. "But why tell me? I'm hardly a senior figure in all this."

"True, but you're the only contact he has with this affair. And he probably prefers to have an unofficial conversation in the confines of his own home, rather than raise the profile and do it officially from his office. He's banking on the fact that through you, his comments will find their way to the right quarters. To me your task here is clear."

"Which is?"

"You have to pass it on to the person in your own office to whom you report. Your immediate boss, in other words. Then it becomes their decision as to what should be done. You are still a trainee after all and you have been there less than three months. It's hardly right that you should make those kinds of decisions yourself."

"Yes, you're right," acknowledged Simon. "It's pretty obvious really. I'll talk to Mary when I get in tomorrow."

The following morning, Roy Partridge and his sergeant were trying to make sense of the confession they had extracted from Carmichael the afternoon before. They were certain they would have to question him again but, for the time being, were content to let him occupy a cell at West End Central, since there were no such facilities at Bishopsgate.

"What are your thoughts, Gordon?" asked Roy.

"It all seems a bit flaky to me," said the sergeant. "And some parts I just don't understand. Why, for example, if he left the ship at Nice for three days did he hide himself away in his cabin the rest of the time?"

"Perhaps he didn't want to draw attention to his absence, so he faked sickness and kept away from everyone for the whole trip."

"Yes, could be. Also why courier a large bundle of euros back to Tilbury? It's not as if he had control of a courier company like Hari Kahn did."

"Agreed," said the chief superintendent. "But have you spotted the inconsistencies, or rather the downright lies?"

"No, what?"

"First, he did not meet Hari Kahn in Bahrain on Thursday, 9 August. That was the day Kahn was having lunch with Watkins at the Mayfair Hotel."

"So it was. Anything else?"

"He could not have sent the euros back to Tilbury. All shipments were being monitored by then and no such packages arrived from anywhere like Monaco or Nice."

"So he's lying, then?"

"Yes, I think so, Gordon. And if he's lying about those things, he's probably lying about everything. It could be the whole story is a complete subterfuge, but I can't imagine what the real truth is. Let's report in to Le Bret before we decide what to do next. I think it would be best if he were transferred to Paris, so I'll see if that can be arranged."

For Mary and her team it was business as usual and had been so for several weeks. There had been no more adverse comments about Nathan Henry from anyone in Lloyd's, especially Darren Black, who seemed to have been absent from the scene for a while. Nigel had circulated a copy of John

Marshall's report following his two weeks in Dubai and the business was beginning to flow. It was, according to the board's estimation, going to be worth at least five million dollars a year in commission revenue, thus ensuring that Mary's team would be even more stretched than they had been all year and may even need to consider taking on another broker. The matter of Hari Kahn had been aired at board level and chairman Peterson had been able to confirm to Sheikh Al Talyani that they, too, were not currently working with any of his companies nor would they be at any time soon. All was looking well in the run up to the year end and their new trading relationship in Dubai boded well for the foreseeable future of everyone. Nigel, of course, was commended for his part in bringing about the forthcoming flood of new business.

Prince Fahd and Princess Laila were on their way to New York, saddened of course by the absence of their business secretary and hoping that he would soon be released and able to join them. He was not about to be. After a long conversation with Lieutenant Le Bret in which he learned that it would take twenty-four hours for the warrant to be issued, Roy Partridge decided that further questioning of Carmichael would be in order. He and Sergeant Bennett therefore made their way to West End Central and their suspect, together with his solicitor, were shown into the interview room.

"Mr Carmichael," began the sergeant. "We have been reviewing your statement and there are certain aspects of it on which we require clarification, if you don't mind."

"Certainly," replied Carmichael.

"When you met Hari Kahn in Bahrain, you are sure it was Thursday, 9 August?"

"Yes, positive."

"And do you know where he had come from that day?"

"No, he didn't say."

"Was it the first time you had met him?"

"Yes, it was."

"So when we asked during a previous interview at Bishopsgate whether you knew anyone by that name and you said you did not, you were lying, were you?"

"Yes, I'm afraid I was."

"And when you couriered the euros back to Tilbury, which company did you use?"

"I don't remember. It was a local outfit in Monte Carlo, just off the main thoroughfare."

"And do you have any documents in support of it?"

"Not any more. I'm afraid I destroyed them."

"It seems to have been a rather foolish move on your part. I don't think I would send that amount of cash by international courier. Why did you do that?"

"It's what Kahn asked me to do."

"And did you have to declare the contents?"

"Yes, but I described them as documents."

"Well, Mr Carmichael," said Sergeant Bennett, summing up. "We don't believe a word of what you have told us. For a start, Kahn was in London on the day you alleged you met him. He was having lunch at the Mayfair Hotel. And we have evidence to support that."

"Well, I might have been mistaken as to the date, I suppose."

"And secondly, you did not send any packages back to Tilbury. What you may not know is that the depot had been under close surveillance for some time now and every package, both incoming and outgoing has been logged and checked by our officers. Nothing was ever received from Monte Carlo. What do you say to that, Mr Carmichael?"

"My client has nothing more to add," said the solicitor. "He has made a full statement to you and will say nothing more. And again, I demand that he be released on grounds of jurisdiction."

"That's not going to happen, Mr Butler," said Roy. "Your client has already confessed to money laundering and now obstructing the police with their enquiries. And it's us he obstructed. As a result, your client will continue to be held here until he is transferred to the police in Paris, which should be within the next twenty-four hours. But for the record, we do not believe anything he has told us. Good day, gentlemen."

"Mary," said Simon when they were by themselves. "Can we have a word sometime? I've something on my mind."

"That sounds ominous," she said, looking concerned. "Is everything all right?"

"Oh, yes," said Simon. "There's nothing wrong at all, but I would prefer it to be in private."

"OK, let's meet after work in The Broker. If should be quiet if we get there early enough."

It was, because they did. Mary bought a couple of fruit juices and they sat at a table at the back of the room away from the front window.

"I've been given some information," said Simon, "about someone who might be involved in the robbery."

"Interesting," said Mary. "Tell me more."

"My girlfriend's father is a Foreign Office official in Whitehall. For a while he was posted to the Middle East and spent time in Kuwait and Bahrain. He told me he knew of Alan Carmichael and that he has something of a chequered background."

"This is the prince's business secretary, right?"

"Yes, that's him. For a while he was commercial attaché in Riyadh before retiring early and joining the prince's staff, except he did not retire early. He was caught taking bribes from foreign business interests to help them get set up in Saudi Arabia, totally against the rules of diplomatic protocol, apparently."

"Yes, it would be."

"More importantly, he did a deal for Hari Kahn which went sour, but Carmichael kept the money, refused to give it back, so Kahn shopped him. The embassy kept it quiet but forced his resignation. He has lied about it ever since. It was some years ago, I think."

"Right," said Mary. "This could be useful information for the police, but I think we should talk to Nigel first. Let's go back to the office and see if he's still there."

They did and he was. Mary asked Simon to repeat what he had told her.

"What's the name of the man in Whitehall, Simon?" asked Nigel.

"George Claremont. He's a good friend of the family."

"Would he be willing to talk to the police, do you think?"

"Probably. My dad says he's as straight as they come, but I think I'd better warn him of the possibility."

"Good. I'll call Partridge and let him know. Thanks for this."

That evening at home, Simon asked his father to let Mr Claremont know what had happened and that he might at some stage be contacted by the police. As it turned out, George was entirely comfortable with it.

In Paris, the Hussain brothers and Yacoub were sticking to their stories and so continued to be in conflict. Lieutenant Le Bret had made no further progress in his investigations, but they had all been charged and the matter was now being overseen by the prosecuting judge, or *juge d'instruction*, in preparation for trial. At some point the judge would decide on what basis they should be brought to court and whether individually or together, but there was a lot of investigative work required before that could happen. Every possible detail of events was being checked and re-checked, but there were still a considerable number of uncertainties in the case causing concern, so it would be a while before proceedings would commence. The judge was particularly uneasy about the testimony against Yacoub, since it came from the Hussains and he was therefore reluctant to prosecute until that evidence had been corroborated by others, whoever they might be. He was content, though, for them all to remain in custody.

But now there was to be another development. Le Bret had advised him that another suspect was on his way, a man who had already admitted to money laundering and who had, by all accounts, been caught lying to the British police about his relationship with Hari Kahn. And, according to information also received, the statement he had made to Roy Partridge was considerably suspect in its entirety. The appropriate documentation having been secured, Alan Carmichael was now on his way to Paris, accompanied by two of Le Bret's detectives. Capitaine Pierrefonds of the Monaco police was also aware of this development and was content for Carmichael to be held in custody in Paris for the time being, while being questioned. He would be up-dated from time to time, the lieutenant assured him. Upon arrival, their latest suspect was duly processed, his personal belongings confiscated and he was read his rights before being locked away in a cell for the night. Interrogation would begin the next day, he was informed, and he would be entitled to a solicitor and an interpreter, if required, since all questioning would be in French. Carmichael confirmed that he would need an interpreter and asked that the Saudi Embassy be informed of his current situation, in order they could pass the news to the prince.

Early the following morning, Carmichael was brought from his cell to an interview room and, with solicitor and interpreter present, his questioning began.

"Mr Carmichael," said Lieutenant Le Bret. "I believe you have made a statement to the British police that you were involved in laundering dollars for a Mr Hari Kahn. Is there anything in that statement you now wish to change?"

"No there is not."

"Are you aware that there are a number of inconsistencies in it?"

"No I am not."

"Are you aware that the British police believe it is a complete fabrication?"

"Yes I am and no it is not."

"Lieutenant, where is this leading?" asked the solicitor.

"You'll see."

"In your statement, for example, you say that you met Mr Kahn in Bahrain on the 9 August and that it was the first time you and he had met. Yet it wasn't, was it? You and he have an unsavoury history. Can you tell me about that, please?"

"I met Mr Kahn on or about the 9 August. I may have mixed up the precise date but it was the first time I had met him. And there is no unsavoury history, as you put it. That must have been someone else."

"It wasn't though, was it? You and he crossed swords some years ago when he bribed you to fix a sponsor for him in Saudi Arabia. It didn't work out but you held onto the money and he reported you."

"Not me."

"Well, it is a matter of record, Mr Carmichael. You were accused of corruption and forced to resign from diplomatic service."

"I was wrongly accused. The matter was nothing to do with me."

"Then why did you let it go? Why did you not take any action in support of your position?"

"The odds were stacked against me. Even though the evidence was false, it appeared to my employers to be overwhelming."

"So you had met Mr Kahn before?"

"No, I never actually met him."

"But you knew of him, something you denied when the British police asked you."

"No comment."

"Mr Carmichael, I don't believe a word of what you have just told me. I think you are deliberately concealing the truth here. Now, let's move to your role in laundering the money. Why did you agree to do that?"

"Because Kahn said he would give me a hundred thousand and I needed the money."

"Lieutenant," said the solicitor, "I think this matter is beyond your jurisdiction. I'd now like to adjourn this interview in order to have some time with my client."

"Very well," said Le Bret. "We shall resume later."

The lieutenant was keen to discover the exact relationship between Kahn and Carmichael and, assuming the latter was lying about it, then it was quite possible that this might be the key to the whole matter. He put an urgent call through to Roy Partridge in London and asked if the exact nature of Carmichael's diplomatic misdeeds could be formally verified.

The chief superintendent confirmed he would do so. He telephoned George Claremont at the Foreign Office and asked if he would kindly call into Bishopsgate Police Station, at his convenience to discuss the matter of Alan Carmichael. George indicated he would do so just as soon as possible. The information he would be giving, he advised Roy Partridge, would be from his own personal recollection and that he would not be disclosing any matters which might be regarded as official secrets.

Later that morning George Claremont presented himself at Bishopsgate Police Station and asked for Chief Superintendent Partridge. Carmichael, he was able to confirm, had been addicted to gambling, which was the reason he rarely had any money but his job at the embassy was well paid and, of course, tax free so he managed to keep his life together, for the most part. Mrs Carmichael lived in the accommodation complex with him most of the time but, because it was not an entirely pleasant lifestyle for women in the Kingdom, she made frequent trips back to the UK. When that happened, he would spend a lot of time in Bahrain, where he could indulge in all kinds of leisure activities not available to him in Riyadh. It was on one of those visits that he first met Hari Kahn. They got to know each other quite well and it wasn't long before Kahn discovered that Carmichael could, it might be said, be rather flexible when it came to protocol and was not above taking the odd backhander in return for commercial favours.

The chief superintendent was listening intently while the sergeant was taking notes. Before very long Kahn approached Carmichael with regard to opening a branch of his freight forwarding company in Riyadh but he needed a local sponsor and that wasn't proving easy. There didn't appear to be enough revenue attached to the venture to interest any Saudi nationals of note, so Carmichael was asked to get involved. Kahn promised him fifty thousand dollars if he could fix it for him and, in due course, a local sheikh agreed to take on the role, in return for fifteen per cent of the profits. In so doing, Kahn had apparently falsified his income forecasts and when it came to light the sponsor withdrew, leaving Kahn high and dry. He demanded that Carmichael return the fifty thousand, but his request was denied on the grounds that it wasn't he who had provided false figures. Kahn was very angry, went straight to an official in Riyadh and told him the whole story, before driving somewhat hurriedly across the causeway to Bahrain.

Carmichael was confronted with his actions and he confirmed it wasn't the first time he had taken bribes. He was forced to resign without compensation and had his pension rights withdrawn. Either that, or the police would become involved. Mrs Carmichael was extremely hurt by all he had done and, as a result, their marriage did not survive. He managed to get a job as business secretary to the young Prince Fahd, presumably by lying about his exit from diplomatic service, and has been in Riyadh ever since. When he returns to the UK he normally stays with his sister, since his ex-wife will have nothing to do with him.

"A very comprehensive account, Mr Claremont," said Roy Partridge. "Thank you very much for that, it has been extremely helpful. I wonder, if I need you to, would you be willing to sign a statement to this effect?"

"In principal, yes," said George. "But I would need official clearance from my superiors before I could agree to that."

"Yes, of course. By the way, how was it that you knew we were interested in Carmichael?"

"Ah," said George. "It was through the son of a friend of mine. The lad Simon, who is a Lloyd's broker, was involved in arranging the insurance in the first place. He's my daughter's boyfriend."

"I see," said Roy. "Well, thank you again very much. If I need to talk to you again I will call you."

Chapter 25

Thursday of that week was the day of the Lloyd's Brokers' Dinner, a sumptuous, black-tie affair that was held each year at the Grosvenor Hotel in Park Lane, with an attendance usually in excess of two thousand people. Nathan Henry took three tables of twelve, allowing eighteen of the senior staff to take one guest each, typically an underwriter. Partners were not permitted to attend, not that any of them would have been the slightest bit interested in going. One insurance broker is bad enough, Mrs Peterson had once said, but a room full of them? No thanks. Nathan Henry had also reserved a suite of rooms in which hosts and guests could assemble, change if necessary and enjoy a few glasses of champagne while waiting for the formal part of the evening to begin, but it wasn't likely that anyone would be staying overnight.

The event was hosted formally by the head of the Lloyd's Brokers' Association and the principal guest was normally the chairman of Lloyd's, both of whom would deliver long, boring speeches on matters that weren't relevant to an audience that wasn't interested. Then there would also be a guest speaker, someone of note and not from the world of insurance, who would lighten the proceedings. The previous year had seen one or two of Nathan Henry's staff letting their hair down a bit, causing the chairman to issue two directives. Firstly, if they went on anywhere afterwards it would be at their own expense, not the company's and, secondly, everyone had to be at their desks by 9.00 a.m. the following morning, whatever condition they might be in. No pulling sickies, last-minute funerals or holidays, which would be bad for office morale.

Very few females from the market bothered to go. Mary did not normally attend, but this year she was being drafted in, much to her irritation, in view of the unavailability of some of the directors. Her chosen guest was none other than the Tellytubby himself, underwriter Martin Jackson. Chairman

Peterson, his deputy Robert Woodhead and head of reinsurance Maurice Jacobs were busy with another matter. They were, in fact, in the middle of take-over negotiations for the acquisition of the broking firm, Baxter Taylor and Black, the attraction being a string of South American agents delivering profitable business, particularly from Brazil and Venezuela. A meeting had been scheduled for Thursday afternoon which was unlikely to end much before midnight, it was thought. Nathan Henry's other employees were, of course, totally unaware of these plans, as were those of the target company, even though due diligence had been underway for some weeks. Both Baxter and Taylor were in favour of selling out, but Black was not, at least not to Nathan Henry, but he wouldn't be welcome anyway in view of his relationship with Hari Kahn. He was, therefore, not planning to be at the meeting, even though he was a minority shareholder in his company. His two fellow shareholders were happy, as it turned out, that they had a chance to be rid of him.

At 6.00 p.m. that evening, Mary took a taxi from outside Fenchurch Street Station, collected her guest from Gracechurch Street and they were driven to the Grosvenor. There were a few others in the suite already and the champagne was beginning to flow. Mary herself stuck to fruit juice.

"Here's to a pleasant evening," said Martin, as he took his first sip. "By the way, there's something I want to tip you off about, Mary."

"What's that?" she asked.

"Your lad Simon is beginning to interest one or two other broking companies. In the short time he's been with you he's made a very good impression in Lloyd's and I don't think it will be long before somebody tries to tempt him away from you."

"I see," said Mary. "Anyone in particular?"

"No, just general interest, but I'll let you know if it gets serious. Meanwhile I'd look after him, if I were you. In a few years' time he's going to be a real asset to anyone who employs him."

"OK, Martin. Thanks for that. He's due for a three month review at the end of this month, so I'll bear it in mind."

After an hour or so, they adjourned to the banqueting room and found their table. The noise level heightened as the tables filled up. It was customary, Mary discovered, for bets to be placed on the length of the speeches. Nigel Watkins, who was also at Mary's table and was the senior man on parade for Nathan Henry, was assigned to the role of timekeeper. They noticed from the order of proceedings that the celebrity guest was cricket commentator David Lloyd, one of the funniest, most popular speakers on the after-dinner circuit and known to those who followed the game as 'Bumble'.

"That'll add some time," said Nigel. "Right, here are the rules. It's a tenner each. Time starts from the moment the first speaker stands up and ends when the last speaker sits down. Nobody can choose the same time as anyone else and the nearest wins. In the event of a tie, in other words if two people are equidistant apart, the pot is shared. For the benefit of anyone who hasn't been before, the speeches normally last at least an hour but probably not more than ninety minutes. OK, who wants to go first?"

Mary went with one hour twenty-seven minutes while her guest chose an hour and sixteen. Other guesses varied from an hour and three minutes up to one hour forty-eight, all of which were meticulously recorded by the timekeeper, who also took charge of the money.

The meal consisted of four courses of high quality food delivered to the tables by an army of smartly-dressed waiters and waitresses, who kept to a strict regime to ensure that every table was served at more or less the same time. Once coffee and after-dinner drinks had been served the first speaker stood up, prompting Nigel to note the time as 9.02 p.m. His address of welcome lasted eighteen minutes before he handed over to the Lloyd's chairman, who droned on about the importance of keeping Lloyd's at the forefront of world insurance. He sat down after twenty-two minutes. Forty gone, forty-seven to go, mused Mary to herself, then I can go home. Bumble received an enthusiastic welcome, prompting him to keep them well-entertained for a further sixty-eight minutes, the cash going to underwriter Cyril Jones who had predicted the total speech time accurately and which immediately prompted a rousing chorus from the other eleven of the 1973 pop song 'Nice One Cyril'.

It being almost 11.00 p.m. by then, Nigel brought the formal part of the evening to an end. Those that were going on elsewhere were, he reminded them, on their own but he bade them all goodnight and a safe journey home, whatever time that would be. Mary had no plans other than to find her way home and, courtesy of her guest Martin Jackson who had pre-booked a car to take him home to East Sussex, she was delivered safely to Liverpool Street Station.

"Thanks for tonight," said Martin, "and don't forget what I said about Simon, will you?"

"I won't," she replied, managing to scramble onto the 11.42 p.m. back to Basildon.

Back at the office the takeover meeting was still going on and looked likely to continue for several hours more. Acquisitions were Robert Woodhead's special area of expertise, so he led negotiations all the way through. According to their management accounts, Baxter Taylor and Black had a current value of six million pounds, the largest and most profitable part of that revenue being generated by Dave Baxter and Phil Taylor. Darren Black's accounts were barely breaking even. At around 2.00 a.m., Robert outlined the basis of the deal, with lawyers from both sides furiously taking notes. A down payment of twenty-five per cent would be made, followed by annual stage payments based on performance of the business going forward. Thus Baxter and Taylor, who each owned forty per cent of their company, would receive six hundred thousand pounds each while Black, who owned the remaining twenty per cent, would get three hundred thousand. The former would each be required to sign three-year contracts while the latter would be expected to find employment elsewhere. Baxter and Taylor would not become main board directors or shareholders of Nathan Henry, but would ply their trade from within the reinsurance division headed by Maurice Jacobs. Their staff would also be offered new contracts. Black would be permitted to take his own accounts with him, but would be bound by a non-compete agreement which would prevent him from poaching any of his former colleagues' clients. Much discussion followed, with Baxter arguing on Black's behalf that he should receive compensation for loss of employment, which eventually Robert agreed to, adding a further one hundred and fifty thousand pounds to the overall acquisition costs, representing approximately three years' salary. At around 5.00 a.m. the meeting broke up. Lawyers were left to draft the appropriate documentation and in twenty-eight days from then, an announcement would be made and the deal consummated. Chairman Peterson and Robert Woodhead stayed in the office and drank coffee, congratulating each other on a good night's work.

Everyone who was out the night before was in by 9.00 a.m., with the exception of Mary. There was still no sign of her by 9.30 a.m. and her team were commenting how unusual that was. It wasn't as if she would have been out on the town like some of the others, so they were beginning to worry a little. Fifteen minutes later Nigel Watkins came into the room.

"Gentlemen," he said gravely. "I had some disturbing news. It seems that on her way home last night Mary was attacked, beaten about the head and robbed. Her mobile, cash and credit cards were all taken. She is now in intensive care at Basildon Hospital and has yet to regain consciousness. It appears to have happened at Basildon Station while she was waiting for her husband Tony to pick her up. He had been slightly delayed when he discovered a flat and needed to change a wheel. Police and ambulance were called and he has been with her all night. Her condition is serious, but stable."

The room remained silent.

"Brian Peterson and Lynne Green, director of human resources, are on their way to the hospital right now. They will call me every so often to give me the latest news. Meanwhile would you, John, take charge of the team for today and we'll see where we're at on Monday."

"Yes of course," said John. "It's going to be all over Lloyd's before long, so I think we'd better tell Martin Jackson at least, plus others that were on her table last night. And if there's anything we can do, please let us know."

"I will," said Nigel.

Essex police were following a number of leads while waiting for Mary to come round. They were at Basildon Station asking rail passengers if they had seen anything unusual the night before but, of course, the evening and late-night crowd would be the most likely source of information. Tony Whitehouse had also discovered, when he took his wheel in to be fixed, that it did not have a puncture, rather it had been deflated. Police were, therefore, not ruling out the possibility that he had been deliberately held up and that Mary had, for some reason, been targeted.

Brian Peterson and Lynne Green arrived at Basildon Hospital at around 10.30 a.m., shortly after Mary had regained consciousness. She was still very groggy and at that point was remembering little from the night before but, according to the doctor in A & E, she was at that point off the danger list. They met her husband Tony and assured him of the company's continued support, and that she should take her time and make a full recovery. The company's private medical insurance would come into play, they confirmed, so she would be assured of priority treatment, her own room, better facilities for communicating with friends and family and a more varied menu, when she was able to eat again. X-rays were due to be carried out later that morning and further information would be released shortly after that. They were then allowed to see her briefly, having been advised that she was still heavily sedated. She recognised them straightaway, a reassuring sign, and thanked them for taking the time to visit her. She wasn't able to tell them much about what had happened but, in any event, the police would be questioning her on that subject, as and when she was up to it. Her husband Tony was also grateful that they had come and promised to keep them fully informed, but he did remind them she had been on company business and that her evening out had, therefore, been for their benefit.

"I wonder if he has in mind some kind of compensation claim against us," said Lynne Green on their way back to the office.

"Possibly," said the chairman, "but I'm not too concerned about that. She is going to be on full pay all the while she's off, however long that is, but I think we'd better notify our liability insurers, just in case. I'm sure they would argue that it's her responsibility to get herself home, not ours, but late-night corporate events are a grey area in that regard. If necessary we'll make an *ex gratia* settlement out of court, but I doubt it will ever come to that. Tony is probably in a state of shock at the moment."

The following morning at the police station in Basildon, the officer in charge, Chief Inspector Hawkins, was reviewing statements from passengers who had been interviewed the evening before. There had been several sightings of two youngish IC1 males hanging around outside the exit from the down platform. They were medium height, aged between twenty-five and thirty, dressed in jeans and hoodies, but unfortunately the CCTV cameras seem to have been put out of action so there were no images of them. There were seen, though, by passengers alighting from trains arriving at 10.35 p.m., 11.05 p.m. and again at 11.35 p.m. and, since Mary had been able to confirm she saw them when she arrived there at just after midnight, there was a strong possibility they were the likely culprits. Further enquiries were being made and descriptions circulated.

Mary's X-rays the previous day had revealed no permanent damage, no fractures and no internal bleeding.

"It was my head, after all," she had said to one of the nurses, "so no real danger of injury." After that they felt she was ready to be interviewed by the police, with her husband in attendance, of course.

"Yes," she confirmed to the officer. "I remember now. When I got off the train at about 12.05 a.m. there were two lads there. I was the only passenger to alight at Basildon and I was surprised that Tony was not already there to collect me. I took out my mobile and, at that point, they came over to me and asked if I could help them get a taxi. I said I would after I had called home, then I remember nothing more until I woke up yesterday morning."

"And can you describe them?" asked the officer.

"Yes," she said, and proceeded to give the same information as the other rail passengers had given later in the evening.

"Somebody sooner or later must recognise them," said the chief inspector to the station sergeant. "We'll need to keep asking rail travellers for several days, I think. Some people don't travel the same route every day, so we might strike lucky if we're at the station next Thursday evening. And put up one of those notices asking people to telephone us if they have information, would you?"

"Yes Sir," said the sergeant.

Simon was at home with his parents on Saturday, having invited Emma to join them for an evening meal. He took the opportunity to talk about the events of the week and especially what had happened to Mary on Thursday night.

"I've been talking to George Claremont," said John Blunt, before Emma arrived. "He was contacted by the police and did visit them at the station in Bishopsgate. He was able to give them a lot of background information about Alan Carmichael, for which they seemed to be extremely grateful."

"Oh, OK," said Simon. "I hope he wasn't put out by that. I don't want to ruin things with Emma."

"On the contrary," said John. "He was very pleased to be able to help. He sees it as his public duty, or so he said."

"Good," said Simon.

Emma arrived and they had a convivial evening together. She was shocked to hear from Simon the latest developments but confirmed her father felt quite good about what he had been able to do to help.

"So what's the latest then?" asked John Blunt.

"Not too sure," said Simon. "I think Carmichael has owned up to laundering the money in Monte Carlo and he's pointing the finger at Hari Kahn as the man who organised the robbery. Carmichael is in custody in Paris but Kahn is still on the run. At least that's what people in the office are saying, but I don't know how true it is."

"I'm really looking forward to meeting your work colleagues at the Christmas party," said Emma. "They sound an interesting bunch of people."

"They are," said Simon. "But before then, there's something else I'd like you to do for me, if you would. The golf club annual dinner is at the beginning of November and I wonder whether you would join me for that? I think it's on the first Friday."

"Yes, of course," said Emma. "I'd be delighted."

"You realise you'll be on the top table this year," said John, "being club champion and all that."

"Oh no," said Simon. "I hadn't thought of that."

"No matter," said Emma. "I'm sure you can handle it."

On Sunday morning the station sergeant at Basildon took a call from a local man who said he had been at the railway station on Thursday evening. He got off the 11.05 p.m., he said, and did notice two men hanging around. He gave the same description of them as others had done but, more importantly, he had seen them before. They were local lads, he thought, who frequented a club called the Cavendish Rooms in Billericay, but he did not know their names. He hung up without giving his name.

"OK," said Chief Inspector Hawkins, when he was told. "Let's see if we can pick them up."

Local police staked out the club and it wasn't long before they were able to identify two possible suspects who fitted the descriptions they had. They were immediately arrested on suspicion of committing aggravated assault and robbery and taken to the police station at Basildon. They were processed by the custody sergeant and gave their names as Liam Byrne and Ryan Mulrooney, aged twenty-eight and twenty-six respectively, both from North Benfleet. Both had large amounts of cash on them which, together with their credit cards and mobiles, were taken from them and held at the station in safe custody. They were questioned at length, neither saying anything to incriminate themselves, and an identity parade, involving all those rail passengers who had been public-spirited to have given their names, arranged for the following day. Warrants were also obtained for searches to be carried out at the addresses they had given and they were then held overnight in separate cells.

At the following day's identity parade, each was picked out by those who had been asked to attend and at the home of Liam Byrne, Mary's mobile was discovered hidden down the back of a sofa. They were charged, despite continuing to protest their innocence and brought before the magistrates the next day. At court, they confirmed their identities and, on the advice of their solicitors, entered pleas of not guilty. Bail was denied and they were remanded in custody to await trial sometime in December.

Despite the overwhelming evidence against them, they continued to protest that they had no knowledge of the assault, that the mobile phone found down the sofa must have been planted there and that those who had formally identified them were totally mistaken. When questioned about the cash in their possession, they each said they had been fortunate enough in recent weeks to have won it during several visits to the races.

"All very flimsy stuff," said Chief Inspector Hawkins to his sergeant. "There is no doubt in my mind we have them and that, however their solicitors may try to defend them if they bother to, we have enough to secure convictions. But we must keep our enquiries going. I think there's someone else behind this and we must find out who it is."

"Yes Sir," said the sergeant. "I agree."

Chapter 26

Like all experienced investigators, Lieutenant Le Bret and his team had, over the years, developed a series of techniques and manoeuvres designed to unsettle a suspect, some of them more legitimate than others, perhaps. Switching between the hostile and the friendly was commonly used, especially when there were two interrogators involved and the pretence that other suspects had provided full confessions was another. Sudden telephone calls providing vital incriminating evidence often helped to create the impression that the interrogators knew more than they actually did and that their information was therefore more up to date. Le Bret and his men also considered themselves able to distinguish between the innocent and the guilty, by the nature of their responses to certain pre-planned questions. Blurred recollection, pauses, avoidance of direct questions, excuses rather than denials, objections, a low-level appreciation of the effects of crime and a softening of hard words were indications of guilt and Le Bret was familiar with them all. He knew what to watch out for and how to deal with it. When shown an item of evidence, for example, an innocent person would wish to examine it closely and ask questions about it, whereas a guilty person would make assumptions about it, show disinterest and even push it away. These methods were, though, made more difficult when lawyers were present and even more so when there was an interpreter in the room.

So it was that, at the police station in Paris, Alan Carmichael was brought by a uniformed officer into a basement room which was windowless and without a clock, designed to increase the level of stress. He was joined by a solicitor and an interpreter. Though Le Bret's English was competent enough, it was not appropriate for interviews such as this to be carried out in anything other than the home language. After a short wait, Lieutenant Le Bret and his colleague Detective Balzac entered the room and sat opposite Carmichael and the solicitor. The interpreter sat at the end of the table, thus not in the sightline of either side. Le Bret was by then in possession of the information that Roy Partridge had obtained from George Claremont concerning Carmichael's slightly unfortunate past and his earlier encounter with Hari Kahn.

"Mr Carmichael," began the lieutenant. "I'd like to begin by reviewing what you told my colleague in London about your involvement in this matter. Is that all right with you?"

"Yes," said Carmichael.

"You say that you were contacted by Hari Kahn and that he asked that you exchange some dollars for him in Monte Carlo. Is that right?"

"Yes it is."

"You say that Kahn sought you out, met you in Bahrain on the 9 August and that it was the first time you had met him. Is that also right?"

"Yes it is."

"No it is not," interrupted Balzac somewhat aggressively. "Kahn was not in Bahrain on that day. You know that."

"My client," said the solicitor, "has already explained that he may have been mistaken about the precise date."

"Is that so, Mr Carmichael?" said the lieutenant.

"Yes it is."

"But, in any event, it was the first time you had met him, was it?"

"Yes, I believe it was. While I was with the embassy in Riyadh I did meet a lot of business people from around the region, so it is quite possible I could have met him, but I have no specific recollection of it."

"You're lying," said Balzac. "We have information that suggests you had inappropriate dealings with Kahn several years' ago, that you double-crossed him and he in turn reported your actions to the embassy and you were fired. Is that true, Carmichael?"

"Where did you get that information?"

"Is that true?" repeated Balzac, shouting.

"I do not recall anything of the sort. I'm sure I would remember if anything like that had happened. Whoever it was that told you that must have been mistaken."

"But we have a written statement confirming it," said Balzac bending the truth slightly.

"My client has made his statement in that regard," said the solicitor. "He has nothing more to add on the subject."

"Let us now move on to the day of the robbery," continued Le Bret. "You say you had no knowledge of it. Is that right?"

"Yes it is. But I now believe it was the work of Hari Kahn who planned it all and had his nephews carry it out. I also believe that the cash he asked me to change for him was the reward money."

"So you say. What about Yacoub's part in all this?"

"I believe Yacoub to have been an innocent victim. He would not have been involved in anything like that."

"You know we have him in custody here, don't you?"

"Yes. What has he told you?"

"And what can you tell us," said Le Bret, ignoring Carmichael's question, "about Al Othaim's murder?"

"I know nothing of how or why he died. I was never there, remember?"

"Now, what you have confessed to is the laundering of Kahn's money. Would you tell us a little more about that, please?"

"I was to collect the dollars from a post office in Monte Carlo and to change them into euros. Kahn had four packages sent by his courier company and he gave me the authorisation documents before I left for my cruise. I left the ship in Nice, hired a car, drove to Monte Carlo, carried out the exchange and posted the euros back to him, having deducted my share."

"You did not," yelled Balzac. "A complete inventory has been carried out on Kahn's company books and no packages were ever received from Monaco. How do you explain that?"

"He must have intercepted them himself before they were officially recorded at the depot."

"Listen, Carmichael," said Detective Balzac. "I think it's about time you stopped lying and told us the truth, or we shall be forced to take very serious action."

"My client is already telling you the truth," said the solicitor.

"What will you do?" asked Carmichael.

"That depends."

"On what?"

"Whether you tell us where the euros are."

"My client has told you that," said the solicitor.

"I think not," said Balzac.

Just at that point, there was knock at the door and a uniformed officer stepped in to tell the lieutenant that there was a telephone call for him. It was urgent, explained the officer, and was relevant to the case. Ten minutes later Le Bret came back into the room.

"I have just had word," he announced, "that Hari Kahn has been apprehended in London and has made a full statement. In particular, he says he never received the euros you say you sent back to him, Mr Carmichael, and he has no idea where they are. He has told us a lot of other information as well, but we will ignore that for the time being. I want to concentrate on the euros."

"What has he told you?" asked Carmichael. "I'd like to know."

"All in good time," said Le Bret. "Now, though, we'd like the truth, please, about what you did with the cash."

"I think it's time for a break," said the solicitor. "My client would like to use your facilities and I would like some time with him. If you don't mind, we'd prefer to stop now and resume in one hour. Would that be in order?"

"Yes, of course," said the lieutenant. "One hour from now."

Lieutenant Le Bret and Detective Balzac withdrew, the uniformed officer escorted Carmichael to the toilet and the interpreter went across the road to a café. Le Bret gave instructions for Yacoub, who did not yet know about

Carmichael's arrest, to be positioned in the same corridor so as to spot Carmichael when he returned from the bathroom.

"What do you think?" asked the lieutenant of his detective.

"He's definitely concealing something," said Balzac. "Did you notice how keen he was to find out what Yacoub had told us and how he didn't like the word murder? He softened it to died instead. His recollection of events was also selective. Sometimes accurate, other times blurred."

"Yes, I got all that," said Le Bret. "So we keep at him then?"

"Yes," said Balzac. "So they've got Kahn then, have they?"

"No, of course not. I made that up. Nobody knows where he is."

"That was good, Lieutenant," said Balzac. "You even convinced me."

The interview resumed as agreed after an hour's break.

"My client has something to tell you," said the solicitor, "but first I'd like to know precisely what information Kahn gave you."

"Not possible to tell you at this stage," said Le Bret. "You will be entitled to see his statement in due course, but not yet. What is it you want to tell us, Mr Carmichael?"

"It's about the money. I did not courier it back to Kahn's depot in Tilbury. I parked it somewhere."

"And where might that be?"

"It's in a safety deposit box in Monaco. The key to it is on my key ring which you have with my other belongings."

"I should add," said the solicitor, "that this changes nothing with regard to my client's position in all this. He had every intention of getting the cash back to Kahn in due course, he just didn't like the idea of it being sent back in the way that Kahn had asked him to, that is to say by courier. He was planning to get Kahn to go to Monte Carlo and pick it up himself."

"Thank you, gentlemen," said Le Bret. "Now we're beginning to get somewhere. We'll take another short break, if you don't mind while I check this all out. I need you to tell me which bank and the number of the box. Is it in your name, Mr Carmichael?"

"No, John Goddard. Have you pen and paper please? I'll write you the details."

"Thank you. Fifteen minutes then."

Le Bret left the room and put a call straight through to Capitaine Pierrefonds at the police station in Monte Carlo. He requested an official police visit to the bank, an examination of the contents of the safety deposit box, confiscation of the cash if that's what was there and a call back in confirmation when it was done. Pierrefonds promised he would see to it immediately. Le Bret then re-joined the interview.

"There's just one more thing, Mr Carmichael, if you don't mind. Did you or did you not plan the robbery yourself, recruit Yacoub and Kahn's nephews to carry it out, ask Kahn to take custody of the reward money before shipping it out to you in Monaco?"

"I did not."

"I think you did."

"Then prove it."

"I intend to. And before very much longer you are going to tell me why."

"I have nothing more to say to you."

"Lieutenant," said the solicitor. "I think this interview is now at an end. My client has given you all the information he has and he's now made a full confession as to his part in the proceedings. Anything more is pure speculation on your part, which we shall not be responding to."

"Very well. Interview terminated."

Carmichael was returned to his cell, the solicitor and interpreter both left the building while Le Bret and Balzac returned to their offices. A short while later, Le Bret took the expected call from Pierrefonds in Monte Carlo, who confirmed there was a substantial amount of euros in the box, that it had been rented to a Mr John Goddard and that the cash was now in safe custody at the station.

"Good," said Le Bret. "Now let's re-interview Yacoub and see if he's changed his story, now that he's seen we have Carmichael."

He was brought to the same interview room, without windows or clock, and with a different solicitor but the same interpreter, questioning re-commenced.

"Yacoub," said the lieutenant. "I have to tell you that your former boss, Mr Carmichael, has made a full confession as to his and your part in these matters and that, as a result, we shall now be continuing with proceedings against you for robbery and murder, both of which you have been charged with already. Hari Kahn is also in custody in London and his statement confirms Carmichael's testimony. What we'd like you to do now, Yacoub, is to provide your own statement for us."

Yacoub was visibly shocked and seemed completely deflated.

"My client has already given you his statement," said the solicitor, "and will not add anything to it."

"Yes I will," said Yacoub, almost in tears. "I'll tell you everything."

"Right, thank you," said Le Bret.

"It all goes back many years to the days when Mr Carmichael was commercial attaché in Riyadh. There was a scandal, the details of which I'm not too sure about, but it involved Hari Kahn and it caused Mr Carmichael a lot of hardship and distress. I believe he lost his job and his wife as a result of what Kahn did to him. May I have some water, please?" he said almost choking.

"Yes of course," said Le Bret, indicating to the uniformed officer to fetch a bottle. "Please continue."

"When the jewellery matter first came up, Mr Carmichael approached me with a plan which, he said, would not cause the prince any lasting harm, but would give us the opportunity to earn some reward money. The prince had chosen Al Othaim to be the main courier then Mr Carmichael put my name forward to go with him. He asked me to arrange a reception committee at the airport in Riyadh, but not to worry too much about who they were, because the jewellery was never going to arrive. He recruited Kahn to find some suitable guys to carry out the robbery and to provide substitute passengers for the flight. He never met Kahn's nephews, but spoke to them using a pay-as-you-go mobile. He referred to himself as the captain, from his early days in the Navy. I was to administer an injection to Al Othaim, which would sedate him but do him no lasting damage and he would be bundled into an ambulance, which would appear as though it were attending an emergency. Then we would be driven away with the jewellery to await instructions from Kahn."

"Do you know who the substitute passengers were and who set off the fire alarm in the departure lounge? And how did you get the syringe through security?"

"No I don't know who those people were, but it was the cleaner, the guy whom set off the alarm, who slipped me the syringe. Then as we drove towards St Quentin, Ali Hussain took a call from someone, I do not know whom, after which we drove to a remote spot where Al Othaim was to be shot, it turned out. I tried to stop it happening, but I was hit in the face with the gun which rendered me unconscious for a few minutes. I did not see which one of them shot Al Othaim but it was Ali who had the gun both before and after. Will the charge of murder against me stick, do you think?"

"It's too early to say. Please carry on."

"We holed up in a deserted farmhouse until there was a call from Kahn giving us a number to call about the reward. Eventually we had instructions for a handover to take place in Kent somewhere, after which we took the reward money to Kahn's house in Chigwell. We then booked into a bed and breakfast place in Barking, while waiting to receive our share of the proceeds, which never came as it turned out. Suddenly there was an urgent call from Mr Hussain senior, saying that Kahn was after us for lying about the amount of the reward money and was on his way to Barking. We didn't understand why, but we got away nevertheless just before he arrived and tried to make it through the tunnel, after which we were arrested."

"Why was it, do you think, that Mr Carmichael chose Hari Kahn for this job? After all, they weren't exactly the best of friends by all accounts."

"Ah, that's easy to explain. It was a matter of revenge. Mr Carmichael wanted to get him back for what he had done all those years ago. He was hoping that the crime could be pinned on Kahn, that he would be convicted of robbery and, more importantly, murder and that he, Mr Carmichael, would get away free. It looks as though it hasn't quite worked out like that. I am a bit surprised that Mr Carmichael told you all this. Was his version the same as mine?"

"It will be, I'm sure," said Le Bret, puzzling Yacoub slightly. "There will be more details we'd like to go through in due course, but for the time being I'd like to thank you for your cooperation here. You will be willing to make a written statement to this effect, won't you?"

"Yes, I guess so. I am really worried about the charge of murder, though. I would like you to understand that I had nothing to do with that."

"We'll bear it in mind," said Le Bret. "Right, I think we can terminate this interview now."

Yacoub was returned to his cell while the two detectives took a few minutes to plan their next step. They decided they would confront Carmichael again, now they appeared to have a full confession from Yacoub, so they re-assembled the same group in the interview room once again.

"There have been two important developments, Mr Carmichael," said the lieutenant. "Firstly, the euros have been recovered by the police in Monte Carlo and are now in their safe custody at the station. They will be held for as long as is necessary until trial and used in evidence. Secondly, we now have a full confession from Yacoub, who has told us everything."

"May I see his statement?" said the solicitor.

"No you may not," said Le Bret. "It seems that you, Mr Carmichael, are the man behind both the robbery and the murder. It was you who recruited Kahn and through him his nephews. It was you who enlisted the help of Yacoub and you who gave the instructions by telephone for Al Othaim to be shot. It was also you who persuaded Kahn to have the reward money sent to Monte Carlo where you planned to convert it and hide it away for your own benefit. At some later date you planned to share some of it with Yacoub but Kahn and his nephews would get nothing. They would be left out in the cold. At the same time you were hoping to pin the whole event on Kahn, which was an act of revenge for the harm that he did to you during your time at the embassy in Riyadh."

"This is complete fabrication," said the solicitor.

"No it is not," said Le Bret. "You knew about the Lloyd's policy, Mr Carmichael, because you had a hand in arranging it and you knew that a reward was likely to be paid for the return of stolen property. You meant no harm to the prince, whose property would be returned, but you meant as much harm to Kahn as you could possibly inflict. As it is you will be convicted and he will get away."

"I thought you said Kahn was under arrest in London," said the solicitor.

"Did I really," said Le Bret.

"Yes, you did and if it proves to be the case that you falsified that information, I shall be lodging a protest on behalf of my client whose confession you have just obtained by trickery."

"Good luck with that," said Le Bret. "It's still a confession, though, and it looks like your client will be charged with conspiracy to commit robbery and murder."

The interview was terminated with Carmichael a broken man, almost in tears and in a complete state of despair. Lieutenant Le Bret and Detective Balzac took stock for a few minutes. Written statements would be obtained in due course from Carmichael and Yacoub in order that Le Bret could make a full report to the investigating magistrate. He was still in two minds about Yacoub's role in the murder of Al Othaim, something he would discuss further at a later stage. He would also report to the Saudi embassy, as he had promised, and to loss adjuster Moore, so that Lloyd's could be informed of the recovery of the reward money. A good day's work all round, they agreed.

Chapter 27

Back at the offices of Nathan Henry, there was better news of Mary. She was recovering well and was expected to leave hospital in a few days' time. She would need to rest at home for a while before returning to work but, in any event, the stitches in her head wound would need to be removed first. Brian Peterson sent a message to her husband that she should stay at home for at least two weeks before even thinking about returning. Tony Whitehouse was a kitchen and bathroom installer with three full-time employees and was in an ideal position to spend time with her at home while his company's contract work carried on. Their two teenaged boys, one in school and the other in sixth-form college, would also be around to lend a hand. They were a close-knit family able to rally round when necessary.

Mary had been interviewed again by Essex police, who were interested to know whether she knew of anyone who would want to harm her and, more importantly, anyone who knew she was going to be late home the previous Thursday. She could not immediately think of anyone. And, as far as they both knew, there was no such person in Tony's life either. Her stock of get-well cards was growing by the day, already numbering fifteen, mostly from people that she worked with, but also from one or two underwriters at Lloyd's, including in particular Martin Jackson. Later that day she recalled the conversation with Darren Black and, having talked things over with husband Tony, decided to mention it to the police.

Byrne and Mulrooney, meanwhile, were being questioned further on the instructions of Chief Inspector Hawkins in an attempt to discover the identity of the person for whom they carried out the attack, if indeed there was one. It didn't seem right, they were repeatedly advised, that they should end up in prison while the other person remained free. Eventually they confessed that there was such a person, but they did not know his name. He was someone they had seen a few times in the Cavendish Rooms in Billericay, who had shown them a photograph of Mary and told them where she could be found. Thus the police concluded he was someone she knew in her working life, able to provide an image of her and who knew that she would be at the Lloyd's Brokers' dinner. When she gave them the name Darren Black, they traced him to an address in Chigwell and he was arrested that evening. He was processed and his photograph shown to Byrne and Mulrooney, both of whom confirmed it was not the man they had met at the club. He was released on police bail on condition he would return for further questioning whenever required to do so.

In Paris, Lieutenant Le Bret had re-interviewed both Carmichael and Yacoub and had been able to clarify many of the points that remained outstanding from previous conversations. He had also questioned the Hussain brothers further and confronted them with what had been revealed, specifically that Ali Hussain was the one with the gun and it was he that shot Al Othaim. Kareem Hussain eventually confirmed the information to be correct while his brother Ali, of course, denied the story, still insisting that it was Yacoub. He did confirm, though, that the telephone call he received while *en route* to St Quentin did come from the captain but, contrary to Yacoub's testimony, he did not carry out the shooting. That was Yacoub. The Hussains also confirmed that their uncle Hari Kahn was the one who had made all the arrangements, who organised the substitute passengers, who paid the cleaner to set off the alarm, who supplied them with the gun and it was to him that they had taken the reward money when they hurried away from the handover in Kent.

Le Bret then made his report to Michel Blanc, the investigating magistrate, who instructed that Carmichael be formally charged. He then raised the matter of Yacoub and his part in the murder.

"It seems to me," he said to magistrate Blanc, "that Yacoub was telling me the truth at that point. He was in full confessional flow at the time and I have no reason to doubt his assertion that he tried to prevent the killing of Al Othaim. I think it would be difficult to make the charge of murder stick when it was an indirect, rather than a direct consequence of the robbery and I think his lawyer would argue that though it might have been Carmichael's intention all along that Al Othaim be killed, Yacoub knew nothing of it and was not, therefore, involved."

"I agree it's a tricky one," said Michel Blanc. "I will give it some thought and call you shortly."

Le Bret then called the Saudi Embassy and gave them a full account of recent developments, asking that the prince be informed. He also called David Moore and gave him the same information, mentioning also the recovery of the reward money.

"How much was there?" asked David.

"Just under six hundred and seventy-five thousand," confirmed the lieutenant, "which is equivalent to about nine hundred thousand dollars."

"OK, thanks," said David. "I'll pass it on to Lloyd's."

A little while later Michel Blanc called Le Bret to let him know his decision about Yacoub, that he should be released from the charge of murder on the grounds that it would be unlikely to result in a conviction. Robbery yes, but not murder. The lieutenant would, he confirmed, advise Yacoub in due course, but for the time being he would hold it back, just in case he needed any further testimony from him.

The prince was astonished when Ambassador Sulaiman al Rahji called him in New York to tell him the news. He just could not believe that his trusted business secretary had been responsible all along for such a crime and, more particularly, that he was the one who gave instructions for Al Othaim to be shot. The princess was equally shocked and suggested they stop off in Paris on the way back to Riyadh to hear more of the detail, particularly with regard to the death of their friend. They would have cut short their stay in New York, but there were only two days left and there were still important business matters outstanding.

"He appears to have been acting out of revenge," explained Prince Fahd to the princess. "He always planned that the jewellery would find its way back to us, but it was the murder he wanted to blame someone else for."

"So it wasn't aimed at us, then?" asked Princess Laila.

"So they're telling us," said the prince, "but the death of my friend I will never forgive him for. He will be punished in France, of course, but I now have to explain to Saleh's family that it was me who chose him for the courier assignment and that it was a member of my staff that had him killed. The least I can do is to ensure his body is returned and laid to rest in an appropriate manner. The family must be distraught that they haven't been able to do that yet."

"Then we shall," said the princess.

"Martin, I've just had word from Oliver Dentham," announced David Moore to underwriter Jackson over the telephone. "According to Le Bret we have the reward money back, or at least the best part of it. About ninety per cent of it was found in a safety deposit box in Monte Carlo having been dumped there by Alan Carmichael. Le Bret thinks he was planning to come back for it later after the dust had settled and that he was trying to hang onto it for himself, rather than share it with the others. We presume he's either spent the rest or has it hidden away somewhere, in which case we might get our hands on that as well."

"Good news, David," said Martin. "I don't suppose I'll get it back for a while, will I?"

"Unlikely to be soon. I think the French police will hang onto it as evidence, but I will take the precaution of formally registering with them the fact that it originally came from Lloyd's who will eventually want it back. Even so, there may be some hoops to jump through when the time comes, which is probably a few months from now. Is there anything you'd like me to do in the meantime?"

"Yes, David. Be sure to tell the brokers so they can officially notify all syndicates that participated in the slip."

"Yes, I will."

"OK. Thanks for letting me know."

The loss adjuster immediately called claims director David Locke and gave him the news, whereupon he made his way over to Mary's room.

"Morning, lads," he said as he breezed in. "Have you heard the news?"

"No, what news?" said Jamie.

"The jewellery matter is more or less resolved now. Most of the reward money has been recovered and guess what? The guy behind it all was Carmichael. I expect Jackson will be kicking himself, he only entertained him to lunch recently."

"How did they catch him?" asked Jamie.

"Well, it was down to Bentham and his gang. First of all they had the police do a raid on Kahn's Tilbury depot and found mysterious packages had been sent to Monaco. They guessed it might have been the cash so went out there and, from CCTV, were able to identify Carmichael. Then someone came up with incriminating evidence about his past history and he owned up to laundering the money. Then eventually he coughed about the whole thing."

"That person was someone Simon knew," said Jamie. "His girlfriend's father. He was a diplomat in the Middle East some years back and knew all about Carmichael. That's what eventually nailed him."

"Good stuff," said David. "How's your boss, by the way?"

"Making a good recovery, we understand. She should be out of hospital in a couple of days."

"I hear Black got arrested for having something to do with the assault."

"Yes, but he was released. The two lads who were responsible didn't identify him as the guy who paid them. We still think he had something to do with it though, because she did rather threaten him when he was found to be spreading damaging rumours about us."

"You do know that Black has a brother who has done time and who lives in Billericay? His name's Steve. A bit of a thug, apparently."

"No. How do you know that?"

"Ear to the ground, old boy. Plus when I first started in this business, Black and I were in the same company. He always seemed to associate with undesirables then and it doesn't look as though much has changed."

"Right David. Thanks. I think we'd better tell someone about that. The police might just care to revisit the Blacks."

"Good idea. See you guys later."

At Bishopsgate Police Station, Roy Partridge was more than a little concerned that Hari Kahn had not yet been apprehended and was beginning to think that he had fled the country using a second passport. The house in Chigwell and the depot in Tilbury were both still under surveillance but there was no sign of him there, nor had he been seen anywhere near his sister's house or his brother-in-law's restaurant. Roy had heard from Le Bret and was aware of all the recent developments, none of which surprised him in the least. As an experienced officer and devout realist, he never took anyone or anything to be true until proven. The biggest blunders, he continuously reminded colleagues, are made by those who presume.

He had also heard from David Moore about the unfortunate incident concerning Mary and that suspicions lay in the direction of Darren Black, a man he had previously questioned.

"Gordon, have you got a minute?" he said to the sergeant who was walking by.

"Yes, boss. What is it?"

"Do you remember the man Black?"

"Yes, the broker. A mate of Hari Kahn, apparently."

"That's him. Well, Essex police think he might have had something to do with the assault on that woman from Nathan Henry, but they've no evidence yet and the lads who carried out the attack didn't recognise him as the bloke who paid them when they were shown his photograph."

"Right. What are you thinking?"

"He lives in Chigwell, doesn't he?"

"Yes."

"So what I'm thinking is whether he's been hiding Kahn there and, more importantly, whether he still might be there."

"It's worth a shot, boss."

"I think so. Would you get them onto it please? Discreetly though. Watch the place for a bit, talk to neighbours, that sort of thing. You know the drill."

"Yes, boss. Right away."

Two days later Mary was discharged from hospital, with instructions to take it easy and get as much rest as possible. Husband Tony collected her and drove her home. A multitude of flowers with goodwill messages were waiting for her and they just kept coming. Nine bunches so far and the household was beginning to run out of vases, so any future deliveries would need to be consigned to buckets. Clearly she was a popular lady.

Later in the afternoon the doorbell rang. It was Jamie Piper-Bingham.

"Well I never," said Mary. "I didn't ever think I'd see you here. Have you been to Essex before?"

"Yes, once. I was lost."

"Very funny. But you are very welcome and it is good to see you. What's the news?"

"We have closure on the jewellery and the reward money has been found."

"Excellent. Tell me all."

Jamie then gave her a full account of the whole matter and she, too, was surprised that the man behind everything was the prince's own secretary.

"But that's not really why I'm here," said Jamie. "You are up to date with police enquiries here, are you?"

"Yes," she replied. "They have two lads in custody but are continuing with their enquiries because they think someone put them up to it. For a while they thought it might have been Black, but it turned out not to be so."

"Right. We still think it's Black. We now know that he has a brother, a guy called Steve, who has done time and who lives in Billericay, apparently. We think it might be worth it if the police follow that up."

"Right," said Tony. "I'll get them onto it. And thanks, it was good of you to come here."

"No problem," said Jamie. "I hope you'll be at the Christmas party."

"Oh yes," said Mary. "But I'll be back in the office before then in any event."

"Good. See you then."

The following day, Essex police arrested Steve Black at his home in Billericay on suspicion of conspiracy to commit grievous bodily harm and robbery. He was taken into custody at Basildon and an identity parade was organised. Byrne and Mulrooney recognised him as the person who had approached them to carry out the assault so he was immediately charged and held to appear in court the next morning. They had also visited his brother's house in Chigwell and, having made enquiries with neighbours, they were able to determine that a man answering the description of Hari Kahn had been staying there. Unfortunately he had not been seen for two or three days, furthermore it looked as though he had disappeared on the day that Darren Black was first arrested. They passed the information to Roy Partridge with the request that Black be detained. Roy sent Sergeant Bennett and two uniformed officers to his office in Pepys Street where he was arrested on suspicion of conspiracy as well as harbouring a wanted criminal. News of his arrest quickly found its way round the Lloyd's market and soon after that to the office of Robert Woodhead.

"This has a slight bearing on the acquisition," he said to his chairman. "It won't stop the deal going ahead, but I think we should make it absolutely clear that Black was never going to be part of it. In fact I think we should make an announcement now about our intentions to take over the business, so as to head off any criticism that might come our way later."

"Good idea," said Peterson. "Let's go public."

"I'll need to get the other two to agree first, of course, but I think I'm going to withdraw Black's compensation for lost employment, since he would have lost it anyway by going to jail. But whether he does or not, he would certainly be suspended by Lloyd's and would never work in the market again. No one would employ him, even in a back office capacity."

"What about his shareholding?"

"I don't think we have much of a choice there, it being a contractual obligation, but he's certainly not getting the extra one hundred and fifty thousand."

"That's in the contract as well, isn't it?"

"Yes, but I think I'll have it taken out, with the agreement of the other two, again."

"Won't he have to sign as well?"

"Yes, I suppose so, but the lawyers can handle that and if he comes after us at a later date, then we'll fight it. He's not in much of a position to argue at the moment, is he?"

"No, I suppose you're right. OK, let's do it."

Simon was at home on Friday evening and beginning to think about his weekend. He called Emma.

"I'd quite like to talk to your dad at some point," he said. "There's been a lot of stuff going on this week and much of it is the result of the help he gave to the police. It's quite a story, in fact."

"Yes, of course," said Emma. "Why not come over tomorrow afternoon? I presume you're at the golf club in the morning."

"Yes, I will be. OK, I'll be over just after lunch. Thanks."

Simon played the customary eighteen holes with his father and two other members, one of whom was Jaffa.

"By the way," he said on the way round, "I'm planning to retire at the end of the year. I'm almost sixty-five now and I've been in the teaching profession for many a long drawn-out year and I now think I'm a bit out of date with modern life."

Simon smiled. "Really?" he commented. "We'd never have noticed."

"Yes," Jaffa continued. "I just wonder where modern education is going. I see highly proficient academic kids doing well enough to go to university, then struggling to find work when they finish. Yet there are chaps who don't do so well at school who fall on their feet and get decent jobs straight away."

"I don't know who you mean," said Simon, looking at his father with amusement.

"Well, you're an example of that, of course, but I don't blame you. It's the system. It makes you wonder whether what I do has any real value at the end of the day."

"Of course it does," said John Blunt reassuringly. "You give them knowledge, if they bother to listen, but you can't give them wisdom and judgement. That has to come from elsewhere."

"You're right John. Anyway I'm getting too weary of it now. And apart from the formal stuff at the school I am planning to have a bit of a bash here one evening, so I hope you'll both come."

"We'll certain try to," said Simon. "You'll be at the dinner I take it?"

"Oh yes. Wouldn't miss it for the world."

After lunch they drove home and Simon walked over to Woodland Drive, where George Claremont was waiting for him.

"I hear you have something to tell me Simon," he said.

"Yes Sir, that's right. It was Carmichael all along. He planned the whole thing, enlisted the help of Hari Kahn, who in turn persuaded his nephews to carry out the heist with help from Yacoub. He was after two things, it seems. Firstly, he was aiming to get his hands on the reward money which he knew Lloyd's would pay and secondly, he wanted Kahn to take all the blame. The reason he had Al Othaim murdered was to blame that on Kahn as well."

"How was he caught?"

"A couple of our investigators tracked the cash down to Monte Carlo and then picked him out from CCTV footage. After that it was largely due to your testimony about his past history. He was really taken by surprise, apparently, when the police confronted him with that and he then virtually caved in and confessed all."

"So it's a good result all round."

"Yes it is. I thought you would like to know the outcome."

"I did get a letter from Chief Superintendent Partridge thanking me for my assistance, but he also told me I wouldn't be needed to make a written statement as Carmichael had made a full confession. He didn't give me as much detail as you just have, so thank you for that. I was pleased to be able to help and I hope it's done you some good as well."

"Yes it might have done. We'll see when my review comes up at the end of this month. By the way, will you be coming to the golf dinner?"

"Oh yes. We'll be there."

"Good. See you there."

Chapter 28

Hari Kahn was, by a somewhat circuitous route, on his way to Pakistan. He did lay low for a while at Darren Black's house in Chigwell but was spooked when the police swooped in one day and took his friend away for questioning. He slipped away under cover of darkness that same evening, took the few belongings he happened to have with him and booked into a cheap hotel near the port of Harwich, where he paid cash for his room. His business depot in Tilbury was functioning normally, more or less, though still the subject of police surveillance and now with the works manager in charge, though the boss had promised to call him from time to time to check on how things were going. On the way he had dropped off his car keys at the works manager's house in Stanford-le-Hope, with instructions to give the Bentley a run out every so often and from then on to park it in the garage, rather than on the drive. The housekeeper would continue her duties until he returned, whenever that might be, but neither she nor his depot manager knew anything of his immediate past history. His sister and brother-in-law refused to have anything to do with him, since they blamed him for the predicament their two sons now found themselves in, so any help from them was out of the question. In fact, they vowed they would help in any way to see him brought to justice if they could.

In Harwich, Kahn went to two different phone shops, bought one pay-as-you-go at each and loaded them with credit. They were linked to different networks. He threw his old mobile, minus its battery, into the nearest bin. The plan was to use one of the new ones for a few days then dump it in favour of the other, and so on. He bought a cheap laptop and set himself up with a new e-mail account, using a different name. He had also changed his appearance slightly, by growing a beard and wearing a cheap pair of off-the-shelf spectacles that did nothing to affect his eyesight.

His UK passport was still in custody at West End Central but, as suspected by Roy Partridge, he had another. Two others, in fact. He had retained Pakistani nationality when he took UK citizenship but, in addition to that, he had a fake one. Some years earlier he had arranged for a friend of his, a known forger, to make him a second Pakistani one in the name of Javed Abbas and, luckily for him as it now turned out, he had been bearded at the time. He had used it only once before, but he knew that it worked, at least on that occasion. His solicitor had managed to retrieve the stock of US dollars from the police after he was bailed, some of which he changed into pounds sterling, others into euros, so he was not forced to use any form of card, at least for the time being. They were probably being monitored, he thought. His escape plan was to leave by ferry, as a foot passenger, and take an onward flight to Islamabad from wherever he happened to end up. From there he could slip in and out of Dubai without attracting anybody's attention, especially if he went as Javed Abbas, thus he could continue to run his businesses as normal.

Two days later, Javed Abbas checked out of his hotel and boarded a ferry bound for Esbjerg. Departure procedures and security checks passed without a hitch, as did his arrival and disembarkation in Denmark. He took a taxi and booked himself into a cheap hotel for two nights, while contemplating whether to take a direct flight, or to stop off somewhere along the way. He decided on the former to cut down on the number of times he would need to show his fake passport. In fact, on arrival in Islamabad, he would use the real one in his own name. Two days later he took an indirect Etihad flight from Kastrup Airport bound for Islamabad, with stopovers in Paris and Abu Dhabi, a total journey time of sixteen hours. He would, though, remain airside all the way through and would not be subjected to any additional passport or security checks. He was by now on the last leg of his journey, having just left from Abu Dhabi on his way to Benazir Bhutto Airport in Islamabad. From then on he would be Hari Kahn again and beyond the clutches of Roy Partridge and his colleagues at West End Central. Again his disembarkation was accomplished without difficulty and he took a taxi to his cousin's house on the outskirts of the city, where he planned to hole up for a day or two while taking stock of things. His cousin, Ravi Kahn, knew nothing of his exploits with the jewellery heist and had no suspicions about the reasons why Hari was back in Pakistan. Ravi knew who the Hussains were, being family members, but he had not had any contact with them for several years. As safe as he now felt, Hari Kahn was not one to rest on his laurels and felt the sooner he moved on, the further from harm's way he would be.

Meanwhile, on his way back to Paris from New York with the princess and their entourage, Prince Fahd was growing increasingly concerned about the fate of Yacoub who, in his opinion, was not the real villain in the scheme and who he now felt had been duped by Carmichael into participating in the heist. He knew how persuasive Carmichael could be and he also knew that Yacoub was very much his subordinate in all matters, so it was quite likely he felt obliged to do as he was told, especially if it was explained to him that no loss would be suffered by the newlyweds in the long run. The prince was keen to do whatever he could to help, though he didn't quite know what, on the basis that Yacoub appeared to have had no part in the murder and was therefore only being charged with his part in the robbery. The prince decided to share his thoughts with Princess Laila.

"I am beginning to change my views about Yacoub," he said, as they were half way across the Atlantic. "I feel a little more sympathetic towards him, now we know that Carmichael was the real villain."

"Yacoub is guilty, though," she said.

"Yes," replied the prince, "but I don't think he's completely guilty."

"Nor is he completely innocent."

"I know, but I feel as though I should help him somehow."

"In that case, you should arrange to speak for him at his trial. You'll have to do something about it when we get there, as well the repatriation of Saleh's body. You need to make your position known to the police somehow. When is the trial?"

"Soon, I think. He's being tried separately from the others, since he only has the one charge against him"

"OK, so why don't you have a word at the embassy?"

"I will."

Upon arrival at Charles de Gaulle, they checked back into Le Meurice, again taking the royal suite and the prince duly called Ambassador Sulaiman. A meeting was arranged for the following morning.

"I just feel a bit guilty myself here," the prince explained. "I know it seems strange, but it was one of my senior staff who is really responsible for all this and it was he who drew Yacoub into the mess in the first place. I know what Yacoub did was wrong and he needs to stand trial for it, but I think I owe him some support here. Do you think there's anything I can do?"

"I'm not sure," said Ambassador Sulaiman. "I'll look into it, though, and let you know. If you give me a few hours I will see what can be done."

"Thank you," said the prince, who then returned to his hotel and, together with the princess, went to lunch at Maximes.

Later that afternoon, the ambassador called him and said he had some news. They arranged to meet at the hotel later that afternoon.

"The trial is set to start on Friday," advised the ambassador. "At the moment Yacoub is pleading not guilty on the grounds that he acted under duress. He's not saying he's innocent, just not as guilty as the others."

"That's my view," said the prince.

"However, his position doesn't stand much chance of holding up in court, apparently, and he's likely to get three or four years inside, maybe longer."

"I see. Carry on."

"There is a better option, though. According to the judge who will try the case, if he enters a plea of guilty, he can then argue mitigating circumstances and if you speak up for him, which the judge has agreed you may do, then he will be treated more sympathetically. You won't get him off, we think, but there might be some relaxation of the sentence."

"Then that is what we should do," said the prince. "Would you see to it that these arrangements are put in place for me, please? I presume his lawyer will need to go along with this plan?"

"Yes, but he has for some time been trying to persuade Yacoub to do just that, so he'll definitely agree."

"Right, I'd also like to see Yacoub before Friday, if that can be arranged."

"Yes, Sir," said the ambassador. "I think that can be done."

"Now," continued Prince Fahd. "I would like also to deal with the matter of Saleh Al Othaim. Is there any news of that yet?"

"Yes, Sir, there is. The judge has agreed that we may make the necessary arrangements to have the body shipped home and I have already been in contact with Saudia, who have agreed to take the casket whenever we ask. It will be on a scheduled flight."

"Excellent. Thank you for that, Sulaiman. I really do appreciate it."

The following day, Prince Fahd met with Lieutenant Le Bret once more and was shown into an interview room where Yacoub was waiting and who jumped quickly to his feet when his master entered the room.

"I can't pretend that I'm not disappointed," began the prince. "I know what you did and there is no excuse for it, but I'd like you to tell me why. How was it that you got involved in such a scheme? How was it that Carmichael was able to persuade you to take part? That's what I'd like to understand."

"I am very sorry, Sir," replied Yacoub, quietly, almost tearfully. "I know it was wrong but I couldn't seem to get out of it. Mr Carmichael was very persuasive first of all, saying that the jewellery would be returned to you in the fullness of time, so you would incur no loss. Then when I continued to say no, he began to threaten me. He said he would see to it that a considerable amount of physical harm would come to me and he knew exactly the people who would be able to inflict it. I was scared out of my life. That's why."

"You should have come straight to me."

"I know that now, Sir, but I was really frightened by what Mr Carmichael said he would do."

"I see," said the prince. "That's more or less as I thought. It's not like you to be disloyal in the normal run of things. Now I understand you have decided to plead guilty and that you will be bringing these issues up in court. Is that so?"

"Yes it is, Sir,"

"Well, for what it's worth, I think it's the best solution. I shall be in court tomorrow and I'm going to be called as a witness. I shall be speaking up for you and letting the court know that I bear some responsibility for what has happened and, as a result of that, I intend to take you back into palace employment, whenever you are free again."

"Thank you, Sir. I do appreciate that."

"The general view is that you will go to jail, but your sentence is likely to be shorter by going this route. And I don't think there's anything I can do to get you back to Riyadh before you have served your time, otherwise I would."

"Thank you again, Sir."

And that is precisely how things turned out. The case was heard the very next day, a much shorter process in view of the guilty plea. The accused stated his mitigating circumstances, asking the judge to take them into account, while Prince Fahd made reference to the reason behind Yacoub's involvement, his previous unblemished record of loyal and devoted service and his willingness to be accepted back onto the palace payroll when the time came. As a result, Yacoub was sentenced to twelve months in prison, less the time he had already spent in custody, which reduced it to about ten. As he was led away, he looked at the prince and nodded his approval.

"I think I made a difference," said the prince to Princess Laila back in the hotel. "Yacoub should be back with us in about ten months, but it could have been a lot longer."

"As long as you're happy with what you did."

"Yes I am. I don't think there was anything more I could have done."

"I also had a long conversation with Lieutenant Le Bret about the others, Carmichael and the two Hussains. There is no likelihood of their court cases being heard much before February next year, since additional evidence is still being gathered, but I am required to be here to act as a witness and I'm afraid we have to bring the jewellery back with us, as well as the documents. I promised to do that when the items were released to us by Lloyd's, all those weeks ago. I think it means you will need to come with me as well, but I don't think they will require you to give evidence."

"Yes, I think we're obliged to be present."

"As far as I understand it," continued the prince, "they will all plead not guilty, each blaming the other two to some degree, but the general opinion is that their pleas will not be sustained and they will all get life. Not a happy ending for them, I think."

"So be it," sighed the princess. "They shouldn't have done what they did. I think they deserve all they get."

That same week Mary was back at work. She bounded into the office on Monday morning full of energy, keen to resume her duties. Her colleagues were pleased to see her and that she seemed totally unaffected by the dreadful attack at the beginning of the month. Her assailants, Byrne and Mulrooney, were still on remand awaiting trial, proceedings she would be required to attend when the time came, while the Black brothers, who had been granted bail were idling their time away in readiness for their trial at some later stage. Darren Black was no longer working as a broker, having been banned by Lloyd's and his ex-partners Baxter and Taylor were by then operating their business from within the reinsurance division of Nathan Henry, along with their remaining seven staff. Black's compensation for loss of employment had been withdrawn by Robert Woodhead and there was little he could do about it. As far as future payments were concerned, he would be denied those as well, on the grounds he had no part to play in the revenue going forward. He had given away his right to receive those in any event, when he signed the contract. There was still no information concerning the whereabouts of Hari Kahn, much to the annoyance of Roy Partridge, though Darren Black had acknowledged his role in giving him a safe place to stay for a while, something else he would stand trial for later.

"So how have things been?" Mary asked her team, when they had all assembled.

"Pretty good," said John. "It was always a struggle without you, of course, especially as we were beginning to get a flow of enquiries from Mike Edwards, but we managed well enough."

"And how are you, Simon? Coping well?"

"Oh yes, thanks," he replied. "It's been a very interesting time."

"Good. It's your review coming up shortly. I think we'll do that in a couple of weeks' time, if that's OK. It will be a formal interview with you, me and Lynne Green so if there are any issues you'd like to raise, please have them ready."

"I will," confirmed Simon.

"And it isn't anything to be concerned about, by the way, I'm sure everything will be fine."

"Thanks."

"Right," she continued. "I'd like us to spend this week getting back to normal. I don't want to interrupt anything you guys are in the middle of, so I'll take anything new that comes in and leave you to finish off what you are already working on."

At that point Nigel Watkins came into the room and was pleased to see Mary was back. He had with him a file of papers.

"Here's a new one for you, Mary. It's a chain of hotels that we've been asked to quote for by Al Talyani. There are others in the market already so we'll need to move fast. The group consists of seven locations in various parts of the Emirates. All the information is in the file and I'd like to be in a position to give them our best quote by the end of Thursday this week. OK?"

"Leave it to us," said Mary. "Right, John and Simon, you can work with me on this. Hand everything else over to Jamie and Craig now and we'll make a start straightaway. This is one I want us to win."

"Back to normal already then," said Jamie.

"Did you ever doubt it?" said Craig.

Chapter 29

Prince Fahd and Princess Laila were finally on their way home. It being November by then, they had spent longer away than had been originally intended, but they were pleased with what had been achieved and it therefore seemed their extended stay was worthwhile. Their flight was, coincidentally, the same Saudia 11.20 a.m. departure that Saleh Al Othaim was originally scheduled to be on back in August, though this time he was in the hold. The coffin had been carefully loaded out of sight without any of the other passengers being aware of it and, upon arrival at King Khaled airport in Riyadh, it was offloaded in the same manner. The family was there to witness its arrival and the prince and princess stood with them on the tarmac directly outside the arrivals hall. Silence prevailed while it was then placed into a waiting hearse, looking more like an ambulance from the outside, but a hearse nevertheless. Four family members were then invited to travel in the ambulance to accompany the coffin back to the house. The prince and princess then met their chauffeur and returned at long last to the King Saud Palace.

The following day Saleh Said Al Othaim was laid to rest with traditional Islamic protocol at the Al Oud cemetery in the suburbs of Riyadh, a ceremony delayed for much longer than the family would have liked, but just as respectful and dignified nevertheless. Prince Fahd and Princess Laila were there, as were Sheikh Al Talyani and Madhi Al Hadda, both of whom paid their respects to the male members of the family, as was customary. They also spent a few moments with the prince who, after all, was still their client. They assured him they would be available for any of his future insurance needs and that the Lloyd's community in London, who already held him in high regard, were happy to continue the relationship for as long as he wanted. The prince acknowledged their presence at the internment of his friend, adding that he held the people of Lloyd's, and those who worked with them, in the highest possible esteem and he would have no hesitation in bringing more of his business to them as and when such occasions presented themselves. Madhi Al Hadda then drove back to Bahrain, leaving Al Talyani to return to Dubai by air.

On Friday evening, the 2 November, the Blunt family and the Claremonts made their way to West Brighton Golf Club for the annual dinner, having arranged a minibus to take them there and bring them home. There had been a minor clash of interests with George Claremont, who was hoping to go to the Amex that evening for the game against Leeds United, but the ladies were against that, as was John Blunt who might otherwise have gone with him, so George was outnumbered. Thus the golf club was the chosen venue for the evening. Simon and Emma were positioned at the top table, as expected, while their parents shared one of the tables of eight, along with two other couples whom they did not know. Simon's cup was taken from its normal position in the club's trophy cabinet and placed in front of him, where it would remain throughout the entire proceedings. Just over two hundred people were there and the club had arranged for outside caterers to prepare and serve the food. Jaffa was there, minus Mrs Gorringe, who had a lifetime aversion to golf and wanted nothing whatsoever to do with the club. Secretly, though, she hoped that her husband would have the chance to spend more time there after his retirement, thus allowing her to continue with her coffee mornings and social afternoons with friends whose company she so enjoyed.

The meal was standard fare and the wine was included in the price of the ticket. Other drinks were not. At precisely 9.00 p.m. the club president rose to his feet and gave a speech of welcome. He thanked club members for their support during the year, one which, despite the wet summer, had been moderately successful resulting in two more cups residing proudly in the trophy cabinet. He acknowledged the tremendous achievement of their youngest ever club champion, who was asked to stand to receive rapturous applause, and hoped that his game would go from strength to strength in years to come. And it was his final duty, he said, to announce the appointment of club captain for the forthcoming year, who this time would be one of their longest-serving members, Mr John Blunt. Much approval and support, John noticed, as he stood to acknowledge the applause.

"You knew about this, didn't you?" said Angela Blunt.

"Yes, but I didn't tell Simon. It will have come as a complete surprise to him."

"And is that why you were against going to the football?"

"Yes. Plus, of course, you would have missed a good night out."

"Yes dear, of course."

Mary had received notification that the following Tuesday was the date set for her assailants Byrne and Mulrooney to appear in court. It was not known how long the case would last, since they were both pleading not guilty, but she would be required to be in attendance throughout. The case was to be heard at Basildon Crown Court, so she would not have far to travel. There was no indication, though, as to when the trial of the Black brothers was going to be. She notified her boss, Nigel Watkins, and Lynne Green of the human resources department, who immediately suggested that she come too to offer support, at least until Mary had given her evidence. Husband Tony would also be there.

At 9.00 a.m. on Tuesday, 6 November, Mary, Tony and Lynne assembled at the courthouse and waited in the foyer. Eventually a clerk came over to them, took their details and advised that the case was not scheduled to begin until around 11.30 a.m., due to some unrelated bail requests being heard, so they were free to relax for a while and to check in again at 11.00 a.m. This did not help Mary's nerves in any way because, as robust as she was, she had not been through anything like this before. Tony was somewhat irritated by the delay, since to him time was money, and it was left to Lynne to settle things down, something she did admirably well. They were back in place at precisely 11.00 a.m. and reported to the clerk.

"There has been a development," he said. "In the last hour the accused have changed their position and decided to plead guilty as charged. This means that you, Mrs Whitehouse, will not be cross-examined after all and you can relax, sit in court and witness the proceedings."

"Thank goodness for that," said Mary, considerably relieved. "Will they be sentenced today, do you think?"

"Probably," said the clerk.

"Good. I'd like to be here when that happens."

Soon afterwards they were seated in the public gallery while the guilty two were led into the dock. Upon request, Byrne and Mulrooney each told of their part in the events of that night, describing how they were offered money to carry out the attack and how sorry they were that they ever got involved in the first place. They said they knew the person who recruited them by sight, but at the time did not know his name. They pleaded that they had helped the police, albeit not at first, in identifying that person, leading to his apprehension and, as they understood things, to that of his brother as well.

The judge listened carefully to what they said, commenting that they had committed a serious assault on a defenceless woman late at night, that they were a serious public menace and their apparent sorrow was probably brought on by the fact that they got caught, rather than any other form of remorse. Without hesitation he sentenced them each to four years.

Friday, 9 November was the day of Simon's review. He and Mary made their way to Lynne Green's office and they sat at a small table with coffee and biscuits.

"This is a performance review," began Lynne, "of your progress to date. It's a two-way thing, so if there's anything you want to raise, please feel free to do so."

"I will," said Simon. "Thank you."

"Mary and I have spent some time on this and we are both of the opinion that you have made an exemplary start to your career with us. We are pleased with the way you conduct yourself and the impression you create with colleagues and Lloyd's underwriters as well. We took you on in the first place because you displayed good qualities and our decision in that regard has proved to be right. In short, things have gone very well and we sincerely hope that they continue to do so. I'm afraid we don't have any bad news for you."

"Well thank you," said Simon. "I don't have anything bad to say either. I enjoy the work, the environment and the camaraderie, and I really hope that I can continue to add value. I am extremely impressed with the way people in this company conduct themselves. They have a way of dealing with serious matters in what often appears to be a light-hearted and casual manner, which of course, is not the case. They are full of dedication and resourcefulness. I hope to be able to emulate those attributes one day."

"Excellent Simon," said Lynne. "Now as a result of this we are going to increase your salary and at the same time remove the word 'trainee' from your job title, probably the soonest in any newcomer's career ever. From January you will be a fully-fledged broker earning nineteen thousand two hundred a year. We hope that will encourage you to continue the good work."

"It will," said Simon enthusiastically. "It will also help with the upcoming increase in the cost of my season ticket."

"Thank you Simon," said Lynne. "That's all for now. Mary I'd like you to hang on for a second if you would. There's something I want to raise with you."

"OK," said Mary. "Simon, wait for me in the office would you. We all need to be in Lloyd's by noon today."

"He's a good lad, isn't he?" said Lynne. "Now, I just wanted to be sure you have fully recovered from your recent ordeal and there are no repercussions."

"Yes," said Mary. "I'm absolutely fine."

"And your husband has got over the shock?"

"Oh yes. Everything's back to normal."

"Good. It's just that when we came to visit you in hospital and spoke to your husband, he did point out that you had been on company business on the evening of the attack, which led us to report the matter to our liability insurers, just in case. I'm just wondering whether you've had any more thoughts on that point."

"Oh, I didn't know that. He's said nothing to me about it but, in any event, I don't think it happened because of my evening out and I think the insurers would say it was my choice how I made my way home. True, I was targeted, but in some ways I brought it on myself, even though I was acting in the company's interests. I think we can forget about any claim for compensation. I'm just happy to be back."

"Good," said Lynne. "I'll let the chairman know."

Mary hurried back to her office and with her team they made their way over to the Lloyd's building, surprisingly thought Simon, without their slip cases. It was approaching noon and as they entered the building there seemed to be a crowd much larger than normal. They stood in the middle of the ground floor at the opposite end from the Rostrum. People were continuing to come in and by 12.15 p.m. there were probably twenty-five thousand or more, as many as there would be at the Amex for a home match, mused Simon.

"We're here for the ceremony of remembrance," said Mary. "You'll see what happens in a minute but it's the moment when our market pays its respects to the war dead."

At that moment two military bandsmen in full dress uniform entered and positioned themselves at the front of the balcony on the third gallery, where they could be seen by everyone. At precisely 12.30 p.m. the sound of the Lutine Bell rang out once, echoing over the entire building and because of the acoustics as loud, if not louder than, Big Ben. The entire crowd fell silent. The buglers then played the Last Post which again rang out across the entire building. No one moved, shuffled, coughed or spoke. Many old soldiers stood to attention. The bugles were the only sound that could be heard. When they had finished, the bell sounded again and the market returned to normal. Mary and her team made their way out of Lloyd's and over to The Broker, where they enjoyed a light lunch before returning to the office in readiness for the afternoon activity.

There was a memo waiting for each of them as they returned to their desks. The subject was 'Christmas Bonuses'. It advised them that they would all be receiving an amount equal to ten per cent of their annual salaries in December, which would be a tidy sum for most people, even though it would be paid through the payroll and subject to tax. In Simon's case this would be an additional seventeen hundred pounds gross and be even more helpful when he came to renew his season ticket in January.

"Is this normal?" he asked.

"Pretty much," replied Craig. "It was seven and a half per cent last year, so we've done a bit better this time around. Everyone is saying we've had a slightly better year than last and the prospects look pretty good for the next as well."

"Great," said Simon.

"Mary," said Jamie Piper-Bingham. "Can we have a private chat sometime, there's something I need to tell you."

"Yes, of course," she said. "5.00 p.m. in The Broker?"

"Done."

"I'm going to be handing in my notice in the next few days," Jamie said when they had settled at their table. "I've decided to move on."

"I'm sorry to hear that," Mary replied. "Has anything gone wrong here and is there anything I can do to change your mind. I know we've bantered a bit about our respective stations in life, but I hope I haven't ever gone too far."

"No, you haven't. I've given as good as I've got. Anyway, it's nothing like that. I've enjoyed my time here very much. I got engaged recently and Lulu and I plan to marry in March. You'll meet her at the Christmas party, by the way. It's the family pile in Hampshire that needs my attention now because old Andy – that's Uncle Sir Andrew the baronet, by the way – is not in very good health and someone needs to be there to take over. He's been coping virtually single-handed for some time now and as I'm his nearest and dearest, he's asked us to move in and run the estate, probably after we're married."

"I see, so you plan to work your three months' notice?"

"Oh yes, I've no problem with that."

"Good. That will give us time to find a replacement. When can I tell the others?"

"Would you leave it for a little while until it all settles down, please? Then I think we can go public."

"Yes of course. And we'll have plenty of time to get used to life without you, won't we?"

"Yes," said Jamie laughing. "I'm sure that won't take you long."

Chapter 30

The day of Nathan Henry's Christmas party was soon upon them. Many would finish work at lunch time, while those who lived further away would start getting ready in the office from mid-afternoon and await the arrival of their partners. Back in the office after their morning session in Lloyd's, Mary took the opportunity to ask Jamie to tell the group about his plans.

"I'm leaving Nathan Henry to take up something completely different," he said. "I'm going to be the estate manager at my uncle's pad in Hampshire. It's a full time job, so Lulu and I will move into one of the apartments and live there permanently. I probably won't start much before Easter next year, so I will be here for the next three months, during which time Lulu and I plan to be married. And we'd love to see you all at the wedding, naturally."

"That's sad news," said John. "Sad news for us, I mean. Sounds pretty good for you, though."

"Yes," said Jamie. "I have enjoyed my time here, but I'm next in line to inherit the place, so I don't really have much choice."

"And will you inherit the title as well?" asked Craig.

"Yes, I think so."

"So you'll be Sir James Piper-Bingham, Bart.?"

"I believe so."

"Well that is something," said Craig. "What will we do without him, Mary?"

"We'll just have to try our best to manage," she replied. "We'll need another person, of course, perhaps another trainee. The last one seems to be working out quite well, doesn't he?"

There was laughter and general good humour all round. At that point they were joined by someone they recognised but whom they did not know. He introduced himself as Phil Taylor, until recently a partner in the now defunct firm of Baxter Taylor and Black.

"I'm just doing the rounds," he said after he had introduced himself. "I thought I'd drop by and pay my respects to you all and to you especially, Mrs Whitehouse."

"Well thank you," Mary replied.

"I and my colleague Dave Baxter, as well as all our staff, were shocked when we heard what had happened to you. Are you fully recovered now?"

"Yes I am thanks."

"I don't know whether you've heard, but our ex-partner was in court yesterday, along with his brother, charged with conspiracy. There were each given eighteen months. Darren has yet to stand trial for harbouring a wanted man, but that is scheduled for early next year we think. Anyway it's the end of him as far as Lloyd's is concerned, thank goodness."

"Oh, good. Thanks for letting me know. What has happened to the accounts that he controlled?"

"Well, there weren't that many of them but we let them go elsewhere. His agents seemed to be just a slimy as he was, as it turned out. Anyway, we're glad to be here and to be rid of him, and them."

"Excellent. Will you be there tonight, Phil?"

"Yes we will. See you there."

Emma Claremont took a train from Brighton Station at 3.00 p.m. which headed for London Bridge where Simon was due to meet her at around 4.20 p.m. She was dressed casually and the plan was for her to change in the office. It was a black tie affair, so Simon would have to change as well. Her train was on time and she and Simon took a taxi to Mark Lane. Mary was still there as was John, but Jamie and Craig had gone home to get ready, since they lived close enough to do so. Introductions were made and shortly after they were joined by Tony Whitehouse and John's wife Christine. Simon had pre-arranged his and Emma's journey home, not wishing to chance the late-night trains on the Friday but one before Christmas and not knowing quite what time the revelry would finish. They were to take a taxi as far as Croydon and Simon's father would pick them up at a prearranged spot and drive back to

Brighton. Emma would then stay the night in one of the spare rooms at the Blunts' house, thus avoiding an early-hours return to her own home and save her mother waiting up, which she would inevitably have done.

By 6.00 p.m. they were all ready to leave the office, so they walked round to the forecourt of Fenchurch Street Station and took taxis to the Café Royale, arriving there just after 6.30p.m. The official start time was 7.00 p.m., so they had drinks in the lounge while they waited for their two colleagues. Eventually they arrived, Jamie with his fiancée Lulu and Craig with his lady, Justine.

"I hear congratulations are in order," said Mary to Lulu after the pleasantries were over.

"Yes," she said. "All very exciting isn't it?"

"How do you feel about moving into the big house in Hampshire and being Lady Piper-Bingham?"

"Oh no, I hadn't thought of that," she replied. "Lady Lulu doesn't sound quite right, does it? I hope it won't hold me back."

Again there was much laughter from the group. Emma was open-mouthed and could hardly believe what she was hearing, after all it wasn't every day she found herself in such illustrious company.

"It's Louisa really," said Jamie somewhat seriously. "That'll be a bit better."

"And what will you do Craig," Mary asked, "when you lose your flat-mate?"

"Not entirely sure yet," he replied. "One possibility is for Justine to move in. That would help us both as she also works in London and currently travels in from Surbiton. Plus the rent at the flat in Kensington is too much for me on my own. We'll just have to see."

"Where do you work, Justine?"

"I'm an economist – a junior one of course - at the Bank of England," she replied, "The journey is OK but it would be a lot better living in town. I hope that's what we end up doing."

A moment later, at precisely 7.00 p.m., the doors of the function room opened and they went in. Their pictures were taken, in couples, by a photographer who was positioned immediately inside the door, who told them that portrait prints would be available later at a cost of ten pounds. The room was organised in tables of ten, positioned around the edge, leaving the centre free for the dancing which would begin later in the evening. Mary's group conveniently numbering ten meant they could all share one table. The room soon filled up and the festivities got underway, making conversation difficult as the noise level rose. There were a couple of table magicians wandering around, doing card tricks and pulling ping pong balls out of peoples ears, while a small group of musicians, two guitars, a trumpet and a violin were doing the rounds offering to play requests in return for tips. Emma was really enjoying herself.

"Is she the one, then?" asked Mary discreetly, while sitting next to Simon.

"Too early to tell," he said in reply. "She's got to go through university yet, but if we survive that, who knows?"

After the meal had finished and coffee and drinks were being served, the chairman moved to the microphone to address them. He thanked everyone for their hard work and dedication during what had been a relatively successful year and welcomed all newcomers to the group, hoping they would find their time here enjoyable and rewarding. He made reference to the recent acquisition and asked those nine people to stand for a few moments so that they could be seen by all. He thanked his directors for their dedication and support, as well as the front-line brokers whose exemplary performance in Lloyd's ensured that Nathan Henry continued to prosper. He paid tribute to the staff who handled all the back-office servicing, reassuring them how important their roles were, along with the secretaries, telephonists and catering personnel. He wished them all a very happy Christmas and hoped that the next year would prove to be even better for them all.

"It's now 9.30 p.m.," he added. "Dancing will begin at around 10.00 p.m., so there's half an hour or so while we take a break, relax and circulate. But before we do that, we come to the prize for employee of the year. This award is for dedication, hard work, integrity, resourcefulness and all those qualities that companies such as ours rely so much on. The prize is a one week family holiday in Barbados, to be added to the recipient's normal holiday allocation. And the winner is someone who has shown dedication and commitment beyond the normal call … Mrs Jacqueline Whitehouse."

Mary was quite taken by surprise but nevertheless went purposefully forward to collect the envelope, amidst a crescendo of clapping, cheering and whistling. As she returned to her table, she passed close to where Robert Woodhead was sitting.

"Wouldn't have been my choice," he commented sarcastically.

"I don't need your opinion right now," she retorted. "You can take your bad attitude and shove it, preferably where it's really dark."